THE WIFE ASSIGNMENT

VICTORIA PAIGE

Content edit by Geri Ejosa
Proofreading by A Book Nerd Edit and Turn The Pages Proofreading

For Geri
Book bestie and dear friend

Kelly's Mafia Family Tree

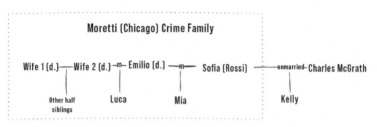

Moretti (Chicago) Crime Family

Wife 1 (d.) —— Wife 2 (d.) —m— Emilio (d.) —m— Sofia (Rossi) ———unmarried— Charles McGrath

Other half siblings   Luca   Mia   Kelly

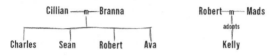

The McGraths

Cillian —m— Branna   Robert —m— Mads

Charles   Sean   Robert   Ava   adopts   Kelly

De Lucci Crime Family   Rossi Crime Family

Cesar —m— Ava   Sofia

*d.=deceased

PROLOGUE

KELLY

"YOU PROMISED."

"I told you something came up." Levi's voice was barely audible over the phone, the background noise too loud. "There'll be other birthdays."

And you've only been home for the first two. The two Ashley won't remember.

"Where are you?" I asked despite the odds against him giving me an answer. Two years before, he'd quit the SEALs to become a mercenary. He didn't say much about that new gig. I figured they were high risk missions of the plausible deniability type. "Sounds like a bar."

"*Kelly*, let me talk to Ash."

"What for?" Levi promised he'd be home. He confirmed a week ago, although those seven days stretched into a lifetime of waiting for his mission directives to change. So, in a way, I should be used to it. But getting used to it didn't mean I was okay with it.

"Dammit, Kelly, I don't have the time to argue with you."

I bit my lower lip, trying my best to restrain the words I wanted to shout at him.

He exhaled an irritated breath. "Did you get the dollhouse she wanted?"

"Yes. It arrived earlier this week. It's still in the box."

"Ask Cillian to set it up."

Again, I kept quiet because I'd been hoping he would do this for Ash. It might help our youngest daughter warm up to him. As it stood, Ash didn't want to have anything to do with her father.

"Can I talk to my girls?"

As my resentment struggled with the need to respect my husband's job, I headed to the kitchen where Ash and Whit were ogling the giant birthday cake. The *Frozen* castle confection sat majestically on the kitchen island. A gift from Gramps and Nana, it was a replica of the yet-to-be unboxed dollhouse. Emotion prickled my eyes. My grandparents were trying to make up for the void left by my children's absentee father whom we hadn't seen in eight months.

"It looks too good to eat, Mama." Ash's awestruck gaze swept toward me.

I tamped down bitter feelings and wrestled to put a smile on my face. "Your dad is on the phone."

My daughters looked at me and then at my chest where the phone was muffled against it. The differences in their expressions stabbed my heart. Whitney—always the Daddy's girl—was all smiles and sprang forward. Meanwhile, Ashley's brows furrowed as she returned her attention to the birthday cake.

"Gimme." Whit shoved her hand toward the phone. I knew Levi wanted to talk to Ash first, because it was her birthday, but I wasn't going to break Whit's heart either. My oldest daughter, now seven years old, had been fortunate to experience "doting Dad" Levi before everything went to hell.

After I handed her the phone, she pranced out of the kitchen.

I edged closer to my youngest.

"Hey." I brushed an imaginary lock from her face. She wouldn't look at me.

"Your dad wants to talk to you."

She pursed her lips and fidgeted with the doilies at the base of the cake.

"Ash?"

She glanced up. "Do I have to?"

Those four words had more heartbreak in them than Levi breaking his promise.

"No, sweetie." It was her birthday dammit. No one was forcing her to do anything. Levi would just have to suck it up. "You don't have to."

A small smile erased the anxiety from her face.

"Mom," Whitney called from behind me. "Dad doesn't have a lot of time," she said, handing the phone back to me. The disappointment on Whitney's face transformed my simmering resentment into seething anger.

"Ash can't come to the phone."

Whit's gaze snapped to her sister's, but I held a forefinger to my lips before she berated Ash.

For a few seconds, all I heard was laughter in the bar, so I knew Levi hadn't hung up.

"Don't know when I can call again."

"I know."

"Wish her a happy birthday. Gotta go."

The abrupt silence over the line told me he'd ended the call.

Gotta go.

This was how he said goodbye to me now? Did he think I encouraged Ash not to talk to him? I realized I still had the phone to my ear listening to nothing. Nothing. Like our marriage.

Goosebumps skated over my skin as I considered the options that had been lurking in the back of my mind.

"I could've talked to Dad longer." Whitney glared at Ash.

My youngest daughter merely shrugged her shoulders, not even looking up from where she'd been mangling the doilies.

"Whit, not today. She can do whatever she wants on her birthday." I stilled Ash's fingers from ruining the lacy paper before grasping her shoulders to squeeze them gently. I made a funny face. "Except ruin the cake presentation."

The girls giggled.

Still, we couldn't recapture the festive mood from that morning, dampened forever by Levi's absence.

My anger wasn't about his job. I had no problems when he'd been with the Teams. He'd withdrawn from us after *the event*. He became a big rock of anger no one wanted to be around, and he refused to get help for it. Ash was a bubbly girl by nature, but in her father's presence, she was subdued. As for Whitney, all she wanted was her dad and welcomed any piece of his time he could spare.

They deserved more.

So much more.

Trying not to rant in front of them about their father was draining. I was reaching my own breaking point.

The doorbell blasted through the cloud of misery hovering in the kitchen.

My two girls glanced expectantly at the entryway. "Gramps and Nana!"

"Don't open the door!" I yelled after them. The exuberance in their stampeding feet trampled the negative vibes that descended over our home. As my hand reached for the handle, I pushed Levi's broken promises away and opened the door.

Tom Roth darkened the entrance.

"Oh my goodness. When did you get in?" He went to

BUD/S training with my brother Callum and had been a longtime friend of the family since.

"Uncle Tom!" Ashley shrieked.

"Happy Birthday, kiddo." He went down on his haunches and gave my youngest a hug before handing her a box wrapped in festive pink paper. My discerning eyes told me it was a Barbie doll. Whitney wasn't as animated with men except around her dad and gramps and didn't rush to meet him. She hung back. Tom was used to it and flashed a grin at my oldest child. "How're you doing, Whit?"

She mumbled a response.

I nodded to the birthday decor that lay on the counter. "You two are slacking. Didn't I tell you to decorate the chairs?"

Getting up from his crouch, he said, "I have a meeting tomorrow but I remembered in our last chat, you said it was Ashley's fifth birthday today so I flew in a day early." He looked around. "Where's Levi?"

When he saw the answer in my eyes, his grin faded. "Shit. Sorry."

I jerked my head toward the kitchen.

Tom followed my lead, giving a low whistle when he took in the cake. "Damn. You sure pulled out all the stops."

"It's from Nana and Gramps. They should be here soon."

"How are they liking LA?" Tom asked.

My grandparents recently moved from New York to Los Angeles. Nana wanted to help with the girls since my career in special effects was taking off. Of course Gramps was fine with the move, especially since the McGraths opened a Whiskey Distillery in San Francisco.

"Nana is ecstatic," I said. "As for Gramps, he's happy that she's happy."

"I'm glad they're doing okay." His eyes bore into mine. "Are you okay?"

Unable to stand the scrutiny, I changed the subject. "Where are my manners?" I feigned a slap to the forehead and headed for the fridge, but Tom snagged my elbow, gently stopping my momentum.

"No rush. It's me, Kelly."

I pinched my lips together to keep them from trembling. He was not wrong. Being a former SEAL himself, he helped me understand Levi and what he went through, and why it was difficult for him to open up after what happened. He kept me sane, helping translate my husband's baffling behavior.

"How are you doing?"

"I'm fine," I whispered.

He cocked his head and looked at me dubiously.

I exhaled a breath. "Okay, I'm not. But you know how the job is."

"I know what I told you before, but you don't have to continue making excuses for him." He let go of me and transferred his hands to his hips, contemplating his shoes before looking up at me. "Do you want me to talk to him next time he's back on the grid? Knock some sense into that mother —him?"

"Oh … no." My heart pounded in horror "Don't. Please don't. The last thing Levi should know is that I'm talking to you about our troubles."

Tom dragged a hand down his face. "I know I told you to give him time, but it's been three years."

"I know."

"I hate seeing you like this. You and the girls deserve more."

Hearing it come from Tom rubbed me the wrong way. It was almost as if I were cheating on my husband.

Still, there was no doubt that he meant well. I put a reassuring hand on his arm. "I'm fine. Truly, I am." I gave him a shaky smile. It had been hard to paste a genuine one on my face today, but this time, it was real. "You know how you can help?"

He stilled, and his gaze turned fierce. "Anything."

"Help us put together the dollhouse."

1

Eighteen months later
Kelly

I was really doing it. Going on a date with a man who wasn't my husband.

As though feeling my gaze on him, Tom put down the menu and grinned at me across the table. "Made your choice?"

I smiled back. "Yes."

Our waiter appeared beside us. "Are we ready for dinner?"

We both made our choices for the evening—prime rib for him, and red snapper for me.

After the waiter left, Tom grabbed his wine and raised it. "To new beginnings."

My smile froze. I reached for my goblet but it stayed glued to the table.

Tom's smile faded, and he lowered his glass. "Too soon?"

The charger plate seemed like a good place to rest my gaze. "It's not that." Finally, I met his eyes. "I just feel sad. But I also know, I need to get unstuck."

He slid his hand across the table and opened it palm up. Tom had been a friendly presence since I'd separated from Levi.

That time Levi hadn't shown up for Ashley's birthday had been my breaking point, so when he finally came home, I asked him to move out. The focus of our separation was his relationship with the kids, especially Ashley. I was proud of him. He'd come a long way in eighteen months. It was time to work on me, to end the cycle of falling into hot sex with my estranged husband.

I looked at the man in front of me.

Tom was the perfect candidate.

We got along. He was good to my children. The fireworks weren't the same as with Levi, but I treasured stability more than anything. Besides, I hadn't given Tom a clear shot yet.

Earlier that evening when he picked me up from the house, looking amazingly attractive in a navy suit, a familiar zing fluttered low in my belly.

And when he kissed me lightly on the lips, it wasn't … bad. It was something I could work with. "Move on" was a repeating mantra in my head, except "liar" kept echoing inside my skull at a louder volume.

Tom's mouth tightened, making me feel guilty. I dodged his invitations for three months, but I finally succumbed to the last one. The thing was, it wasn't even because of him, but something irritating my husband had said that became the catalyst.

"It's fine." He chuckled in self-deprecation. "But I don't want to be your rebound man."

"You're not." The first goal was to quit rebounding into my husband's bed. "But I'm really sorry, Tom. It's just that this is the first time I've been on a date in forever."

I raised the glass to my lips to take a sip before I blabbered my misgivings about this dinner. My babysitters—Nana and Gramps—had been full of encouragement.

"I understand," he said wryly, taking more than a sip of wine. "I consider this a victory after you've repeatedly turned me down."

Our appetizers appeared, so we shifted to less touchy conversation, namely the girls' summer activities.

"So, they're skipping camp this year?"

"Nana and Gramps are taking them to Disney World and Universal Studios. They'd cry if we sent them to camp." Both girls hated outdoor activities when it had nothing to do with the characters they loved on television. Love for movies was in our genes.

"And Levi?"

"He still has his weekends with them."

"But he's been out of town for the past three weeks, right?"

"He gave me a heads up about it." Sharpness entered my tone. One of the causes of the breakdown of our marriage was that Levi didn't communicate enough when he took off for missions. It hadn't always been that way.

I gave myself a mental shake. I also promised myself I'd give Tom my undivided attention.

"Sorry." He exhaled a breath. "I didn't mean to be an asshole about it. He kept doing it——"

"Let's not talk about him or what happened in my marriage."

"I witnessed enough of what did happen."

"*Tom*," I said. "Agreeing to go out with you doesn't give you the right to criticize my hu—the father of my children."

He winced. Even when I caught myself before I called Levi my husband, which technically he still was, he had caught the almost slip.

"I'm sorry," he repeated. "I'm making this awkward for you."

If there was one thing Tom Roth was good at, it was the aw-shucks Southern farm boy persona. He forgot I knew him when he was a SEAL. He was as deadly as Levi. His current business was security installations on the West Coast which made his job more stable than my husband's. Funny how I never considered this when Levi swept me off my feet at twenty-two and asked me to marry him. Having Whitney and Ashley changed my priorities.

I shrugged. "You can't help yourself. You've been so much a part of my life. You're not a stranger."

"Let's make this easy," Tom said. "Let's not call this a date."

"Okay." I stifled a small laugh. "I smell a catch here."

"No catch. I'm failing miserably on this date and I want a do-over."

"Oooo-kay, we haven't even had dinner."

"Let this be a no-pressure dinner between friends …"

My brow arched.

"Who could potentially be more," he added. "Our inter-actions have always involved the children. We don't know how to act around each other when they're not around."

It was painfully true.

He raised his glass of wine and said, "To friends who could be more."

I clinked my glass to his. "I'll drink to that."

But then Tom's expression changed, his jaw hardening as he looked past my shoulder. A tingle snaked up my spine, before my whole body stiffened.

I turned in my seat, my stomach dropping when I spotted all six-five, two-hundred-thirty pounds of brawny man at the seating hostess' podium. I wasn't the only one who had noticed him. Several female—and male—patrons' attention angled his way. The man's eyes met mine across the room and my treacherous body came alive. Not exactly sexually, but with the exhilaration of seeing him.

My husband, Levi James.

Along the heels of exhilaration followed biting jealousy.

My eyes frantically searched around him to see if he was with another woman.

And … that irritated the hell out of me.

Moving on, remember?

He started across the room, his gaze unwavering on me.

"Fuck," Tom said. "What do you want me to do?"

My unfocused stare returned to my dinner companion. "You think I have an answer?" Irritation morphed into worry, spurring me to snatch up my phone to check for any urgent messages from my grandparents.

Nothing.

Dizzy with the pendulum of rapid-fire emotions, my swoosh of relief swung back to irritation … and a conundrum.

First and foremost, how to handle my husband advancing upon us. His electric stare narrowed briefly on Tom before slicing back to me, pinning me to my seat as if I'd committed a grave crime.

When he reached us, he stole a chair from an adjacent table, twisted it around, and sat beside us.

"This is cozy." Levi surveyed the wine glasses on the table. He picked up mine and downed its contents.

"Ahh, tastes expensive." He and Tom locked stares. He was acting like an asshole and he knew it.

"Do not cause a scene," I hissed.

"Is everything okay here?" A man in a suit, I presumed to be the restaurant manager, hurried to our table. Levi's attire was out of place. He was in tactical cargos and a tee in a room full of suits and ties.

"We're fine," Levi said. "I was late."

The manager kept a neutral face but glanced at Tom who was murdering Levi with his stare. My husband simply cocked a brow at my dinner companion, daring him to say otherwise.

Tom looked at me. "I'll do whatever you want, Kelly. If

you want to have this asshole thrown out of here, I'll do that too."

"I'd like to see you try, bro," Levi said lazily.

His nonchalant reply was at odds with the tension radiating from him. It was suffocating the air in the restaurant.

"Don't." One word was all I needed to communicate with him.

"That'll depend on you, beautiful."

"Mr. Roth? What do you want me to do?" The manager fidgeted beside us.

I turned pleading eyes toward Tom and I was crushed at his resigned look.

Damn Levi.

"We're fine," Tom said.

"We're more than fine." Levi captured my gaze. "Because she's my wife."

"Soon to be ex," I hissed back.

"You wanna play that game here? You know what happens when you do that?"

Every nerve-ending in my body woke up in response to the threat in his voice, sparking a pornographic reel in my head. Over those eighteen months we'd been hooking up, and depending on our situation, the hate fucks were explosive.

"I don't even know why I'm in denial," Tom said, drawing both our gazes back to him. He pointed his finger between the two of us. "That's chemistry."

My husband smirked. "You're the moron who tries to get in between us"

"Levi," I snapped.

"But you know what they say about chemistry"—Tom took a deliberate sip of his wine—"burn too hot and you burn to ash."

Levi's brows drew together dangerously.

"I was a chemistry nerd in high school," Tom explained.

"I would've been a college professor instead of a SEAL, but I like a challenge. Get me?"

"I'm not seeing your point, Roth, so spit it out."

Tom slouched back in his chair. "It's all about finding the right composition to start a slow burn. Burn too fast and ..." He let the words hang and pointed at the two of us again. "How's that working for the both of you?"

I heard Levi growl and I glared at Tom. "Not helping."

"If he's got something to say, he can say it to me now."

"You idiots," I whisper-yelled. "People are starting to notice." I ducked my head between my shoulders while my eyes darted around the restaurant, painfully aware of the interest of the patrons who were not so subtly glancing at our table. "Maybe have the server pack up the food," I told Tom before addressing my husband. "Thanks for ruining my dinner with a friend."

"A friend?" Levi's heated eyes scanned me up and down.

Okay, so maybe I dressed a bit too sexily. I was feeling empowered to finally go on a date. Well, a friendly date as it appeared.

"Yes. Friend," Tom said. "I realized I needed to go slow with Kelly. Slow burn, remember?"

I slid my chair back and got up. "I'm taking an Uber. See if I care if you two beat the crap out of each other."

With a huff, I grabbed my purse and left the two aggravating males at the table. Tom's response to Levi surprised me. Baiting my husband that way was a brawl waiting to happen.

I stopped by the ladies' room first with the need to catch a breather. I had given my dark hair a blow out to compliment my little black dress, but now the curls were irritating my flushed face. I dug out a clip I always kept in my purse to put it in a ponytail. Snapping up several paper towels to run under cool water, I cooled my heated cheeks. Flushed mostly from embarrassment, no doubt partly from my husband's heated gaze that promised retribution of the claiming kind.

I repeated the mantra in my head.

"Move on, dammit." I pressed my palms against the sink and leaned into it, sucking in a couple of breaths, still disbelieving that Levi crashed my date with Tom. After calming down, I slipped my phone out and called my grandmother. She answered immediately. "Did Levi find you?"

"Nana, why in heaven's name didn't you warn me?"

"And say what? Your husband is about to descend on your date? I didn't want to worry you for nothing in case he didn't. Guess it was too much to assume he wouldn't."

"How did he find out I was on a date?"

"I think he talked to Whitney yesterday."

"And you told him which restaurant?"

Nana made a sound as if I was even wrong to ask that question. Levi had tenacity stamped on his forehead.

"You have to be impressed. Wasn't he clear across Europe for a job?"

"I don't know what to do now. I don't think he'll let me leave with Tom."

Nana sighed. "Didn't I tell you to make it clear to him?"

"He was being bullheaded."

"And this date with Tom was you being defiant. You wanted to prove Levi wrong and that you could move on."

"What a mess."

"Where are you calling from?"

"The ladies' room."

"You think it's a good idea, child, to leave those two men alone."

"Shit." Images of overturned tables, broken chairs, and shattered porcelain flashed through my head.

With those thoughts scurrying in my mind, I wrenched the ladies' room door open, sprinted out, and smacked into a solid wall.

Steadying hands gripped my elbows, and before my gaze reached the face of the man I ran into, I knew who it was.

"Where's Tom?" I asked.

Levi's jaw clenched. I shouldn't be poking the bear, but my irritation was at its peak.

"He's waiting for the packed food."

"I came with him, Levi. It's only right that I go home with him."

"Over my dead body."

"This is not the place," I hissed.

His eyes narrowed. "Don't make me prove otherwise, Kelly."

His voice was soft; the threat wasn't. I felt a zap between my legs. Stupid chemistry. I wished it would burn the hell out.

All I could do was glare at him.

"Let's take this outside," Tom said behind the mountain that was my husband.

I pivoted on my stiletto and stalked out the rear exit of the restaurant and into the parking lot.

The two men seemed to fall back. Harsh whispers were exchanged behind me, but I continued walking until I realized I didn't know where we were parked.

I spun around to face them. "I'm Ubering it." Dammit, I forgot to order my ride, but they didn't know that.

"Hell no."

"Fuck no."

I split a look between them. "This is ridiculous."

Tom raised a brow. "We were having a friendly date when this jealous gorilla crashed our dinner."

"Friendly?" Levi scoffed. "There was nothing friendly about the way you were looking at my wife."

Tom folded his arms. "Soon-to-be ex."

Shit.

I surged forward just as Levi punched Tom across the cheek. "Stop it!"

Tom staggered back, but before I could get between them, he launched himself into Levi's torso, sending them crashing to the ground. My attention momentarily flitted to the takeout containers where the contents of steak and fish met their demise. I paced around the grappling pair rolling on asphalt and exchanging punches. Growing up with brothers, I knew better than to try and break them apart.

"Stop it!" I shouted.

But the two were lost in a flurry of fists, grunts, and cursing.

A crowd started to form including two parking attendants who stood there gawking at the men.

"Do something," I yelled at them.

They both looked at me like I was crazy.

"You two are going to kill each other if you don't stop!" They didn't seem to hear me, and the crowd was already taking bets.

Unbelievable.

I stomped my foot. "I'm leaving."

I spotted the restaurant manager in the crowd. He glared at me as if it was all my fault. I fished my phone out and brought up the transportation app and started walking.

"Kelly," Levi shouted.

I continued walking, but it wasn't long before the grip on my arm slowed me down.

I stopped and glared at him. "Is he alive?"

"For now," he responded.

"That was a joke."

"I don't joke when it comes to you, Kelly."

He tugged my arm and guided me to his Escalade.

"You had no right to show up at dinner."

He didn't answer me until we arrived at the vehicle.

"Kelly." Tom limped over to where we were. He was bleeding from the nose and lips. Meanwhile, my husband only had a cut on his brow. His nickname with the SEALs was Iron Jaw. He credited his "jaw of steel" to his Samoan-Irish blood.

"You okay?" I asked my doomed dinner partner.

Levi grunted his displeasure beside me.

"I'm fine. You sure you want to go home with this asshole?"

Levi broke into a sarcastic chuckle. "You seriously didn't learn your lesson—motherfucker."

"You're not the only frogman here."

"Enough!" I pushed the mountain out of the way to talk to Tom. Levi hesitated, but emitted a grunt and circled the SUV toward the driver's side.

"I'm sorry," I said. "We probably shouldn't have done this."

Tom shot a long look in the direction of my husband who slammed into the Escalade before returning his attention to me. "Don't. Not your fault. But maybe you should clear things up with him first."

"He's stubborn."

Tom smiled wryly. "Or he's determined not to lose the best thing that ever happened to him. I can understand that."

The Escalade started, and the window on the passenger side rolled down. "Let's go."

"Call me when you get home," Tom said.

"Okay."

The men exchanged one last daggered look before Tom sauntered away.

I opened the SUV door, slid into my seat, and turned to my husband. "Did you really have to—"

He dragged me over and slammed his mouth on mine.

2

LEVI

THERE WAS no stopping to think if the moment would come back and bite me in the ass. No way was I waiting a second longer to remind Kelly she was mine.

I yanked her over the console and sealed my mouth on hers.

Her fist punched my shoulder. I wasn't being fair, but I knew exactly what my wife wanted and how she wanted to be kissed. An all-consuming need engulfed us each time our bodies collided.

When she gasped, my opportunistic tongue slid between her lips. Her muffled resistance soon turned into a moan of overpowering need, and my dick roared up in challenge, pushing against the restrictive zipper.

I tasted her mouth. It tasted of the wine she drank with that fucker, but she was so damned sweet. After making sure I'd branded her mouth, I ended the kiss.

She thumped me on the shoulder again. "How dare you."

"How dare I?" I'd shrug off her indignation had I not

been nursing my fury all the way back from Germany. "I'm not the one who went out on a date while we're still married."

A chill fell between us.

I eased the vehicle out of the parking space and snaked around the crowd milling around the restaurant. After rolling onto the main road, I glanced at her briefly. "All right, that wasn't a fair statement."

"I'm glad you clarified that because I've been trying to talk to you about how to move forward and you kept brushing me off. And last time when I said maybe we should start seeing other people, you scoffed and told me to go ahead."

"I was pissed."

"Then you left to go on that assignment."

I shot her a glare. "I didn't expect you to go through with it."

"Why? Because you're that confident of your hooks in me?"

I didn't reply because said confidence was taking a beating right now. I couldn't say it didn't serve me right. Thinking that just because I had Kelly where I wanted her in the bedroom didn't mean I had her where I wanted her outside of it. And right now, it was outside of it that needed work. But me being me, I fucked up again last year when I went to Ukraine to rescue my friends without telling Kelly where I was going.

It seemed easier that way. Until I returned.

Kelly didn't even ream my ass. The extremely calm way she told me to think of the girls and her not knowing how to explain why Daddy missed his weekend showed me clearly how I'd fucked up. I couldn't come up with a good reason for her to give me another chance after that.

Silence.

I side-eyed her, but she was staring straight ahead.

I swallowed the fucking lump in my throat, my saliva drying up. "Things are good between me and the kids now. I don't want Roth mucking up all the progress I've made, especially with Ash."

"This thing with Tom is separate from what he is to Ash."

The surrogate dad while I was off on my merc missions? A bitter taste saturated my tongue. But fair was fair. I'd been a stranger to my youngest daughter. But things were different now.

My fingers tightened around the steering wheel. "So, you're admitting there's a thing."

"Hardly," she scoffed. "I figured if I said relationship even if it's not in the sense of romantic love, that wouldn't go down well with you."

"You know me so well, wife. So, moving forward," I said. "I'll state it clearly. I want you to give me a fair chance."

She was already shaking her head. "I don't know, Levi."

"Things were going well. I already admitted I fucked up."

"I never held your job against you," she said. "You know that. I stuck with you when you were a SEAL. I knew what it meant to be a SEAL wife. But after what happened, you stopped communicating."

"I'm trying. I've been good since the Ukraine fuck-up. I don't up and leave."

"Thank you for that." There was sincerity in her tone, but it only wrapped a web of panic around my lungs. Was being a good dad all she wanted from me?

With the way she was holding herself against the door and with her exit coming up, there was no way I was getting invited into the house. Cillian and Branna had the kids, which meant Kelly had planned on staying out late with that fucker. Bile churned in my gut. In the eighteen months we'd been separated, we'd only slept with each other. It was an unspoken understanding. But again, the situation changed last October, and it was all my fault.

I didn't know what else to say. That she came home with me and not Tom had been my sole objective for the evening.

The thought that she was out with another man burned a hole of jealousy in me so deep, I didn't know how to handle it. My default mode was to fuck her to prove my point, but that was why we never fixed our marriage. We didn't communicate outside the bedroom.

And Tom's words about chemistry ate through me like acid.

That motherfucker. He enjoyed watching me squirm.

The SUV made it to Kelly's street. I didn't want the night to end there.

"Kelly …"

"I'm not inviting you in, Levi."

"But you're alone … maybe we can talk."

"I need time to think." She glanced at me. "Since you're back, do you want an extra weekend with the kids?"

I stared straight ahead. "You know I do." I didn't ask the obvious question.

"I'm *not* spending it with Tom. I have extra work at the studio, and the kids are staying with Nana and Gramps but I'm sure they'd love to see you."

"Works for me."

If I could slow the speed of the vehicle more than the crawl I was already driving it, I would. Too soon, I coasted the Escalade into her driveway. I could force the issue about having it out tonight, but I didn't. I was aware I was navigating a razor thin line when I crashed her dinner date.

She came home with me.

Punching Tom also gave an outlet to the simmering rage that had festered since Germany. We had it out. That was what frogmen did.

"You're not going to apologize, are you?" The tone of her voice held resignation as well as fond amusement.

"Apologize for stopping my wife from going on a date with another man? No. Apologize for my words that made you do it? Yes." I didn't wait for her response and unlatched my seat-belt. "I'll walk you to the door."

"I don't think that's a good idea," she whispered.

My muscles tightened. "Why?"

"Because ..." she huffed. "You're going to kiss me, and then we're going to have sex."

Exasperated, I shoved out of the SUV, and glanced over my shoulder. "I'll walk you to the door."

"Bossy," she sassed as she exited the vehicle.

"You like bossy," I called after her strutting figure. Didn't she know better than to run from a hunter? The thin fabric of her dress hugged her shapely ass and hit the middle of her thighs. It wouldn't take much to shove the skirt above her waist, push her panties to the side, lift her against the wall, and thrust into her.

Fuck. The visual made my erection uncomfortable even in the relaxed-fitting pants. Red edged my vision when my thoughts rambled onto a different track. What if she did go home with Tom? What if they made out in his car? It would've been easy for him to snake his fingers up her thigh.

Kelly whipped around. "Did you just growl?"

I stepped right into her, took her keys, unlocked the door, and crowded her into the foyer.

"Levi!" she snapped.

I slammed the door, grabbed her purse and tossed it on the couch. Then I spun her around and caged her against the door.

"Yes, I did," I muttered against her lips. "I was thinking how short your dress was, and how you were out on a date."

Her breathing hitched.

"Have you fucked him?"

"No!"

Truth.

"Have you kissed him?"

Her chin dipped. I tipped it back up. "Have you?"

"You expect me to answer with you looking at me that way?"

I leaned back, brows furrowing. "You know I would never physically hurt you, right?" That was our dominance play. Kelly sassed me all she wanted outside the bedroom, but when it came to our sexual proclivities, she loved being bossed around.

"I'm not afraid for me," she retorted. "After what you did to Tom, you expect me to answer that?"

"He tackled me."

"After you punched him, but I'm not taking his side either. You both were morons."

"Agreed. But you haven't answered me."

"There may have been a kiss."

A rumble rose in my throat.

"No tongue."

"I suppose," I said finally. "That's a bit better." Kelly averted her face. "Right?"

She nodded vigorously.

"Why can't you look at me?"

"Don't be mad."

"Babe, mad is if you don't tell me what the fuck's going on with your obvious evasion."

She sighed and mumbled something.

"I didn't hear you."

"I thought the kiss was nice and I felt a tingle."

I did not like the sound of this tingle. It came back to what Tom said about chemistry. To keep from roaring at her, I flattened my mouth.

She sneaked a look at me again. "Are you mad I told you the truth?"

"I'm not happy," I said. "I'm not pissed at you, Kelly, but I'm not denying if Tom was in front of us right now, I'd want him to see this."

Her eyes widened. "What?" The way her husky voice washed over me made me hard all over.

"Chemistry." Then I kissed her, pressing her into the door with my body as my hands snaked down her sides. She moaned and opened her mouth, allowing my tongue to invade and conquer. Fuck, it didn't take much for her to turn me on. But throw in some competition, and the green-eyed monster threatened to consume me.

A warning in the back of my head told me to rein it in and not maul my wife, making this another desperate attempt to connect with each other through sex. That cycle had to stop. Still, I needed to know if she was wet. She was. I could smell her arousal, but I wanted her to admit it was for me.

I was a needy fucker.

While still devouring her mouth, my fingers gripped the edges of her skirt and shoved it up. I answered her moan with a gratified grunt and let my fingers stroke between her legs finding her drenched. I tore my mouth away, but kept it a scant breadth away. "This better be for me, beautiful."

"You know it is," she said.

Our breaths mingled, thick and heavy with the want between us.

I gave her a quick kiss before sinking to my knees, inhaling her through the fabric of her panties. I tugged them down exposing her pussy. Her skin was smooth as silk there and I gave it a tongue lashing, feeling her fingers dig into my hair.

"We shouldn't do this." She moaned from above me.

I clenched my jaw. She was right. Though we hadn't fucked for six months, it was mostly because I was avoiding the talk about how we were taking our separation to the next level—meaning divorce.

Kelly definitely pushed me to face that inevitability.

But, plot twist, babe, I was never letting you go.

I slid her panties all the way down, but she refused to lift her stilettoed foot and let me have them. "I'm stopping, but I'm keeping these."

She emitted a brief laugh that was laced with annoyance and amusement. "What is this … spoils of war?"

"Battle." I told her. I hadn't won the war yet. She lifted her foot and finally awarded me possession of her panties. I stuffed them in my pocket.

I rose to my feet and cupped her face. "Ask me to stay."

She shook her head. "I told you, we shouldn't do this."

"No sex."

She raised a brow. "After that display, you think we'll have self-control?"

"You're admitting you can't resist me?"

"I don't want to hurt your feelings if I succeed."

I barked a laugh. "Oh, beautiful." I kissed her again out of fondness, but she moaned and again, I had to remind myself of the long game.

I reluctantly pulled away. "Just so you know … Tom knows dick about chemistry."

"He has a point about—"

A change in my stare had her clamping her mouth shut. Good.

Fuck Tom Roth. He wasn't stealing my wife.

I planted a kiss on her forehead. "You think about whatever is bothering you tonight, but this limbo between us has gone on long enough. I'll pick up the girls tomorrow."

I eased her from the door and opened it. Oxygen rushed into my lungs and cleared my head. I strode to the SUV without looking back.

3

Kelly

"I want to bring Snuffles."

Looking up from cramming more clothes into a suitcase than what two girls would need for a weekend stay with their dad, I stared at Ashley in her dark purple tutu. Mr. Snuffles was her gray two-foot long stuffed hippo.

"You don't want to leave him at your dad's by mistake, right?"

Her bottom lip stuck out. "But Daddy went to pick him up anyway and brought him over."

My girls were experts in getting their own way with their dad. I wasn't sure where they'd learned the art of cute manipulation, probably from my cousins on the Italian side of the family.

Whitney walked in and dropped her pajamas into the already-bursting suitcase. I blew imaginary hair from my forehead. "Do I need to remind both of you that this is only for a weekend?"

"Why can't we stay longer with Daddy?" Whitney asked.

I long suspected Levi was letting them get away with things. He and I had this co-parenting stuff down, but it took a while for us to get there, especially since Ash hadn't been comfortable around her dad without me. But I was proud at how far Levi had come to earn our youngest daughter's trust. He'd lowered his pride, sought counseling, worked on his anger, and accepted what *happened* was beyond his control.

"Because both of you have school on Monday. You two can run circles around your dad and trick him into playing hooky from school."

Ashley rolled her eyes. "It wasn't hooky, we had tummy aches. For real."

I lovingly pinched my lying daughter's cheek. "It was also the season premiere of *Hodgetown* season five."

I needed to have a chat with my … what do I call him? My cheeks heated, remembering our encounter last night. Surprisingly, Levi was the one who put the brakes on it. Sex couldn't fix what was broken between us. Neither was love the problem.

The D-word hung between us, and in a way I understood why he didn't want to talk about it. I didn't either and I was the one who wanted the separation. At the time, it was all about the kids. And now? Every time I thought about legally ending our marriage, my stomach churned in a sickening way. It was only in the last time we talked that I pressed for a serious discussion on how to move forward.

A vehicle pulled into our driveway. My girls perked up and rushed downstairs. I ran after them. The last time Whitney threw open the door without being sure who was on the other side, Levi took me aside and chewed my ass out. He was a stickler for security and overprotective as hell.

"Ashley! Whitney! Remember what I told you girls the last time?" I yelled after them.

My youngest fidgeted by the door, beside herself with

excitement when the doorbell rang. I was happy Ashley had gotten closer to Levi.

As my hand tightened around the knob, I looked into the peephole to check if it was him. I tried to calm my heart rate, convincing myself that it was running after the children that caused it to accelerate, and not the anticipation of seeing him again after our explosive encounter the night before.

Opening the door, he darkened the entrance because there was so much of him.

When my brother Callum brought his SEAL buddies to New York during one of their downtimes, it was love at first sight.

Levi's hair used to curl around his neck but he'd shortened it recently into a tapered crew-cut. His jaw sported a sexy perpetual three-day stubble. With a towering build, people moved out of his way. What they didn't know was how his caramel-colored eyes melted at the sight of his girls.

However, at the moment, they were focused on me, and I resisted backing away when they flared. He stepped into me and planted a kiss on my mouth. "Hey, beautiful."

When he pulled away, cockiness tilted the corner of his mouth. He knew I wouldn't berate him in front of our daughters.

Before I could reply, he'd moved past me and gone down on his haunches, welcoming the tackle from Ashley and Whitney.

"Daddy. Daddy."

While the two girls competed for their father's attention, I headed for the stairs. "I'll bring their suitcase down."

"I'll get it," Levi called, getting up.

"I got it," I told him. "Stay with them. They missed you."

In three strides, he closed the distance between us, gripped my arm and turned me around to face him. "I missed their mother too."

"Levi—"

His jaw clenched before gesturing for me to precede him. "After you."

"You just want to look at my ass," I retorted.

His eyes widened and then crinkled at the corners, his mouth splitting into a full-blown grin.

"Mama said the A-word," Ashley told her sister.

I regretted my comeback as I ascended the steps. Besides not winning any mother-of-the year awards, it called attention to my backside which only reminded me that he'd snagged my panties the night before.

When we reached the top, I couldn't look at him. I went straight to Ashley's room and pointed at the suitcase. "Try and get that closed."

"What are your plans after work today?" He asked casually, zipping the suitcase with ease and hauling it off the bed. I grabbed Mr. Snuffles.

I shrugged. "Same old, same old." I had no plans to see Tom. He didn't call after our failed date nor did he respond to my text this morning checking how he was. Not that I'd accept if he had suggested we see each other this weekend.

"You should have dinner with us," he told me as if sensing the battle inside me. "I'm cooking the Levi special spaghetti with cream cheese."

I laughed. "My hips expanded just hearing that."

"So?"

My smile was apologetic. "I can't."

"Why not?" He stopped in the hallway and frowned at me. "Why not?"

"It's your weekend with the girls."

"What's wrong with eating together as a family?"

Sometimes I wanted to whack my estranged husband over the head. He had no concept of being separated—and about to get a divorce. "Because we might give them the wrong idea."

He lowered the suitcase and crossed his arms.

"I think the kids and I have the same idea. We're waiting for their mom to catch up."

"That's not fair. We have things to discuss."

"Exactly. So, when are we going to get a chance to do that?"

"Not when the girls are around."

"So, when?"

"When? When?" My second "when" was almost shrill in disbelief. "You kept brushing me off before and now you want to talk?"

"Because I knew you were going to ask me for a divorce."

I blew out a breath. He was not wrong. "I feel like we're in limbo and I think something's got to give."

"Your answer was to go on a date with another man?"

"I thought we'd already talked about this last night."

"About how my words sent you to the arms of another man?" A muscle ticked in his jaw. "I already apologized for that. It won't happen again." He muttered something else, but I was too pissed to discern his words. "If that's a way for you to get my attention and make me talk to you, then it worked."

I glared at him. "You arrogant ass. Is it always about you? What about maybe I'm sick and tired of being lonely?"

"I'm not the one who wanted this separation."

"But it was needed!" I stomped my foot.

He looked away. "I've fixed my shit with Ashley." His gaze returned to mine. "The girls ... they want us back together."

My chin lifted. "That's the thing, Levi. It's time to work on me."

"You mean us."

I shook my head. "No. I mean *me* separate from *you*."

Our girls made noises of impatience from downstairs.

"They're waiting for you."

His eyes narrowed. "We're not done talking about this."

Why did it take the threat of another man in my life for him to be willing to talk?

Fed up, I snapped, "Fine."

"Tomorrow. What are you doing?"

I shrugged. "Laundry."

His eyes darkened and the gold flecks in them disappeared. "Call you with the details."

"But the girls ..."

"We'll figure something out. We can't dance around this shit any longer."

With that statement, he turned and returned down the stairs.

Both of us plastered smiles in front of the girls who seemed oblivious to the discord between us. Ashley grabbed Mr. Snuffles from me. I walked them to the Escalade.

"The girls heading out for the weekend?" A voice called from across the street.

It was Nana. She and Gramps lived a couple of streets down and made terrific babysitters when I had to work late or travel with the production crew and Levi couldn't take them because of his own job.

The girls greeted Nana briefly, but were clearly excited to leave with their dad.

"Levi," Nana said. "How's work?"

"Keeping me busy."

"Daddy promised to make his special spaghetti." Ashley looked at me. "If Whitney and I don't eat it all, we'll bring you some, Mama."

I smiled at my youngest. "Thanks, baby."

"We need to leave. Traffic." He stared at me. "Don't work too hard, and the offer for dinner stands." He nodded at my grandmother. "Branna."

When they left, Nana turned to me. "You two seem to be fine after what happened last night."

"He wants to talk about it."

"I thought you said he gave you his blessing."

"He did."

Nana raised a brow.

"Okay, he said it was because he was pissed off. He said he didn't expect me to go through with it."

My grandmother snorted a laugh. "Men. They should know better than to issue a challenge like that." She looked at me knowingly. "Especially to a McGrath." Amusement glinted in her eyes. "Tom is a good guy, but I don't think he's for you."

Annoyed, I looked at Nana. "Why do you say that? You like Tom. You and Gramps encouraged me to date him."

"Seeing you with Levi, it's clear you two have—"

"Please don't say chemistry," I groaned. "That's what got us into trouble in the first place."

Nana looked at me speculatively. "Do you want to come over for tea?"

I checked my watch. "I need to get ready."

"All right, but I need to get out my piece."

"I knew it," I laughed, though not so much in humor since "come over for tea" meant a lecture.

"Don't get smart with me, young lady."

"Not that young anymore. I'm thirty-two."

She tipped her chin to where Levi's Escalade disappeared. "Your husband is trying, but I'm not seeing you trying hard enough."

"That's not fair, he—"

"He still loves you."

"Sometimes love isn't enough."

"Marriage isn't easy. Having one foot out of a relationship isn't commitment. And now look where that got you."

"Don't you think I know that? Why do you think I wanted to talk to him about a divorce? Maybe a clean break is what we need." Again, my bravado at saying those words belied the sickening feeling in my gut. But I was tired of running in place. Something drastic needed to happen to force a change.

"I was against you marrying a sailor, if you remember."

"I know, Nana."

"But you couldn't see past the stars in your eyes."

"We'd been fine for four years. I really thought we would make it." My voice broke with emotion.

Nana's eyes etched with pain. The pain of losing my brother, Callum ... his death had a rippling effect on the McGraths, Levi, and even Tom.

She cleared her throat. "As I was saying, your husband is trying. I understood the separation for working things out. But this has gone on long enough. My advice, and I say this with much love, either work on putting your marriage back together or let him go."

Let him go?

Thinking it to myself already made me sick, but hearing it coming from someone else was like a shot to the heart.

He was willing to talk now.

It was time to decide whether to give our marriage a second chance.

Levi

It took the possibility of losing her to another man to face my fears of a divorce. It burned a hole in my chest from Europe all the way to the U.S. With my luck, she would be serving me those papers tomorrow instead of having a chat. In a place like Hollywood, anything was possible for a price. Kelly had friends in high places who could have a lawyer draft divorce papers overnight.

I was a pushy asshole, but seeing her with Tom lit a fire under my ass.

"Daddy, are you mad?"

Ashley, my ever-inquisitive angel, asked from the back.

"No. Why do you ask, sweetheart?" I forced a smile on my

face.

"'Coz, you've got those lines between your brows."

"I'm thinking how to get around this traffic, sweetie." This was partially true. The 101 was always a nightmare. The weekend was no different.

"I think Dad didn't like Mom going out with Uncle Tom," Whitney said.

My fingers tightened around the wheel. I *did not* like my kids calling him "uncle". That indicated he was family. He needed to stay in the friend zone, preferably in the end zone. "Does he come over often?"

My two girls exchanged looks, but didn't answer.

I realized my brows had drawn together again. "Did your mom tell you not to say anything to me?" Goddammit. I had sunk to my lowest ... milking my daughters for information. "Don't answer that."

Whitney giggled behind me. "Which one don't you want us to answer?"

I gritted my teeth and changed the subject. "How's school?"

"School is boring," Ashley piped in. "Miss Harrington told me to write 'I will not put gum in Samantha's hair ever again' a bajillion times."

Kelly texted me about that while I was on assignment in Europe. I tried not to laugh, but I couldn't keep the amusement from my voice. "That was not nice, pumpkin."

"She makes fun of Ashley," Whitney defended her sister. "She says you and Mom hate each other. That's why you don't live together."

Words stuck in my throat. I didn't know what to say. It wasn't the first time our kids asked us about the living situation. In the beginning, I didn't even have days where I could keep them. Kelly and I wanted to make sure Ashley was comfortable being around me without her mother. It took months. And then, so as not to disrupt their routine, we kept them in the same house while Kelly and I switched out places. That went on for a year. I'd since bought a house in Los Angeles as a way of proving I was here to stay and my nomadic days were over.

"Your mom and I are working things out," I gave our agreed-upon standard response. I seemed to keep messing up. It wasn't that Kelly was opposed to the nature of my job as a SEAL and later as a private military contractor. She was handling that part fine. It was when I was stateside and still not mentally present with anger issues. She'd repeatedly asked me to seek help and to go to couple's counseling. I was too cocky, thinking she loved me enough to deal with my bullshit.

"Do you still love Mama?" Ashley asked.

Heat burned up my throat. "Yes, baby girl, I do."

I never stopped loving Kelly. From the moment I laid eyes on Callum's sassy sister, I was smitten. Her dark hair was the color of midnight, and her blue eyes flashed translucent when she was emotional. I called her "beautiful" from the beginning because I felt that to my core. I still remembered that time when I knew she was going to be my future.

As a product of foster homes, I was used to being unwanted and avoided invitations from my teammates to visit family because I was so used to being alone. But I was so damned glad Callum's persistence got through my stubbornness. We were at her family's Irish pub, Eamonn's. Kelly had never been impressed by her brother's SEAL buddies, so when one of my drunk teammates made fun of an equally drunk homeless man, she reamed his ass. Not only was she beautiful, but she stood up for the less fortunate. At that moment, I fell in love. After Callum's death, I lost my way, but I have never stopped loving her.

I glanced in the rearview mirror at my girls.

They deserved more. My wife deserved more.

All I needed was to convince Kelly to give me a second chance.

4

KELLY

THE HOWARD SPECIAL EFFECTS studio was quiet this Saturday. It was unusual. On any given day, there would be an army of SFX artists working around me, but the team was up in Vegas doing finishing touches on a big budget superhero movie. As the clutch-time designer on the production, the director and costume designer tasked me with the key pieces for the final desert showdown.

Currently, my attention wasn't on the silicone masks on the table. My thoughts were on my marriage.

On Levi.

On the girls.

On my brother, Callum.

Invisible claws dug into my heart.

The film was based on a comic book he loved as a kid. I took on the project on the condition that his name would be included in the dedication.

A lump formed in my throat. Callum's death triggered the death spiral of our marriage. A SEAL mission went sideways in the Gulf of Aden. Details about the op weren't made public until two years after the event. Levi couldn't give me the info, and I knew that killed him, and it was why he stayed away from us. He couldn't get to Callum when an explosion rocked the ship and killed my brother.

I inspected the paint job on a silicone mask and decided it was good for now. Only when it was dry could I decide if it was perfect, but my years of experience indicated it would be.

I checked my watch. Nine o'clock.

I didn't need an alibi not to make it to Levi's dinner. Our marriage was stuck in an endless cycle of one step closer, two steps back. At one point in the last three weeks, I was feeling strongly about divorce. A clean break. But Levi muddled my resolve, showing me how far he would go to keep me. Surprisingly, he didn't do that by fucking me senseless.

I had a million reasons to end our marriage.

But I held on these past eighteen months thinking I needed that one good reason for me to stay in it.

The failure of our marriage was my fault as much as his. It certainly had a lot to do with my own baggage.

The line of silicone masks blurred as I processed when our marriage started to crack.

After Callum was killed, my husband transformed into a stranger I couldn't bear to be around. Withdrawn. So angry at the world that even our youngest daughter avoided him. We were supposed to grieve the loss of Callum together. Instead, we did it separately.

Tom had been a bigger support than my own husband. But even Tom gave excuses that it was probably survivor's guilt. I asked Levi to seek help. But he quit the SEALs and became a mercenary instead and drifted further and further away from his family.

What was bad became worse.

When the mask came back into focus, I bit back a smile and thought of Callum. This particular piece was his favorite character from that superhero world. Bittersweet memories washed over me.

Cal looked out for me especially when my mother's side of the family were being assholes because I was a scourge to their family name. I was a result of a love affair between Charles McGrath and Sofia Rossi. As her bastard daughter, I was an obstacle to an arranged marriage between the Rossis and the Chicago Crime family. My biological father was in jail at the time I was born, so I was adopted by Cal's parents, Robert and Mads. Charles was Robert's brother. So, technically, I was Cal's cousin but he'd treated me no different from his other siblings.

When Callum left for BUD/S, I was the one who cried the most. He was my partner in crime when special effects interested me after I watched *Galaxy Quest*. He liked it when I used him for a guinea pig. He even covered for me when I crazy glued cheap silicone pieces to his and our youngest sister, Alana's, foreheads.

When I was in high school, I stole ingredients from the chemistry lab so I could make my own gel. The commercial mixture was expensive, especially to a teenager who was on an allowance. Working extra hours at the pub bussing tables didn't cover the expenses either. So, I bought cheap molds from the backs of vans that trolled Times Square and tried to cook my own gel mask in our brownstone. It started a kitchen fire. Cal took the blame for that, and our parents punished him instead of me. Though I had a feeling they knew the true transgressor, they took that opportunity to ground Cal when he started hanging out with a shady crowd.

Callum was my person until Levi came into my life. There was an unprocessed guilt for myself. I couldn't completely grieve with the McGraths, so maybe I understood why Levi pulled away from me after my brother died.

There was survivor's guilt.

Then there was also a different kind.

Before my mind could prod deeper into my complicated emotions, the studio's guard poked his head into the SFX department.

"Miss James?"

"Yes?"

"There's a Detective Woodward here to see you."

Gabby's here? "Can you show her in?" I proceeded to transfer the masks to the curing rack so they would dry right.

The guard nodded and closed the door.

What did Gabby want from me? She was married to one of Levi's teammates. Teammate sounded too organizational and there was nothing organized about Levi's team. They didn't have an outfit name. Everyone appeared to be a contractor. Even though John Garrison, their CIA handler, was running the show and throwing them jobs, none of them really answered to anyone. Going rogue was a constant refrain. I shook my head. That's what you get when you put all alpha males together. No one was the boss of anyone.

The door opened again, letting the detective through. She was dressed in a chic sports suit but still gave off the no-nonsense detective vibe. Looking at her, one couldn't tell she used to be a popular teen star of a zombie series that I loved. Her son, Theo Cole, was the star of the Primeflix money-making series, *Hodgetown*. Hollywood royalty certainly ran in their bloodline.

"Gabby, this is a surprise." She and her son were the main stakeholders in Revenant Films which produced the *Hodgetown* series. I had the pleasure of working with Theo in previous seasons.

She looked around. "So this is where all the magic happens."

As an artist, I noticed the contours of her face, the shape of her eyes and their unusual chestnut color. She and her husband Declan made a gorgeous couple. Levi's friend was no slouch in the looks department but I was biased. I thought

Levi was the sexiest among the bunch. But then, I loved brutish looking men who dwarfed me. Scratch that. There was only one and it was Levi.

"Kelly?"

Crap. I realized Gabby was waiting for my answer, and instead I was daydreaming about my estranged husband.

I grinned wryly. "Sorry, I'm always awestruck by the color of your eyes."

Gabby laughed. "Now, you're going to make me blush."

I snorted. "With all you see as an LAPD detective? I doubt anything makes you blush nowadays."

"True." But her cheeks did heighten in color, and I bet it wasn't my comment about her eyes, but more about what made her blush. And I didn't need two guesses to know she thought about Declan.

"What brings you here, detective?"

"RHD is spread thin right now and requested our assistance on the case. It's not a priority, but Kelso and I offered to do the groundwork."

Working in LA, I'd learned that RHD meant Robbery and Homicide Division. My gut tightened and my gaze lowered to the rest of the masks, my mind racing. "Who?"

"Don't be alarmed. Everything is still sketchy."

A chill rose up my spine. "You know that's the wrong thing to say if a person shouldn't be alarmed."

"Tom Roth."

My jaw dropped. "What?"

"His office asked us to do a wellness check when he failed to show up at an important meeting this morning."

"He missed that?" Tom had mentioned we could spend Saturday evening together to celebrate closing a big deal.

Gabby nodded. "LAPD sent patrol officers over to his West Hollywood residence." She was watching me carefully when she added, "There were signs of a struggle. Coffee table smashed, chairs overturned, and more."

"Oh my God."

"No body. Nothing on the security cameras. No sign of forced entry."

"Do they know—" I cut off. My mind scrambled. Sooner or later they would discover the altercation at the restaurant. "It's not Levi."

"Don't tell me anything," Gabby warned. "Kelso is on his way to Levi's now. Anyone with a brain would agree that it would be stupid to go after Roth after that scene in the parking lot last night."

"Shit."

"You were in the appointment book for dinner last night. RHD contacted us because they knew you assisted the department last year. I was surprised when I saw the footage from the restaurant though." Gabby shook her head. "These men. Why am I not surprised?"

The detective regarded me carefully. "He took you home afterwards?"

"I'm not saying anything else until I talk to my husband."

"Fair enough."

Levi

"CAN WE WATCH TV?"

I glanced away from my phone and looked at Whitney. "Sure, princess."

My focus scattered between entertaining the girls and figuring out how to convince Kelly to give us a second chance. I hoped she'd show up for dinner and obviously she wasn't or she'd be here by now. But she hadn't called to check on the girls and wish them goodnight.

I pushed away thoughts of her and Tom together. She said she wasn't going to see him, and I trusted her word.

"It's Saturday night, go ahead and find something." Once I repaired my relationship with Ashley, they became effortless to manage. If they had their way, they'd sit in front of the television for hours. But in an attempt to establish well-rounded children, I had to cajole them to leave their preferred entertainment on the couch and go to theme parks or go hiking.

"Yay," they both squealed, and it was like a stampede to the living room. Kelly chided me about letting them watch too much television, but I knew she was secretly pleased our little heathens carried that McGrath trait. Besides, the same thing happened when they were at their grandparents.

"There's a new PrimeFlix movie. I think it's a vampire," Whitney called.

I hurried to the living room to make sure that it was PG at least. It wasn't. Rated R for sex and violence. "Pick another one."

"How about this? It's a cartoon." I checked the synopsis and rating. Sometimes these cartoons were too scary or too adult for kids. PG. No warnings of any sort. "That's good. Start the movie. I need to tidy up the kitchen."

Unable to help myself, I swiped Kelly's number, but it went immediately to voicemail.

"Hey, babe, you're probably swamped. But I wanted to let you know the girls are fine." I started putting away the dirty dishes. "No matter how late it is, if you want to come over. Please do."

I ended the call, hoping I didn't sound like a pathetic bastard. I lingered in the kitchen, hoping she'd call back immediately and pretended to still be putting the dishes away.

"You're making too much noise, Daddy," Ashley yelled.

Shaking my head, I asked, "You girls want anything from here?"

"Chips and soda?" Whitney asked.

"Didn't you both wolf down two plates of spaghetti and slices of cheesecake?"

"Then why are you asking if we need anything?" Ashley asked.

"Water?" I asked.

"Just you, Daddy."

My heart rolled under my chest. My talk with Kelly could wait, but I couldn't help thinking if she were here, it would make our family complete. Why couldn't she see that?

I filled a pitcher of water and took out a plate of fruit and cheese from the fridge. These kids might have just finished dinner, but watching television made them hungry. Popcorn probably at midnight. I was certainly in the running for father of the year.

As was their routine, Whitney and Ashley sat on opposite sides of the couch to make room for me in the middle. Afterward, they'd attach to my sides like a pair of barnacles.

Twenty minutes went by and the cartoon couldn't hold my attention because my eyes kept straying to my phone on the side table, willing it to ring. Unable to stand it, I leaned over Ashley and grabbed it.

"Daddy, no phone," my youngest pouted.

"I told your Mom to call me back."

"Oooh, maybe if we all leave her a message, she'll come," Whitney said.

I grinned at my girls. "Good idea." Maybe it was time to use our girls as bait. If there was one thing I couldn't fault Kelly for, it was how much she loved them. Although she was less susceptible to their manipulation than I was, it didn't take much more to have her cave.

They were great kids, and I couldn't have asked for better.

We paused the movie and all of us went to the kitchen. I checked her location again with my girls on either side of me. I broke into a smile. Her dot was a few miles from the house.

I called her number again to tease her. I didn't care if she knew I was stalking her. But it went to voicemail again. Whatever. Maybe she wanted to surprise us. I was all for that.

"Is that Mom's green dot?" Whitney asked.

"Yes."

"Does that mean she's close to the house?"

I grinned at Whit. "Yup."

The excitement on my girls' faces made me exhale my mixed emotions. Hope. Anxiety. Fear. Uncertainty. I was seventy percent sure Kelly showing up was a sign our conversation was heading in the right direction. But it didn't matter because whatever she decided, I wasn't giving up.

The doorbell rang.

I frowned and checked my phone. Her dot was still two miles away and it had just updated. I needed to talk to Bristow about its accuracy. A retired SEAL, he was our team's comms and surveillance expert and his experience as a medic saved my ass when things went FUBAR in Mexico. The girls, as usual, ran to the door, but had the sense to glance back at me, and I gave them my stern dad look.

Checking the peephole, I was surprised to see Kelso.

Did my wife have an accident on the way here? My anxiety spiked to dangerous levels. Was that why she wasn't answering her phone?

It felt like an eternity to open the door.

Kelso frowned when he saw my face.

"Did something happen to Kelly?" I snarled.

His frown cleared, and he started shaking his head, easing my worry a bit.

"No. Sorry, man, she didn't call you?"

I wasn't about to admit to stalking my wife to anyone else except myself.

I shook my head.

"Come on in," I invited.

"Hey, girls," Kelso greeted.

"Why don't you head back and watch the cartoon? Kelso and I have something to discuss."

The girls dawdled in the foyer for a few seconds, their faces etched with disappointment. But kids being kids, they bounced back into the living room to continue the show we'd been watching.

I gestured to the sitting room. "What's going on?"

"Tom Roth. How well do you know him?"

I stilled, then a wave of fury swept through me. "Roth filed an assault complaint? He had it coming." But then Kelso was a homicide cop. Cold sweat dampened my forehead. "Fuck, he didn't have a condition, did he?" What if that motherfucker croaked?

"Not that I'm aware of. He didn't show up for an important meeting this morning and beat officers did a wellness check. His house had been ransacked and there were signs of a struggle."

"All right." I crossed my arms. "You guys saw the surveillance at the restaurant and naturally, I'm the first suspect."

"You're the obvious, yet unlikely, suspect," the detective said. "Because why attack a guy for everyone to see and then turn around and assault him at his home?"

I shrugged. "Act of passion."

Kelso barked a short laugh and pointed a finger at me. "Don't say that in front of the detective in charge."

"I'm pretty sure I could clear myself." Still, I did a mental check that I had my bases covered. "Do you want me to come into the station?"

"Looks like I don't need to coach you on anything. RHD is overwhelmed with cases. I doubt they'd hold you for long. And, no, not without a body. Gabby and I were making sure you both knew what was coming."

I raised a brow. "Isn't that a conflict of interest?"

"You're friends of the LAPD. You've helped us nail down

several terrorist threats. We've grown fond of your hulking ass."

The doorbell rang again. As I was walking over, Kelso said, "That's Gabby. She has Kelly with her."

I opened the door to his partner and my wife.

I caught a glimpse of Kelly's worried face before she stepped into me and hugged me.

5

KELLY

"DON'T SAY ANYTHING. I know a good lawyer." My arms tightened around his torso as I stared up at him.

Levi's brows rose. "Do you now?"

"What's going on? Is Dad in trouble?" I peeked past him at Whit and Ash. Their deflated faces made me want to kick myself.

I didn't think about the kids.

Great going, Mom.

Extricating myself from my husband, I walked to my girls and put a hand on each of their shoulders. "It's nothing. We'll get it sorted out."

"But why are they here?" Ashley asked, pointing to Gabby and Kelso. "They're cops. Did Daddy do something?"

Levi went to my side. "Just a misunderstanding, baby girl. Go back to your movie."

"Is this a discussion for grown-ups?" Whitney scrunched her nose.

A brief laugh escaped me despite my anxiety. That excuse

wouldn't fly with my children for long. "Yes. Everything will be fine. Promise."

"Okay," Ashley said. "We got interrupted at a good part of the movie. Come on, Whit."

My youngest skipped back to the living room, but Whitney hung back, brows still knit with worry.

"Go ahead," I said. "Keep Ash company."

When my eldest returned to the living room, our group moved to the sitting area.

"I should've let you stay with me last night," I told my husband. "Then you'd have an alibi."

Levi winked at me. "See, that would've solved our problem."

"I don't know why you're so relaxed about this," I snapped. "Tom is missing." I was worried about my friend, too, and my husband finally cottoned to this. "And you could be a suspect," I added.

"So which aspect are you more worried about? That Tom is missing or your husband could be charged with his murder. That is … if they could find his body—"

Kelso coughed into his fist. "Cops present."

"Not to mention I *am* the father of your children."

Levi's expression turned stone cold. When he did that in the bedroom to mess with me, it turned me on, but when it was a matter of life and death—not to mention his future as a free man was at stake—it pissed me off.

"Don't be an ass about this." I glanced at Gabby who was looking at me with sympathy. A potential candidate as a man in my life was missing while my potential ex-husband could be the suspect.

"You're putting her in a difficult position," Gabby said.

"It was already a difficult position to be in last night," I grumbled, glancing at the detectives. "It would be too stupid for him to go after Tom after everyone in the restaurant witnessed their fight."

"I don't know, Kelly," Kelso said. "Levi said it could be an act of passion."

I spun on my husband who still had his poker face on. "Are you fucking kidding me?" Then remembering that the kids had a penchant for eavesdropping, I lowered my voice, "Are you trying to get thrown into prison?"

"Oh, so now you care?" he said. "Wouldn't that clear the way for Roth? Oh wait, he might be at the bottom of the lake somewhere."

I snapped my mouth closed.

Kelso and Gabby turned away but their shoulders shook with laughter.

I was about to explode on my husband.

I was speechless.

Speechless.

That was when I saw the glint of amusement in his eyes.

"You have an alibi," I whispered.

He snagged me around the neck in that possessive hold that made my knees go weak and brought his mouth to my ear.

"Maybe. But can't say I'm pleased you're worrying about the other guy."

"I'm worried for a friend."

"A friend? One you said you felt a tingle when he kissed you." He leaned away to watch my reaction.

I glared. The desire to knee him in his groin was as overwhelming as my desire to ride his dick.

Levi, very slowly, swiped his tongue on his lower lip.

Or I could ride his face. Gah!

Stop.

"Is it getting hot in here?" Kelso teased.

We both turned to the detectives who were looking everywhere but us.

Levi chuckled. "Sorry. You caught us at a heated moment."

"Obviously," Gabby said dryly.

Kelso checked his phone. "The detectives on Roth's case are ready to see you."

"It's ten." It was a weak protest. Crime doesn't have a time in LA.

My husband shrugged. "Let's get it over and done with." He looked at me. "Can you stay with the girls until I get back? I'm not sure what time it'll be. Plan on staying the night, hmm?"

"Of course."

"Use my bedroom." His face was unreadable. "I have shit in the two other rooms."

"You haven't unpacked?" I rolled my eyes.

"I was hoping you'd help me." He winked at me.

This man. "Go." I gave him a shove. "Hopefully, there'll be no problem."

"Pretty sure it's simply a formality." Gabby split a look between us. "They may talk to you about your relationship with Tom, too."

"There is no relationship," Levi growled beside me.

I yanked him around and cupped his jaw with my hands. "Do not fuck this up, okay? Don't let the detectives egg you into admitting something that will incriminate you."

His jaw clenched tight before he gritted, "Not my first rodeo."

"You know what I mean." I cocked my head at Kelso. "Does he need a lawyer present?"

"We know Delgado and Chen. They're good people," the detective said. "I don't think they're going to look hard in Levi's direction."

That gave me little assurance.

Levi squeezed my hand. "Don't worry. It'll be fine. I promise."

. . .

AFTER THEY LEFT, I rounded the girls back into the living room. Ashley was in tears while Whitney was close to breaking down, her face mottled red.

"But why did they take Dad away?" Whitney asked, her mouth trembling.

"They want to ask him a few questions. Your Uncle Tom is missing."

"Is it my fault? I told Dad you were going on a date."

As much as I wanted to lecture my daughter with a lesson about manipulating her parents, this wasn't a teaching moment, especially since the consequences were unknown. I tried to beat back my own worry for Tom.

"No, honey. Tom's disappearance had nothing to do with what you told your Dad."

"Gramps said Dad could make people disappear," Whitney declared.

"What?" I need to have a chat with my grandfather. "When did he say this?"

"A long time ago … when there were bad people going after Theo."

I relaxed. "Well Tom isn't bad people."

"So bad people are after Uncle Tom? Does that mean Daddy will help find him?" Ashley asked pensively.

"There are cops for that." Whit scowled at her sister. "Don't mention that to Dad."

I rubbed my brow feeling the beginnings of a headache. Even though Ash and Levi had come a long way in their relationship, and there was no doubt that my youngest daughter now favored her father over her Uncle Tom, it would still sting if Levi heard that statement. Any mention of Tom seemed to trigger my husband nowadays.

"Everything is going to be fine," I repeated. "It's getting late. You both need to get to bed."

"How about you, Mom?"

"I'll wait up for your dad, but if I can't, I'll sleep on the couch."

"Dad has a real big comfy bed," Whit grinned.

Oh my little matchmaker. "Go on, go brush. Lights-out in thirty minutes." My daughters must have sensed my exhaustion and did as they were told. They shared a bedroom in Levi's house that had an ensuite bathroom. After I made sure they had everything they needed, I did a little exploring.

With a four bedroom house, Levi's crap occupied two of them. My husband still had the boxes packed up from when he moved out. I made my way to his bedroom. I had nothing to wear to bed so he owed me a t-shirt to sleep in. Without feeling guilty, I entered his master bedroom and couldn't resist looking around.

My eyes caught a piece of black fabric on the nightstand. My panties from last night.

I couldn't even summon feelings of outrage. Immediate heat pulsed between my legs. My pervy husband perving on me was hot as hell. Did he inhale my underwear last night as he jacked himself off on the bed?

Or did he wrap the scrap of fabric around his erection while he fucked his fist?

Oh, my God, my daughters were in the next room, and I was having X-rated visions of Levi's massive body writhing on the bed.

Shaking my head, I reclaimed my panties and rummaged through his dresser for a t-shirt, opting for the softest and most threadbare one. I sniffed it. It smelled so good.

I took a quick shower and laundered the two panties I now had in my possession and ran them through the drier for a few minutes before hanging them up. Hopefully, by the time I actually went to bed, one pair would be dry. I wasn't getting into Levi's bed. I didn't want to give him the wrong idea. The couch was comfortable enough, and it was only for a night.

I settled in front of the television with a bowl of cold spaghetti and turned on the television.

KELLY

"BABE ..."

A rumbling voice was so soothing in my ear, I tried to burrow further into the pillows.

But they were hard. Not exactly rocks, but there was no give, and they were oddly warm.

Someone was carrying me.

"Levi?"

"Shh ..."

"Did you just come home?"

"Yes."

"Put me down. Tell me what happened."

Wakefulness battled with my heavy lids.

"Tomorrow. I'm not rehashing anything tonight. Everything's fine."

"Okay." My mind drifted off again.

"Why did you sleep on the couch?"

I inhaled his scent. He always smelled good. Sandalwood and clean soap. Comforting yet all man. "I was watching reruns." I yawned. "I fell asleep."

"Obviously."

"I didn't finish an episode I think."

"You're tired, babe, from working all day and the excitement of tonight."

I let his voice surround me with serenity. Things might be really fine.

I was placed on the softest mattress. Consequences flew

out the window. "You won't fit on the couch." Another yawn escaped me, and I rolled over to one corner of the bed.

"I don't plan to sleep on the couch."

Hmm, I muttered. "Put a pillow between us."

"That won't stop you." There was laughter in his voice.

"I borrowed your shirt."

"I see that."

"I took back my panties."

"I see that too."

I yawned. "I'm not wearing any."

I never heard his reply as sleep claimed me once more.

Levi

My hard-on kept me awake all night.

I needed sleep after the night I'd had, but did I think to move to the couch? No. For the obvious reason that it would be damned uncomfortable, I would cut off a finger before I gave up the chance to finally share a bed with my sexy-as-sin wife.

Not that it wasn't heaven and hell. With sweat beading my skin, and my poor molars grinding against each other, I fought the urge to crawl between her legs and bury my face in her sweet pussy.

I put the pillow between us as she requested. Somehow, in her tossing and turning, she'd grabbed the stupid thing and had thrown it somewhere on the floor.

She'd been plastered to me for the last hour, a leg thrown over my thighs. Every time I ran baseball stats in my head and I thought I'd survive, she'd rub her bare pussy on my leg.

Jesus Christ.

That was sweet fucking torture.

I didn't want to move.

I didn't want to wake her.

I did not touch her inappropriately or seduce her.

One would say I was the one being seduced.

Again. Jesus Christ.

The back of my neck was drenched.

My cock was rock hard. It would take only a few strokes to give me relief. But since I liked to torment myself where Kelly was concerned, I refused to budge.

Sometime before dawn I fell asleep, but it must've been short since I was jolted awake to the sensation of fingers fluttering over my skin, inches above my morning wood.

Kelly was awake.

The hitch in her breathing was different, more pronounced, its rhythm erratic.

"Any lower and I won't be responsible for the consequences," I warned.

"What happened to the pillow?" Her husky voice was sex itself. Everything about this woman did it for me.

I choked with laughter. She was too cute. "I told you that wouldn't work, beautiful. Hasn't in the ten years we've been married." When she was pissed at me, and we hadn't settled our fight before bedtime, she always put a pillow between us.

The heat of her pussy branded my thigh. Our bodies were frozen, but need throbbed between us.

"I don't know if this is a test from the powers above," I groaned.

"You should have left me on the couch."

She tried to extract herself, but my arms automatically came around her, locking her in place.

"Levi," she mumbled. "We shouldn't."

"What were you about to do before I interrupted you?"

"Nothing," she whispered.

"Don't lie, babe."

"I wanted to see your cock," she said.

I inhaled sharply. "Do you want to take it out?" I wore athletic shorts so I wouldn't be tempted to roll over and shove into her.

"I shouldn't."

"But you want to … You don't have to finish me off," I said. "I can take care of it myself."

"What's in it for you?"

I was staring up at the ceiling the whole time, but when I felt her gaze on me, I turned to look at her. "You know you're gorgeous when you're just waking up?" As much as I loved our scorching tear-your-clothes-off sexual encounters, sleepy Kelly sex was also a turn-on. She was extremely pliable, and she would take however I gave it.

Pre-cum beaded my cock. Could I really hold out and beat one out in the shower?

"Hmm." She rubbed her face against the side of my chest. "That's not an answer."

"It's going to be all about you, babe."

She laughed briefly. "Somehow I think I'm going to be the recipient of endless orgasms. Need I remind you our kids are in the next room?"

"Then you'll have to be quiet. Take me out."

"Levi …"

"We're not having sex. Not in the real sense. Consider this foreplay."

"Foreplay to what?"

"Take my cock out, Kelly. Inspect it. You know you missed him. "

"Since when do you talk about your cock in third person?"

I chuckled as I unwrapped my arms from around her so she could move freely. I crooked them under my head.

She propped up on an elbow and shot me a suspicious look. "I thought we weren't going to confuse our talk with sex."

Grinning at her, I said, "Don't worry. I'm in control. We won't have sex. And you're not sucking me off either."

She raised a brow.

I puffed a laugh. "Even if you insist, I'm not gonna fuck you."

She narrowed her eyes as her hands slipped under the band of my shorts. "You seem so sure of that."

When her fingers encircled my shaft, I groaned in pleasure. "Fuck, yes. That's it, babe." She squeezed. "Good girl." I started to pump my hips.

"Are you sure I can't lick it?"

"You're killing me ... just ... just do that..."

"Levi, I don't get it," she whispered. "I can give you relief."

I realized my eyes were shut. I popped one open and said, "Touch yourself."

"What?"

"Tell me if you're wet."

She bit her bottom lip. And with one hand still holding my cock at her mercy, her other one reached between her legs. Her immediate whimper almost had me busting a nut. "So, so slick."

"Fuck, you're so hot right now." I gritted and pumped my hips against her hand.

"I don't see the point in this."

"Don't get yourself off," I warned.

"You don't make sense," she whined. "I need ... need ..."

"I know what you need, beautiful, but you have to be quiet."

"What?"

I pulled her over me, having her straddle my hips. She scooted her ass and rubbed her pussy against my shaft, and I could have exploded right there. I held back, keeping us on a razor's edge of one of the most erotic mornings we'd had in a long time.

"Levi," she moaned again. "I need you inside me." Her wet rimmed the bulb of my cock that wanted inside so fucking much.

"Come up here."

"What?"

"Ride my face, babe," I ordered.

Without giving her a chance to protest, I hauled her up and sat her wet heat over my mouth and thrust my tongue right in. Her wetness gushed all over my mouth.

She was saturated with her juices, and I greedily consumed every last drop that fell on my tongue. Her musky scent surrounded me, and I didn't care if I suffocated under the weight of her cunt.

She squealed. I gave her thighs a squeeze and got out, "Hands to the headboard and keep a lid on it."

"Oh my God, oh my God," she continued moaning. "Levi, oh my God, that's so good."

I assaulted every part of her pussy, putting as much of her swelling flesh into my mouth and went to town licking and sucking until her reedy cries reached my ears.

"I can't anymore…"

She tried to climb off, but I held on fast to wring every last bit of her orgasm.

"Levi! Stop," she hissed, but then promptly moaned again.

I flipped us over and braced my elbows on either side of her head, pumping my painful erection against her. It didn't help that my cock happily found its place at her entrance.

Her legs went around me.

"I can easily shove in," I said quietly. "But I won't."

"Why would you torture yourself?"

"Because I promised I wouldn't fuck you until you gave our marriage a second chance."

She looked away. "How is this different?"

I cupped her chin and angled it back my way. "I care more for your needs than mine. This is a shallow way to prove it, but it's a start. I want to give you everything, Kelly. All I need is a clear shot. A clean slate."

Kelly shook her head. "It's not fair to ask me this right after giving me a mind-blowing orgasm."

A grin curved my mouth. "That good, huh?"

She rolled her eyes. "You know it was."

A timid knock sounded on the door.

Kelly and I looked at each other before I said quietly, "It's not locked."

I flipped on my back and shoved a pillow on my crotch just as the door opened and our two heathens peeked in.

"See, I told you it was just Mom making those strange noises because she's with Dad," Whit told her sister.

Kelly muttered something behind me, and I tried not to glance back at her with an I-told-you-so look.

"I thought it was that ghost from the cartoon we saw yesterday," Ash whispered back.

I gave a choked laugh while Kelly punched my shoulder from behind.

"Can we come in?" Whit asked.

I checked to make sure their mother was decent enough. She'd gone to her knees, but her cheeks were flushed, and she sure as hell had the freshly fucked look.

I was a proud motherfucker to put that look there. "Sure, sweet pea."

When they ran into the room, I braced for impact.

My six-year-old scrambled right over me to get to her mother. Thoughts of a broken penis flashed through my head. Whit, thankfully, approached from the foot of the bed and crawled between us.

The girls gave a satisfied stretch. A tangle of skinny bodies, skinnier limbs, and long hair separated Kelly and me, yet it was the closest to her I'd ever felt.

A feeling of family.

Her eyes caught mine and she mouthed. *Talk later.*

We stayed that way for a while until Ash complained about being hungry.

"I'll get the girls fed. Why don't you freshen up?" She probably wanted to put on panties and wear her own clothes from the night before.

"I want waffles and bacon, Daddy," Ash put in her order. "Don't forget maple syrup."

"Is this how you spoil the kids and why they're excited to see Daddy?" Kelly raised a brow.

"Busted." Whit giggled.

"Oops," Ash whispered and grinned her gap-toothed smile. "I forgot."

"Looks like your dad and I need to have a conversation about your diet."

6

KELLY

WHILE LEVI DISTRACTED the girls with the promise of breakfast, I went into the bathroom and turned on the faucet. His words asking for a second chance echoed in my head and sent my thoughts back to the night I had asked him for a separation.

I put down the fairytale book and looked at Ashley. She'd finally fallen asleep. My daughter was unsettled with her dad prowling around the house like a storm cloud. Even I wasn't comfortable with my husband anymore. He'd become a stranger.

At least he wasn't a drunk, and at least he didn't yell at the girls. Sometimes I wondered if it was better if he stayed away. Ashley didn't want to be in a room with him when I wasn't around. She said he was like that angry bear on TV. Whitney would get mad at Ashley because my oldest was closest to Levi. But my girls didn't deserve this.

The door to our daughter's room opened. I could feel his presence even without turning around. It wasn't warmth or cold, it was just … dead presence. Something that put me on edge and wrapped me in despair. I couldn't live like this anymore. I couldn't grieve Callum or the slow death of a relationship that cannibalized my soul.

"Can I talk to you?" *His voice was rough.*

I kissed Ashley on the forehead and got up. He wasn't at the door. He'd already gone down the hallway and down the stairs. I followed him to the outdoor patio.

"My company is reorganizing," *he said.* "I've asked for most of my assignments to be here."

I raised a brow. "Here? What kind of jobs?"

"Celebrity protection."

"That's not going to make you happy."

"Oh, what do you think will make me happy?" *he sneered.* "The SEALs? They fucked us over, didn't they? Being a security contractor? The government found a way to fuck us over again."

I didn't point out that a few of his team went rogue against the U.S. government. It was a wonder they weren't in Leavenworth.

I folded my arms. "Are you still going to travel?"

"Probably. I'll try to stay local."

"Is anything going to change?"

He glared at me. "What do you want from me, Kelly?"

I stared at him. I didn't even know anymore. And his declaration that he was staying didn't bring me joy. A slither of unease wrapped around my heart. Even before he came home this time, I knew I'd already made a decision.

"Are you willing to go to couple's counseling?"

He snorted. "The last thing I want is for a stranger to tell us how to fix our marriage."

"How about a grief support … "

He flipped the patio chair over, startling us both. He scraped a hand over his face and muttered, "Sorry." *And then stalked to the far edge of the patio. He looked out into the darkness of the garden for a few minutes before he turned around.*

"I can't bear to see you slip away from us like this, Levi." *I walked slowly toward him. I saw a man vibrating with rage. Deep down inside,*

I knew he would never hurt me physically. Emotionally, he was tearing me apart.

"I'm right fucking here," he growled. "I'm moving here. And I'm asking you again. What else do you fucking want from me?"

I knew for a fact that the private military company he'd been working for had been dissolved by the JAG. If it hadn't, would he be here right now?

I raised my hand and touched his cheek. "I'll always love you, Levi," I said softly.

I saw the moment the anger bled out from him, and I hated the stricken panic in his eyes. "Babe?" he asked hoarsely. "What ... what's going on?"

Staring up at the night sky as though it would keep the tears at bay, emotion was a ball of pain pushing up my throat.

He gripped my shoulders. "Why does this feel like goodbye?"

"I need to think about Whit and Ash." I started crying. "You need to seek help for your anger, your guilt over what happened. I can't live like this anymore. Think about our girls ... what you're doing to them. The children and I are leaving you and there's nothing you can say or do to stop me."

I leaned into the sink, becoming aware of the water running, as the physical pain of that night drilled into my chest. He tried to convince me he would do better, but after a week he realized I was right. We'd become strangers, and he had trouble interacting with Ashley.

But Levi had changed. He sought counseling for his unresolved anger and grief. He even joined a veteran support group. He was a teddy bear around the girls, and they loved their daddy. The first year we devoted so much time to making sure the girls didn't suffer because of our separation. I didn't cry around them. I kept my pain to myself including my own guilt and our inability to talk about Callum's death. There was still something I was ashamed about that I hadn't told anyone, but if there was anyone who would understand me, it was my husband.

Lately, we'd been at each other's throats, hence, that night when he challenged me to find someone else.

Maybe it was because we never worked on our relationship or talked about the possibility of getting back together.

We were scared of how to move forward and the possibility of losing each other forever.

Divorce was a life-changing event that would jolt us out of the limbo we found ourselves in.

It was time to see if we had another shot.

"I WANT ANOTHER ONE, DADDY!"

Ashley certainly had a bigger appetite when she was with her father. It didn't take much analysis to figure out that Levi fed them more sugar and fat on the weekends. It was why I balanced their diet when they were with me. No parenting competition existed between us because of our separation. I never bad-mouthed their father to the girls and, as far as I knew, Levi never did that either.

I took in the entire tableau of him bantering with our kids and tried to remember the last time we'd been around the kitchen for breakfast like that. Last August, Levi sustained a bad concussion during a mission to Mexico and needed someone to look after him for a few weeks. When Bristow called me, the first thing he said was that my husband was okay—alive, but injured. It triggered flashbacks to the devastating day we were told of Callum's death. My body froze and my fingers grew so numb, I nearly dropped the phone. It took me a few seconds to understand that Bristow was telling me my husband was alive. Relief washed over me, but I later worried his frustration from his temporary disability would erase all the progress he'd made with Ashley. But unlike that time after my brother died, Levi hadn't withdrawn from us. His orneriness was physical—dizziness and short-term forgetfulness—plus he seemed to enjoy the pampering and the opportunity to spend the downtime with family.

It gave me hope we had resolved our issues, and we could talk. Then came the confusing time when he disappeared to Ukraine to rescue Garrison and Bristow. With no word of warning, he missed his weekend with the girls. Trying to hold it together while trying not to worry the kids should've earned me an acting award when my insides were webbed with anxiety. He called the next day, and I was too relieved to be pissed at him. When he returned, everything was fine … at first. But I pulled away from him again before I realized what I was doing.

I thought divorce would make this arrangement less wishy-washy and define our boundaries. He could be free to do what he needed for his job. No expectations. No resentment. Simply living our own lives, stepping up for the girls when the other one was busy. But if I was honest and I dug deep down, the thought of divorce left a bitter taste in my mouth.

"Waffles?" Levi asked me.

"No. I'm good."

"Can we ask her now?" Whitney was looking at her dad.

"Ask me what?" *Hmm, I smell an ambush coming.*

"Well," Ashley huffed, glancing at her father. "Daddy and Gramps said we need a puppy and responsibi-li-ties."

"That's right!" Whitney asserted. "And, Mom, we need extra protection when Dad's not around, right?"

"That's right, princess," Levi said and then turned to me as if I was going along with it.

"Hmm." Looked like I needed a mimosa for the conversation. But since orange juice was the only beverage available, I took my time filling up my glass with it, then took a longer time taking a measured sip before saying, "Having a dog is not as easy as it sounds."

"We're ready," Whit said.

"But who's going to feed it, walk it, brush it?"

"I can teach them," Levi said. "And before you balk at the walking, we do have a backyard. We don't have to get a puppy. Bristow and I looked at the available protection dogs that our friend has. He trains dogs for the DoD. We're thinking German Shepherd given the temperament of the one he has. Great family dogs, but protective of the little ones. Malinois and Dutchies have too much drive."

"Visits to the vets? Bathing?"

"I can handle that," he said again. "Cillian said he'd pitch in too, and I have no shortage of buddies around here who I could count on. But" —he glanced at the girls—"you'll need to play with him, throw balls for him. Interact with the dog. We have pools at both houses. He should be trained for that too."

"Yes, Dad."

"Yes, Daddy."

"Promise?" he pressed. "Because we don't want to make your mom regret giving her permission."

"Promise!" Again, their voices rang out in unison.

I loved seeing the excitement on my children's faces and bringing a dog into the family would certainly help them learn responsibility, but adding that complication while Levi and I were trying to figure out our marriage was awful timing.

"Mama?" Ashley prodded.

"I'm not saying no," I said before awarding Levi a look full of censure. "But your dad and I have to discuss this first."

Levi took the hint, his eyes communicating he understood. He addressed our kids. "How about this? When you girls spend the summer with Gramps and Nana, you take over some responsibility for Ruger. See how it feels to take care of a dog? Brush him, feed him, walk him with Cillian."

"But he's not a puppy," Whitney mumbled.

"And all puppies become grown-ups like Ruger," I reminded my daughter. "They don't remain all cuteness."

Lesson number one.

The girls looked at me doubtfully and then turned pleading eyes on their father.

Levi came to my side and put an arm around my shoulder. "Sorry, girls, Mama Bear has spoken and I agree with her."

Levi used that term when I had the final say about something. I hadn't heard that endearment in years. Something rolled under my chest. It was the closest joint discussion we'd had as a family.

Whit and Ash looked like they wanted to say more, but Levi must've used some secret coding language because they pressed their mouths together and didn't say another word.

I glanced up at my husband. His eyes gleamed with affection and amusement. Levi James was definitely drawing me back into his web, and, together with these two munchkins added as helpers, I didn't stand a chance.

They resumed attacking their breakfasts. As soon as they finished, they excused themselves and ran off to the backyard.

Alone with Levi, I helped him clean up. He was an expert when it came to loading the dishwasher. He approached it with mathematical precision in maximizing usable space.

I started rinsing the dishes and handed it to him. "A dog, huh?"

"We talked about it at Cillian's before I left for this last job. He wants a companion for Ruger, but then the girls mentioned wanting a puppy."

I shook my head. "And knowing Gramps, he suggested one without thinking of the consequences to the parents."

"Hey, you need to give Cillian more credit."

"Levi, I say this with a lot of affection about Gramps, but you know he loves pleasing the girls, sometimes to the detriment of everyone else."

"I know, babe." He grinned at me.

"Okay, don't keep me in suspense. What happened at the station last night?"

Levi shrugged. "They asked me how I knew Tom and asked me point blank if I knew where he was. I said no."

"Okay, but you stressed how stupid it would be for you to go after him after the fight at the restaurant, right? They agreed."

His mouth twitched.

"What?" I fumed. "You didn't go off and tell them you had thoughts of murdering him, right?"

"No, I didn't."

I was still far from calm, because now my worry turned to my friend.

"So, do they have any idea who could have done something to him?"

"Several actually, but I found this out after my meet with the detectives. It might be his rival in the security business of the resort hotel or a rival of the resort hotel itself. Bristow is digging into it."

"Uncle Cesar is a silent partner." I blew out a breath. Tom did frequent business with my aunt's husband, Cesar De Lucci, who had a slew of casinos and resort hotels in Vegas.

"Did the detectives still want to talk to me? Do they have this info?"

"No. I don't want you getting involved. I'll pass along Cesar's information. I'll call him."

Levi straightened from loading the dishwasher and leaned a hip against the counter. His eyes grew heavy lidded and shivers went through my spine. "Is there something else?"

"I told the detectives that Callum was a common acquaintance between Tom and me. You were more a friend to him than I was, although it seemed he wanted to change that."

"Not this again," I groaned.

"But my exact words to the detectives were this: 'Tom Roth didn't deserve death by my hands. But make no mistake, I would kill anyone who would hurt you.'"

A growl crept up my throat. "Did you have to add that?"

Levi shrugged. "Can't help it. I think they need to see I was honest with them about my feelings when it came to you. More believable."

He had a point.

He cupped my cheek, staring intently into my eyes. "I told them I didn't kill indiscriminately even in my job. I told them —" He let it hang as though the next words warranted my complete attention. "I don't know how I'd react if you chose him over me. If he won you fair and square, I had no idea how that would make me feel. I didn't mention the killing again."

I exhaled a pent-up breath. "Thank God for that."

He continued holding my gaze captive. "Would I be willing to lose you to another man without a fight? I don't think so. I don't have a lot of quit in me, Kelly, especially when it comes to you."

Whether it was part threat or part vow, I couldn't quite describe the feelings those words evoked but it sent a shiver through my body.

He held my eyes for a second longer, as if making sure those words sunk in before taking a step back.

"I don't want you anywhere near this," Levi said. "If the detectives don't need to question you, and just need Cesar's information, I'll be the go between." A corner of his mouth tipped up. "Although, chances are your uncle already knows more about this than we do since his guy didn't make the meeting with Tom."

I puffed a short laugh. "Probably."

"So." He crossed his arms and glanced out the kitchen window briefly to check on the girls before returning his attention to me. "How about we talk about us?"

I nodded. "Tonight?"

His brows drew together. When he was about to say something, I added, "I still need to do a turnover of the masks I did yesterday."

"Ah …"

"Hopefully that will be the last reshoot."

"I'm surprised they didn't ask you to go up there."

"I have a capable department. And I accepted this job on the condition I wouldn't have to leave Los Angeles on short notice."

"I'm proud of what you've accomplished in the past several years, babe. To be able to dictate your terms in a place like Hollywood is huge."

"I've worked with great people."

His smile held some sadness. "I wish I had been here to witness all those milestones."

He'd missed one of the award shows where I won best special effects that year.

"There'll be more," I said, then laughed. "I hope."

"Well, I'll definitely make sure I'm going as your date." His eyes narrowed. "No more dates with other men for you."

He started to get worked up again. I could usually tell because a muscle started ticking in his jaw and his eyes turned from warm chocolate to flint.

"Hey, you told me to go on one," I countered.

"I did not," he enunciated.

I tapped my lips. "Let me refresh your memory. I told you we need to talk."

He winced. "Yeah, I said I was short on time."

I pounced on that admission. "You couldn't stand to talk two minutes after you dropped off the girls. I know you were pissed at me last Christmas when I took them to spend it with the McGraths, but it was my weekend with them."

"I thought we were making progress and you pulled that shit," he retorted.

"I think we should table that discussion for tonight, but I want it out of the way right now that we were both at fault with why I went out with Tom."

His jaw clenched. "I already apologized for that."

"Because when I wouldn't sleep with you when you wanted to scratch an itch—"

"I wish you wouldn't call it that," he growled.

"You immediately made it about sex, and I was using sex to force you to discuss our marriage."

"I thought you were going to ask for a divorce."

"And what if I was? It was time."

"You still think that?" he gritted.

I waved an arm. "Tonight, we'll talk, but for now, let me get this off my chest or it will bug me all day."

He smirked. "Feeling guilty"

"Levi!"

He held out an arm. "So, speak."

"You made it about sex. You told me if I went through with the divorce, I wouldn't find another man who could fuck me like you did."

His eyes darkened. "That's the truth—"

"You're so cocky. But let's not forget what you said, 'Have at it and see if you can find a fuck like me.' and then you left for a three-week mission."

The silence was louder in our stare-off, but I wasn't backing down.

Finally, he blinked. "I was an asshole and an idiot."

"Agreed," I exhaled an annoyed breath."But now I feel guilty because I led Tom on."

"Woman," he muttered. "You feel guilty about leading another man on, how about your poor husband?"

"Might I remind you Tom is missing?"

"How can I forget? Now that you're certain I won't go to prison, all your thoughts are on him."

"This is not a competition!" I yelled.

The backdoor slammed, and our two munchkins ran back in. We glared at each other.

"Mom, are you hanging with us today?" Whit asked hopefully.

"I need to do some work, but I'll see you guys tonight."

"Tonight?"

"Yes. I'll see if Gramps and Nana can take you, so your dad and I can talk."

My heart clenched at the hopeful looks our two girls split between us.

I looked at Levi again, and his eyes softened from his sharp stare earlier. He clasped my nape and brought my fore-head to his lips, planting a kiss there before another light one on my mouth.

Then he stared into my eyes. "Tonight, babe."

7

KELLY

I WAVED off the driver of the production van carrying the masks I made the day before. One of the production assistants supervised the loading, and a few members of the SFX team gathered to receive last-minute application instructions from me.

Now that everyone was gone, I walked back into our department. It had been a hectic few weeks, but my exhaustion didn't stem from my job, but from my personal life. Nervous energy bounced inside me like a closed circuit. I surveyed my surroundings and sighed. I left the facility with Gabby so abruptly the night before, I didn't get a chance to clean up. I was a stickler about keeping my station clean. After packing up my make-up into my rolling cosmetic case, the next step was to check what silicone adhesives I could repurpose. I made my own special mixture.

If there was one area in my life where I was OCD, it was in my job. I grabbed the hand vac and tidied up further. While the noise of the vacuum drowned out everything else, my thoughts automatically went to our upcoming discussion.

I still loved Levi.

I doubted I could love another man as much as I loved him.

Lost in my thoughts, a movement at the corner of the studio startled me. My heart almost beat out of my chest when I saw an unfamiliar man in a suit standing there. He wasn't looking at me but at the workstations in the studio.

"Excuse me?" I called. "You can't be in here." I was used to studio executives strutting around like they owned the place. At least this one didn't have an entourage in tow. Yet despite the squarish dark glasses and his slicked back hair like an Elvis pompadour or a bad comb over, there was something unsettling about him that made the hairs on the back of my nape stand up.

The man shrugged and started my way. "Just wanted to talk to you."

"I'm calling the guard." I walked to the nearest wall with an intercom.

"I'm afraid Freddy won't answer."

The chill around me dropped further, and dread displaced the air in my lungs. I slowly turned to face my unwanted guest. "What did you do?"

"Oh, he'll be fine. The man has a wife with a third kid on the way. I have no reason to be heartless."

He stopped in front of me. My purse with my phone was hooked over the handle of the makeup luggage.

"What do you want?"

"A friend of ours. Do you know where he is, Mrs. James? Can I call you Kelly?"

"I don't know who you're talking about." Tom. This man was looking for Tom.

He grinned and reached out to brush the back of his fingers along my cheek, but I recoiled.

"Ah, so beautiful. Our friend Thomas Roth. Who else?"

"Then you should know he's missing."

"That's what the cops know. And they sure as fuck didn't figure it out yet."

"What?"

"You see, the man I sent for him didn't come back."

A glimmer of hope rose inside me.

"You really shouldn't play poker," he said. "Now I know you don't know anything. I'm worried your boyfriend bested my man. Admittedly, he's not the brightest bulb, but he's good muscle."

I held back a retort that muscle wasn't everything.

"Where's your phone?"

Oh, hell no is this man ...

It happened so fast. Pain exploded on my cheek, and my whole body twisted around and crashed against the table, bumping my hip so hard, I crumpled to the floor and emitted a distressed cry.

Black glossy shoes appeared in my line of vision, and he yanked me to my feet by my hair. "I'm not asking again. Now, I don't want to hurt you more than I have to. You want to get back to Ashley and Whitney, right?"

"Don't you dare mention my children," I spat.

Using my hair as leverage, he brought me closer. "I know where they are. They're with your husband. Big man, that Levi James. I'm surprised Roth had the balls to lust over his wife. But you're separated, aren't you?"

Who the hell is this man? Violated didn't even begin to describe how I felt.

He released my hair and shoved me in the direction of my things. He stalked over and grabbed my giant purse and rummaged through its contents, carelessly tossing things on the floor. I gritted my teeth, part in fear, part in outrage. Finding my phone, he woke it up and held it to my face for authentication.

Then he scrolled through my contacts.

"Guess this is him?"

He showed me Tom's name. Without even waiting for my response, he proceeded to check our message stream. "Guess he never responded to your text or calls."

He lowered my phone and studied me. "Now what use are you to me?"

"Please let me go," I whispered. Now more than ever I wanted my girls and Levi.

Why did it have to be a life-or-death situation before what mattered the most became clear?

The man studied me further. "No. I might have more use for you."

He reached inside his coat and drew a gun, pointing it at me.

Blood left my face and my legs threatened to buckle.

"You have a choice. Either you walk out on your own, or I carry you. And I'm telling you right now, it would piss me off if I have to carry you. And you don't want me pissed."

"You don't need me," I begged.

Bang!

A pitiful cry escaped my lips. My whole body started shaking and I couldn't keep the tears at bay. They scalded my eyes and rolled down my cheeks. "Please don't. My girls need me."

The man advanced on me and pointed the gun at my head. "Then you better do as you're told."

ELVIS TIED my wrists behind my back and dumped me in the trunk of a sedan. He also bound my ankles. I saw his accomplice briefly. A man with strange tats on his neck. I would've paid more attention to his facial details if I wasn't still shaking from when Elvis shot at the wall to my right, missing my ear by millimeters.

All I could see were the faces of Ashley, Whitney, and Levi. What the hell had Tom gotten me into? Then I was immediately ashamed for blaming him. He'd been so supportive when Callum died, more so when Levi had become distant. I hated depending on anyone because I hated that they left, and I would be stuck by myself.

It was one of the reasons I thought I had to let Levi go, but I realized more than ever that my husband never left, not even when he was grieving my brother. People had different ways of handling grief.

The ride was bumpy. I tried to recall everything I had learned in movies and wished I'd paid attention to Levi's self-defense lessons. But with my hands and feet bound, it was hard to get leverage to kick out the tail lights. And then what?

After what felt like forever, the vehicle crawled to a stop. I heard its door open and slam.

The trunk opened, and Elvis dragged me out. Dusk was descending judging from the dark orange sky. His cohort was nowhere in sight. He let me fall to the ground so he could untie the rope around my ankles. Then he hauled me up again.

"Move."

He certainly didn't like carrying stuff.

We were on a property with high elevation. I tried to discern landmarks around me that could clue me in to where we were, but it was too dark, and the property too recessed from the access road to orient myself with which part of LA we were in. Our trip was about twenty minutes so we couldn't have gone too far from the studio.

We entered the house, a fancy log home by LA standards. He nudged me toward a sunken living room, then took out his phone and made a call. He moved to the window, looking back at me every now and then as he conversed with someone. His other hand held the gun loosely by his side.

I was too disoriented, too pissed, and scared shitless. But I was not stupid enough to know that if I did something remotely irritating to that man, he wouldn't hesitate to shoot me and bury me in his backyard.

My imagination was always on overdrive when I was scared. I held on to the thoughts of my family again. Ashley in a purple tutu taking a bow. Whitney in her first softball game. The first time I laid eyes on Levi James.

Images of the cocky SEAL showing up at our house in Brooklyn one summer flashed through my mind.

Levi. He'd be worried.

He would call my phone and … shit, what did Elvis do to my phone?

"Da." He ended the call and turned to face me.

I did not like the blackness in his gaze.

I did not like the way he stalked toward me.

Instinctively, I backed away.

"Don't piss me off," he said. "I could just shoot you."

"What do you—" I didn't finish responding. His right arm crossed his body and cut an arc. The force slamming against my face sent me spinning and I landed on the couch behind me.

Too stunned, I tried to speak, but my throbbing jaw refused to obey.

He jumped on top of me.

Air left my lungs when he pushed his knee against my ribcage. He set aside his gun and started to choke me.

My feet kicked out.

Oxygen. I needed air.

I was going to die.

I was going to die.

Black dots danced behind my lids. The end. Just nothing-ness. Pressure everywhere. My head was about to explode.

Then ... freedom. I gasped, swallowing a box of razor blades. My eyes struggled to find focus before falling on my captor's form.

Elvis came into focus. He was typing on his phone.

"Let's see what Roth will do now."

"I thought ..." I wheezed. "I thought you couldn't reach him."

"The image was sent to a chat room. He'll see it."

"Are you going to let me go now?"

"Hmm ... you *have* seen my face, and I know your husband has connections in high places."

"Then I'm more of a liability. Let me go. I won't say anything." *I'm going to make sure you burn in hell, asshole.*

He sank to his haunches. Dead eyes reminding me of Hannibal Lecter when he was about to make a kill. I was doing everything in my power to withhold the outrage inside me that wanted to break this asshole's nose. Only self-preservation to live and see my family again held back the retort on my tongue.

God, what did Levi do in situations like this?

When Elvis reached out, I turned my face away, but all he did was tuck a hank of hair behind my ear.

"I won't hit you again," he said quietly. "I got what I needed."

"Please let me go," I pleaded again.

For the first time, I saw a flash of regret cross his face. "That depends on what Roth does. I have my doubts of your importance to him. He didn't put up much of a fight when your husband reclaimed you." He smiled faintly. "Yes, I was watching." He looked at his phone. "Now we wait."

8

LEVI

"Daddy, I'm hungry," Ashley said. "Where's Mama?"

I glanced up distractedly from my phone. Kelly's was still pinging at the studio, but she wasn't answering.

"No luck?" Branna asked by my side.

I shook my head. A sense of foreboding replaced the anticipation of seeing my wife. "Why don't you let the girls eat?"

"I want to eat with Mama." Ashley's lower lip quivered. "Where is she?"

"She's still at work, baby girl," I told her. "She's probably stuck again."

"Let's eat," Whit told her sister, then she glanced at me and winked. Everyone in here knew my youngest daughter turned into a little monster when she was hungry. And after her daddy-of-the-year fed her all those waffles drowned in maple syrup, I was only collecting the spoils.

"Come on, girls." Branna ushered them to the dining room.

I glanced over to where the door to the garage opened, but it was only Cillian coming in with groceries. "Where's Kelly? Her car isn't here yet, and it's almost seven."

"I've called her a couple of times," I said and nodded to the bags in his hand. "Need help?"

"Nope, this is all of it. Not like her to not give a heads up." Kelly's grandfather lowered his load on the center island. Branna returned to the kitchen and started browsing through the bags. "The girls started eating. Kelly can catch up later. Sometimes the production vans run behind schedule."

"She would have called." Cillian repeated his earlier statement.

Nana shrugged. "She usually calls, but I recall a time or two when she was delayed for a couple of hours and couldn't let me know. Remember this production is in a time crunch. She's probably in last minute meetings."

I tapped the phone on the table. It wasn't unusually late, but it was two hours past when she said she would be here.

I swiped another number. I needed eyes on her.

"Yo, man," Bristow answered. "What's up?"

"Are you sober?"

He chuckled. "Had a beer. About to start on the heavy stuff, what's going on?"

I excused myself from Kelly's grandparents and headed to the backyard. "I need a favor. Check security feeds at the studio and see if Kelly's car's still there."

"Ooohkay," Bristow responded but there was laughter in his voice.

Fucker.

"She was supposed to be here two hours ago and she hasn't responded to my calls or texts. It could be she's busy, but I—"

"Say no more." I could hear him move around and get settled. Bristow was a retired SEAL like I was and he was the comms expert on the team. "Howard Productions, right?"

"Yup."

"Give me a few. I'm still hooked in with LAPD access, so shouldn't take too long."

I paced the backyard. "Heard anything new on Tom?"

"Yes. I'm chasing a lead on the rival corporation of the De Lucci-owned resort … hmm … this is strange."

I stopped pacing. "What's strange?"

"No … I have the correct address and network …"

"What's going on?"

"Surveillance is dead. The feed is blank."

"What?" I was already heading back into the house. "I have a bad feeling about this. Can you see if her car is still there?" I sent him the information to access the StarLink car security.

After a few minutes, Bristow said, "It is."

"I'm heading there." The bad feeling had just turned into full-blown concern.

"Coming with."

I wasn't going to turn down any help I could get. "Thanks. Meet you there."

"Copy that."

I ended the call and contemplated what to tell my girls without worrying them. I hated to lie, but not knowing the real situation, I had to err on the side of not upsetting them.

"Everything all right?" Branna asked.

"I'm going to check on Kelly."

"Need company?" Cillian asked.

"I'd rather you stay with the girls."

"What if she's on her way home, and you pass each other?"

"Her car is still there."

"Oh." Branna narrowed her eyes at me. "Is there something you're not telling me, son?"

"Nothing concrete. Just not like Kelly to not call." Especially when she knew how important our talk was going to be.

I returned to the dining room. Whit was happily tearing the meat from a chicken leg while Ash was pouting at her plate.

"What's the matter, baby girl?"

"I want Mama."

"She'll be home soon," Whit told her sister. "You better eat that up, or she'll remove the crispy skin, and you'll be left with breast meat."

"I like breast meat," Ash said, but her lips turned down. "But I do like crispy skin."

Whit winked at me, but the smile died. I struggled to put back a neutral face. "I'm going to go get her."

"What's wrong? Did she finally call? Did she have car trouble?"

The inquisitiveness of my youngest gave me the perfect evasive response. "Something like that."

I kissed the top of their heads. "Don't give Nana and Gramps any trouble while I'm gone, okay? And Ash, eat the chicken and the peas, or you're not getting more waffles tomorrow."

My youngest emitted a resigned sigh.

I didn't linger and grabbed the keys, hellbent on finding out what was going on with Kelly.

THIRTY MINUTES LATER, I arrived to my worst nightmare. Police lights were flashing right in front of the studio and the area was cordoned off.

I squeezed my Escalade into a tight spot, slammed out of the vehicle, and jogged to the entrance. Bristow was rapidly walking my way, and we met at the perimeter of the police line.

"You know what the fuck is going on?" I asked. "Anything on the police scanner?"

"Yes. One of the production vans came back to pick up something and found the guard unconscious behind the desk. They thought it was a medical issue, but when he came around, he said he was tased."

"Where's the guard now?"

Bristow nodded to an ambulance. Walking over to the emergency vehicle, someone was already asking questions—a detective of the West Hollywood bureau probably—while the EMT worked on the guard. .

"Have you gotten a hold of Kelso or Gabby?" I asked Bristow.

"Left them messages."

His phone pinged. "Kelso is on his way."

I tried to beat back the panic rising inside me, the urgent need to run in there. With no "in" with the scene's law enforcements, it was a waste of time, and the person who had the most answers was in front of me.

"Is there anything else you can tell us?" I heard the detective ask.

"I'm sorry, I—" The guard Freddy saw and recognized me. "Mr. James."

"What happened?" I cut between the detective and the guard.

"Excuse me, who are you?"

"I'm Kelly James' husband," I told the detective. "She was working."

"Nobody else is inside," the detective said.

Freddy shook his head. "Before I got tased, she was still on the premises. I didn't see anything else."

"Surveillance?" I asked.

"We're getting a warrant for that now," the detective told us.

"Kelly's phone is inside," I said.

"That's going to be evidence."

"Are her things in there?"

"Sir," the detective said in exasperation. "I know you're worried about your wife. But let me wrap up here and we will interview you at length."

"You don't need to interview me," I snarled. "I need to be in there. See what happened. My partner and I have worked for the LAPD before."

The detective squinted his eyes at me. "Even so, I'm afraid that's not possible. It'll be my ass on the line if you screw up our crime scene."

I spun away from the man to hide my frustration. Where the fuck was Kelso?

"That was a Hail Mary request," Bristow said.

I knew better than to argue and lose my shit and get ejected from the premises, but the dread in my gut had escalated into something close to terror.

Someone took Kelly.

"Kelso's here," Bristow said. "He was closer than I thought. Let's see if he could pull any strings and get us inside."

After arguing with the detective-in-charge of the case, our friend managed to get us into the studio with the promise not to disturb the crime scene.

I wanted to snarl and snap, but like everyone else, they were just doing their jobs. I stalked ahead while Bristow updated Kelso on what he'd found regarding the Roth case. If he in any way put my wife in the crosshairs of the people after him, I was going to hunt him down, and there was no telling what I would do when I found him. This could be one of those cases where I was willing to murder a person who got my wife hurt.

The acid scalding my gut intensified when we entered the studio. My eyes went to Kelly's purse on the floor and its scattered contents. Her makeup case was sitting in the middle of an aisle.

Kelso flashed his badge at the patrol officer who approached us.

"Detective Burns radioed and gave the go ahead to share information," the officer said.

"What you got?" Kelso asked.

"There are signs of a struggle …"

The cop looked at us before returning his attention to Kelso. "We found a bullet casing."

"Fuck …" It was as though my spinal cord snapped, and I hunched down to rest my palms on my knees. My breathing serrated. Bristow's hand on my shoulder did nothing to quell the warring rage and fear in my heart.

"His wife is Kelly James," Kelso explained my reaction to the officer.

"Shit, man, you should have warned me."

That made me straighten up. Now was not the time to go pussy. Kelly needed the SEAL and mercenary to find her, not the worried husband.

"I'm okay," I said. "Was there any blood?" It was like a string of tacks passing through my throat to get that out.

"No. No blood. And we haven't identified the spot where he fired yet. Still waiting for a warrant on surveillance to see what happened here."

"Do you mind if we look around?" Kelso asked.

"Not at all."

"Bristow," I murmured out of the corner of my mouth.

"Got it."

We approached the scene where all the struggle happened. "He made her get her phone, but then left it."

"This has got to have something to do with Roth," Kelso said.

Bristow casually lowered his messenger bag beside Kelly's phone that was left on the worktable.

He was cloning the device. I had an app installed on it for cases like this but hadn't activated it. The initial activation had to be a close proximity thing.

I fucking hoped it was going to work.

A few minutes later, Bristow gave me the thumbs up.

I had a feeling we stood a better chance of finding Kelly on our own without the red tape of waiting for a warrant.

9

KELLY

MY CAPTOR WAS ALTERNATELY CHECKING his phone and looking out the window. Was he expecting Tom to simply swoop in and save me? He and I weren't at that level.

"What's your name?" I asked.

Elvis turned his attention to me distractedly, then he shook his head. "My name's not important."

"Well, if you want me to continue calling you Elvis."

For the first time since I'd met this man, which was all of three hours, he burst out laughing. Like real laughter. And as if the sound was foreign to his ears, he caught himself. He cleared his throat, but his mouth twitched. "Let me guess, it's the hair."

I shrugged. "Could it be anything else? But it does suit the shape of your face." This man could only be from Vegas. Maybe he moonlighted as an Elvis impersonator. Or, shit, maybe that was his cover?

"You can call me Blaze."

"Is your name really Blaze?"

His face slowly lost its laugh lines. "As I said, it doesn't matter, but I'd prefer it if you didn't think of me as Elvis in your head."

"What do you have against the King?"

"I'm not doing this with you," he muttered, switching his gaze back to the phone.

But, of course, I held on to my advantage. Revealing a name, even when it was false, meant that I might have gotten a bit under that tough exterior. I pushed through the tenderness of my throat, my voice still raspy. "So, do you have family?"

He cast me an irritated glance. "Men like me don't have families."

What, assassins? Mercenaries? Clean-up crew for the mob? But the mob was all about family.

"What do you mean 'men like you'?"

"You ask too many questions," he snapped.

"Just curious."

"Do I look like a family man to you? You think I'm anything like your husband."

Levi is a hundred times the man you are.

"My children," I said. "Seeing their faces greeting me after a hard day of work is like a stress relief. Makes all the hard work worth it." Maybe I was pushing it, so I added, "But I'll admit, sometimes I come home exhausted, and all I want to do is crawl into bed and ship my kids off to my grandparents."

His mouth quirked into a smile and I thought I was making progress, but his next words chilled me. "You think I don't know what you are doing?"

That was when I realized his eyes were still deader than dead.

I cast him an innocent look. "I don't know what you mean."

"You're trying to humanize yourself so I won't hurt you further. Ahh ... Miss James, that won't work. You want to know about men like me? Our empathy was beaten out of us a long time ago. We will only destroy the people we love and that includes children." His eyes lost focus for an instant before all traces of his smile disappeared. "But I won't bore you with the details. So, are we done here?"

I decided the best option was to shut up. He was a trained professional, not a man driven by his emotions to take me hostage. Not a casual mob leg-breaker who went home to a wife and children after collecting on a gambling debt. Blaze was a real-deal assassin. The ones who did business on the Dark Web and whose fees were astronomical.

His phone beeped. He speared me a warning look not to move and went to a different room. I heard his hushed voice. He didn't seem pleased.

When he returned, his face was more unreadable than ever. "Get up."

I struggled to my feet. "Did Tom respond?"

"No. Your disappearance has become bigger news than my employer was willing to undertake."

"What do you mean?"

An eyebrow rose. "I'll drop you off at your house."

I wasn't even surprised he knew where I lived.

But my self-preservation was screaming not to trust him. My mind was trying to reason with myself that it would be messy to kill me. But was that the plan all along? Blaze didn't bother to hide his face from me unless it was deliberate.

He could easily shoot me from across the room if I refused to comply.

All these thoughts trampled through my head as I made my way toward him. And when I was within reach, he made a grand gesture of letting me walk first.

He didn't seem like a man who would shoot me from behind.

"We're taking another car. It's parked in the back."

The back was darker.

"I'll have you know," my voice was strangled. "I'm not having good feelings about this."

"Fair enough." Our footsteps crunched on gravel. My sense of foreboding escalated when I saw a clearing surrounded by woods. It was too dark. Too menacing. Too easy for him to kill me and bury my body.

The edge of the clearing revealed an outline of a car.

Blaze slowed his steps, falling back.

I turned.

———

Levi

"What do you mean it ended?"

Bristow made me take the exit to Laurel Canyon Boulevard. I probably shouldn't have been the one driving, because I was close to losing my fucking mind, but my partner was better liaising with Nadia, the LAPD crime analyst. They were able to track two vehicles exiting Howard Studios at around the time the abduction happened.

Kelso and Gabby were following one; we tracked the other and ended up at the foot of Hollywood Hills.

"No traffic cams," Bristow replied.

I pulled into the parking lot of a burger joint while he figured out where to direct me next. Kelly's phone yielded nothing useful. There was a text from an unknown number that said: "There's something you need to know. Meet me at the gate." Everyone agreed it sounded bogus and planted to make it look like it came from Roth.

As much as I hated the man, I didn't think he'd take Kelly away from the kids without letting them know where she was. We also questioned the security at the studio, but the SFX department was in a separate building apart from where the studio had the sets. The gate had been rigged, and the lever was up, allowing whoever took Kelly to stroll right in.

I cursed and pounded the steering wheel. "What the fuck do we do now?"

Bristow gave me the side eye. He knew better than to tell me to chill. I was frothing at the mouth and ready to burn the entire city of Los Angeles down to find my wife. Whoever thought it was a good idea to abduct her had taken the wrong woman. Because I would make it my damned mission that my face was the last thing those fuckers would see on this planet.

Right before I blew their brains out.

Stewing in my rage and thirsty for retribution, I almost failed to notice the message that popped up on my phone.

"What the fuck?" I grabbed the device and showed Bristow the screen. "An address."

THE PROPERTY WAS on Laurel Canyon Boulevard, just past Mulholland Drive. Kelso and Gabby were en route because their lead ended up nowhere when they found an abandoned vehicle in a shopping center parking lot. But we weren't waiting for backup. Bristow had deployed a drone and scoped out the property.

There was only one heat signature in the house and none around the perimeter that would indicate a hostile lying in wait. I turned into the property and pulled to a stop right in front of the house. I just cleared my seatbelt while shoving open the door when Kelly stepped out of the house.

Relief hit me hard.

Words choked up my throat and my feet knew only one direction to move. I had her in my arms and I held onto her like she was my lifeline.

When she cried out, I immediately dropped my arms and stepped back, castigating myself for not checking her for injuries.

I blinked. My eyes not trusting what it was seeing. Kelly was lit from behind, and I stepped aside to let the headlights illuminate her face.

The crushing weight on my chest made it difficult to breathe or speak. The relief at seeing my wife alive was quickly replaced with thermonuclear-level fury fueled by her battered condition.

Somewhere I heard another vehicle arrive and doors slam.

"Kelly?" My fucking hand was shaking as I brushed the back of it gently down her face. My heart roared in anguish when tears brimmed her eyes and rolled down her cheeks.

"Is it okay to h—"

She dove into me and cut off my words. My arms came around her again, gingerly this time as though I was about to cradle a newborn. Without being sure of the extent of her injuries, I was lost on how to hold her. Her heartbreaking sobs ripped through my soul.

"I thought … I thought," she hiccupped between sobs. "I wouldn't see you or the girls again."

"Fuck, Kelly." It was a struggle to keep my voice level, to relax the tension in my body so it wouldn't transfer to her. "Who did this to you?"

My eyes met Gabby's over my wife's shoulder. I gave a brief acknowledgment, glad to know the detectives had arrived and another woman was present just in case the unspeakable had happened to my wife. My mind drew a blank, refusing to consider such a scenario.

"I don't know," she gulped, and looked up into my eyes. "A man called Blaze. He spoke Russian to someone on the phone."

"You getting this?" Gabby asked her partner.

"Where's this Blaze now?" Kelso asked.

Kelly's eyes dropped to the ground. The detectives and I exchanged glances.

"Who sent the address, Kelly?" Gabby asked.

Kelso looked up from typing information. "Would you be able to describe him to a sketch artist?"

"Can we save the questions for later?" I snapped.

"Every second counts if we're going to catch this bastard," the detective shot back. "Did he just let you go?"

Kelly stared at my chest and shook her head.

"She's in shock, you morons," Bristow cut in. He'd done additional checks around the property. "House and perimeter are clear." He addressed Kelly. "I want to look you over. Make sure everything is fine. Unless you want to go to the hospital."

"I don't want to go to the hospital."

"Babe," I gently pulled back and stared at her. It was hard not to react to the giant bruise on her face and its swelling, but the marks around her neck were pushing me off the ledge of my control. Someone choked her. Someone grabbed her around her neck and fucking choked her. "We need to have you looked over."

"I wasn't raped."

I carefully folded her in my arms again and rested my chin on her head. I was a Navy SEAL, had been a ruthless mercenary, but if a man had brutalized my wife, there was no way that wouldn't bring me to my knees. And there was no fucking way I wasn't tearing that fucker apart with my bare hands.

For my wife, I'd be a stone-cold killer.

"Let's move inside and have Bristow look you over," I said.

I watched my wife for signs of distress as we entered the house and settled in its sunken living room. She was limping and I had to beat back a roar every time she winced.

"I'm really okay," she said in an ultra-soft voice as if a squeak from her would send me into a rage. She was not wrong. I was a hair-trigger away, but it wasn't directed at anyone at the moment. I didn't know if that made it worse. But this wasn't about me. This was about trying to get my wife to talk.

"Babe," I tried again. "Can you tell us what happened?"

"Blaze took me from the studio. He threatened me." She told us how he tied her up and dumped her into the trunk of the car and took her here.

Bristow returned with his medical kit and I reluctantly vacated my place in front of her. The fucker hit her twice, pinned her with his knee, and choked her.

Someone needs to die.

"So he sent a picture to a chat room," Kelso repeated what Kelly had told us. "Is this about Tom Roth?"

She nodded.

"Kelly, does that mean Roth is not missing?" Gabby asked.

Her mouth pressed into a straight line before she looked at me. "He was the one who saved me."

What the fuck?

10

KELLY

"WHERE'S ROTH?" My husband was a volcano waiting to explode.

Both detectives glared at him, but it was Gabby who said, "We're asking the questions."

Levi gripped his hair and turned away before violently dropping his arms by his sides in frustration. He reminded me of the Hulk in smash mode. I'd never seen him that pissed.

Well, tough. This whole shit storm happened to me. He was worried, but I was the one who had been kidnapped by a lunatic and physically abused by a man who was after the guy I had dated once.

Once.

I wouldn't even call it a date.

"He left as soon as he knew you guys arrived."

"The drone didn't see any other heat signature around the house," Levi said.

"He must have been watching from the property across the street," I said.

"How did you get away from this …" Kelso looked at his phone where he was taking notes. "Blaze?"

"He said he was letting me go." My whole body shuddered. "He took me to the back of the property and …" Words stuck in my throat, my words trailed off. I squeezed my eyes shut momentarily before I exhaled a painful breath. I focused on Gabby's calm eyes. "It happened too fast. One moment I see Blaze raising his gun toward me and then gunfire exploded."

Levi cursed at no one in particular but continued to be a looming presence pacing behind the detectives, flicking sharp glances in my direction.

"I dropped to the ground." I hitched my shoulders. "Blaze staggered and ran toward the front of the house while shooting at someone to my right."

"He got away?" Gabby asked.

"Yes."

"Roth was alone?'

"I don't know."

"What do you mean?"

"I …" I hissed when Bristow touched my face with a dampened gauze but the sting gave me a momentary respite to collect my scattered thoughts. "Tom was talking to someone … he was wired … comms."

"He didn't mention any name?" Gabby was asking all the questions.

"No."

"I was hysterical," I admitted. "I'm not sure I remember much after that."

"You've been beaten up," Bristow said. "You are in shock."

"Tom tried to ask me things … I don't even remember what those questions were."

"Did he tell you who was after him?"

"No," I whispered. "I didn't even think to ask him." I

broke Gabby's gaze and stared at Levi who'd stopped prowling around and looked at me. "I just wanted to go home."

"Fuck this," Levi muttered and squeezed in between me and the detectives. "Can we do this tomorrow?"

Gabby nodded and looked at Kelso.

"Fine with me," her partner said.

"I need to check your neck." Bristow tipped my chin up, smiling at me briefly before I tilted it for his inspection. He asked me questions as he pressed gently on my throat.

"Does it hurt when you swallow?"

"A bit."

"He didn't fracture your larynx, otherwise you wouldn't be able to speak and it would be too painful."

"Good to know."

"Do you have difficulty breathing?"

I shook my head. Bristow asked more diagnostic questions. I assured him I didn't black out and didn't need a hospital.

"Your voice should be less scratchy in a few days."

"For reasons we're not clear about," Kelso said. "Roth didn't give any indication why you were abducted other than to get to him."

I nodded.

"You think you remember Blaze enough to work with a sketch artist?" Bristow asked. "Not tonight of course. You're about to crash."

I gave a tired smile.

"We might get a hit on the agency databases if he's not in the Fed's." And without missing a beat, he added, "Mind if you lift your shirt so I can check your ribs?"

Levi scowled at Kelso who mumbled about checking something in the car. Bristow had me stand up. As I lifted my shirt, the SEAL started prodding my rib area. Meanwhile, either my husband was glaring at his friend for inspecting the bruising on my torso or he was glaring at the discoloration in that area.

"It's bruised, not broken."

"I feel battered. It could've been worse."

There was a pregnant silence, then I became aware they were waiting for me to answer Bristow's question. "His face is stamped in my memory. I'm probably the worst person to abduct and not wear a mask since I study facial contours as my job. I could sketch his face out myself. But I also think he's in disguise."

"But you said he was not wearing a mask?"

"No. His features looked natural, not even a prosthetic appliance, but he appeared sophisticated in the way he presented himself."

"What do you mean?"

"You know the hitmen you see on TV, like the guy who went after Jason Bourne?"

Bristow chuckled. "I doubt they really look like that. Majority of them are the *Goodfellas* types. Now if we're talking mercenaries, it's different."

"I'm not sure he had military training. He said something about losing empathy at a young age."

"Russians are known to train their assassins from childhood."

"What the hell did you discuss?" Levi growled. "You were having a heart to heart with a hitman?"

"Hey, you know what they say when someone kidnaps you?"

"Not when it's a professional, much less a top tier hitman, which this Blaze appears to be."

"He mentioned something else," I said. "He said there was another hitman sent for Tom. But obviously they're not very good if Tom got away ... And now this."

"Roth is a frogman," Bristow said. "Woe to anyone who underestimates our kind."

Gabby rolled her eyes. "When Kelly gives us a sketch of this guy, think you can run him through your databases?"

"Sure," Bristow said, but he was looking at me. "How's the adrenalin crash?"

"This is probably what I'm feeling." I was wired, tired, and in between. Mostly, I was irritated and relieved.

"You need to rest," Levi said, kissing the top of my head. I loved it when he did this. I leaned into him. I tucked away that sentiment for further evaluation. It was not the time to get all emotional about our situation going forward.

"Are the girls still awake?"

"They are." A muscle ticked at Levi's jaw. "Trying to figure out what to do tonight."

I touched my swollen cheek. "I don't want them to see me this way but ..." Anxiety riddled my chest. "But what if Blaze comes back for me? Or his employer sends someone else..." Rising panic shrilled my voice. "Oh, my God, who's with them?"

Levi settled his hands on my shoulders. "They're fine. When you got kidnapped, Kelso immediately ordered a patrol in front of Cillian's house." He glanced at the detective who returned from the outside. "Right, man?"

"Yes," the detective said. "The watch officer assured me there's a patrol parked in front of their house."

I relaxed a little. "I don't want to be separated from them tonight."

"Same," Levi said. "But know you bought yourself a body-guard, babe. No arguments."

"I'm not arguing," I mumbled.

"We'll think of something," he assured me then glanced at the detectives. "Let's reconvene tomorrow."

Bristow packed up. "As soon as you're up to it, Kelly. We'll need that sketch."

Levi

"I FORGOT to tell them about the other guy," Kelly said after we made a short stop at her house to pick up some clothes. She and I had discussed how to hide her battered face from the kids. The swelling had worsened, and the discoloration was darkening.

My brows drew together. "Blaze had a partner?"

"Yes, but he was only at the studio."

I whipped out my phone and did a group message to Bristow and the detectives. "There's another player."

Kelly glanced at what I was typing and continued, "I only caught a slight glimpse of his profile and hair, but I noticed neck tattoos." She rubbed her temples. "How could I forget that there was another?"

I sent those details over and pocketed my phone. "Let's focus on our current problem. I'll carry you in from the vehicle. Hide the bruised side of your face against my chest. I'll handle them."

"Thanks," she whispered. "I'm so sorry I worried you tonight."

"Not your fault."

"I know you blame my relationship with Tom."

My hackles bristled at the term relationship, but Kelly hadn't noticed.

"He's really just a good friend."

I ushered her to the door. "I don't want to discuss Tom Roth right now. Let's get you settled at Branna's. I've already told her we're sharing a bedroom."

Kelly eyed me through her swollen eye. It was difficult to hold her gaze and not want to kill someone. Not having an image of Blaze in my mind was eating my insides like acid. Reminding myself that my wife was alive and with me was the only thing that kept me from going feral.

We didn't say anything else on the short drive to her grandparents' house. When we pulled into the driveway, Cillian was waiting.

He went around to Kelly's side. My own anger was reflected on his face as he stared at his granddaughter.

He softened his features when he opened the passenger door. "Oh, princess."

"I'm okay, Gramps. It looks worse than it feels."

"Now I know that's a lie," Cillian said. "But we won't discuss that tonight."

"I'll come get you," I told Kelly. "Don't move."

"Not moving."

I came around and scooped her against me. My heart expanded when she tucked into me. No matter how much I wanted her back in my arms, this wasn't how I wanted it to happen. I'd willingly crawl over a bed of nails if I could spare her that pain and horrific experience.

Cillian was a silent mountain of anger by my side. In the world he'd lived in, the only appropriate response was revenge.

"Mama!"

"Mom!"

The girls rushed to us at the door.

"She's out of it," I told them. "Let's save this for tomorrow, okay?"

"Sorry to worry you, munchkins," Kelly mumbled, turning slightly to face the girls but keeping a good deal of her swollen cheek hidden.

"I'm glad you're okay, Mom," Whit said in a shaky voice. "Did they get the driver who tailgated you?"

"Kelso and Gabby are on it." I strode into the house. "We'll talk tomorrow. Your mom is getting heavy."

Kelly turned into my chest and pinched my nipple.

"Fuck."

"That's what you get," she whispered.

I double-timed it up the stairs and into the guest bedroom Branna prepared for us. The girls wanted to follow, but luckily, she intervened. "Come on, you young ones. I only let you stay up this late so you could say goodnight to your mom and dad."

"Whew, that was close," Kelly said. "Can't wait to take a shower."

"I'll help you."

"I think I can mana—"

"I'll help you," I repeated, lowering her onto the bed. When she was about to protest again, I put a finger on her lips. "Give me this, beautiful. Please."

"—kay."

Looming above her, I said, "Don't move."

I MET Cillian and Branna in the kitchen. She was preparing tea for Kelly.

"I brought in your duffel," Cillian said.

I thanked him.

"The girls?"

"They're settled in bed," Branna said. "They'd been getting all worked up with worry."

"Sorry."

"What are you apologizing for?" Cillian said. "Who else would take care of your girls if Kelly needed it? You always have us to rely on."

I huffed a short laugh. "Well, thanks then."

"Do they know who took her?" Branna asked. "Please tell me that part is over."

"We're not sure yet, but it might have something to do with Tom."

"Tom?" Cillian's brows drew together. "I've known that lad a long time. He's a good kid. Have they found him?"

I evaded his question. "He's mixed up in this shit somehow."

"Something's not right," Branna said. "How did Kelly get away?"

"The detectives are investigating. I'll tell you soon. It's not bad, but it's not good either because we're not sure if they'll send someone after Kelly again."

"Did they just let her go?"

"Someone rescued her," I hedged and tipped my head to the tea. "I'll come back for that. Kelly wants to freshen up and needs my help."

11

LEVI

WHEN I GOT BACK to the room, it was to an empty bed. I dropped the duffel and marched to the bathroom.

With a towel wrapped around her naked body, she was gingerly leaning over to turn on the shower.

"You never listen," I growled.

She spun around and looked at me sheepishly. "I got impatient." She gripped the towel closer. "And I can manage this."

I pulled my shirt over my head. "Maybe. But I'm not going to let you."

Her eyes flashed. "Levi, I'm not in the mood."

My fingers stopped at the button of my jeans. "Woman, the last thing on my mind is sex. I want to take care of you."

"I'm perfectly fine. I just got knocked around."

"You're pretty banged up."

"Seriously, Levi, I'm made of sterner stuff. You forget I can take a hard pounding from you."

Images of me rutting between her legs with headboard-destroying drives flashed through my head.

"Jesus Christ, Kelly," I grumbled, quickly lowering my zipper over my rapidly hardening cock. "Now is not the time to give me a hard on."

Her eyes tracked my movements. She was making it difficult to remain clinical. If it wasn't for her battered face, I'd say she wanted to jump my bones given how her tongue came out to swipe at her lower lip. Her cut lower lip.

She tipped her chin. "Then what do you intend to do with that."

"It's my problem. You're not showering alone. Deal with it." I stalked toward her.

"I can give you a hand job," she mumbled.

"What in the hell did Bristow give you?"

"No idea," she shrugged. "Typical pain killer. I still feel the pain, but I don't care."

I kicked off my jeans and my boxer shorts. My mouth twitched when her eyes widened, taking in my erection.

Clearing my throat, I moved past her. "Okay. Come on. Let's get you in there." I checked the water temp and adjusted it so it wasn't too hot.

"Nooo," she whined.

I glanced at her. "Warm and cold. You don't want your bruising to get worse. Bristow gave us ice packs." I nodded to the towel. "You can let go of that now."

She gave a huff and stripped it off to hang on the hook by the shower door.

While I helped her settle under the spray of water, staying detached was a struggle. My head and emotions were still consumed with rage. I tried not to think about her bruises, because she'd feel my fury in the close confines of the glass enclosure, but when her naked body pressed against my swollen shaft, I couldn't help groaning into her hair. My go-to method of running through baseball stats to keep the blood in my head and not in my dick went down the drain.

She turned around and pressed her tits against me. "I can feel you."

I was hard as a rock, but, somehow, I managed to grab the shampoo and started lathering her hair. While she rested her cheek on my chest, her arms wrapped around my torso. "All I could think about was you and the girls," she whispered. "That I needed to get back to my family."

Words backed up in my throat. Hope rose inside me. "What are you saying?" She glanced up, smiled, and raised a hand to cup my jaw. Then she turned away from me, leaving me reeling.

She could've said she just wanted to get back to the girls and left it at that. I wouldn't have felt hurt or resentful if she didn't think of me when she was in captivity. I was prepared for a long road to win her back.

Lust had long abandoned my body. Instead, it was filled with so much more. And as I gently helped Kelly wash away the traces of the night, I realized what I felt was hope, that this time, I'd get my family back and do it right.

KELLY

I woke up to light peeking through the window. It wasn't the window of my bedroom. Disoriented, I turned my head to the right and immediately regretted it. My whole body, including my face and neck screamed at me. But the sight of my husband's broad back inked with various Nordic symbols was a welcome sight. His right arm was cocked at an angle and a Spartan helmet tattooed on his bicep with the words "with it or on it" was on full display. A bittersweet smile touched my lips. Callum had the same tattoo. It was from the movie *300* where the laconic phrase meant to come back with your shield in victory, or die on it if defeated. That movie was iconic with the SEALs.

The events last night came filtering back. It was almost as though I dreamed it. Was it real? I couldn't believe I was kidnapped, beaten, and rescued.

I shifted on my elbow and let my gaze enjoy the line of my husband's back that led to his muscular butt. He was wearing boxer shorts now, but before our girls got into the habit of visiting us early in the morning, he slept in the raw.

I sighed wistfully. Was it only yesterday morning we'd woken up together?

"I can feel you admiring my ass," an amused gravelly voice said.

"It's a very fine ass."

"The front is better." He slowly shifted onto his back, casually folding his arms and putting them under his head as though he were a sultan about to be serviced by a harem.

I rolled my eyes and scooted away so I could see him better. "Thanks for taking care of me."

"It was my pleasure, beautiful."

It took all my willpower not to touch my face, because I knew my husband enough that it would destroy his mood to be reminded that he hadn't protected me from Blaze. He would always be a protector. And given how he and the kids were first in my mind yesterday when I thought I would die, he had always been the one. We just lost our way and let our issues come between us.

"So, I fell asleep on you last night," I said.

"You had a horrific day." His sleep-roughened voice was incredibly sexy. I didn't know why I was love-doped over my husband when I couldn't have sexy times with him in the state I was in. Well, maybe I could, but … stop! Obviously it had been a while since I woke up in bed with a man.

Yesterday morning didn't count because the kids interrupted.

"We didn't have our talk about … us," I said. Funny how I wanted more than ever to put the decision behind us. What happened yesterday was an eye-opener about what was important.

"No, we didn't." His eyes grew hooded. "Could you give me a hint which direction you're heading?"

"Whether it's divorce or reconciliation?" I asked. At his scowl, I quickly added, "I think we should give our marriage another chance."

A broad smile transformed his face. He sat up on the bed and leaned against the headboard. "This is progress."

I laughed lightly. "Tell me about it." Then my face turned serious. "I'm scared and I'm still working through my aban-donment issues. I felt like a single parent even when you were home and whenever you disappeared without a word—"

"I fucked up last year," he cut me off abruptly. "When I went and rescued Garrison and Bristow's asses and didn't tell you I was leaving for Ukraine. That won't happen again. And, if it's classified, I'll just tell you it is."

"Thank you." He'd been good about it since that happened, and I'd stopped waiting for the other shoe to drop. It took our separation for him to see what he'd been missing out on with Ashley, and he accomplished that goal beautifully with the tenacity I knew he was capable of. "You've done a great job with Ash. You're her favorite person now. Sometimes I get jealous."

"It's because I let her get away with a lot of things," he puffed a short laugh. His sheepishness was adorable although adorable was the wrong word to use. Hot. He was hot.

"No, the turning point was when you danced with her after she messed up at that recital."

Levi's face turned fierce at the memory. "When your little girl is miserable and she asks you to wear that pink tutu, I don't care if you're a badass SEAL or a ruthless mercenary, you fucking wear that tutu and put that smile back on her face."

I stared at him, taken aback by the emotion and conviction evident in that declaration. It was a foregone conclusion that I'd never fallen out of love with the man. I might have fallen deeper.

A knock on the door interrupted our heart-to-heart.

I panicked and touched the side of my face. "Shit."

He jumped out of bed. "I'll take care of them. Do whatever you need to do."

12

LEVI

THAT DAY STARTED with moving myself into Kelly's house. Dropping my duffel in her bedroom, I smirked. She could kick me out later, but as far as I was concerned, she'd earned herself full-contact protection.

Bristow came by to help me upgrade her security system. After years of putting me off, she didn't argue. The girls tried to bring up the puppy conversation to segue into the security around the house, but their mom was onto their antics and tabled that talk for another day. They were as opportunistic as I was, and that made me a proud dad.

Kelly's expertise in SFX came in handy. The blue-black discoloration and swelling on her face became mere smudges the kids didn't fuss over. She mumbled something about contour makeup.

That evening, Kelso filled us in on the investigation's progress. In addition to the detective, Migs Walker, who was a part of my team, came by with Ariana. Kelly spoke to her after lunch, and Migs' wife suggested a vitamin infusion to help with the recovery and the stress. The men gathered around the kitchen drinking beer while Kelly was in the living room with the girls, hooked up to an IV bag. Ashley and Whitney kept asking questions, fascinated by the yellow liquid dripping into their mom.

"Any lead from the sketches Kelly provided you?" I asked Bristow.

"Not yet," he replied, glancing at the detective. "Sent you a link to download it."

"I'll get Nadia on it."

Bristow said, "There's also a partial sketch of the man with Blaze at the studio. I'm thinking he's the one who messed with the surveillance."

The man was in profile, not much to use for facial recognition, but once we identified Blaze and his associates, I was sure the rest would follow. The sketch of Blaze, however, was detailed and even included specific lines of his face. I hated that it was etched in my wife's memory. It was etched in mine too. If I could conjure up that fucker, I would. But killing him seemed too easy for retribution. The way I was seething inside, torturing him for days before ending him was what I had in mind.

"I called my friend in the Vegas PD," Kelso said. "Since Roth's been doing business there, I wonder if he got mixed up with the ROCC."

"Russian Organized Crime Collective," I said. It was the official term LEOs used for the Russian mafia. Cadres were the smaller groups who controlled each location.

"Yup," Kelso said. "Simon Stepanov is the man who runs the Vegas cadre, but he is the head of Murder Sanctum."

"I've heard about the organization," Bristow said. "They're like the modern-day Murders Inc."

"You're talking about the society of hitmen in the 50s?" I asked.

"Yes," Kelso said. "Blaze could be one of theirs. Since it

was a De Lucci resort that Roth was dealing with, I've reached out to Kelly's uncle and he pointed me in a different direction when it came to Stepanov."

I stilled at the detective's next words. "Kelly's Chicago family."

"You think they're involved?" I asked.

The detective shrugged. "Anything is possible at this point and Chicago has had dealings with the ROCC, especially the one in Vegas."

"Are you saying this is about Kelly, rather than Roth?"

"We can't confirm until we identify the men involved in her abduction."

"Don't forget there's also the one who tried to whack Tom."

Kelso pinched the bridge of his nose. "Yeah. I have a feeling we're only scratching the surface here and this shit gets deeper."

"Man, and I thought my wife was complicated," Migs said. Ariana was the sister of a former crime lord of Los Angeles who had deep connections to the cartels. "But your wife is connected to both Chicago and New York, right?"

"Don't remind me," I muttered. I hated both sides of her Italian family. Her abandonment issues ran deep because of those assholes. She was lucky she grew up with the McGraths.

"Nadia is going through old files to find a link between Murder Sanctum, the Vegas mob, and Chicago—the Moretti Crime family," Kelso said. "Emilio Moretti broke ties with the ROCC a few years ago. A disagreement over something, no one is talking."

"Everything about mob activities is rumor," I murmured to no one in particular. "When does she go on maternity leave?" Nadia was married to our seemingly cold-hearted, invincible leader John Garrison who had succumbed to true love. They were expecting their first child in a few weeks. We got a kick out of teasing him because despite the many times he'd escape gunfire, terrorists, and a near beheading, his downfall was a broken condom and a nerdy crime analyst.

"When the baby pops she says," Kelso laughed. "If Garrison had his way, she'd be on bed rest. You should see those two argue."

"He seems busy enough with prospective fatherhood, he barely checks in with me," I said.

"He said you're in charge," Migs said.

"Did you all have to have babies at the same time," I groaned. "When's Ariana due?"

"Six weeks." The soft smile that curved Migs' mouth was a familiar one. That was the same smile I had when I was in pictures with Kelly and my girls.

"Man." Kelso glanced at Bristow. "Aren't you freaked out hanging around these dudes? They're falling like flies."

Bristow eased back in his chair and drew on his beer. "Terrified."

Everyone burst out laughing.

I walked to the edge of the kitchen and leaned against the entrance to the room. "You ladies need anything?"

"Almost done," Ariana replied. "Tell Migs to get out the carnitas and cheese dip I have in the cooler."

"You didn't have to bring food too," I told her.

"Hey, no rejecting tacos, bro," Bristow said from behind me. A scuffle of feet and a hushed argument ensued between Bristow and Migs.

I glanced over my shoulder to see Ariana's husband warding off Bristow's hand on the cooler.

"Just helping out," Bristow protested.

"Helping out? You're going to eat everything. Let the pregnant woman and the kids eat first."

"Migs," Ariana called. "There's plenty. I made extra for Bristow."

"See?" Bristow grinned. "Your wife loves me."

"How about I punch that smirk off your face?" Migs shot back.

A tug on my shirt diverted my attention to Ashley's upturned face.

"You hungry, baby girl?"

She shook her head.

"What's going on?"

"Auntie Ari has a big tummy."

I didn't know whether to laugh or worry about my child's tact. "You didn't say that to her face, did you?"

Again, she shook her head.

"There's a baby in there," she said not so quietly, then her eyes widened. "I felt it move!"

I grinned. "You moved too." I sank to my haunches. "But it's not really in the tummy. There's a part of women called a womb."

"But how do babies get in there?"

I realized that the men had stopped arguing, so I glanced behind me again. Motherfuckers' faces were red from trying not to laugh.

"Well?" Ashley insisted, pulling my attention back to her.

"Uh …"

"Having problems explaining the birds and the bees, Daddy?" Kelly called.

I rose, lifted my curious daughter in my arms and walked over. "Did you put her up to it?"

"She asked Ariana," Kelly couldn't help laughing. The minx. "We just needed a little time to frame our response properly."

"Well, baby girl, I'll leave it to your mom." I lowered Ashley and might have double-timed it back to the kitchen, but not before hearing the egg and sperm conversation. When Kelly asked for a separation, I had to read up on parenting books and learned it's around six years old when kids become curious about shit like that. According to the book, it was also important to use the right terms and not dumb them down. I certainly didn't remember Whitney asking about it.

"Chickened out, Dad?" Migs chuckled.

"Wait until you have to explain it to your kid," I mumbled.

"But how does the baby come out?" Ashley asked loudly.

Kelly calmly explained the birth canal and the vagina.

Migs continued pulling out the food containers from the cooler and transferred the items to the kitchen island. "Ariana is handling that talk. When my son comes of age, I'm just going to throw a box of condoms at him."

KELLY

"WELL, THAT WAS FUN." I told Levi as we waved off Ariana and Migs. Kelso and Bristow left an hour earlier, the former saying he had to leave early the next day for Vegas. As for Levi's buddy, he was a bachelor so I guess he had better things to do on a Sunday night than to hang around a married couple and their kids.

"Ariana's belly is huge," I added.

"Yes, your daughter mentioned that."

I laughed lightly and shook my head. Straight from the mouth of babes. Wasn't that the saying? Thankfully, the girls had gone to bed.

We headed up the stairs, my mind on our sleeping arrangement. Levi dropped his things in my bedroom. I was conflicted about his presumptuousness. In his defense, the kids did catch us in bed for two straight mornings, and I couldn't deny we were doing naughty things that first time. My cheeks flamed at the memory.

"Ari told me it's only one baby. Twins do run in Migs' family." The man had five sisters. Five. Ariana also told me what an amazing brother he was, and it just made her fall for him harder.

"What's that sigh about?" Levi asked with amusement.

"They look so in love." I glanced behind me and nearly rolled my eyes. Predictably, he was staring at my ass.

"Hey, are you saying we don't?"

We reached the top floor. "I think ours is a mature love."

He pulled me into our bedroom and boxed me in against the wall. "That sounds boring." His eyes scanned my face. "Don't I give you butterflies anymore, sweetheart?"

He'd given me a lot of stomach flutters lately, and he hadn't said sweetheart in a while either. When we'd still been together, he used that endearment often, usually in a sexy drawl invoking a tingle from my navel to the core. I didn't recall him calling me sweetheart during our separation, and most definitely not during our random hookups. And I annoyed myself for being annoyed because he had every right to withhold a part of himself while being uncertain about us. Something had changed when I gave him the green light that we had a second chance. Somehow my observation of another married relationship had challenged him, but it also made me want to tease him.

"You do," I admitted, but since he was cocky enough, I added. "Sometimes."

"Sometimes only, huh?" The gleam in his eyes told me he knew I was totally lying.

"When you don't piss me off," I retorted, but it came out a bit breathless. "By the way, it was quite presumptuous of you to put your duffel in my room."

He glanced over his shoulder at his things and shrugged while still having me caged in. "Sleeping in different bedrooms will confuse the girls. They've seen us in the same bed the past two nights. Has your decision changed about giving a go to our marriage?"

"No," I said. "But I thought we could take it slow, and sleeping in the same bedroom could muddle things."

"Things were already muddled up anyway when we weren't sleeping in the same bed and just fucked to scratch an itch."

I winced at his language, but he was not wrong.

"But the problem is not about sharing a bed," he said. "Besides, I'm not going to fuck you despite those damned mixed signals—"

I gasped in outrage and glared at him

He stared at me steadily. "Not after you've just been attacked."

"But I feel fine," I whined.

His brow arched. "You mean you want me to fuck you right now?" He leaned in closer and my nipples reacted like Pavlov's dog, aching to be touched.

"Well, not exactly put like that." I was unsettled from the mixed signals comment. "And they weren't mixed signals. It's conflict. You know our chemistry in bed always gets in the way of us having a conversation."

He raised a hand to my mouth and stroked the cut. "I want to kiss the shit out of your beautiful lips, and it's not possible right now." His fingers stroke down my jaw, down the side of my neck and circled around the bruising hidden under the concealer. Then they traveled down the side of my breast before tracing lower.

"Levi," I whispered.

His chocolate eyes turned molten. Finally, his fingers reached the waistband of my lounge pants, and he didn't hesitate to slip his fingers inside. I arched and moaned when he touched my clit. He never failed to find the mark.

"Damn, you're so wet."

I didn't answer him, just gave in to the way his fingers massaged the tender flesh.

"That's it," he said. "Ride it, babe."

It didn't take long. It never did. I should be embarrassed but I shuddered as the ripples of my orgasm hit me. He kept the heel of his hand at that sweet spot and prolonged my pleasure. And as my shudders faded away, he withdrew his fingers and I watched him lick them.

My filthy lover.

He loved my taste.

"Delicious," he said as if he'd had the most satisfying dessert. I frowned when he backed away.

Again?

He was hard.

"This is getting ridiculous, Levi."

He adjusted his cock, and I nodded to it. "That must be begging for my hand."

He backed up to the bed and sat on it, tapping the mattress. "I'd pass on the hand job if you let me sleep with you tonight."

My lips twitched. "Would you now?"

"Sleeping beside you tonight would be more satisfying," he paused. "Well ... for now."

"I'm getting the sacrifice of it all and I appreciate it." I approached him and got between his knees. His arms came up automatically to caress my backside. "But don't you think it's ridiculous?"

"No, I don't, because I don't want to pass up the opportunity to get things off my chest. If we fuck, we'll never talk."

"That's my line."

"Kelso wants you to call Chicago. See if they know anything."

Blood left my face and I sank beside him. "Are they ... are they involved?"

"Don't know yet. Straight up, I hate that you have to deal with them."

Thinking of Chicago brought my insecurities into focus. I was five when I found out that Uncle Charles was my biological father. No wonder he'd been trying his best to take me to parks and even my first day of school. He just wasn't cut out to be a parent though. At Aunt Ava's wedding, I was brought in front of this old forbidding-looking man who asked me questions I didn't want to answer. He was Giovanni Rossi, my grandfather, and was the boss of the Rossi Crime family at that time.

When I turned ten, the McGraths sat me down and explained to me the whole sordid story. I knew Charles had been in jail when I was born, so it wasn't like he had a choice to abandon me. I think the hardest part was knowing my mother Sofia Rossi gave me up voluntarily when she wasn't destitute at all. Nona Rossi took her to Italy and kept her hidden until she gave birth. They returned in secret and reached out to the McGraths. And the rest was history. All rights to me were surrendered. So legally, I was a McGrath. Charles' older brother Robert and his wife, Madelyn, were my parents. And although Charles tried to be a real dad, he never got his shit together, and I was already too attached to Mom and Dad and my brothers, Callum and Ronan. That hurt a lot too, knowing they weren't really my brothers but my cousins. But they never treated me as the outcast of the brood even when our youngest sister, Alana, was born.

My head throbbed just thinking about my family history.

"Say the word, I'll tell Kelso to forget about it," Levi said. "Or I could be the one to talk to Chicago." He took my hand and said, "Give me your eyes, beautiful."

I did.

"I know there's something messed up in there." He tipped his chin in the general direction of my head. "I know it's not because of me, but it's because you never fully got over what Sofia did. It's rooted deep in you, babe." His face grew troubled. "I may not have been the cause of the initial mess, but I made it worse."

When I was about to open my mouth, he narrowed his eyes, so I said nothing.

"I shut down on you in the two years following Callum's death. That mission took him from us, and it wasn't my fault. I accept that now. What I can't accept is what I did to you. How it only made your abandonment issues worse. A reopened wound takes more time to heal. The scarring is deeper, uglier. The mark may never go away, and that's on me." His grip on my hand tightened. "I think I got some things right in these past eighteen months trying to get us back on track, like dealing with my anger and Callum's death. They were sort of related. Being a better father to our girls. I also understood why you wanted to keep my shit from them. What I got wrong was using our physical connection to keep my hooks in you without talking about what's broken. And you telling me to leave your bed before the kids wake up is telling me we're still broke. But we're making progress, and I'm not fucking that up. I don't want to fuck you and have you kick me out of bed the next morning. That's a vicious cycle. It's got to stop." He looked at me without saying a word for a long time and then, "Well?"

My smile was small, but he smiled wide.

It was the most words Levi had spoken about our problems, about understanding how his actions had affected my own deeply rooted ones. "We're making progress. But you seem to be shouldering the blame. I got comfortable ... you let me get comfortable. And the sex? I didn't just fall on your cock, right? We were both consenting adults. I'm not a damned underaged virgin. And Levi?"

"Hmm ..."

"We can sleep together."

He exhaled a long shuddering breath, got up, and started to pace, rubbing his fingers across his jaw.

Confused, I asked, "Was that not what you—"

He surged to his knees in front of me, and pushed mine

apart. He raised his hands to cup my face tenderly. "Thanks, babe, for giving me this chance."

Then he kissed me gently on the lips, but I felt the zap all the way to my toes.

Guess my husband still gave me butterflies.

13

It had been ten days since my kidnapping. The man I knew as Blaze was Hans Ulrich. That was what was on his American passport, but he had several aliases. The guys referred to him as Blaze Ulrich. He was part of the Murder Sanctum network. On the surface, little was known about him but several hits could be attributed to his specialty. He earned his moniker because he liked to set things on fire and blow things up. He was known as the ordnance expert of the mob.

The kids were in school. I was lounging by the pool, finally feeling more like myself since I didn't have to take pain killers any longer or have to cake my face with foundation and concealer. The Brazilian balm from Bristow, which I suspected contained arnica, plus the two vitamin infusions I received from Ariana helped me heal faster. I was no longer swelling, and my bruises had faded into a greenish-yellowish hue.

The main thing in the past few days was the need to gird my loins and call my Chicago family.

I could only put it off for so long because the detectives

were hitting a dead end. Levi also threatened to call them himself. Kelso indicated he was swinging by for dinner after a lead on the Russian gang in Vegas yielded interesting intel.

Intel. My mouth quirked up. I was beginning to sound like my husband.

My biological mother answered the phone on the second ring. "Kelly?" Her trademark husky voice made me think of a 50s era actress wearing a wide-brimmed fedora and double-stranded pearls around her neck.

"Yes. It's me."

"So good to hear from you, darling."

After we exchanged awkward pleasantries and boring weather commentary, I said, "I left messages for Luca but he hasn't returned my calls."

"What do you need from him?" Sofia asked, her tone turning wary. My stepbrother was the current boss of the Chicago Mafia. After Sofia's husband, Emilio, died, there was a brief power struggle between the cousins but it was obvious who was favored to become king. It was not out of the question that what happened to me could be blowback from that.

"I guess it would be useless to ask if Luca has enemies," I said.

"What happened?" That time Sofia's voice turned sharp.

I sighed before giving her a gist of what had transpired since Tom's disappearance to my abduction, and rescue.

"And I'm only hearing about this now?" she screeched. "Are you all right?"

"I'm fine." I'd been wondering why I was calmer about what happened. It was either being around my husband made me feel safe, or it was in my blood to deal with situations like this.

"I have been calling Luca since yesterday." Okay, 'have been' was pushing it. I called twice and left a message once. I could hardly tell Sofia it turned my stomach every time I had to do obligatory calls to her side of the family. The less I contacted them, the better for my mental health.

"You have to be careful about the Vegas mob," Sofia whispered. "They have ears everywhere. I will talk to Luca, but do not call me on this number again."

The line went dead.

Puzzled, I stared at my phone.

She really did hang up. I looked at it a while longer, not really surprised with the way Sofia acted. What else was new? And as I'd practiced over the years, I shrugged it off. I was nothing to them.

"Doing all right out here?" Levi's voice spoke behind me.

My heart jumped. "How do you sneak up like that?"

He just grinned and gave me a peck on the forehead before handing me a tall glass of iced tea.

"Hmm, special service," I said. "I can get used to this. My own personal pool boy."

He sat on the lounge chair beside me. "Were you talking to Sofia?"

I side-eyed him. "Spying on me?"

"Just wondering when you were going to call them. I offered, remember?"

"I can fight my own battles. I just needed time."

Levi sighed. "That was a brief call."

"She hung up on me."

"What?"

I shot Levi the side-eye again. "Luca hasn't returned my messages. Sofia doesn't appear to know anything, but she warned me about the Vegas mob. Something smells fishy."

"And?"

"And nothing," I said. "She hung up." I was getting irritated with my husband. I didn't need him to needle me about how I chose to communicate with my family.

"I'll call her," Levi said, getting up from the lounger, but I tugged him down.

"Don't," I snapped. "They have better things to do than attend to a Kelly problem. I'm the poor relation, remember?"

"But their shit is affecting you," he gritted.

"We don't know that yet."

"Chances are they'll deny it and do something else in the background to try and fix it," he said grimly. "I'm not down with that. I'm not down with not knowing what the Chicago mob will do to ensure your safety. They could make it worse. If you don't want to deal with them, I will. Got it?"

How could I stay irritated with my husband when he turned all growly and protective. So freaking sexy. Still, I didn't want him sticking his nose in my Chicago business. That was like stirring a hornet's nest. I knew he had friends in high places on speed dial, but we just needed to let Luca respond in his own sweet time. If there was something I knew about my stepbrother, no one forced him to do anything before he was ready. I knew that by rumor. How Luca once shot a business partner during a dinner meeting because he was being a pain in the ass and wanted Luca to sign off on a deal.

I took a sip of iced tea. "You don't have to wait on me hand and foot. I can also do the cooking, and help with chores around the house."

Levi exhaled a long sigh and said, "You did the same for me when I was laid out. But no, this is not me returning a favor." He leaned forward and looked me straight in the eye. "This is me taking care of my wife."

"We don't seem to have a problem picking up where we left off." The morning after we decided to give our relationship a try, save for a little bit of awkwardness in the beginning, we'd adjusted smoothly. Then I grinned. "Except the other part."

The sex. We hadn't had sex.

Levi's body froze. "I wanted you to be physically ready." The heat in his eyes gave me a hot flash, and I gulped down the cold tea. "Having you sleep beside me, sometimes tucked into me … you don't know how many cold showers a day I've taken."

"We don't have problems indulging," I teased. "You're the one who keeps putting off the real thing."

He sat back, but the heat between us escalated. "Because sweetheart, the kids shouldn't hear what I really want to do to you. I'm making sure you're strong enough too."

"I think I'm physically able to take that pounding now," I whispered.

He gave a measured nod. "Yes. But I'm afraid your flimsy bed can't withstand my pent-up hunger for you. We should do it at my house."

I rolled my eyes. "What's wrong with my bed?"

"It creaks."

"Hey, I bought that at an auction from the Great Gatsby remake." As soon as the words left my mouth, I smiled sheepishly. "Well …"

"Christ. How much did you pay for that thing?"

"It all went to charity," I defended. "The studio hired a craftsman from France." He stared at me dubiously, so I changed the subject. "But what do we do with the kids?" I asked.

"They're a pair of cock-blockers, aren't they?"

"Levi, shame on you."

He smiled wickedly. "Aren't you looking forward to a Levi-headboard-wrecking pounding?"

"Oh my God," I whispered. I definitely was. The evidence of wetness between my thighs confirmed this.

A knowing smile spread across his face. He leaned closer, a hand resting on my lounger, pressed his lips on mine and swept his tongue into my mouth. Heat exploded between us, and I was dragged from my lounger onto his. He reclined and let me stretch on top of him. We got into the rhythm as we went at it with our tongues and lips, grinding against each other. I was glad the property had high walls because I was about to be ravaged on top of a pool lounger.

His hands went under my shirt. "You have too many clothes on." His fingers glided to my butt and squeezed the globes. "Why couldn't you have worn a skirt?" he groaned before resuming to devour my mouth.

I rubbed my pussy over his hardness.

When I finally came up for air, I breathed, "You don't want me to make it easy for you, do you?" I said it with my tits brushing up against his chest. I could feel the vibration of his groan.

"You never make it easy, beautiful."

"You're a SEAL. You never want easy," I murmured, my lips teasing him, not letting him catch them.

"That's right."

He stilled, angling his head toward the entrance of the patio like something caught his attention. "Kids are here."

Levi

KELSO DIDN'T TURN up until after dinner. Branna and Cillian, ever the reliable babysitters, came by that evening with their German Shepherd, Ruger, to help entertain the kids so they didn't have to listen to the detective's update.

I lowered a slab of sizzling ribeye in front of Kelso and sat beside him.

"Man, I do nothing here but eat." He stole a quick glance at Bristow. "Is that why you've turned bodyguard for the kids?"

Bristow volunteered to pick up the girls from school that afternoon. "Contrary to my legendary appetite," he replied.

"I'm just helping out a friend. Besides, what will I do with my downtime?"

"You need to find a girlfriend," Kelly told him, taking her seat on my left.

"Kids doing okay?" I asked.

"So far," she said. "I warned Ashley not to taunt Ruger with Mr. Snuffles."

"We've discussed Ruger's need to hunt down an object." I arched a brow. "I don't think Mr. Snuffles will survive him."

"Your daughter can be stubborn. Gramps said Ruger doesn't become aggressive with a toy if you try to take it from him, so I'm not worried."

"That dog has a playful streak," Bristow said. "He sure liked playing keep away with his ball when I was over at the McGraths. That should wear out your girls."

I tipped my chin at Kelso's plate. "How's the steak?"

"Rare, just the way I like it."

"So what's the news from Vegas?"

Kelso chewed slowly before unlocking the tablet he had with him and sliding it over to us. "There was a gang encounter that left a couple of Vegas mobsters dead."

Kelly leaned in to look while Bristow left his chair to peek over my shoulder.

"All of them have a record," the detective said. "Those are their mug shots. Any one of them look like the guy who was with Blaze?"

My wife scrolled through a few. "I'm pretty sure it was this one." She tapped on the screen. "The tattoo definitely matches."

"He fits the profile," Kelso said. "Jude Eisenberg—a known member of Murder Sanctum and a hacker, so that answers how he rigged the surveillance and the entry gate at the studio. He owns a seat at the Sanctum table which means for him to be involved in your studio abduction shows how important getting to Roth was."

"Couldn't he have hacked the surveillance remotely?" Bristow asked.

I leaned back in my chair. "He could've, but maybe they were short on time and had to do it quickly."

"From his file, he owns the drug territory in West Hollywood," Kelso said. "He might have been in town at that time, so Blaze tagged him."

"What exactly happened in Vegas?"

"I came straight from there which was why I was late," Kelso said after gulping down the next bite. "I have a buddy with the Vegas PD. He told me there's an ongoing gang war with money laundering at the casinos from drug revenue. It's messy. Assassinations were carried out yesterday. Eisenberg was one of them."

"Was one? Someone else was killed?"

Kelso swallowed another bite, chased it down with beer, and tipped his chin toward the tablet in my hand. "Keep going."

There were three more guys, but Kelly shrugged. "I don't recognize any of them."

"They're all associates of Simon Stepanov," Kelso said. "Which only confirms that Murder Sanctum is heavily involved." He glanced at Kelly. "Were you able to contact Chicago?"

"I left a message for my stepbrother," she answered. "I talked to Sofia, and she said she'll get back to me."

A look of frustration crossed the detective's face like he wanted to push Kelly. I caught his gaze and shook my head.

The detective's jaw hardened before continuing, "According to my friend, it's a case of gangs jockeying for heroin territory. It'd been a headache for them and it's becoming one for us because Moscow White is reaching LA." The detective glanced at Kelly. "It's heroin spiked with a compound that gives it a special hit. Several deaths had been attributed to it. It's surpassed the high of the ones cut with Fentanyl."

"Damn," I interjected.

Bristow went back to his seat and fired up his laptop.

Kelso finished eating and drained his beer.

"You eat fast," Kelly said. "Want another one?"

A thoughtful look crossed the detective's face. "No. I'm good."

"Dessert?" My wife prodded. "Nana brought her famous Irish Cheesecake."

"Ahhh," Kelso said sheepishly. "You may not want to serve me dessert after my questions."

"What questions?" she asked.

"Could it be possible it was your stepbrother who called the hit on Eisenberg?"

"What?" Kelly's tone was of genuine surprise.

"You said Blaze took pictures right? He posted it in a dark web chatroom. I'm sure Roth wasn't the only one who saw it. I bet you Moretti would've caught wind of it too. As payback, he killed Eisenberg and took their drugs."

My wife gave a mirthless laugh. "You overestimate my importance to the Chicago mob."

"Cards on the table," Kelso said. "You say you're not important? Vegas is a mobster's lair, we know this. So, my buddy up there has a file on you too. Why wouldn't they? You are the granddaughter of the former Rossi crime boss. You're the daughter of Sofia Rossi Moretti, the widow of the former head of the Chicago crime family."

"The Rossis only acknowledged me during my aunt's wedding," Kelly whispered. She stood and walked to the kitchen window, staring into the backyard. "I've never been anything special. I was never invited to Rossi gatherings. I'm considered an embarrassment. Robert and Madelyn McGrath are—and always will be—my parents. It's on my birth certificate." She turned back to Kelso. "I don't think I merit any attention from the Morettis."

"Crime families are about blood. You are still one of them. What if Murder Sanctum thinks because you're outside the immediate protection of both families, you'd be an easier target?" Bristow floated up the idea that had been echoing in the back of my mind.

"I don't think Luca would be outraged on my behalf enough to retaliate," Kelly said. "That would be risky for the *family* with little benefit."

"Mafia ties are deep and complicated," I told her.

"You can't help but wonder if Chicago whacked Eisenberg because of what he did to our mafia princess here ..." Bristow said.

Kelso started nodding his head. "That idea has merit."

"Ugh, I'm not a mafia princess," Kelly griped.

Everyone chuckled around the table.

"The Eisenberg homicide belongs to the Vegas PD, and they will keep me apprised on the investigation," the detective told us.

The door to the backyard swung open and Cillian walked in. "Did you all get my granddaughter squared away?"

"There's been a slight complication." I gave her grandfather a gist of what Kelso had told us.

"Simon Stepanov ... interesting." Cillian looked thoughtful. "Do you remember Isaac Ford, Kelly?"

"Ford ..." Kelly said. "Are you talking about the son of the former senator of New York, Walter Ford?"

"The one and only."

"How is he connected?" I remembered the scandal regarding the senator's son. He was found guilty of securities fraud. The senator resigned his post. The man was a billionaire. He didn't hurt for the salary of a public servant, but it was the embarrassment stemming from his son's actions that caused him to resign.

"The younger Ford was convicted of insider trading and short selling," Cillian said. "SDNY hired McGrath Investigations to dig into the anomalies in the case. It was Robert's findings that allowed the U.S. Attorney to prosecute."

"Yes, so?"

"Murder Sanctum was rumored to be behind the prison riot that killed Isaac Ford."

Kelso and Bristow straightened in their seats. Kelly's grandfather had a captive audience.

"There were speculations in the mob that the riot was deliberate to mask the hit on Ford," Cillian said.

"He ordered his own son whacked?" Bristow asked incredulously.

"Ordered it?" Cillian scoffed. "No. I'd say he was fatalistic about it. The Russian oligarchs made the old man rich. He knew it was coming. Isaac was a scapegoat if you ask me and the kid knew too much. It's Walter who was secretly manipulating things behind the scenes. He didn't order his son killed, but knowing the older Ford, he had no choice. How old is he now? Seventy? Back in the day, there were rumors the New York mob got him his seat in the senate. In return for favors, of course." He glanced at Kelso. "After RICO took out most of the Italian bosses, they decided to lie low when it came to whacking people. They never do that anymore, preferring to outsource it to the Irish or to the Russians. That's where Simon Stepanov came in with Sanctum."

"I thought Stepanov was an associate of Chicago?"

Cillian shrugged. "Chicago used to run Murder Sanctum, but they had a falling out in the past six years."

"Right around the time the younger Ford got whacked."

"Who would know more about this?" Kelso asked.

"I could ask around," Cillian said.

"Gramps," Kelly chided. "I don't want you calling any of them. You promised Nana."

"But if it's going to help you, pumpkin." Her gramps' face

grew tender. Branna and Cillian had an on-again-off-again marriage mostly related to his life of crime. He and his son Charles went to prison in '89 on racketeering charges. Charles was released earlier, Cillian in '96. The way the McGraths had told it, Branna had been adamant about not taking Cillian back because he ruined Charles' life who was twenty-one at that time. Cillian pursued Branna for the next five years until she relented. He stayed away from mob business. Over twenty years later, they're as strong as ever. I wondered if all this turmoil in Kelly's life influenced her leeriness of getting back with me. She had to know. She and the girls mean everything to me.

"It would help if you could ask around," Kelso hedged, casting Kelly another wary look. My wife could be downright scary when she wanted to. She had the McGrath crystal blue eyes that flashed almost translucent when she was emotional.

"Will do."

"Dad! Mom!" Whitney burst into the kitchen, her eyes full of excitement. "Ruger tore up Mr. Snuffles."

Fuck.

Branna walked in with a teary-eyed Ashley dragging Mr. Snuffles on the floor. A Mr. Snuffles eviscerated by a rambunctious Ruger judging from the stuffing hanging from the ripped fur.

"I thought I told you to get Levi," Branna told her husband.

"Got sidetracked with business."

"What business?" the McGrath matriarch demanded.

"Oh no, sweetie." Kelly crouched in front of our daughter. I didn't doubt that was also to distract her grandmother from ripping Cillian a new one.

"You were right, Mama," Ashley's mouth quivered.

"I tried to take it from him." Whitney panted as though she'd run in a marathon.

"I'll get him." Cillian walked to the back door before

throwing over his shoulder. "He was playing keep away, that's all."

When Kelly's grandfather returned with the German Shepherd, he called my girls over. "Now make up with each other."

"Hmm … I don't know." My youngest pouted. "He destroyed Mr. Snuffles."

"And your mom warned you not to bring him out," I said. "Ruger thought it was one of his chew toys. You can't do that to him, baby girl. You can't set him up to fail just because you want to tease him. If you can't learn that, we're not getting a dog."

Ashley turned teary eyes up at me, her mouth struggling not to quiver, and I thought she was going to bawl her eyes out. But I stood my ground. It was probably the harshest I'd ever been with her, but I didn't budge.

"Nana said she'll fix Mr. Snuffles for you," Kelly added.

Ashley returned her attention to Ruger. "I guess I forgive him."

"Now, that's settled," Cillian said with satisfaction. "How about you all come over to my place on Sunday for a barbecue?"

I could see Bristow's eyes lighting up like a spotlight.

"Kelly's cousin is flying in from New York." Cillian split a look between the two unattached males in the room. "She's single and smart."

"Oh my God, Gramps, stop matchmaking," Kelly groaned.

14

KELLY

AFTER KELSO LEFT, sleeping arrangements seemed to be up in the air.

"But, Mom, I want to make up with Ruger," Ashley said. "Besides, Nana is bringing Mr. Snuffles home."

I glanced at my grandmother.

"I'd love to have them over."

My attention returned to Ashley. "Nana will fix Mr. Snuffles tomorrow."

Ash's lower lip trembled and tears came to her eyes. "But I want to sleep with Mr. Snuffles."

"It's late," Whit told her sister.

"No, no, it's okay," my grandmother said. "I'm not sleepy at all."

Levi, who was talking to Bristow and my grandfather, approached our huddle. "What's going on?"

"Kids want a sleepover at Nana and Gramps."

"Excellent!" my grandfather boomed.

"Wait a minute." I glanced at my husband. "Are you okay if the girls are there without us—?"

"I'll stay over," Bristow said. "And the patrol car will be making the rounds anyway."

He and Levi exchanged a look.

Hmmm …

"Great, we can shoot the shit and drink whiskey," Gramps told Bristow.

"I'm up for it."

Bristow was Irish. He seemed to hit it off with my grandfather. They would've shared the same hair color if Gramp's ginger hadn't faded to golden.

I glanced suspiciously at Levi, who, interestingly enough, had averted his gaze to look at the girls, a smile playing at the corner of his mouth. He tousled Whit's hair before crouching in front of Ash. "You behave for Gramps and Nana, baby girl."

"I will, Daddy."

"No more taunting Ruger," he added.

Ash gave a series of vigorous nods.

"Who knows?" Levi glanced over his shoulder at me and winked. "Your mom might be so impressed with your dog care-taking skills, she'll agree to a puppy."

"Nice try, Dad." I joined their trio and addressed Whit. "You need your iPad? I saw it on the charger upstairs."

My eldest daughter shrugged and left to get the device.

"They still have clothes at our house, so no need to pack," Nana informed me with a knowing smile on her face before pushing Ashley out the door. Gramps and Bristow mumbled they would wait out front.

"You guys don't have to rush off," I called after them, partly from amusement, but mostly from embarrassment because it was so obvious they were pushing for Levi-and-me alone time.

And judging from my husband's expression, I had a feeling he was the instigator of the sleepover.

Our gazes locked. The smolder in his eyes was enough to melt an iceberg. It certainly turned my legs to goo.

"One of our ... girls is still upstairs." And apparently electricity zapped my brain too since I had momentarily forgotten my daughter's name. "Whit."

His eyes crinkled at the corners. "I know."

"Do you want cheesecake?" I scrambled for something to say as the implications of being left alone with my husband elicited a wet spasm between my legs. "You haven't had dessert yet." He loved Nana's cheesecake.

He raised a brow, the corners of his mouth twitching. "I had a different kind of dessert in mind."

Footsteps plodded down the stairs, and Whit appeared. I glared at my husband to behave.

His twitching mouth became a full-on smirk.

"Did everyone leave?" Whitney asked.

"No. They're outside." Levi put a hand on our daughter's shoulder and accompanied her to the walkway where Gramps and Bristow were waiting.

"Have fun. Don't stay up so late with that iPad." I watched them for a beat before deciding I was the one who needed some cheesecake. Or maybe I was just delaying the inevitable.

In the kitchen, I busied myself and plated a slice.

A voice rumbled behind me. "So, where were we?"

I jumped and spun around. "Don't sneak up on me."

"Can't help it."

I put a hand over the hammering in my chest. I knew that. It was part of being a SEAL. Stealthiness was part of his training. Doing it while being the biggest man on the team was hard, so he'd worked harder on it than most, and it had become second nature to him.

I sat on the barstool and dug into my dessert.

"I'll have a bite of yours." He sat beside me.

"Who said I was sharing?" I mock-glared at him, spooned cheesecake into my mouth, and watched him watch me draw the spoon slowly from between my lips. I savored the whiskey-infused sweetness around my tongue before swallowing.

His eyes hooded. "Fuck, that's sexy."

I regarded my spoon and gave it another lick.

"Babe," he groaned.

Grinning wickedly, I lowered my eyes and spooned the dessert and held it up to him, catching his gaze.

"Thought you weren't sharing." Levi opened his mouth, and the spoon disappeared into its depths. He ate while holding my eyes. I slowly extracted the spoon. A crumb of cheesecake settled at the corner of his mouth.

"You missed a spot." I tipped my chin to where sticky creaminess decorated his lips.

He made no move to clean up.

I bit my lower lip before I edged closer. "Allow me."

I leaned in and licked at the crumb. His tongue shot out and tangled with mine before fully capturing my mouth. Groans filled the kitchen. I wasn't sure if they were from him or me, but when my hand landed on his chest, I felt its vibration all the way to my core.

He dragged me closer until I was straddling his lap. His fingers dug into my hair and I started squirming on his rapidly growing erection.

I jerked away. "Dammit, I'm not done with dessert. Why are you so hard already?"

He tugged on my hair exposing my throat and nibbled his way up my neck to my jaw. "Because I've done nothing but think of fucking you. I want my dessert, woman."

"Slow down," I gasped. My nipples felt scratchy against my bra.

"Stop riding my crotch," he growled.

Oh right. I was rubbing my pussy against his erection, but

I was so close, the pinnacle was right there. The friction and his big dick. Oh my God.

Before I knew it, he was lifting me up and sitting me on the island.

"We shouldn't let good cheesecake go to waste." His voice was strained.

"What are you proposing?"

He snatched the spoon, and cut through the dessert, and held it in front of my mouth. "Open."

I obeyed and opened my mouth, but, apparently, my legs did the same and my opportunistic husband immediately wedged his hips between my knees. He teased the edges of my mouth with the cool silverware before he smeared the cheesecake against my upper lip, dropping crumbs of crust into my low neckline. They settled between my cleavage.

"Oops," he murmured, lowering the spoon. "Guess I need to clean you up."

He leaned closer and licked my upper lip. I started panting, my breath hitching when he trailed kisses down my neck again, lingering on my collarbone before sweeping up to where my pulse was beating, giving it special attention. When he pulled away, I was on fire, my insides screaming for him to take me right then and there.

He dragged his knuckles against the dampness between my thighs. "Are you wet, sweetheart?"

"You know I am."

His eyes were dark pools of desire before I lost sight of his face. When he lifted my top over my head, a bra strap fell to the side. His eyes followed its movement before glancing down at his fingers. He was too busy getting me naked. He tugged on the ribbon holding up my light linen lounge pants.

"I guess we're doing it right here?"

"No. But I want to eat you before I pound the fuck outta you." He freed my pants from my legs and then leaned into me, our mouths a hair's breadth away. "But I want to make sure you're soaking and limber."

"How considerate."

"That sass," he growled before he shut me up with a deep devouring kiss that stole my breath. Our tongues dueled and explored each other. I tasted sweetness and Scotch. My fingers clutched his shirt, desperation evident in my movements. I was chasing my orgasm, rubbing against his hard length ... almost there.

He tore his mouth away and growled. "The first time, you come on my mouth. Got me?"

Then all I could see was the ceiling. Cool air caressed my nipples before his hot mouth took over. He sucked on a taut peak while his other hand kneaded the one that was free. He licked my cleavage, before he moved to my other breast.

"Levi," I moaned, my fingers digging into his hair. "... need more." Why was he torturing us with slow mode? That wasn't our speed.

He released the nipple he was teasing and said, "What's the matter, sweetheart, you hurting right here?"

His knuckles stroked through my panties.

"Yes."

"You want me to suck this needy pussy?"

I nodded, still staring at the ceiling. His head started going lower, and I let go of his hair.

"Let me see how wet you are, beautiful." His fingers nudged the fabric aside and slid through my folds. "Damn, babe, you're soaked real good." He inserted a thick finger, and I could tell just how slick I was.

"Fuck me," he groaned. His mouth was below my belly button, lips moving in a rhythm timed to the pumping of his fingers in and out of me.

I rotated my hips to hurry him along, but he pressed down on my pelvis to keep me steady. When his warm breath fanned the apex between my thighs, I was breathless with anticipation and my legs started to shake.

"Goddamned beautiful ... all this wet for me." The first hard lick had my back arching again. No tentativeness. Levi knew where all my trigger points were.

"Oh ...oh," I moaned. He hit them every single time. Lick, flick, and stab. Roughness circled around my clit. Pleasure, indescribable pleasure, built with his fingers doing magic inside me while his tongue masterfully danced around my sensitized flesh. The pressure increased. I was breathless with my need to come until he scraped my clit just as his finger rubbed that sweetest spot inside me.

My hips bucked against his mouth as starbursts exploded behind my lids. My climax rippled through me. Clenching my thighs against the head that gave me a second rush of pulsing sensations, I cried out. I sobbed for him to stop because I couldn't breathe. And yet I kept pushing against his mouth to give me more.

"Oh my God, ahhhh," I yelled again as another wave washed over me. I struggled to draw in oxygen. "Stop ... enough ... I can't take anymore."

Levi

DELICIOUS.

I couldn't stop eating my wife's pussy. Every drop that fell on my tongue left me craving for more. Her agonizing cries of pleasure only spurred me to lick harder. And my fingers loved getting sucked inside her.

"... enough!"

She'd been screaming that for a while, but I was an addict with an insatiable need. Her clit swelling against my mouth exhilarated every goddamned cell in my body. I could've come while tongue-fucking her. But I was a fan of delayed gratification, edging to the point of losing control.

I was dangerously close to that limit.

After giving her clit one final pinch between my lips, I surfaced from between her quaking legs to see her naked tits rising and falling from exhaustion. Damn, I loved this view.

"You're the devil," she mumbled. Her flushed face glistened with sweat, her arms cocked beside it in total surrender.

It was possible I grew even harder.

Christ.

"Up," I dragged her to a sitting position.

"Ah …" she moaned.

My heart plummeted. "What is it? Did I hurt you?"

She glared at me. "Not that. My ass feels numb and—"

I chuckled and tossed her over my shoulder.

"Levi!" she screeched.

"Heads up, babe. First time is going to be rough and hard." With her muttering unintelligible phrases, I might've heard the word 'caveman.' I took the stairs two at a time, passed the landing, and turned into her bedroom. We needed a bed. Having her sore before we even fucked was a travesty, because I had many plans that involved making up for lost time and blue balls.

Prowling toward the bed, I threw her onto the mattress, watching her bounce once before landing on her back, legs cocked at an angle.

Impatience tormented my every move as I turned away from the breathtaking sight of my wife and sat on the edge of the bed. Unlacing my boots, I kicked them off along with my socks. I stood, taking a deep breath, as I tore my shirt over my head and started undoing the button of my jeans, wincing as I lowered my zipper over my bulging erection.

I could feel her eyes on me, so I glanced over my shoulder.

Yep, she was up on her elbows, and she was eating me up

with her eyes. The need in them became my undoing. She was begging for a fuck all right.

I stared straight ahead again, clenching my jaw. "You keep looking at me that way and it'll be over before I even get started." This was it, I was claiming my wife again. And I was making sure she knew I was the only one capable of fucking her the way she deserved. Stomping out of my clothes, I turned around and couldn't help the corner of my mouth lifting when her lips parted and her eyes widened.

"Oh, my God," she whispered. "I forgot how big that thing was."

"Thing?" I raised a brow.

"It could be its own entity."

I choked on a laugh and put a knee on the bed. "You make it sound like an alien."

"Monster," she whispered. "Are we having monster sex?"

"Need to spread those thighs wider, babe." Her legs fell open, and I fell on top of her. My hands tangled in her hair, framing her face and tipping it up so I could see her eyes. "Should I be jealous of monsters now?"

"No. Not if you give me that hard pounding."

Damn … this woman. Could she be more perfect? I rocked into her, wetting the tip of my cock against her entrance. "Feel that, babe?"

"Yes." Her eyes glazed with need.

So responsive, so perfect, so fucking mine.

I shoved inside her. We both groaned—mine strangled and hers breathless.

"Jesus, you're tight." I gritted as wet heat clamped down on me.

"Haven't had sex in … in a while."

"I don't think I'll survive the first stroke."

"Don't move yet." Kelly hissed, her eyes scrunching shut. "I take back what I said about monster sex."

I buried my face in her hair and smothered pained laughter because my dick was aching to thrust. "Too late."

"Give me a few seconds."

The seconds felt like an eternity until she whispered, "Okay."

I lifted my head and searched her eyes for any sign of discomfort. There was none, only need, impatience, and excitement.

"Grab my shoulders and round my ass," I ordered. "You want to hang on for this." I shoved my hands under her ass to pin her in place for my thrust. "Tap my shoulder if it hurts."

"Hell, we're not stopping." Her eyes flashed.

Her heels dug into my ass, and I sank deeper. "You're so fucking beautiful, taking every inch of me." I rotated my hips and ground against that spot I knew was still sensitive.

Her breathless cry was all the answer I needed. Withdrawing my shaft was agony, her channel suctioning tight around me. With my next measured thrust, heaven jolted from the base of my neck and zapped the length of my spine.

I wasn't going to last if I concentrated on how her pussy gripped my length.

I concentrated on the expressions of her face, matching my rhythm to how her mouth opened, how she moaned my name, how she cursed me for being such a beast in bed while praising me for it.

My pounding accelerated, and in the back of my mind, the mattress was unsteady and damned creaky. But I was beyond caring. I drove into Kelly over and over, making sure to grind against the sweet trigger sitting behind the tip of her clit. Her head tilted back, mouth gaping in another sob, and she rippled around my cock.

Then the weirdest thing happened.

A cracking noise filled the room.

The mattress tilted to the side.

What the fuck? My pumping slowed.

"Don't stop. Don't stop," Kelly yelled.

"Not stopping, but holy fuck …" I increased my pace, but it was getting hard to bottom out since, apparently, we'd broken the damn bed and were sliding to the corner.

"I need more," Kelly wailed. "Harder."

"Jesus, fuck, your pussy's greedy." Staying buried inside her, with my left hand gripping her ass, I stretched my right arm overhead and gripped one of the headboard railings and hauled us against it. Her back was against the pillows, and she was partially sitting up.

I resumed pumping, desperation trickling sweat down my face as I clung to the headboard for leverage while I hammered into her over and over.

Her muscles clenched around me, and I felt her go over the edge with another cry. When her screams faded, all that was left was creaking, and the strokes and slapping of wet flesh.

"You good?" I grunted.

"Yes," she moaned. I wasn't even sure where her head was positioned, somewhere against my chest. The way I had her curled couldn't be comfortable. But at least she was responsive, and I hadn't suffocated her.

I gave in to my own beast and chased my climax. It didn't take long since I'd been riding the edge all night. I emptied inside her for what felt like forever. Months of frustration followed by hope poured into her.

I was slowing down my strokes, preparing to ease off my wife, when the headboard broke.

15

KELLY

"TOLD YOU IT WAS FLIMSY."

The morning after "the broken bed" incident, I still couldn't believe the bed shattered around us. One of the feet cracked under all the weight (and banging), and when the mattress sloped, Levi continued pounding into me by grabbing the headboard. Well, that gave way too.

Talk about crazy.

We stood side by side, coffee in hand, surveying the carnage. A flimsy silk robe cloaked my body. He was in his boxer briefs.

I arched a brow his way. "Someone wanted to pile drive me into the bed."

Levi barked a laugh. "As if you didn't encourage me?"

I smiled into my coffee. I was quite the wanton, wasn't I?

He wrapped an arm around me, pulled me close, and kissed the top of my head. "I think that's symbolic, don't you?"

"What? A broken bed?" I laughed.

"You replaced our marriage bed," he accused.

"It was too big," I said. "And there were too many reminders."

"I'm in there, babe. You can't get me out."

So cocky.

"Remember the last time you challenged me with that?"

He glowered. "Let's not bring that up again. It makes me overly possessive, and you need a break from fucking."

After the broken bed, we simply migrated to the living room couch.

"Got that right," I retorted. "Maybe we should stay over at Nana's for a few nights."

"That's not a bad idea. We could get a new bed. I have a solid one over at my house. But what do we really want to do, Kelly? Stay here?"

I sighed. "It's too early for this conversation. Let's check on the kids before they trick Gramps into giving them pop tarts."

"It's six," Levi said. "Think I have time for a run?"

"What? You still have energy after last night?"

He shot me a devilish grin. "Months of frustration, babe. I guess if we're staying at your grandparents for a few days, I need to work more of it off."

"Sex machine."

He drew me into his arms so quickly, I nearly dropped my coffee. It did spill a bit, and I glared up at him. But before I could bitch, he swallowed my protest with a deep searing kiss. I couldn't help but melt into him and was breathless when he let me go.

"Only for you." He winked at me and left me standing there trying to remember what I said before the kiss.

An hour and a half later, I was in Nana's kitchen supervising breakfast. I found out Gramps had fed them Oreo cookies with their milk last night, and I had to level up with scrambled eggs, ham, and sautéed peppers wrapped in a whole wheat tortilla. I also packed their lunch boxes with cut-up leftover steak that was trimmed of fat, peas, carrot sticks, and apples.

My grandparents were in the backyard with Bristow. He was trying to convince them to put in perimeter surveillance. Good luck with that. Levi had been trying to convince my grandparents of that for the past year. Hell, I only agreed recently.

"Can I stay home, Mama?" Ashley asked plaintively.

Whit speared her younger sister a look. "Why? So you can play all day?"

"No, because everyone will be here. It'll be fun." Ash unrolled the burrito I so painstakingly wrapped and started plucking at the filling.

"Ash, you need to eat the wrap so you'll have more energy during the day."

"Can I have cookies instead of the apple for my lunch box?" my youngest daughter scrunched her nose.

"That will make you tired," I said. "The carrots and apple are healthier because it's natural sugar." It wasn't the first time I had explained this concept to my youngest. Sometimes it needed to be repeated.

Levi appeared in the kitchen, freshly showered after his run. "Listen to your mom, girls." He walked by me and brushed my lips with his before heading to the girls to plant a kiss on top of their heads. "You've got thirty minutes before we take you to school."

"I want to stay home," Ash continued to whine.

Levi sat beside our youngest and ruffled her hair. "You've got to go to school, baby girl. How about you get a cookie after dinner tonight, hmm?"

He glanced at me. I mouthed the word "sucker." He and I needed to have a serious conversation about his compromising skills.

His eyes crinkled at the corners, but he changed the subject. "I see Bristow is trying to convince Cillian and Branna of additional security."

"Is it working?"

"Looks promising. Cillian appears interested."

I laid a plate with a giant egg white burrito in front of him. "Made to order." I winked.

"Thank you, beautiful."

Our eyes locked, and the heat in his eyes momentarily blocked out Ash's laments until …

"Stop your freaking whining," Whit yelled. "Maybe if you'd go to school, you wouldn't act this dumb."

Levi froze, and I gaped at my oldest.

Ash's lips trembled, and she blinked back tears as if shocked her sister yelled at her before lowering her head to stare at her plate.

"Whitney James," I said sternly. "That's no way to talk to your sister."

"Why? I'm telling the truth," she continued to rant. "You all baby her. Everything is baby girl this and baby girl that. Dad reads her bedtime stories at night and what do I get? I get asked if I did my homework. She's dumb. Maybe if—"

Ashley started bawling and I automatically moved to her and hugged her, still glaring at Whit.

"That's enough," Levi said sternly. "You don't talk to your mother that way either."

"Then how, Dad?" Angry tears rolled down Whit's cheeks. "I've tried so hard to be good. I make good grades. I try to be the best older sister. I got in trouble for pushing a boy in my class when he made fun of Ash. I got sent to the principal's office. All he talked about was following the rules and poor Ashley's hurt feelings."

Levi and I were speechless. A vise of I'm-the-worst-mom-ever squeezed my chest.

"I'm done with this family," Whit declared. "Done with this." She jumped off the bar stool, knocking it over, and ran upstairs.

The slam of the door on the second level reverberated around the house. Ash's crying had slowed to hiccups.

I didn't know what to say. How could I have been so oblivious to my older child's feelings?

"I think …" Levi whispered. "I'm at fault here."

"It's both our faults," I said. "But maybe you can explain better to Whit that we don't love or care for her any less?"

He compressed his lips, gave a brief nod, and abandoned his breakfast to follow our daughter.

"Whit hates me," Ashley said through her tear-streaked eyes.

"She doesn't." I kissed the top of her head. "Your dad and I misjudged what you both needed from us. This separation was difficult, and it caused a lot of confusion." I turned her toward me and cupped her cheeks. "But we're going to fix this, okay?"

"Okay, Mama."

Nana, Gramps, and Bristow walked in and noted the vacant seats, abandoned breakfasts, and teary-eyed Ashley.

"What happened?"

Levi

I TRUDGED up the steps to the second floor, trying to come up with what to say to my oldest child as a niggle of fear tugged at my heart. Had I fixed my relationship with Ash, only to ruin the one I had with Whit? Playing favorites was not my intent. I had missed so much of Ashley's growing-up years, and I might've overcompensated giving her my attention to the detriment of Whit.

Being a parent was hard, and I admired Kelly for holding down the fort while I was gone on missions. I was surprised she put up with my shit as an absentee parent for two years.

One step forward, two steps back.

That shit stopped now.

I rapped lightly on Whit's door. "Princess, can I talk to you?"

No answer.

I opened the door anyway. Whit was lying on the bed facing the wall. Her thin shoulders shook. Whit was tough. She wasn't a loud crier. All I heard were sniffles and the occasional hitch in her breathing.

I sat on the edge of the bed. "Can you turn to face me, sweet pea? I want to see your pretty eyes."

"They're not pretty. They're swollen," she sniffed.

She still didn't turn over, so I continued, "I'm sorry if I made you feel like Ashley was the favorite. I don't love her more than you. I love you both equally." I sighed. "I just made mistakes in the way I showed it. I wanted my family back. I just had to work harder with Ashley, because she wasn't close to me like you were ... because I wasn't around much when she was born."

Whit finally turned to face me. "Uncle Callum died, and you became sad." She blinked and a tear fell to the pillow. "I don't remember him, but I think I was sad too. So were Nana and Gramps. Everyone was sad. But Ashley was too small to be sad." She looked at me earnestly. "She did not understand your sadness. You didn't want to talk or go out, and that was okay. Ashley likes to chatter about fairytale princesses and going out for ice cream. All I wanted was for you to be home, Dad."

Was it possible to have my heart excavated out of my

ribcage? Emotion burned the back of my eyes. "Thanks, Whit."

I tucked a dark curl behind her ear. "But you have to know … I love you as much as Ashley. As much as your Mom. The three of you are my world. It's just that I was overcompensating … you know what that word means?"

She nodded. "Doing too much?"

"Yes, but in the wrong way … I see that now because I neglected you. I tried reading to both of you, but you and Ashley liked different things and you get bored with what she likes."

"I don't need you to read to me, Dad, but I understand now." Her mouth twisted. "Ashley has just been so whiny lately."

My brows shot to my hairline. "I think you were that way at her age. You just have to be patient with her, all right?" I poked at her chest. "That's your responsibility as her older sister. Don't call her names, but tell her when she's doing things wrong or she's being a pain in the butt. You have to know, sweet pea, hurtful things you say are like nails hammered into a fence. Do you know why?"

She shook her head.

"When you remove the nails from the fence, what do you see?"

"Holes."

"The holes are the damage from those nails—your words. They'll remain there forever. They'll leave scarring. So, what am I trying to tell you?"

She sighed heavily. "Words I say can hurt really bad and it will stay with a person forever."

"That's right. That's one of the reasons your mom and I separated. I had anger issues because of Uncle Callum's death. If we didn't separate, if I didn't fix myself, I might've said hurtful words to your mom and to you girls that I could never take back. Come here."

I patted the space beside me, but Whit crawled onto my lap instead, and my arms convulsed around her. It reminded me that I hadn't hugged her this way in a long time. It was always her younger sister who got first dibs. I hadn't tried to be an equal-opportunity dad. I shouldn't let my guilt dictate how I treated my girls any longer. Christ, parenting shit wasn't a one-and-done. As the girls grew older, different challenges would sprout out of nowhere. I was given a second chance both with Kelly and the kids.

I wasn't wasting that chance.

Five minutes later, we returned to the breakfast room.

Ashley had finished her breakfast, and Kelly was drinking coffee.

Whitney approached her younger sister. "I'm sorry I said mean things to you. You're not dumb, Ash."

"I forgive you," Ashley said in a serious tone. "But you better hurry up and finish your breakfast, or we'll be late for school. Mama said if we're good and help Gramps with Ruger this week we could look at puppies this weekend."

Surprised, I crossed my arms and arched a brow at Kelly. "Really?"

"You said I had the final say." She chewed her bottom lip. "That is … if your friend has a dog ready to go."

A grin split my face. "I'll check with Mike."

16

LEVI

EARLY THAT SATURDAY MORNING, I packed my family into the Escalade on our way to Barstow, California where my SEAL buddy Mike had his kennel. The drive was through the desert on route 15.

"We're coming up on Victorville," I said. "Anyone need to pee?"

"I'm fine, Dad," Whitney said, busy on her tablet.

"Ashley?"

"No, Daddy," she murmured sleepily.

Kelly was on the phone with Alana, her cousin back east who'd been kicking ass as a private investigator for their dad's agency. The phone call gave us a respite from Ashley and Whitney singing a popular song from a Korean pop group. I loved my kids, but I'd heard that damned song more times than I cared to. The chorus had been hammered into my brain like a mantra—and not in a good way. I glanced over at my wife and she shot me a quick smile before giving her attention back to the phone.

We attended our first couple's counseling session the day before. I still thought it was a waste of time. If we'd put our minds to it, we could've come up with a solution ourselves. I wasn't down with putting the pause on sex as the counselor suggested while we worked through our issues. That was a problem before when we just used sex to scratch an itch. In my damned opinion, it was the not talking and just having sex without sharing a bed afterwards that caused the problems. Admittedly, staying with her grandparents put an automatic moratorium on our sexual activities, but thank fuck we managed to get it out of our systems a couple of days ago.

I passed the exit for Victorville and checked the clock on the dash. We were making good time and should be there in thirty minutes.

"I'll see you and Charles tomorrow," Kelly said. "I'm really fine. You all don't need to be here. LAPD is on the case. Seriously, when you do get here, please don't interfere and question the detectives … ohmigod, I'm not giving you their names. Just chill, okay?" Kelly paused for a while, just shaking her head. "All right, all right. See you tomorrow."

After ending the call, she turned to the kids. "Your aunt Alana says hi."

"I can't wait to see her," Whitney said. "I miss her."

"She's got business in Vegas, but maybe you all can hang out after," Kelly said.

"Is she putting away the bad guys, Mama?" Ashley asked. "Maybe she can help Uncle Kelso."

I chuckled. "Didn't she get in trouble with one of the Harlem detectives?"

"That was because she showed them how sloppy they were and helped them solve the case. She didn't get the credit, but she got paid. Alana doesn't give a hoot about prestige. She just wants to get the job done." Kelly paused. "Like you and your team."

My hand reached over to take hers, and I gave the back of

her fingers a quick kiss and shot her a quick glance. "Thanks, beautiful."

She inhaled sharply, and her eyes glimmered with what suspiciously looked like tears. I returned my gaze to the road but observed from my peripheral vision that she had turned her head to look out the window while surreptitiously swiping her eyes at the same time giving my hand a squeeze. In the past two days, despite what happened between Whitney and Ash, my heart swelled with hope at how quickly we fell back into being a family. I loved it. There was still a lingering regret of missing Ashley's first steps and every single *first* I would never experience again. I unloaded that in our counseling session. I didn't resent Kelly for insisting on a separation, but I copped to frustration and anger when she put up that wall between us last Christmas. It blindsided the fuck out of me. I'd never been more miserable in my life.

"Are we there yet, Dad?" Whitney asked.

Ah, the perpetual question.

"About half hour," I said.

"Mom, do you have beef jerky?"

Kelly looked into her tote bag of snacks and handed Whit the jerky. "Don't eat too much. We'll be having lunch before we meet your dad's friend."

"I'm excited," Whitney said as she tore open the jerky. "Dogs can eat jerky, right?"

"Yes, but I'm not sure we should give him the human kind. Too much salt," Kelly said. "Which reminds me, drink water after you eat that. How about you, Ash, are you hungry? Want some snacks from here … what's wrong, sweetie?"

"Daddy is going to be mad at me," Ashley whimpered.

I glanced at the rearview mirror upon hearing the misery in her voice. "What's wrong, baby girl?"

"I need to pee."

KELLY

"CAN you hold it for a while longer?" Levi asked.

"I really, really need to go, Daddy."

I felt for both Levi and Ashley. There wasn't anything for miles and miles. Just the road and desert on both sides. The shoulder wasn't an option either.

"Dad asked you earlier if you needed to pee," Whitney told her sister.

"I really didn't need to."

"Maybe you should have worn a diaper."

"Whit," I admonished my older daughter. "Not helping."

"She's gonna pee in the car, Mom," Whitney grumbled. "Then she'll ruin this entire trip."

Ashley started to cry.

"It's just a car," Levi cut in. "Whit, remember what we talked about? Ashley, baby, hold it for a minute longer, all right? I see an exit coming up."

Levi told me about his conversation with Whit so I'd be aware of what was simmering between our girls. Even with that setback, I felt like we were becoming a team again. Neither of us expected an overnight miracle. Anxiety didn't help either. My oldest was eager to see the puppy and her sister was the obstacle.

"The desert?" I saw where there was a crossroad ahead.

"No choice," Levi said. "You're going to have to tough it out, baby girl." He glanced at the rearview mirror. "So, I'll need you to stop crying."

After trying several attempts to stop crying, Ashley gave one last ragged hiccup. "Okay."

The exit Levi was talking about was a crossroads that led to nowhere. There was nothing on either side of it but sparse low-lying shrubbery. He went off the highway into an intersecting paved street before off-roading it into the desert, coming to a stop beside brush and rock.

"I'm not getting out," Whitney declared.

"That's fine." Levi shot me a look, and I guess I knew what to do.

He got out of the SUV and opened the door to Ashley's side, unbuckling her from the child seat and jogged off with her to the nearest shrub.

"Aren't there rattlesnakes?" Whitney asked, watching her dad and sister move away from the safety of the vehicle.

"They're around, but your sister is fine. That's why your dad didn't want us along, so he can keep an eye on her." I peeked over at Whitney. "What you said to Ashley hurt her feelings."

My daughter pursed her lips and lowered her eyes to the iPad. "I know. Dad explained to me how words could hurt and stick. I'll apologize."

"Good. This is an exciting day for both of you. You need to be patient with her. You're the big sister, Whit. You know what that means, don't you?"

"I look after Ashley when you and Dad can't."

"Yes. I know Ashley is at that age where she can irritate you."

Whitney grumbled, "She can be annoying and stuff. But I love her and I want to be a good sister."

I reached out and patted her hand. "Thank you."

She looked past my shoulder. "Looks like she's done."

Levi had Ashley piggybacked over his brawny shoulders. She had her arms up in the air and was giggling. An indescribable emotion shot through me. It grew too big to contain in my chest. Was this it? Was this us being a family again? I wanted that desperately.

"Are you getting back with Dad?" Whitney asked.

It used to be, I'd shrug and give a non-committal answer.

This time I turned in my seat and looked her in the eye. "We're working on it."

And I felt those words to the bottom of my heart.

Things went more smoothly from there. When we reached Barstow, we had lunch at a local family restaurant that served farm-to-table all-American food. They made everything in-house from their bread to the mayonnaise they put on their sandwiches. My daughters especially loved their house-made potato chips. Sated from lunch, we drove another ten minutes to his friend's kennels.

A mile of unpaved road with pastureland on either side stretched before us. Levi said his friend bought the place to breed horses, but ended up going after his other passion of training protection dogs. The ranch house was massive. The barn had been transformed into kennels.

Our girls had their faces plastered to the windows.

"Look to your right," Levi pointed to a man wearing a padded suit that made him look like a sumo wrestler. In front of him was a German Shepherd being restrained by his handler. "They're doing bite exercises."

"I see that on TV," Whit exclaimed. "That's so they can chase the bad guys when the cops can't, right?"

"Yup."

We had originally planned on an already-trained protection dog, but Levi and I thought it over and agreed that we couldn't deny our kids the experience of raising a puppy.

The Escalade pulled up to a parking space in front of a ranch house.

A man in a ball cap stepped out. He was about five-ten and had a lean muscular frame, wearing a tee with the company logo imprinted on the front.

Levi exited the vehicle and extended his arm. Handshakes were exchanged and then slaps on the back. I slipped down from the vehicle and opened Whitney's door while Levi went back to help Ashley out of the child seat.

The children pulsed with excitement.

Holding Whitney's hand, we met Mike in front of the SUV.

"Beautiful kids." Mike sank to his haunches and bopped Ashley lightly on the nose. "Ready to meet the new member of your family?" He glanced over at Whit and ruffled her hair.

There were bobbleheads and grins all around. Ashley's gapped-tooth smile was adorable. Even Levi's tough-looking friend was charmed. "Come on then."

The men walked ahead while the girls and I followed more slowly. There was controlled chaos, barking, and shouting around us that made our daughters a bit tentative. We passed by the space Levi pointed out and saw a dog take down the guy in the puffy suit.

Ash and Whit's hands tightened in mine. A sense of foreboding dropped in my stomach wondering if they should be witnessing that. Watching it on TV was different. It also reinforced our decision to start with a puppy rather than a fully trained protection dog.

"Is that what our dog will do to a bad guy, Mama?" Ashley asked, her face serious.

"Yes, honey." I put my arm around her.

"That's so cool," Whitney said.

"That boy over there is going to a federal task force." Mike glanced back at us and pointed to the dog in question. His eyes softened when he saw the girls plastered to me. "You're getting a teddy bear compared to that one."

"But he's so cool!" Whitney enthused.

"Too much energy for all of us." Levi winked at his daughter.

Ashley exhaled a big breath. "I don't think I can keep up with that one. He's fast."

Mike led us into a corralled area where a gaggle of rambunctious puppies tripped over each other to greet us.

"Oh my gosh, Oh my gosh." Whitney let go of my hand

and crossed in front of me, not sure where to look, while Ashley was more reserved. My youngest continued to cling to me, but the big smile on her face reassured me she was happy and excited.

Levi came to my side and grasped my hand, giving it a squeeze. Our gazes met and communicated the same thing. Seeing the sheer joy and wonder on our children's faces were moments to treasure.

Our attention shifted to the kids and the puppies. Ashley finally let go of my hand and joined her sister.

Levi wrapped his arms around me, and I leaned into him. Whatever doubt I had about getting a puppy dissipated. Two hours later we were on our way back to Los Angeles.

Levi was on the phone with Bristow who'd been tracking our vehicle and following us at a distance. He waited for us in a Barstow coffee shop while we selected the addition to our family.

My husband wasn't taking our security for granted, but at the same time he wanted us to do this important occasion on our own as a family.

I looked over to where my girls were taking turns petting the male puppy they called Scout. The nine-week-old shepherd was sleeping quietly now after the poor thing threw up twenty minutes into our drive home.

As we got closer to Los Angeles, I was thankful for our broken bed that sent us to stay with Nana and Gramps for a few days. They said it took a village to raise a child. Somehow, I had a feeling it applied to puppies too.

17

KELLY

"So, let me get this straight, you're staying here because you and Levi broke your bed?"

Alana McGrath was my youngest sibling. She was twenty-seven years old, and a licensed private investigator working for our dad's family business. Arriving that morning with Charles, they were just in time for Gramps' Sunday dinner. No matter how many times I told them I was fine, they were still concerned about a possible link between Stepanov and one of Dad's most controversial cases.

"Well ..." I angled my eyes slyly at my sister, before smiling into the salad I was tossing. "We did."

"Holy fuck. What did he do? Ram you against the head-board?" Alana's eyes were saucers, and I couldn't help laughing. She leaned over and scrutinized the guys outside who were kicking back some beer while Gramps smoked the meat. He'd been experimenting with barbecue and made damned succulent brisket and falling-off-the-bone rib. He gave *finger-*

licking-good an exalted meaning. My Aunt Ava, who was a restaurant maven, wanted to open a barbecue restaurant.

That idea was still up in the air. Nana worried that attention may veer away from the Eamonn brand which was our chain of Irish pubs, but I could see where Gramps wanted a stamp of his own legacy.

We were helping Nana with the sides. All the McGraths were put into training at the pub at a young age. I started bussing tables when I was twelve, and occasionally worked the cash register. Though not all of us were savvy cooks, we were at least passable at knife skills and cold station preps.

Nana made the collard greens and the girls' favorite, macaroni and cheese. The cheese sauce was made from béchamel and four cheeses, including white cheddar, which gave it that sharply robust taste I loved. Maybe Gramps was onto something after all.

"Well, I could believe that," Alana continued our 'broken bed' conversation. "I always thought Levi was a monster."

"Hey—" My cheeks reddened as I recalled my monster sex comment.

"Although …" It was her turn to look at me slyly. "Remember that time we were drunk, and you raved about his goods?"

I bit my lower lip at the memory, trying to suppress my horrified sheepish smile. It was during one of our distant cousin's bridal showers. A male stripper was flaunting his silk covered package in front of me and I waved him off. "Don't remind me."

Alana laughed harder. "You told the poor guy your husband's was twice as big as his—relaxed."

Thankfully, Nana walked into the kitchen, and my sister couldn't keep teasing me about my drunken blunder.

My grandmother checked the sides in the oven. "We should start serving soon." She looked at us distractedly. "What's this about Levi?"

"Nothing." I changed the subject. "I say we give this barbecue restaurant a try."

Alana's mouth was twerking in an effort to contain her mirth.

"But who's going to run it?" I continued, trying to keep my face serious when Alana was getting crosseyed trying to keep a lid on her laughter. "Ava's more of a figurehead now and is stepping back. She loves traveling with Cesar." Off the record, although common knowledge because no one admitted directly to being a mafia associate, Cesar was a scion of the De Lucci Crime Family which was currently being run by his nephew.

Our mob relations ran deep, though I didn't mind the De Luccis because they were one of the organizations that still didn't deal with drugs and human trafficking. Their real estate business was immense, and everyone was mum on what was legitimate and what wasn't.

Such was the morally ambiguous nature of the clan I grew up in.

I thought about my cousins—Uncle Sean's kids—who were more business-oriented and financial whizzes like their dad. "Sara loves Gramps' barbecue so I think she'd be all over it. Besides, she loves to cook and has a good head for business like Aunt Ava."

"I can't even think about opening a new restaurant and starting from scratch." Nana sighed. "Kelly, can you check with the guys if they're ready to eat?"

A cooler of beer sat beside the men. Bristow was talking to Gramps, and, from their gestures, they were probably discussing the finer points of the smoker in front of them. Levi and Charles were off to one side. My husband's attention kept drifting to where the girls were sitting on the grass beside Scout who was currently pouncing on a dozing Ruger. After we returned from our puppy field trip, Levi and I laid out the ground rules. The girls were to wake up early to feed the puppy which meant they adhered to bedtime without fuss. Levi would do the first and last walk of the day. Since it was a nine-week-old pup in need of housebreaking, there would be plenty of chances taking turns for walks. According to the book I was reading, every two hours seemed the norm.

"Nana asked if you guys are hungry," I called out. "The sides are ready."

"Bring it," Bristow said.

"Where's Kelso?" I asked.

"He's on his way," Levi said. "He should be pulling in any time now."

"We can eat out here," I said. Bending over the cooler, I checked its contents. "You guys have been busy. Need me to bring more ale?"

"The Belgian one," Levi said.

All the men concurred with the suggestion.

"You got it." I craned my neck to Ashley and Whitney. "You girls good?"

They gave me two thumbs up, too tired to vocalize their answer.

"That pup runs them ragged," Gramps said. "See? Told you a dog is good for them. They don't spend that much time watching TV any more."

I laughed. "Sounds like it. I'll head in and tell Nana and Alana to set up out here."

"I'll come help." Charles fell into step beside me.

"You don't have to," I said. "We can manage."

"But I haven't gotten a chance to talk to my favorite girl."

I jerked my head. "Come on then." Even if Charles was my biological father, our relationship had always been indulgent uncle and niece. Even then, I knew he would've done right by Sofia if she hadn't ditched me to marry into the Chicago crime family. I didn't get the idea that he'd been in love with her. When Charles was released from prison, he did his best to be present in my life, functioning the best as the cool uncle who did all the fun things with his niece before returning me to my parents to handle the more serious disciplinary stuff. Which was why I could never repay Mads and Robert enough. They never made me feel like I was the reject of the brood. My issues had gone on long enough. I didn't want it having a negative impact on my girls. "Any second-best girl right now?"

He grinned widened. "I'm happily unattached."

"Probably best for your commitment-phobic ass."

"Hey, we McGraths have the wild side. Ask your Aunt Ava. She has that streak too. I think Bianca is the same. Cesar is going to have a headache with that one."

We laughed. "That should be interesting. She's what? Turning twenty?"

"I think so," he replied. We entered the kitchen.

"What are you two laughing about?" Alana demanded.

"Bianca," Charles said.

"That one has a lot of Ava in her," Nana confirmed.

"And she wants to join the family business," my sister informed me.

"The restaurant?" I thought that was a given.

"No. McGrath Investigations."

"What? This should be interesting. Tell Uncle Cesar to be ready with bail money."

Everyone found that funny.

"We do have interesting clients," Alana said. "A mafia wife wants me to track her husband who's currently in Vegas with his mistress."

"I thought mistresses were an accepted custom."

"Apparently this particular wife expects more fidelity. The Omertà is so open to interpretation nowadays anyway," my sister said.

"Just be careful," Charles said. "Omertà or not, these

Made Men value the brotherhood first. At least those who adhere to the old ways."

Nana huffed. "The old ways? They choose which fecking rules to follow to suit their purpose. Don't get me started when they start spouting this Men of Honor bullshite …"

"Okay, Mom." Charles hurriedly rounded the counter to give Nana a hug because when she started cursing with a hint of Ireland and it wasn't nipped in the bud, you were in for a fifteen-minute rant, maybe longer.

"We better set up the table," I said. "Charles, can you grab the ale you guys wanted?" I walked over to the cabinets beside the sink to get the plates. When I looked out the window, my brows furrowed. The men's attention was drawn in one direction toward the street. The sharp and short burst of a police siren alarmed me even more. I abandoned the plates when Bristow started charging for the street.

As I exited the back door and sprinted parallel with the guys moving from backyard to front, I heard Levi instruct Gramps to watch the kids.

"What's going on?" Alana was at my heels. Charles was already a step ahead of us.

Levi looked over his shoulder. "Stay back."

Bristow and Alana got into it.

"Get out of my way, ginger," Alana snapped.

"We don't have time for stupid shit," Bristow growled. "Stand back while we handle it."

"Oh, boy," Charles chuckled. Keeping Alana out of perilous situations was like waving a red flag at a bull.

A standoff was taking place. Three black SUVs were in front of the house. Two cops from a patrol car had their guns drawn and pointed at our surprise visitors. Levi threw out an arm to prevent me from moving forward.

Kelso had arrived and was approaching the driver's side of the first Suburban, his hand on the gun at his waist.

Bristow and Alana quit bickering. Tension throbbed in the air surrounding us, making it difficult to drag in oxygen.

The first SUV's middle passenger window rolled down to reveal the handsome face of a man I wasn't expecting to see.

"This is quite the welcome party, sis."

18

LEVI

FUCKING LUCA MORETTI.

Beside him was Sofia.

"Son of a bitch," Charles muttered.

I didn't know anything about Charles' feelings for his ex. What I did know was I didn't trust Kelly's stepbrother, but he also wouldn't put Sofia at risk.

"What the hell, Luca?" Kelly yelled, but my arm prevented her from leaving the front yard.

"Fucking great," Alana said. "What are they doing here?"

"We need to talk," Moretti told Kelly. "We dropped by your house but no one was home."

"A phone call would've sufficed," my wife told him. "You didn't have to come all the way from Chicago."

"I like face-to-face meetings," he returned smoothly.

Kelso walked grimly around the SUV and came to stand in front of me. "Family?"

"Unfortunately, yes," I told him. "Kelly's Chicago folks."

The detective nodded and waved off the patrol officers to lower their weapons.

Luca stepped out of the vehicle. He was in a suit. I'd never seen him not wearing one. After the death of his father, Emilio Moretti, almost two years before, he'd become the head of the Chicago Crime Family. He smoothed his threads before turning around to assist Sofia out of the SUV.

"I'm going to have one of my men with me," Moretti said.

"What's the matter, Luca?" I scoffed. "Afraid to be outgunned?"

Kelso shot me a look before turning to the mobster. "Two vehicles need to leave. I'm not down with having them here. I'm certain if I search them, I'll find weapons and that's not going to help shit right now."

Luca grinned at the detective. "I like this guy."

"Don't get complacent," Kelso bit out. "I'm not on your side. I'm avoiding unnecessary conflict or possible bloodshed. Not to mention, I hate paperwork. If you give us useful information, we could work something out. My men have called this in. If you do have weapons in the remaining vehicle, tell your men to move them elsewhere. Or all the vehicles could leave and come back when you're done."

"I wasn't expecting a police patrol," Luca muttered, walking back to the SUV to have a chat with his soldiers.

Afterward, he turned back to us. "Shall we take this inside?"

Our group moved away from the street. One of Moretti's men stepped out of the lead Suburban and taunted the patrol officers with a mock salute. Kelso frisked him to make sure he didn't have a piece on him. The guy had one tucked away in an ankle holster.

The detective glared at Moretti's soldier. "Really?" He handed the weapon to Bristow.

"Are you expecting trouble?" I asked Kelly's stepbrother.

"Nothing more than usual," he told me. "There's always

someone who wants to whack a boss." He smirked at me. "The question is if it will be worth the hellfire my outfit will rain down on them if they fail."

Kelso walked past us. "Not something you want to talk about in the presence of a cop."

I always thought Kelly's stepbrother was an arrogant son of a bitch. I wasn't surprised because with my intel on him through my Fed and CIA connections, he was well protected by political families in Chicago and probably had half of the Chicago PD on his payroll.

Kelso appeared to have done his own research and understood that the value of Luca Moretti was not in putting the man behind bars but in his cooperation. And my mafia princess, even one with a tarnished crown, certainly gave me a view of the symbiotic relationship between organized crime and law enforcement.

Someone else wasn't pleased with the arrival of the Morettis. Kelly's grandmother was prowling out of the house with a shotgun.

"Jesus Christ," Kelso growled. "Mrs. McGrath, I strongly advise you to put that weapon down."

"It's my property, and they're not welcome here," she shouted.

"Nana," Kelly snapped, and then split a look between her grandfather and Charles. It seemed her uncle welcomed any excuse to get away from Sofia and walked ahead of the group to take the shotgun from his mother.

"This is why I hate organized crime shit," Kelso muttered to me. "So much family drama."

"I hope you're not expecting me to feed them." Branna reluctantly surrendered the firearm to her son.

I was pissed Moretti put my wife in a difficult situation. Despite reminding Kelly she didn't owe jack shit to the Chicago side of the family, she kept up with them out of obligation. However, I'd bet my left nut that, save for Branna, every single person present was dying of curiosity about their reason for leaving their lair to deliver a message to Kelly.

"No, we don't want to disrupt your plans," Sofia said coldly.

"If that were the case—" That was Alana putting in her two cents. "Maybe you shouldn't have shown up without warning which nearly caused a shootout."

"All right, everyone calm down," Cillian boomed. "There's plenty for everyone—"

"That's not the point, Cil." Branna glared at her husband. "They have no business showing up here unannounced. They're not family."

"I consider Kelly my sister," Luca said. "And no need to feed us, Mrs. McGrath, but whatever is cooking in that smoker sure smells good."

"Well, don't expect me to serve you." Branna turned away to head into the house. "You all take care of them."

"Awkward." Bristow walked up beside me and flicked his thumb over his shoulder at the unexpected visitors. "What do we do with them?"

"Keep an eye out for short tempers," I said. "We've got Irish and Italian hotheads. Not a good combination."

"Should be interesting."

KELLY

"THIS WAS EXTREMELY INCONSIDERATE, Sofia. What if I showed up at your doorstep unannounced?" I put the iced tea pitcher in front of her and poured her a glass. I went through the trouble of preparing a fresh one because I didn't trust Nana not to dump a container of chlorine into it. Thank goodness the patio had two outdoor dining tables. It was an unspoken understanding that I should keep Sofia away from my grandmother's table.

Levi handled the drinks for Luca and his bodyguard.

"You're family. Of course, it's okay," she said.

I stared at her dubiously. "Really."

"I'm not expecting you to feel an attachment to me," she said. Sofia Moretti was a beautiful woman. She was dressed in a black Chanel suit like a tragic Jackie O., complete with large-framed sunglasses. "But I hoped you'd be closer to Mia."

"Where is she?" I asked.

"Luca didn't want her coming along, she's back at the compound."

"Figures." My half-sister was the typical treasured mafia princess.

"She wanted to come," Sofia added. She glanced wistfully over to where Whitney and Ashley were hanging around the other table with Nana. "They don't like me. I bet that hag poisoned your children—"

"There are many things I will take from you," I said. "But never insult Nana or Gramps, or any of the McGraths for being protective of me and mine."

Sofia's mouth tightened. She plucked the sunglasses from her face and contemplated the hinges on the stems. "You never understood, did you? Life in the family is different. I explained it to you."

"That I was an embarrassment? Grandpa Rossi acknowledged me."

"Emilio is old-school. If I wasn't his third wife, he wouldn't have married me because I wasn't a virgin. You're a reminder of that."

"Plus, I'm half-Irish," I added.

She ignored my sarcasm and continued, "The only way I could ensure no harm would come to you was if there was no communication between us."

I'd asked Sofia a long time ago if her husband was

abusive, and she'd said not physically, only mentally and verbally.

"And Luca? Is he good to you?"

She nodded, finally meeting my eyes. "I breathed a sigh of relief when he took over. He's overprotective of Mia. I always have to referee between them. But Luca is the boss now, and he's not making me marry someone else and trusts that Mia will keep me loyal to the Morettis."

"Conversation seems to be so serious here." The man in question eased himself into the chair opposite me. "Cillian was telling me about his plan to open a restaurant. He gave me a taste of the ribs and brisket. Good stuff."

Oh, God, please no. Though I was excited about the barbecue restaurant idea, I did not want my Chicago family involved. "That's wishful thinking. No one wants to manage a new concept."

"Besides New York and LA, Chicago is restaurant central, and I know some people who'd be interested."

"Let's not discuss this," I said. "How about telling us the purpose of this visit?"

Alana brought the side dishes to the table. "Yes, Luca. How about getting straight to the point?"

"The point doesn't concern you."

My sister glared at Luca. "Kelly is a McGrath. Therefore, it involves me."

My stepbrother eyed the dishes set in front of him. "Should I be worried your grandmother is going to poison us?"

Alana smiled sweetly. "That wouldn't be such a terrible idea, but since my dear sister is eating at the same table, you're quite safe." She winked at me. "For now." She sashayed away.

"That's Robert's youngest, right?" Luca asked.

I smiled into my iced tea. "Yup."

"She and Mia would get along," he muttered.

"Well she and I get along," I said, feeling possessive of my McGrath family and wondered what part of me was Sofia.

My mother looked amazing at fifty-two. She must've been a stunner in her twenties. As a makeup and later SFX artist, I had to keep up to date with the latest skincare trends. It also made good conversation with actors and actresses.

"You still look fantastic, Sofia," I said in all sincerity.

A genuine smile curved her mouth, and it reached her soulful brown eyes. Was that how she attracted Charles? "I'm happy you're taking good care of your skin. You take so much after Charles' family including that stubborn chin, but that flawless complexion came from me."

"That sounds like a backhanded compliment. I'll take it."

Her eyes flashed with irritation.

A clearing of the throat came from my left. Levi approached with the platter of brisket and ribs. With him were Bristow and Kelso. They must've had a quick meeting while I was entertaining Sofia, and Luca had been chatting with Cillian. I wondered if Gramps ever worked for Chicago.

"Cillian should open a restaurant in Chicago," Luca repeated what he told me just as Levi reached my side. "It's probably safest for you to move there, too."

"What the hell?" I frowned. "Where is this coming from?"

Levi looked like he wanted to murder my stepbrother, maybe death by rib platter to the head.

"Wishful thinking, Moretti." Levi's voice was icy. "'My wife stays with me."

"He didn't mean to be so blunt," Sofia said.

I glared at my mother before awarding Luca the same censure. "Again. What the hell?"

Levi dropped the serving dish on the table before taking his seat beside me. Bristow and Kelso flanked my stepbrother in a move meant to intimidate.

Luca shrugged. "So, I can keep an eye on family, dear

sister." His gaze shifted lazily toward my husband. "Besides, I thought you were separated."

Before I could answer, Levi said, "We're back together. So, start talking before you find my boot up your ass."

A muscle ticked under my stepbrother's right eye as he sought confirmation from me. "You're back together?"

"Yes." Under the table, Levi's hand slipped into mine and squeezed.

"Then you're lucky," he told my husband. "Because I don't allow anyone to speak to me that way and live."

"And you're lucky that Ash and Whit are close by, or I wouldn't hesitate to plug a bullet between your fucking eyes."

Sofia gasped and made a distressed whimper. I held fast to Levi's hand, hoping I could communicate for him to keep his temper in check. Luca should've known better than to taunt my husband about taking me away from him. The two men locked eyes, skyrocketing the testosterone around the table to uncomfortable levels.

"Amusing how you talk like that in front of a cop." Luca glanced at Kelso. "You let him disrespect your badge that way?"

I'd only known Kelso as affable, but the way he grinned reminded me of a shark scenting blood in the water. He grabbed the serving spoon and helped himself to mac and cheese. "You come and pull shit in my city, I have no trouble helping Levi take out the trash. So don't think I'm not willing to bend the rules like the many cops you have in your pocket. But, unlike your fuckers, I'm on the right side of the law."

"Don't start shit and start eating," Bristow added, shoving the beans toward Luca. "Or start talking."

"Rogue cops, huh," my stepbrother sneered.

"You're imposing on McGrath hospitality," Kelso said. "Make it worth their time, pal."

"Tell us why you're here," I said, irritated with Luca's mind games.

He exchanged a look with Sofia. "Better eat first because after we're done telling them what we know, we might be shown the exit."

"Did you have anything to do with Murder Sanctum sending a hitman after me?" I asked.

"No. But Simon Stepanov is stirring up shit with Chicago."

"Because of his dead gangsters in Vegas?" Kelso raised a brow.

"That wasn't us." My stepbrother seemed unperturbed, picked up a rib and started tearing into it while Sofia picked up her utensils and demurely tackled her plate. The meat was falling off the bone, so it didn't cause any projectiles into her clothes.

"We don't deal with that shit," Luca said after polishing off the rib as well as two slices of brisket. For an elegantly dressed man, he ate barbecue like the rest of the guys. "Though I *had* weighed going after them after what they did to Kelly."

"Enough hedging." Levi tossed a bone on his plate. "It seems you're the one on a fishing expedition."

"All right." My stepbrother leaned forward. "I'm trying to prove that it wasn't us who hit Vegas." He glanced at Kelso. "But Stepanov is more concerned with the missing drugs."

"They're missing?" Bristow asked.

Luca exhaled in resignation when he saw the genuinely surprised expression on the detective's face. "Shit. Shit."

"Should I arrest you now?" the detective asked dryly.

"You know I wouldn't be asking this in your presence if I had anything to do with it," Luca said.

"How do you know it's missing?" Levi prodded.

"Stepanov thinks we did the hit on his men and took the drugs. I informed him we didn't, but he doesn't believe me."

"So he could still go after us?" I asked.

"I don't know," Luca acknowledged. "But then the other rumor might be true."

"What rumor? Levi asked.

There was silence and contemplation around the table until Kelso asked the obvious question. "Did you guys ever see the video Blaze took of Kelly?"

Luca nodded. "It was a common chatroom for organized crime and other players in the underworld."

"You know my friend Tom Roth, right?" I asked.

Her stepbrother smiled grimly. "Of course. He's in the middle of all this fiasco for thwarting a Sanctum assassin."

"He's a SEAL," Bristow smirked.

"I find it interesting that he's supposed to be a security specialist for big name hotels, yet he has a small office in Downtown LA," Luca said.

"I think he has a warehouse and another office in Vegas," I said. "He travels all the time."

I refused to look at Levi. He could be jealous all he wanted, but Tom and I were friends. A friend who saved my life. Although it could be argued I wouldn't have needed saving if he wasn't embroiled in underworld activities.

"Travels, huh?" Luca smirked. He slipped out his phone and scrolled through a few pictures before sliding the device toward Levi and me.

Levi cursed.

"The man with Tom looks familiar," I said.

Levi passed the phone to Kelso. The detective's jaw tightened before he handed the phone over to Bristow who mouthed, "Fuck."

"Would someone tell me who that is with Tom?" I asked.

"Dmitry Vovk," Levi and Kelso said in unison.

"We know the LAPD had custody of Dmitry but had not charged him. He was let go." Luca's eyes studied everyone's reaction. "There's also a rumor that it's not really the LAPD, but the CIA. That's making more than a few people nervous. Roth is clearly in that picture."

"This changes the whole angle," Kelso said.

"So, Dmitry is involved with what's happening?" I asked.

"If Roth is involved, then I'm pretty sure he is," Luca said.

"You know we're hearing something else interesting about Stepanov, Emilio Moretti, and one Walter Ford," Kelso said.

Luca stilled, his face showed surprise before he smiled slyly and relaxed, shooting a quick glance to where Cillian was sitting. "You guys know more than I thought. I suspect ole' McGrath isn't cut off from the life after all."

"He is," I snapped. *And don't you dare pull him back in, asshole.*

"You don't think, dear sis, I don't know when questions are being asked of my associates and *my men?*" He leaned forward, and it was the first time I'd seen the charming façade fall off. "I make it my business to know—"

"Dial it back, Moretti," Levi warned.

"And if you returned my call and didn't hide things from us, Gramps wouldn't have had to do that," I snapped. "You keep talking about family, but it's only *family* when it suits your agenda, isn't it?"

"You've got a live wire there." Luca smirked at my husband before returning his attention to me. "You're right. I'm sorry, but like I said, I was preoccupied."

"Luca," Sofia said softly. "You have to tell them."

"All right." My stepbrother pushed his plate away. "But the Isaac Ford thing is all speculation. Even I'm not sure if Emilio and Stepanov engineered the whole thing. However, two years after his son was killed in prison, Ford met with my father. There was arguing … as though Emilio owed Ford something."

Kelso propped his elbow on the table and steepled his fingers, stroking his chin with it. "Any proof of this?"

"They were in the study. I was pretending to arrange the flowers in the hall," Sofia said.

"You spied on your husband a lot?" Kelso quirked a brow.

"Insurance in case I couldn't bear staying married to him anymore, I'd have something against him. He would never let me leave with Mia, so I stayed."

And yet she had no problem giving me away.

"Anyway, Ford said, 'A son for a son, that was the deal'," Sofia said. "I moved closer to the study that time, but Emilio saw me through the crack of the door and walked over to close it."

"What did he mean by that?"

"A few weeks later," Sofia stared at me steadily. "Your brother was killed in the SEAL operation."

The world tilted, and my lungs refused to work.

Levi stood so fast the chair he was sitting on nearly toppled over. He slammed both palms on the table and leaned forward. "What the fuck are you saying?"

"A year after Isaac Ford died, the prosecuting attorney's son perished in a car accident," Luca said. "The following year, Callum McGrath was killed. You follow? Sheer coincidence?"

My pulse pounded in my ears, and I wracked my brain to remember what Dad told me of the accident that claimed the life of the prosecutor's son. We'd always accepted that Callum's job was dangerous, but he lived and breathed the SEALs. He embraced it. We accepted that he died doing something he loved while protecting our country. We did not expect him to be betrayed.

Levi's hands curled into fists, and he sat down again, grabbing my hand in his, both of us clinging to each other for support. "Who?" His voice cracked, echoing my question because words choked in my throat. "Who betrayed him?" he rasped.

I glanced at the other table. Nana and Charles were watching us but Gramps and Alana were chatting with the girls.

"I don't know. I suggest you find Roth—"

"Tom would've said something," I argued. If Tom had known all along, the betrayal I felt …

"Not if he was working with the Gray Wolf—I mean, Dmitry. One of them is the key." Luca eyed me intently. "Something has spooked the Russians and there will be terrible blowback if they can't keep the lid on this."

"On Walter Ford?" Bristow said. "Maybe higher. Because who would have classified information on a covert op?"

Kelso said, "Give us a name."

"I don't have it. Roth and Dmitry are your leads," Luca said. "I'm thinking now, if Roth was able to get the jump on Blaze, he killed Eisenberg, and took the twenty million in product. I'm not sure how Ford figures in all of this." His gaze scanned the table. "I haven't had dealings with the old man. We terminated business with him before my father died."

"Let's get this straight," Bristow said. "Isaac Ford was killed in the prison riot seven years ago."

"The following year it was the prosecutor's son." Kelso was entering information in his phone. "Callum McGrath was killed five years ago."

My throat closed up as I remembered getting the news that ripped the family apart. Mom was inconsolable for weeks and had to be sedated. Ronan and Levi couldn't accept that Callum was gone and dealt with the grief in their own destructive ways. It took a while before everyone could move on, and now with new information, it was like receiving the tragic news all over again, except this was worse.

"If an American conspired to derail that SEAL op, that's treason," Levi gritted.

"Exactly."

I stared at my mother. "You've had this information for years and you never spoke up?"

"No," Sofia said. "No, darling, I didn't. I only made the connection when Luca and I talked about it this time which triggered my memory of that conversation. I keep a record of what I hear. Luca provided the dates on Isaac Ford and the prosecutor's son's death. Everything suddenly made sense."

"Remember this is all speculation," Luca cautioned. "One of the men who knew for certain —my father—is dead. That leaves Ford and Stepanov. This is assuming Stepanov through Murder Sanctum brokered the deal with his Russian contacts to subvert the op." He looked at Levi. "We can pull what we know together and determine what happened. To see if the theory checks out." For the first time since he arrived, exhaustion lined Luca's face. "They say Stepanov has dirt on everyone."

"More than you?" Kelso derided.

My stepbrother narrowed his eyes. "As I was saying, Stepanov may have the proof we need. He's known to keep recordings of conversations as insurance so no one can take him out."

"So, we flush out Stepanov?" Bristow said.

The men continued to plot, but a silent scream started forming inside my chest, as if my lungs couldn't contain the pain and anger that deep-dived in my heart so quickly.

Callum was murdered!

"Kelly," Levi's concerned voice and a tug on my hand finally pulled me out of my spiraling anguish.

I turned to him—the man who carried the pain of losing my brother for so long. An apology wanted to form on my lips, but no words came.

When his face turned soft with understanding, it made me feel worse.

My chair scraped back. I stood and fled into the house before I broke down in front of everyone.

19

LEVI

EMOTIONS HIT US SO FAST, Kelly was up on her feet and gone before I could stop her. But maybe having it out in private instead of rehashing our issues in front of everyone was for the best.

"I'll go after her," I told the table and stood to rescue my wife from Alana and Branna who surged from their chairs. I reached them in time and blocked them from following Kelly. "I got it."

"What did that asshole say?" Alana jerked her head in Luca's direction.

"Useful information," I said.

"Is Mama okay?" Ashley tugged on my tee.

I glanced down at my youngest. "I promise she will be."

"Did Uncle Luca make her cry?" Whit asked, glaring at her step-uncle.

"He's trying to help," I said. "I need to check on your mom." I speared the adults a look. "Stay here. Please don't interfere. When we're ready, we'll share."

I kept my face neutral and my voice firm. They had every right to know, but not when I didn't have the facts. I turned away from them and disappeared into the house. As I suspected, Kelly was in the powder room. The door was locked.

I rapped on the wood lightly.

"Give me a minute," a garbled voice filtered through.

"Babe, it's me."

Silence reigned for a few seconds, and I didn't know what else to do but wait. Eventually, the knob turned and Kelly opened the door. I caught a glimpse of her ravaged face before she turned away to hug her arms.

I slipped inside, and closed the door, locking it.

I went to her.

The second my hand touched her shoulder with the intent to pull her into my arms, she twisted around, crashed against my chest and started crying.

I held tight.

I held tight through her wracking sobs with the emotions of bewilderment that reflected my own, and the questions thrumming through my head.

I held on to her because I sure as fuck was holding on to our marriage. I wasn't letting go. I wasn't letting her down again. Anything she needed. She was my priority. Not my anger at the betrayal that killed Callum, but Kelly, Ash, and Whit. My family.

After a few minutes, she glanced up. "Callum didn't need to die. He didn't deserve that." Her words were still warbly. "And I pushed you to move on when you said something was off about the op."

"Hey. Hey. None of that now."

"That's why you quit. Because your command refused to listen to your team on the ground. That's why you were so angry." Tears continued to stream down her cheeks, and I swiped them away with the pad of my thumb. "In a rage ...

but I wanted you to move on because it killed me to see you blame yourself, Levi—"

"You were hurting too." I hated to see self-recrimination in her eyes, and reminded her she was right to ask for a separation. "My headspace was fucked up at that time. I refused to get help. It wasn't healthy for our kids, for our marriage. It took the threat of losing everything to face my shit." When she continued to look at me in that heartbroken way, a fierceness overtook me. "I was angry at myself. Angry that I didn't have Callum's six, angry that the mission went FUBAR, angry that my command didn't seem to give a shit."

"You listened to your gut feeling that whole time," she said softly.

"But at what cost?" I growled, trying to keep from coming out of my skin. "I lost sight of my priorities. For Christ's sake, I have two small children and I managed to be home six weeks in two years. All because of what? My anger? My cowardice? I was too chicken shit to face you—face the McGraths because I came home and Callum didn't."

Kelly inhaled sharply. "I understood your guilt, Levi. More than you know."

There was an earnestness in her voice that made me pay attention.

"I never told you this," she said. "Callum used to be my person before you came along. So, when news came that there were casualties, my first thought was of you and then him." A ragged breath escaped her as more tears spilled from her eyes. "When you came home, I was ashamed at the tremendous relief I felt. I couldn't face my parents because of that. We were all heartbroken that Callum was gone, but my mind didn't want to dwell on this other feeling. The relief …"

"Oh, beautiful," Fuck. I didn't even think about how complicated losing Callum was for her. There were no words I could say that would comfort her in the guilt she was feeling. I knew how much she loved Callum. She had survivor's guilt in another form.

I hugged her and let her sob into my chest. And all I could muster was "McG wouldn't hold that against you." And he wouldn't. When I told my friend I was marrying his sister, he said I didn't deserve her and if I made her cry, he was going to kick my ass.

Kelly pulled away and gave me a small smile. "But having Ash and Whit helped me through that and I think they're helping you too because they are the future you and Callum were fighting for."

I cleaved to her. "With this piece of information from Moretti, we're handling this together. And I swear to you, I'm going to put all my resources behind it to discover the truth."

She exhaled. I wasn't sure if it was in relief or resignation. "You think Garrison can help us? He's on an extended leave right?"

My mouth quirked up. "That man couldn't resist a lead like this."

Her eyes grew troubled again. "Beautiful," I said firmly. "We're going to find out more in the coming days. We both had different experiences and responsibilities back then that colored our judgment. We need to let the past go. We're going to find out the truth—together. Find out what the fuck is going on. Get me, babe?"

A watery smile curved her lips. "Got it."

I grinned, lowered my head, and sealed our new-found understanding with a kiss.

Afterward, Kelly sent me on a mission to look for cucumbers in her grandmother's fridge. I was instructed to cut her six rounds, so that was what I did. Alana came in and gave me a strange look.

"How is she?"

"Still in the bathroom." I transferred the small slices onto a plate and put them in the freezer for a few minutes.

Her cousin frowned. "Her eyes are swollen?"

"Yes, she didn't want to go out there looking like that."

Branna walked in. "Is Kelly okay?"

"She's fine, just got some news, that's all," I hedged. Shit, I wasn't ready for this inquisition from the McGrath women.

Alana crossed her arms. "And you can't share it right now?"

"Nope."

"Does the Moretti or Rossi family have anything to do with this?"

"Look," I said. "It's complicated, and there's a lot that is rumor. You know how organized crime works. No one wants to go on record. It's always Tony A said this but Big Sal said that. Nothing written, nothing recorded, which is why Luca came over personally to tell Kelly what he knows."

"We have resources, too, you know," she said. "We don't need the Morettis. If it's the Russians we should be looking into, then the De Luccis can help with information."

"Your eavesdropping was not obvious," I told her, thankful I had to turn away to get the chilled cucumbers from the freezer. "Gotta get this to my girl."

On my way back to the powder room, I swiped Kelly's purse along the way and tucked it under an arm. Kelly said she had her life stashed inside, its weight heavy enough to engage the sensors on a passenger seat.

I rapped on the door, and she let me back in.

Her face was scrubbed clean, and she was gorgeous despite the remaining discoloration from the bruises and redness around her nose. The blotches around her eyes made them look bigger, more soulful. Her lips were also swollen and a deep red.

"You look perfect."

"No need to flatter me," she mumbled.

"No, really." She took the plate from my hand, sat on the toilet and put the circles on her eyes.

"I have chilled aloe vera soaked cotton pads at the house," she told me. "It's so good to wake up the eyes."

"Is that a trade secret?"

She laughed lightly. "It's not a trade secret, but every makeup artist worth her salt will go for a natural remedy first before attempting to cover puffy eyes with product."

"I know this really good makeup artist," I deadpanned.

"You're so good for my ego," she grinned. "You even listen to me go on and on about healthy eating and vitamin infusions."

"Always good to learn something new."

She lowered the used cucumbers and picked up a set of new ones. "Yes, but right after, you grill a thick hunk of meat with a big layer of fat."

She resumed her cucumber therapy shit.

"Hey, I'd never hear the end of it from Cillian if I served him anything short of a perfect steak. You know he's all about the marbling. Besides," I argued. "You saw his brisket and that layer of fat. You're the one who mentioned he should open a restaurant."

"Yes, I'm ambivalent about that now."

"Because your stepbrother is interested in partnering up?"

"That," she said. "And because it reminded me that Gramps got the recipe and technique from a fellow inmate. I wonder if it became popular and that person found out, if he would sue or try to cut into a partnership."

"Hmm, that's an interesting thought. Might ask Robert." Before her adoptive father opened a private investigation firm, he used to be a prosecutor for the New York Southern District. It was when a McGrath wed a De Lucci that caused a conflict of interest on so many levels.

After my wife was done de-puffing her eyes, as she called it, I watched her put on makeup and watched her transform into another version of herself. I couldn't decide which version I loved more.

"You're going to make me self-conscious if you continue looking at me like that," she murmured while crimping her lashes with a torture instrument.

"Don't make me laugh, Levi," she muttered.

"What was I doing?" I asked innocently.

"You wince whenever I use the eyelash curler."

"I don't know why you need it. Your lashes are curled."

"Not enough. And it's habit I guess."

"You know you don't need makeup to look gorgeous, babe."

A smile played on her lips, and her lashes swept down so I couldn't see what she was thinking, but it was a familiar look. It was one she made when my compliments pleased her. She lowered her instrument of torture and turned to step into me. My arms instinctively wrapped around her.

"Thank you." She tilted up her chin. "Now give me a kiss, sexy man, before I put on lipstick."

"I don't mind ruining it for you," I teased before I claimed her lips.

KELLY

As I WATCHED Sofia and Luca leave, I was surprised how I wanted them to stay longer. I wasn't sure what changed. Maybe it was the new understanding of my biological mother's reasons for giving me up. I gave her a small smile before she raised the blackened windows to finally hide her face from us.

"She's very pretty," Whit whispered as the SUV pulled away.

I glanced at my eldest daughter. "You look like her."

"How about me? Who do I look like?" Ash asked.

Levi, who was standing beside me, answered, "I think Ash takes after the McGrath side with that chin."

"I agree."

We walked back to the gathering. Kelso and Bristow gave us the privacy to say goodbye to the Morettis and chatted with Cillian. After my girls ran back to play with Scout, Levi tugged me close to him. "What are you thinking?"

"What do you mean?"

He eased me into him. "I know the expressions of your face, beautiful. You were sad when you watched Sofia go. That wasn't there the last time we saw them."

I shrugged helplessly. And for the rest of the day, it nagged at me. It wasn't until I checked on the girls at bedtime that I finally figured out where those wistful feelings came from. I tucked it in the back of my mind. I'd probably stay awake at night turning it over in my head.

Whit was reading on her tablet, while Ashley was reading one of her fairytale books.

"Lights out, girls."

"Just one more chapter, Mom," Whit said.

Ashley closed her book without another word and turned away to sleep.

"Did you do your homework?" I addressed my oldest daughter.

"Yes."

"You didn't run it by me."

She lowered her tablet. "I'm eight years old. I've got this."

My mouth turned down in disbelief, not knowing whether to smile or be annoyed that she was growing up too fast.

"What?" said the grumpy child.

"All right, I'm going. Last chapter, okay? Then lights out. I don't want to—"

"I got it."

I closed the door and ran into Levi.

"They're all tucked in?"

I walked past him. "Yes. They're growing too fast."

"Yeah, I noticed. Ashley suddenly wanted to read her fairytales on her own."

"I wonder if it's because she didn't want to bug her older sister. Maybe Ash is considering Whit's feelings."

"Probably. Or they're just tired and don't know it."

"How's our other child?"

"All walked and pooped," Levi said. "Wanna say good-night to him?"

We encountered Cillian at the bottom of the stairs.

"Great barbecue, Gramps."

He nodded wearily. "Yes. But I must be getting old. Couldn't stand drinking late with Bristow."

"That's why he left early," Levi said. "Perimeter secure?"

My grandparents had finally agreed to have security installed.

"*Shite*, forgot about that," Gramps said. "What with Alana and Charles staying over, maybe it's not a good idea to turn it on. There's a patrol car out front."

"You still need to make it a habit. I'll take care of it for tonight," Levi said. "I'll be up early tomorrow to walk the dog anyway."

Gramps shot my husband a relieved smile and trudged up the steps. Ruger followed his master.

After we checked on Scout who was already upside down in his crate snoring, Levi pulled up the security app on his phone while I went on to take my nightly vitamins. I was contemplating the epiphany I had about Sofia when I felt his warmth behind me. His arms wrapped around me, pulling me against a warmer chest. "You look lost in thought, beautiful."

He let me go, turned me around, and caged me against the counter.

"I had an epiphany today."

"About?"

"My relationship with Sofia and how she gave me up

seemed to be the root of how I react to my relationships. Why I wanted independence at the first signs of cracks in our marriage."

"How you wanted to rely on yourself?"

"Yes. I'm trying to protect myself from disappointment. But when I analyzed what she'd done given the nature of a mob family, I couldn't say I totally blamed her." Levi's body grew more alert. He was staring at me like he wanted to say something but was waiting for me to say more. "The first time I saw Sofia, I was ten. Her explanations about protecting me didn't make sense then, because I didn't understand the nature of crime families. When I grew up, I found out for myself how complex the family works. I found out that my stepfather considered me a blight. I found out that probably Sofia was right in giving me up, but it still didn't lessen the feeling that my own flesh and blood deserted me, especially after I saw how happy Mom and Dad were when Alana was born. I think that's when I felt the difference, you know." I looked apologetically at Levi. "Sorry, I'm rambling but I just needed to think this through."

"I'm all ears, beautiful."

I gave him a brief smile. "Thanks. Of course, everyone's attention was centered on the new baby. Suddenly, I wasn't the youngest kid anymore. There was nothing special about me. Then Uncle Sean got married and had kids. I was the only one whose real parents were not married, whose mother willingly signed away her rights to me. So, getting to my epiphany today …hearing how Sofia kept track of Emilio's conversations so she might be able to escape one day?" I gave a shake of my head. "For the first time, I saw how her gilded cage was a prison in itself."

"She didn't have to marry Emilio."

"She was nineteen, born into the *family*, and raised with its rules. They could have disowned her. They had enemies who wouldn't blink an eye striking back once she was out of their protection. I mean, Grandpa Rossi didn't acknowledge me until I was five and I think it was only because the McGraths became aligned with the De Lucci's through Aunt Ava's marriage. If I was, indeed, the fallen mafia princess that Sofia was, whose own baby was in danger because of its mixed blood, wouldn't I do everything in my power to protect it, even give it up? I look at Whit and Ash. I have the support structure of the McGraths backed by the De Luccis. But most especially"—I raised my hand and cupped his jaw, and his gaze darkened—"I married a man who loves his kids and would do anything to protect them."

Levi's mouth twitched. "You're forgetting, I'm very much in love with their mother."

Our lips met in a long, sweet kiss. "But after all that rambling, all I'm saying is I'm doing my best to put this abandonment behind me. Now that I'm a mother, knowing Sofia's circumstances when she had me, would I have done the same? Was I too harsh in my judgment of her? The other thing was … Mom, Dad, Ronan, Alana." I let out a rough breath when I said, "And Callum? They never made me feel like an outsider. They loved me like I was their own, so I had no reason to hold on to this issue any longer. It's become an excuse more than a reason."

"I'm glad you're letting go, babe." Levi stared at me with all warmth and tenderness. It seeped into my skin and blanketed me in security. "You're wrong about one thing," he said. "There's no doubt you would have fought tooth and nail to keep the kids. You're not a spoiled mafia princess. You forget that you have McGrath blood in you. That alone would make you react differently."

I thought back to my polished biological mother who remained as beautiful as ever. She always wore the best labels, had perfectly coiffed hair, and was a favorite of the Chicago society pages. In a way I think my preoccupation with skin care had everything to do with appearing as perfect as she was, to be worthy of being Sofia Moretti's daughter. Yet, I'd been introduced to honest labor by the McGraths who put me to work at an early age at the pub.

My lips quirked. "I had another epiphany."

"What's that, babe?" There was an amused glint in his eyes.

"What I am now is the best from both sides of the family."

"I picked the right woman to be the mother of my children as well," he murmured and kissed me again.

Later, as we settled in bed after fooling around without actually having sex, we cuddled together. I was falling asleep when I felt Levi kiss the side of my head and say, "You're worth the wait, babe."

20

KELLY

THREE DAYS LATER, Alana went to Vegas to pursue the cheating mobster case, while Charles left for San Francisco to check on the McGrath Distillery. As for the rest of us, the housebreaking of the newest member of the family seemed to take over our lives.

It was like having a newborn baby all over again.

Scout was adorable. It amused me to see how Levi and the girls did their best to take care of the pup without putting any pressure on me. After giving the pup his last walk for the evening, they deposited him into the crate.

"When can he sleep with us?" Ashley asked with pouty lips when Scout gave a little whine and shot her his soulful brown eyes.

"When he's fully housebroken," Levi said.

"Gramps told us that, remember, Ash?" Whitney reminded her. I noted that my older one was learning to be more patient with her sister.

"I know." Ashley squatted in front of Scout. "Night, Scout.

See you tomorrow. Don't pee in your crate, okay? Or you might not get to sleep with me soon."

Standing up, Ash announced she was going to brush her teeth.

"I'll read you a story after," Levi said.

"I'm tired, Daddy," she said. "Plus, I need to wake up early tomorrow and feed Scout."

"We'll come by and say goodnight."

"I'm tired too." Whitney yawned. We followed them out of the mudroom and watched them drag their feet up the steps. They passed their great grandmother on the way down.

"Night, Nana," they chorused.

When my grandmother reached us, she said, "Seems like a win-win getting the pup for the girls. I've never seen them so ready to turn in."

"And they hardly watch television anymore," I said.

"Well," Nana grumbled. "I guess that's good, but I miss my binge-watch buddies."

I laughed. "I could be your binge-watch buddy."

"Don't listen to this old woman. You and Levi go make more babies."

"Nana!" My eyes widened even as I heard Levi chuckling behind me. "Two isn't enough?"

"Four is a good number. Look at Robbie and Sean. And Ava for that matter."

"Times have changed."

"Bah," Nana emitted a non-committal sound and suggested tea in the kitchen.

Levi and I sat on the barstools around the kitchen island.

Nana put the teakettle on the stovetop and fired it up. "Broken bed aside, what are you going to do with the housing situation now that you're back together?"

"Seems easier to stay at Kelly's house." Levi winked at Nana. "Free child-care."

"The house a few blocks down is for sale," Nana said with

a twinkle in her eyes. "It's a lot bigger than the one you have now. Plus, you have a pup to consider, and Cillian could do the dog sitting."

"I know you all are trying to make it easy for me and I really appreciate it," I told my grandmother. "And I also see how the girls are bonding over Scout. Have you seen any troubling behavior, Nana, since that incident with Ash?"

Nana shrugged. "Kids will be kids. They go through mood swings. And Whitney is eight. That's the age where you wonder where your lovable and good-natured child disappeared off to. I've been through that stage several times with all my kids. Add in the grandchildren too. It's common."

"That's a relief," Levi muttered.

The front door opened and Gramps and Bristow strode in, with Ruger trotting behind them.

"Well, I'm taking off," Bristow said.

Levi stood to give his friend a hug and a back-thump. "Tomorrow?"

"Yeah, Garrison said he might have something for us."

I grew interested. "Anything to do with Tom and his friend?" We hadn't mentioned Dmitry to my McGrath family yet because that would mean revealing the sabotage of Callum's mission. Without all the facts, I wasn't willing to send us into that tailspin of grief again. Especially Mom. That news might just kill her. It was only during the past two years that she'd come to terms with Callum's death.

Bristow shrugged. "He isn't saying."

"Well, I hope they can get to the bottom of who wants to hurt my granddaughter." Gramps glanced at Levi. "If Stepanov, indeed, gave the order, I want him dealt with. I want that Blaze guy found. I want the mastermind. We're not letting them get away with shite."

"We're not," Levi's jaw clenched. "Kelso is keeping in touch with Vegas PD who has a line on Stepanov."

"No mob justice, Gramps," I said. "We do this by the book. I want them prosecuted."

Under the island, Levi reached for my hand and gave it a squeeze. That was all there was to it, wasn't it? Though I knew deep inside my husband wanted vengeance, I wanted more than anything to put everything behind us.

"All right, but keep me updated." Gramps stalked off to the mudroom. I heard him say good night to Scout before whistling for Ruger and heading up the stairs.

"Can't take the enforcer out of the man," Nana sighed. "He's only known one way to take care of things."

"I know that," Levi said.

"I'd rather you stay out of jail than get caught taking the law into your own hands," my grandmother warned.

"Me too," I said.

We changed the subject to the girls' upcoming summer activities.

After Levi tossed back his whiskey and I finished my tea, we all went upstairs to retire for the night. As Levi and I turned into our bedroom and closed the door, he backed me against it and put his forehead to mine.

"A part of me thinks Cillian is right," he said. "Stepanov may not have physically hurt you, but he gave the order."

"What are you saying?"

"If Roth is working with Dmitry to take down Stepanov," Levi said. "I want in on that. And fuck waiting for Roth to show his mug again. It's pissing me off."

"Wouldn't it bug you for the rest of your life if you took matters into your own hands."

"Can't answer that for sure, babe. Going rogue has never been a problem. What matters to me is you. That this wouldn't change the way you look at me."

"It's just that." I raised my hand to his cheek. "I don't want anything to happen to you, but I think we also need answers about Callum."

He grabbed my hand. "Bristow is working on that."

Something vibrated between us. It was his phone.

Levi checked his message. "It's Garrison. He wants a meet."

"When?"

"Now."

"He's here?"

"He's outside." Levi shot me a heated look I felt right between my legs. "Why don't you get ready for bed? I'm thinking of making love to my wife slow and sweet."

"Hurry back."

"I will." With those sexy hooded eyes, he gave me that lazy grin that definitely made my lady bits quiver some more.

"Garrison's waiting," I reminded him breathlessly. "I think I'll soak in the tub."

"Do that."

After Levi left the room, I couldn't wait to strip free of my clothes. In the bathroom, I started filling the tub, but decided to take a quick shower first.

I welcomed the quick rinse, and after I exited the glass enclosure, the tub was almost full. Steam snaked up from the surface of the water. I didn't need to dip my fingers in it to tell it was scorching. Emitting a brief laugh, I adjusted the temperature. Levi tolerated baths with me but it wasn't his favorite activity unless he'd had a strenuous workout and there was a promise of sex afterward.

Just as I shut off the water, I thought I heard a scream.

Then a dog started barking furiously.

Was that Ruger or the television?

My heart thudded.

Did Nana get the kids out of bed to watch TV? I sprinted out of the bathroom, throwing on clothes not caring if they were inside out, because my instincts were clawing at me. A muffled angry voice that sounded like Gramps filtered up from the first floor.

I left the bedroom and dashed to the girls' bedroom. Ash was sitting up on the bed, dazed.

"Mama," she whispered.

"Where's Whit?"

"She went to check on Scout."

I plucked her out of the bed and deposited her into the closet. "Do not come out unless I say it's okay. Stay quiet."

I ran back into the hallway and smacked into Nana. "What's going on?"

"Someone inside the house," she hissed, holding the shotgun.

Ruger's bark turned frenzied. Men started shouting. I ran back into the bedroom. "Have you called 911?" I threw over my shoulder.

"Yes. What the feck are you doing?"

"Shit, shit." My phone was in my purse, and it was downstairs. I spotted Levi's duffel of things and rummaged through its contents and found what I was looking for. "Come on."

I led the way to the staircase.

"Gramps!" A scream came from downstairs.

Whitney!

"Run!" Gramps yelled.

My lungs and heart jockeyed for space as I sped down the steps, but when I reached the bottom of the stairs, my blood plummeted to my feet.

Whitney was hurtling toward me, and a man was limping after her. Another was holding Gramps at gunpoint. I grabbed my daughter and shoved her behind me at the same time I withdrew the taser from my pocket and held it up. The man after Whitney paused.

"That's a bad idea," Limping-Man growled.

I fired my taser past him right at the black-clad man holding Gramps, hitting him right in the chest.

"Fu—" the man dropped and started to convulse.

The man before me grinned. "Missed your shot, sweetheart. Think you can take me on?"

All I could hear was the pulse in my ears and Gramps' muffled yelling. I slowly backed away with my daughter, down the hallway, past the mudroom on the way to the backdoor that led into the yard.

"You're going to leave your other child?" the man grinned and stopped at the bottom of the stairs. "She's up—"

The ratcheting of a shotgun commanded everyone's attention. I instinctively rounded over Whitney, sending us crouching on the floor.

"Stay away from my grandchildren, you fecking bastard!"

21

LEVI

SCOUT DECIDED to delay my meeting with Garrison. The German Shepherd plopped itself on the sidewalk, refusing to walk. I stared at the pup but he ignored me.

"Come on, little guy, you were whining in your crate. Thought you needed to go." I gave his leash a tug and walked forward, but he wouldn't budge. I waved at the officers sitting in the police cruiser across the street. Fuckers probably thought my predicament with Scout was hilarious.

I glanced ahead. Two blocks up, headlights flashed.

I scowled at the errant puppy again. "Fine. Just this one time." I bent forward and picked him up. "You little cock-blocker." I was anxious to get back to Kelly. Images of my wife currently soaking in a tub flashed through my head. I made it only a few steps when the pup squirmed and I had no choice but to set him down. He waddled to a grassy area and rolled on his back.

Seriously?

"Last chance, bud," I told him in a stern voice. The pup gave a sigh, rolled to stand, and started trotting beside me.

On our way to John's car, Scout made a stop to do his business. Fortunately, not one I'd have to pick up. Finally, we reached Garrison's Escalade and got in.

"Did you have to park this far?" I shut the door behind me. Scout bounded up to Garrison.

"I didn't want your patrol to get suspicious and investigate."

I would have done the same if the situations were reversed, but I had to share my grumblings.

"Little thing giving you problems?" he chuckled.

"Tell me about it."

"I might get one when our kid turns two." John scratched the dog's ears while Scout gave a satisfied groan.

"Surprised you're here." With Nadia so close to her delivery date and knowing how Garrison was so paranoid about schedules, I doubted he'd leave her side. "How's the missus?"

"She's about to pop," he said. "At this point she's tired of being pregnant."

"Kelly was the same way. The last month is hard for them."

"She's taken to sleeping on the recliner," he grumbled. "Anyway." He switched to his business tone. "I got hold of Dmitry. He's in the U.S."

I stilled. "Did he say anything about Tom Roth?"

"He admitted the plan was for Roth to infiltrate Murder Sanctum. There appears to be bad blood between Stepanov and Dmitry, but I have a feeling it's more about Ford."

"Our Walter Ford?"

Garrison nodded. "Stepanov is only a middle man. But it's Ford's business with the oligarchs that Dmitry has a beef with."

"How about Stepanov's deal with the Russian mafia and its connection to the op that killed Callum?"

"Dmitry has information, but he won't give it to me."

"Fuck that," Levi snarled. "He owes us. He's a CIA asset, right? Why—"

"Dmitry will only turn the intel over for a face-to-face with Kelly."

I wasn't sure I heard him right. "What?"

"Kelly. It seems he has something to say to Kelly."

"Why can't he hand it over to you? Or to me."

"No fucking idea," Garrison muttered. "Look. I tried. All Dmitry asks is to speak to Kelly."

"I'm not down with that shit. Is Roth making him do this? Because if he plans to steal my wife …"

"James—"

"No fucking way."

"James!" Garrison snapped. "Table that jealousy shit for a second, would ya?"

I scowled at him. It was on the tip of my tongue to tell him he was just as bad when it came to his own wife.

"Nadia is working with Bristow to figure this shit out, although I'm telling you now without Dmitry's input, they're not getting very far."

"Have you looked into Stepanov's organization?"

"The Sanctum has flown under the CIA's radar because they usually deal with mob business, but this one involves a SEAL op, and if anyone in our military and our government is complicit, that's treason. If it's proven, this is going to be a big scandal not only on the Hill, but U.S. Central Command as well. We need to tread carefully, not go off half-cocked, and make sure we have evidence."

"Damn it."

"Glad I'm not in the middle of that shit," Garrison muttered. "This is sensitive intel, and any leak might trigger a cover up."

Garrison's phone mounted on the dashboard flashed and read "Red" which stood for Bristow calling in.

"What's up?" John frowned and glanced at me. "Yeah, he's with me, but why call me and not him? ... What? Fuck."

A bad feeling crawled up my spine. "What?"

"You're on speaker," John said.

"The perimeter alarms on Cillian's property have been breached," Bristow said. "I'm sending the screen to you right now."

"Why didn't you call me?"

"Safer to call G, just in case you were in covert mode and didn't turn down your ringer. Outside infrared shows two vans parked behind the house."

"Fuck." I made to get out of the vehicle, but John stopped me.

"Do you have a weapon on you?"

"No."

"Leave the dog in the car, I'm coming with."

I didn't argue and met him at the back of the vehicle. He handed me a silenced Glock, several magazines, a knife, and a compact submachine gun. Shutting the cargo area, he said, "Let's go."

"John ..." I thought about Nadia.

He glared at me. "If you think I'm letting you walk into an ambush by yourself, then I'm disappointed you still don't know the man I am. Either we argue here or go secure your family."

I shut my mouth, rabid to get back to the house. I stuck the comms device in my ear.

Bristow guided us. "Shadows moving in front of the house. They might have someone posted who saw you leave. Approach from the back, more concealment with the trees."

"Copy that." Garrison and I acknowledged. We sprinted down to the cross street and approached from the road running through the back of the property. We spotted the vans.

"Shit. Wish I had a drone to deploy for heat signatures," Bristow said. "Going by the infrared. I see two hostiles in the backyard. And I just spotted one detaching from the trees beside the police cruiser."

"We need to assume they got the cops," Garrison said.

"I've alerted Kelso," Bristow said. "A nine-one-one call originated from the house."

"I can take those two hostiles," I said. "John, take the one in front. We can't have him rushing in when we breach the house."

"Wow, you're giving orders to G," Bristow chuckled.

"It's about damn time," I muttered.

John gave me a brief nod and made tracks to the side of the house that would lead him to the entrance.

Having confidence in him went a long way in keeping me calm. My panic was buried deep inside, and my training kicked in. I scaled the eight-foot concrete fence and sidled over to the tree beside it just inside the yard, making a mental note that it was a security weakness. I dropped to the ground in a crouch.

"Two tangos," I whispered to Bristow. "Anyone else?"

"No, you're clear."

"Engaging." Fishing out my fixed blade, I approached one of the hostiles who had his back to me. I put my hand over his mouth and slit his throat and tried as quietly as possible to lower him to the ground, but his partner saw me. We were about to open fire on each other when a blast came from the house.

I drew my gun first, fired, and dropped him with a head shot. Noise erupted in comms.

"What the hell was that?" John growled. "Other hostile is moving in."

"That sounded like a shotgun."

"Cillian or Branna," I muttered. Scooting to the back door, I peeked through its glass panel and spotted the silhouette of Kelly and ... Whitney. My girls!

I crashed through the door. "Are you all right?"

"I'm gonna kill him," someone shouted. I raised my gun over their heads.

"Cillian," Branna appeared at the bottom of the stairs and stepped over a body. The splattered blood and the hole on the wall above it painted the entire story.

Branna was fumbling with the shotgun, blocking a clear shot to a hostile who seemed shaken, but with enough wits to point a gun at her.

Cillian launched himself at the man, knocking him over.

Police sirens blared outside.

I shoved Branna aside and saw another dazed hostile lift a gun toward Cillian. I shot him in the head.

Garrison crashed into the house from the front door just as I pulled Cillian off the man he tackled. I kicked his gun out of his reach. With John watching my back, I let loose the rage I fought to contain when I realized my family was in danger.

"You piece-of-shit son of a bitch," I roared, cracking his jaw with the force of my gun. I flipped him over so his chest was on the floor. "Don't you fucking move, asshole. Or better yet, give me a reason to shoot you."

I fixed my gun to the back of his head, hand tightening around its grip, my finger brushing the trigger.

"Dad," Whitney's voice broke through my blind fury.

I eased my finger on the trigger, lowered my gun, and turned to my girls. I stood just as Whitney dove into me. "Daddy!"

My arm went around her and with the other, I hauled Kelly into my embrace. Tremors wracked my insides. "Ashley?"

"She's upstairs," Kelly cried.

"Ruger," Whitney wailed, tearing away from me and dropping to her knees.

I saw the German Shepherd on his side. He was barely moving, but alive.

"Shit."

Kelso and a couple of uniforms appeared inside the house.

"He saved me and Gramps," Whitney sobbed. "Is he going to be all right? There's so much blood."

"Hey, buddy." I kneeled beside Ruger.

He gave a soft whine and nuzzled my hand.

"Fuck." A voice uttered behind me.

I'd never been more relieved to hear Bristow curse in front of my daughter. "About time you got here."

The house erupted with activity. Kelly broke away from me to check on Ashley.

"Oh, man." Bristow's attention fell on Ruger. "I'll get him stabilized and take him to the emergency vet."

"Is he going to be okay?" Cillian asked hoarsely.

I glanced at Kelly's grandfather. "Your head's bleeding."

"Just got pistol whipped. Ruger first."

"Ambulance is on the way," Kelso told us.

Rising to my feet, I glared at him. "All bets are off. You know this, right?"

The detective's jaw hardened.

Stepanov had gone after Kelly before, and now, he'd gone after my entire family.

This was fucking war.

22

LEVI

THE NEXT TWENTY-FOUR-HOURS were a rush of activity. We moved the McGrath family into a safe house close to Assassin's Hill. Cillian had a concussion. It didn't take long for the lone surviving assailant to tell us who sent mercenaries after my family.

It wasn't Stepanov.

"Something set off Walter Ford," I informed the team.

Bristow, Garrison, and I were gathered in the basement of the safe house. Declan was keeping watch on my family. I still hadn't told Kelly about Dmitry wanting a face-to-face because our girls needed her first. Whitney was traumatized by what happened. Watching her gramps get knocked down, a dog she loved shot, and then her grandma going all Rambo on their assailant, I was glad my wife had the presence of mind to shield her from the actual carnage of witnessing Branna scatter the mercenary's brain on the wall. There was no way the kids were going back to that house anytime soon.

"I've confirmed cryptocurrency transfers to several accounts belonging to our mercenaries," Nadia said. I couldn't believe she offered to help us. But according to John, she would go into premature labor from an argument preventing her from getting involved. Bristow was more than capable, but with both of them tackling the intel we'd gleaned from the surviving attacker, details were getting slotted into place quickly.

Nadia said. "They were already waiting in the wings and were just waiting for a go ahead."

"It came from a Ford shell company you say?" Garrison verified.

"Yes," the analyst said. "It's the same one we suspect sponsored the Gulf of Aden attack on our SEALs."

"What set them off?"

Bristow brought up a screen. "This happened yesterday at a Las Vegas club right before a concert."

"A shootout?" Garrison asked.

"Yes."

"Any casualties?"

"Vegas PD is still investigating," Bristow replied. "So far three bouncers at the club were killed, but according to witnesses there were more, but the attackers cleaned out their casualties. Video footages had been wiped. I'm going through social media footage, too, but so far all I'm seeing is shaky video."

Further digging linked one of the owners of the club to Simon Stepanov.

"Too much of a coincidence?" Nadia postulated.

The door to the walk-out basement opened to the arrival of the detectives.

"Have all the McGraths reported in?" Garrison asked Bristow. "Because if this is Ford going after the McGraths again, they should be put on notice."

"So far Ronan and Alana are not responding," Bristow

said. "Mrs. McGrath and Kelly have been trying to reach everyone since everything went down."

"Ronan goes to Montauk in the summer," I said, trying to beat back the worry. "They're concerned with Alana since she went to Vegas."

"She's using a burner," Bristow said. "Wasn't she tracking a mafia soldier there?"

"Shit. And she hasn't reported back?" I asked.

"No."

"Alana is missing?" Kelso asked.

"I wouldn't say missing yet. It hasn't been twenty-four hours," Bristow said.

"Anything else from the crime scene?" I asked the detectives.

"CSI is finishing up. We don't have enough to prosecute Ford until we can confirm that the shell company is undeniably his," Gabby said. "So far, it's covered with layers of ownership."

"Yes, but Ford has the most to lose here. Where is he right now?"

"His personal assistant is giving us the runaround," Gabby said.

"Last known location?" I asked.

"Chicago," Nadia said. "He had a flight plan scheduled for Seattle, but it was never executed."

"So, either he's still in Chicago or he took a less trackable route."

Garrison crossed his arms. "Could he have left the country?"

"Fuck, I hope not," I growled. "I want to hang him by his nut sack and make him pay."

"Easy there, tiger," Kelso said.

I glared at the detective.

The team discussed other possible locations for Ford.

"How are your kids holding up?" Gabby asked.

Words clogged my throat and I swallowed, instinctively looking up at the ceiling. They were at the pool or maybe playing with Scout. "I don't know yet. But they don't want to be alone without one of us."

"You took the big bedroom with that supersized bed, right?" John asked. "Because, I think you and Kelly will have those two sandwiched between you for a while."

"Fine with me. Anything to help them feel safe."

"My two cents," Bristow said. "Ash and Whit are resilient. I've been around them, and they're tough kids. Just think about it, man. Whitney just saw how tough the women in her family are. That's role model for you." He coughed. "Not that I'm suggesting dispensing of your enemies with a shotgun is the way to go. All I'm saying is, they know their dad is tough. I'm sure they've heard stories about their gramps. Now they know that their nana and mom are tough too."

"Thanks, man. Coming from you, that's something."

"I still haven't told Kelly about Dmitry."

Garrison regarded me thoughtfully. "There's time. In light of these circumstances, I'll see if he'll agree to an alternative." He walked toward me and clapped my back. "Your family comes first."

KELLY

LEVI'S TEAM came around the corner to the pool area where the girls were spending time with Scout. My eldest child was still understandably withdrawn, although there were moments when she smiled when the pup did a cute head tilt. Gabby recommended several child trauma psychologists she'd worked with.

Nana kept Gramps indoors because bright light hurt his

eyes and he'd been ordered to rest. Everyone worried about Ruger. We'd called the emergency vet clinic so often, I was certain they were going to send our numbers direct to voice-mail. The vet wanted to keep him one more night. He certainly wouldn't be lacking attention when he came home, and the girls were anxious to pick him up the next day.

Meanwhile, I was irritated and worried that I couldn't reach Alana. Her voicemail box was full. But Mom and Dad were worried because after what happened to us, they couldn't get a hold of their kids.

Levi watched me end the call, and I shook my head.

"No luck?"

"None."

I heard the sliding door behind me, and Nana asked, "Have you gotten hold of Alana yet? Cillian is driving me crazy."

I knew it was her own concerns, but she was laying it on Gramps because it was the tenth time she'd asked me today. "Ronan might simply be out of pocket in Montauk, and you know how Alana is."

Nana harrumphed. "We shouldn't have let her go to Vegas."

"You didn't know this would happen," I reminded her.

"When was the last time you had contact with her?" Kelso asked.

"She called us when she arrived," Nana said.

Nobody wanted to make speculations or give false hope. I could see it on everyone's faces. Which was why, when Nana invited the detectives and the Garrisons for dinner, everyone declined. Bristow was staying with us to provide added security.

I trailed Levi's team to the door and tugged on Nadia's elbow. "Thanks for helping today."

"John wouldn't have been able to keep me home despite this big girl wanting to come out."

"You're due any day now, right?"

Nadia gave a light laugh. "Yes."

I glanced at her husband who was talking to Levi.

My hand involuntarily went to my chest. "No words can express how thankful I am that John jumped in to help Levi yesterday. I—"

"Not another word," Nadia said sharply. "John wouldn't be the man I married if he abandoned his friend. That's not in his vocabulary."

"But—"

"John and I discussed this. He'll try not to put himself in a situation where he'll have to choose between me and his job. And it wasn't a job. It was an intrinsic reaction of the man he is. The choice he made yesterday, Kelly, was a choice he could live with."

"What happened last night puts a perspective to the situations Levi faces in his job."

Nadia tried to hug me, but her stomach came between us. She settled into giving my shoulder a squeeze. "Now you know. You can never predict decisions they make in life-or-death situations."

"What's going on here?" John asked, putting an arm around Nadia.

"Just thanking her for her help today and what you did yesterday."

John emitted a non-committal sound. "You're family."

"Annnnd, you should be honored to hear John say that," Levi chuckled.

"I'm a changed man," he shot back.

"Not too changed," Nadia glanced at her husband, and the way they looked into each other's eyes made me lean into Levi. I had a feeling it was the same look I gave my husband.

AFTER LEVI'S TEAM LEFT, dinner was a muted affair. Only Bristow seemed to be alive at the table. Occasionally, Scout elicited laughter when he decided attacking our feet under the table was an accepted behavior.

"Why does he do that?" Ashley wailed. "Ruger never nipped our ankles."

"That's instinct," Gramps told her. "It's the way shepherds herd, but we need to redirect him because it's unacceptable for him to do it to us."

After dinner, Gramps declared his head was killing him and retired to the bedroom with Nana. Bristow offered to let Scout out in the yard. The girls, fortunately, seemed ready to crash.

Ashley asked. "Can we sleep with you tonight, Mama?"

"Sure, sweetie. How about you, Whit?" I asked.

"I don't want to be scared," she whispered.

"It's not being scared." Levi put a hand on her shoulder. "This will be us being a family, okay?"

"Just like the time we watched that scary cartoon?" Ashley asked.

"Exactly like that time." When Levi had his concussion and had to stay with me, there was a night when we watched an animated film that was too adult for kids. Whitney was fine after one night, but Ashley demanded Levi and I sandwich her so she would be safe on both sides. That lasted a couple of nights.

"Can Scout sleep with us?" my youngest asked.

"Hmm, better not," I said. "He's not fully housebroken yet." We didn't tell the kids that Scout had chewed through the leather seats of Garrison's SUV. But Bristow was a godsend. Though Levi's team helped move the big stuff into the safe house, he ran errands around town for us, ferrying stuff from my grandparents' house we might have forgotten, even following up with Ruger. Plus, Whit and Ash loved him. My husband's bachelor friend who could be bribed with food was proving to be an ideal babysitter and dog sitter.

"Okay, but soon?" Still from Ashley.

"Not promising, baby girl," Levi said. "It's up to Scout to show us he's ready to be trusted outside his crate."

"Okay, Daddy."

With that settled, we thanked Bristow again for helping us and went to the second floor. The bedroom we occupied was furnished with a California-sized mattress. The draperies were all basic beige and the bedding was white. Like a hotel, I figured it was easier to throw in the washer with bleach if necessary.

The pantry and fridge in the kitchen and the basement were fully stocked with food and could feed a large family indefinitely for months. I wondered if it was more than a safe house. Judging from the walls and the security, it was possible to retreat into this property in case of a cataclysmic event. I'd heard Levi mention Assassin's Hill a couple of times before. Gabby and Declan lived close by. Garrison and Nadia bought a house at the bottom of the hill. LA had faced several terror threats in the past two years, from an ebola-virus scare to a ransomware attack that took down the utilities during Stream-Con. I shuddered at the memory. Levi's team were on top of both threats.

It was easy to take Levi's job for granted when he'd been a SEAL. It was harder when he took private contracts because the missions weren't always about protecting the country, and I didn't doubt it benefited people with questionable moral compasses. I also didn't doubt having to work for such people contributed to Levi's anger.

"Wow, this room is huge," Ashley exclaimed. "This is bigger than any room I've seen!"

"But not cozy," I told her. I glanced at Whitney. She was looking around but remained subdued. First chance I had, I was taking her to the counselor. "What do you think, Whit?"

She shrugged. "It's okay."

"What's wrong, sweet pea?" Levi asked.

"When will Ruger come home?"

"Tomorrow," I said, but an idea struck me and I glanced at Levi. "Road trip? Think they'll let us see him?"

Levi's eyes flashed with determination. "I'll make that happen."

As it turned out, the whole troop wanted to visit our heroic wonder dog. Renewed energy sparked in our girls. There was no stopping Gramps either from seeing his dog.

We all piled into the Escalade on a trip to the emergency vet's clinic. The receptionist accommodated our request.

Ruger was in a sectioned-off area for critical care animals. He was curled up in the corner of a huge crate with an IV line running in. The vet tech said he was lightly sedated because of his stitches and they didn't want him moving around too much. It also helped him with the pain.

Poor boy.

Whitney and Gramps crouched in front of him.

"You saved me, Ruger," Whit whispered.

Tears pricked my eyes.

A soft whine sounded from the crate.

"We love you," Ashley said behind her sister. Somehow my youngest knew this was Whit's moment and hung back. "Get well soon, okay? Scout needs his big brother."

We also brought the younger German Shepherd. Scout was plopped on the tile floor, blissfully unaware of his surroundings.

Gramps mumbled something in Gaelic, and I saw him wipe his eyes.

Levi put his arm around my shoulder.

And together in the emergency room of a vet clinic, we gathered around as a family, thankful for being together and surviving an attack that was designed to destroy us. Levi told me those who attacked us were Ford's men and I was more convinced this whole chain of events had something to do with the McGraths rather than Tom.

It was the wrong time for my mind to mull what I remembered of my father's case. I was antsy to get hold of Alana, but I was more than worried that she was in trouble. I carried the anxiety in the pit of my stomach on the ride home.

Levi stopped at a twenty-four-hour fast-food joint to get burgers, fries, and milkshakes. The kids were thrilled because now that they'd seen Ruger, their appetites returned and were ravenous. Even Gramps was hungry.

My troubled thoughts about my sister and Ronan continued to hound me. It didn't help that Levi and the girls—suitably wired from sugar and carbs—decided to stream a series while sitting on the bed. The sounds from the television competed with my dreams, so when my phone rang, I was startled awake to silence, in a strange bed with half the weight of my youngest daughter piled on top of me.

"Phone," Levi grunted.

I grabbed the device from where it was charging.

It was from an unknown number.

My sister?

"Alana?"

"It's Tom."

23

_____

Levi

"Why didn't you tell me Dmitry wanted a sit-down?" Kelly asked me.

We were in the bathroom. Thankfully, the kids were dead to the world after having fallen asleep watching television for three hours. It was already nine in the morning but with the black-out-shades, one couldn't tell.

"There was no opportunity to bring that up." I crossed my arms, hanging on to my displeasure with Roth's phone call.

"My sister is missing," Kelly said. "What if Dmitry has information about her whereabouts?"

"Garrison already asked him and he had no clue. What does Roth want?"

"A face-to-face."

I tried not to grind my teeth. My back molars had already taken a beating with the jaw clenching that man had given me with the way he'd been after my wife.

"Perhaps you should remind him that the LAPD and Vegas PD want him for questioning."

"He said Dmitry couldn't make it, but the message he has for me is time-sensitive."

"Oh, he would just jump at the opportunity."

"Levi," Kelly snapped. "Now is not the time to get jealous. Alana and Ronan are missing. He has information on the op that killed Callum. Don't we want closure on this?"

Tears glazed her eyes, and I felt like a fucking asshole.

I scraped a hand over my face. "Shit, you're right. I was going to tell you today."

Her eyes narrowed.

"I was." I honestly was. "I was going to call Garrison and check where he was with Dmitry first."

She relaxed. "I believe you."

"I don't want you anywhere near Roth."

This time it was she who crossed her arms. "I don't think that's your decision."

"The fuck it isn't. You're my wife."

"Yes. And I need you to do what you do best."

I exhaled heavily. "And what is that?"

"Keep me safe. Have my back while allowing me to do what I *need* to get us closure."

———

"Enjoy your stay, Mr. and Mrs. James."

I grabbed the keycards from the check-in staff and turned to usher Kelly aside.

"Here." I handed her one of them. "Remember to stay close to me."

"Jeez, Levi, that's the hundredth time you told me that."

"This is no joke," I warned on our way to the elevator banks. "I could call this whole thing off."

She stuttered a few steps before glaring at me. "You wouldn't do that. You're just as eager to find out what the hell happened on that mission."

"Test me. Just test me." We waited for the car to arrive wrapped in a pissy mood. We'd been at each other's throats since Tom called her. The person of interest in both the LA and Vegas PD cases contacted her instead of the cops.

Fortunately, Ronan surfaced from his break in Montauk. Alana was still missing, so Kelly knew I was all bark about calling it off.

All intel indicated Dmitry and Roth were allies and no imminent threat came from them, but it did nothing to lessen my annoyance with Roth who seemed to be handling the liaison between us and Dmitry.

"Relax," Kelly said. "Between you, your team, and Uncle Cesar, I feel safe."

I tightened my grip on her hand, letting her know I appreciated the sentiment, and partly to remind her not to talk about it until we got to our suite. The elevator arrived and took us to the penthouse.

The hotel's security had done a sweep, and Kelso did the same prior to our arrival, double-checking behind the hotel's team. Only a few people were in the loop with none of the feds or Vegas PD involved.

When we entered our room, I still ran through the usual security protocols. After I finished my review, I turned to Kelly.

"Any change in plans?"

Roth had been messaging her.

"The last instruction from him is still to be at the Lorian Casino at ten tonight."

The message was sent when we first rolled into Vegas. The meet would occur in less than two hours.

"I'm sorry Kelso is going rogue again," Kelly said. "I hope he doesn't get suspended like last time."

Despite my misgivings about getting a friend in trouble, I grinned. "Don't worry about it."

"But if Gabby is covering for him, that would mean she'll get in trouble too."

I put my hands on her shoulders to reassure her. Making her feel bad about it didn't even cross my mind. I didn't need to use guilt to have her back out. That wasn't my style, and it had no place in the scheme of fixing our marriage. "Babe, one thing you need to know about our friends, they don't have a problem battling through the bureaucracy and red tape to get things done. We need that intel from Dmitry, not only for this, but our detective duo hopes it will help their case in keeping Moscow White out of Los Angeles. And, beautiful, I'd want nothing more than to put the people who hurt our family behind bars." If not six feet under.

I gave her a nudge toward our bedroom. "Go freshen up. I'll bring the suitcase to the bedroom, and let the guys know we're here."

"I'll call Nana and Gramps before I shower and check on the girls. Let them know we've arrived."

She disappeared into the bedroom while I called Bristow.

"Yeah."

"Any update?"

"Nope. No sign of Roth or Dmitry. No sign of Ford or Stepanov's men that we have on file. Nadia hooked me up with several surveillance videos running the new facial recognition software and still nada."

"I don't know why Dmitry couldn't just agree to meet with me or Garrison."

"Uh, maybe because Dmitry knows you're pissed at Roth for getting Kelly involved, and they're partners in whatever shit this is all about."

"I hate getting Kelly into the middle of it and Roth is leading this meeting while he's wanted by the LA and Vegas PD."

"Just keep your cool," Bristow reminded me.

"I'll try," I grunted, trying not to froth at the mouth with the situation.

After I ended the call with him, I brought our things into the bedroom, setting the suitcase on the luggage rack and hanging up the garment bags. The bathroom door was closed. I smirked and glanced at the king-sized bed and remembered the night we'd broken hers.

I adjusted the thickening erection behind my jeans and sat on the side of the bed, kicking off my boots, settling against the headboard and brooding over the closed bathroom door.

I couldn't wait to sink into my wife again. The frustration of the past few days with our arguments led to disgruntled pecks on the mouth. I wanted to grab her and kiss her hard. Our girls being constantly attached to us was the only reason that prevented me from flinging their mother over my shoulder, marching into the bedroom, dropping her on the bed, and fucking her raw.

Shit, that image wasn't helping. I checked my watch. And there wasn't any time either. Kelly was hungry, and I knew a hangry Kelly wasn't conducive to the kind of fucking I envisioned.

The water turned off, so I pulled the shirt over my head in preparation to take my turn in the bathroom. I forced myself to get up from the bed because it only gave me an uncomfortable stirring in my groin. I was dragging down the zipper of my jeans when Kelly stepped out in a billow of steam with nothing but a towel wrapped around her chest, her wet hair in a twist.

My saliva dried up, and when all the blood rushed south of the border, I got lightheaded. "Sure hope you left some hot water for me."

She paused just inside the bedroom, her eyes darting from me to the suitcase and back to me again, or more specifically to my cock that was pushing past the waistband of my boxer briefs.

"We don't have time," she mumbled.

I choked a laugh and advanced on her. "Don't you think I know that?" I was barely hanging on to my self-control, but fuck it, I needed to feel those naked tits against my chest.

"Levi," she warned in a breathless voice.

I hauled her against me and stripped away the towel. Fuck, her tits felt good. I crushed her mouth in a fierce, bruising kiss before breaking away. "I've been wanting to do that for the past three days."

Her eyes flashed. "You annoyed me."

"Yeah, well you annoyed me too. Doesn't mean you should change to those little pecks and act like you hadn't been creaming over my tongue a week ago."

She stared at my chest and huffed. "It's just … never mind."

"What? I wanna know."

"We're late." She glared at me.

I raised a brow. "We can be later."

"All right. What I really wanted to do was bite your lip and shut you up because you tried to keep me out of a solution when it was me that Dmitry specifically asked for."

"Really? And that's a surprise when you know I'd lose my shit if he touches a hair on your head?" I stepped back from her and folded my arms over my chest. Her nipples were pouty and begging to be sucked. "Also, you know there are other ways to shut me up."

She gave another irritated exhalation, covering her breasts with her arms. "Go! You'll be needing that cold shower."

"Oh, my cold-hearted queen," I murmured, walking past her and glancing down at my erection. Yeah, my balls needed a deep freeze.

KELLY

. . .

LORIAN WAS one of the lowest stakes casinos in Las Vegas, which also made it the most crowded. Levi said he wasn't surprised Tom chose this spot because of the variety of guests who came in—from sneakered, Hawaiian-shirt wearing retirees to starry-eyed honeymooners to people in suits and fancy clothes warming up their gambling hands for the night. No one looked out of place.

The casino floor was vast, but the crowd was so crushing this Saturday night, I could sense Levi wanting to leave the second we crossed the threshold. He communicated with the rest of the team using a collar-mic. Kelso was around some-where, but I hadn't spotted him. Most of the crowd flocked to the slot machines, roulette, and craps table.

We tried our luck with roulette and Texas Hold'em. Finally, we settled on the Blackjack table. Levi seemed to do well, squaring off against the dealer. It helped that the other players around the table were not idiots.

As Levi's chips piled higher, we started getting more involved in the game. My husband had just scored Blackjack and was done with the round. The remaining players started calling me Lady Luck. On my left, a man in a cowboy hat who'd been winning around fifty percent of his hands glanced at me. "What do you think, Lady Luck?" He showed me his cards of double eights. The dealer was showing a seven.

"Split it," I told him. That was the only logical play, but apparently me giving the blessing seemed to be the supersti-tion at the table.

"Sounds good."

He won both hands. Everyone started cheering around me.

Every time the dealer shuffled his cards, I checked my phone. Nothing from Tom.

"Think our friend isn't coming," Levi murmured. Our

success in the card game seemed to have loosened our anxiety about the meet. Gambling did that—gave you the high of winning and desperation for more.

Gramps had explained why loansharking was a lucrative part of mob business. The collections made from high-stakes gambling loans were crazy.

"I don't know," I replied.

By the time I had the urge to pee, I realized an hour had gone by. "I need to go to the ladies' room."

"I'll come with. You want to play slots afterward?"

I shrugged. "Doesn't matter. How long are we going to wait?"

Before my husband could answer, the dealer asked, "Leaving already?"

"Yeah." Levi grinned. "Leave while you're ahead."

"That's smart," Cowboy man said. "Thanks for the wins, lady."

Now that I was a few steps away, I could study the guy instead of talking to his hat. He had a dark full beard, but I still couldn't quite see his eyes.

Levi felt me hesitate. Cowboy man was still grinning at us before he tipped his hat and turned back to the table.

My husband ushered me toward the hallway leading to the restrooms. "Bristow," he said. "Any update on cowboy guy from our table? An associate of Dmitry, Ford, or Stepanov?" His hand tightened on my arm and I glanced up at him.

"What?" I asked.

"What? … Fuck!" Levi growled before pushing me toward the ladies' room. "Go. Kelso has eyes on Roth"

"Well, I really need to pee." I hurried into the ladies' room. Women at the sink glanced up and scowled at my husband who retreated immediately.

"Sir, you're not allowed in here," a restroom attendant barked at Levi.

"I'll be right outside," he muttered.

Shaking my head, I told the women, "Sorry, he's overprotective."

"If my man was that hot, I'd have him follow me everywhere," one of them quipped.

Several women giggled.

The ladies' room was huge and was divided into two sections with attendants milling around, making sure guests had everything they needed. A half-wall of sinks in the middle divided the two areas. I found an empty cubicle on the other side of the door from where I entered. As I took care of my needs, the cacophony of chatter was everywhere—women complained or swooned over their men, excited patrons talked about the shows they'd seen while others planned what club to hit later.

After I was done, I exited and went to the sink to wash my hands. When I looked up at the mirror, I was startled to see a large woman behind me dressed in an attendant's uniform. Her hair was in a braid and she was wearing dark square-rimmed glasses. Even with lipstick and garish foundation, she had distinctly masculine features. But since it was Vegas, nothing surprised me. He could be a drag queen or she could be a transgender or she could be a woman who just looked more masculine.

I smiled in the mirror and froze when the attendant came closer.

There was something oddly familiar about that face. Goosebumps dotted my skin when I looked around and realized I was alone in the area with her.

The attendant stared into the mirror and our gazes locked while recognition jolted my heart.

"Hi, Ki," he said.

"Callum?"

24

KELLY

SPINNING AROUND, my mind tried to make sense of what I was seeing.

"Callum?" I repeated in a raspy whisper.

Lightheadedness swept through me. I blinked at the face smiling at me in a lopsided grin ... an endearingly familiar grin.

"Oh God!" I didn't know where to look. I didn't know how to feel. Fear and anxiety burst inside me. My trembling fingers reached for his face. "Are you real?"

Deep in my heart, I knew it was my brother. The glint in his eyes, the exact way he smiled couldn't be faked under the layers of caked makeup.

He covered my hand with his. "I am. Who else calls you Ki?." Lowering our clasped hands, his eyes hardened in determination before he started pulling me toward an employees-only exit.

Jolted from my trance, I resisted. "Wait, we need to get Levi."

"No time."

"I can't leave—"

My brother grasped my shoulders and hauled me close. "Roth is providing a diversion. We suspect Ford or Stepanov has a man on the floor."

"The man in the cowboy hat."

He nodded. "Yes."

Levi's voice called. "Kelly?"

Female chatter rose in indignation.

"Seriously, dude? Let her pee in peace."

"Another impatient man. Figures."

"But …" I began, torn.

"Trust me, Ki. You want answers to where I've been. Come with me now."

A split-second decision had me following Callum through a cleaning supply closet that opened to a hallway leading into the casino's alley.

"Give me your phone," he ordered.

"What? No!"

"I can't have anyone tracking us."

Even when I was shocked from seeing Callum alive, I had the wits to dig in my heels. "You mean Levi? Are you mad? He's my husband!"

Cal glared at me. "I know. But I can't risk it."

My purse started vibrating. Digging my phone out, I knew it was my husband, but before I could swipe to answer, Callum snatched it from my hand.

"Hey!" I snapped.

He was as bossy as Levi. He strode over to an open dumpster, tossed the phone over, and continued walking.

"You get rid of my phone and then leave me here?" My feet were compelled to move in his direction.

"You're following me, aren't you?" He threw over his shoulder.

He stopped beside a white work van, slid behind the wheel, and started the engine.

I hurried around the other side. What the hell was I doing? I climbed in beside him. "I haven't seen you for five years. I'm trusting you now, Cal. I swear if you sell me to human traffickers or get me killed, I'm going to come back as a ghost and haunt you."

My brother chuckled darkly, guiding the van down the alley, but was blocked from exiting into the road because of traffic.

"Kelly!" Levi roared.

I turned in my seat and saw my husband barreling toward us. "Shit."

"Fuck," Callum muttered. "Forgot what a big sumbitch James is."

"He's going to be pissed."

"I think we're past pissed, honey."

My husband appeared at my brother's side.

And he had a gun pointed at Callum.

Levi

"Track her!" I yelled into my mic, slamming through the exit into the alley.

"You're there," Bristow said. "You're right on top of her signal."

I glanced to the side. "Fuck. It's in the dumpster. Disable and wipe it, then get hold of Kelso. Does he still have eyes on Roth?"

"Yes."

Up ahead, the flashing tail lights of a van caught my eye

and my fear escalated alongside the speed at which I pumped my arms to get to her faster. "Kelly!"

I sprinted toward the vehicle and prayed the traffic would prevent it from escaping. I would chase the damned van all over the strip if I had to. On my approach, I rattled off the license plate to Bristow. Drawing my gun, I reached the driver's side. Identifying my wife as the passenger, I pointed the gun at the driver. "Kelly, get out!"

She made no move, increasing my frustrations of not being able to grab her, but my gaze was locked on the driver.

He rolled down the window. "Hi, James."

That voice. McG? I couldn't believe my fucking eyes.

"Levi, it's okay," Kelly said in a rush.

"What the hell is this?" I snapped.

"Dump the phone, get in, and I'll tell you."

"No."

The traffic started moving.

"Then we're not stopping."

"You're not leaving with Kelly." I stepped in front of the vehicle. He'd have to get through me before I'd let him take my wife—brother or not.

"We're sitting ducks out here, motherfucker."

Even before he shouted those words to me, my senses were alert to the surroundings. My peripheral vision caught a lurking form to my right.

Cowboy from the Blackjack table appeared and he reached inside his jacket. Before he cleared his gun, I swung mine his way and shouted, "Drop it."

Gunfire exploded.

The guy dropped to the ground, but I wasn't lingering to find out if he had any friends around.

I circled the vehicle to Kelly's side. She had her head down, hands over it in a crash position. I pulled the door behind her open and jumped into the van. Before I got it closed, Callum burned rubber to get out of there. I was thrown from side to side as the van avoided other vehicles, rode the sidewalk for a few seconds, before settling into a smooth ride. When I found my bearings, I got on my knees between the front seat in time to see us run a red light.

My wife was white-knuckling the dashboard and the door handle.

"You all right, Kelly?"

"I forgot," she panted but continued, "What a terrible driver Cal is."

"Someone was shooting at us," Cal glanced at me. "I'm not kidding, bro. Ditch the phone."

"No."

"Then I'm dropping you at the corner."

"You contacted us. You must need us."

"I need Kelly and Kelly alone."

"You seem to misunderstand. I'm not leaving this vehicle without my wife."

"There's more at risk here if we're followed."

"Alana is missing," I told him.

"I know," he replied. "That's why I need Kelly."

"Do you know where she is?"

"We've been sent a picture of her. Proof of life."

Kelly gave a strangled cry. "Who?"

"Dmitry is chasing down the source with Moretti."

The van swerved again to avoid a red Porsche.

"Moretti?" I clipped. "Is that fucker involved?"

"Other than Stepanov's previous link to Chicago? No idea. But the pictures were mailed to one of his restaurants. Old school mail drop."

"That's why there's nothing in the chatroom," Bristow said through comms. I forgot he was still monitoring.

We made a sharp right turn on a red light. Irate motorists blared their horns. "Keep driving like a maniac, you'll be stopped by a cop."

He cursed, turned the vehicle to an on ramp before

glancing at the rearview mirror. "I trust you, James. But I'm not onboard trusting anyone else, especially that detective guy who's tailing Roth."

"Kelso is good people," I said.

"And he's got friends in the Vegas PD who want to shut us down."

"Who shot at us?" I asked as the van got on the interstate.

"Ford's man," Cal said. "That's why he targeted the McGraths. Because he found out I'm alive. Ford is getting more desperate by the day."

"Do you know who fucked up our op?"

"Yes. But we still need hard proof."

"Stepanov?"

"He's just the middle man. Look, it's a long story, I'll tell you all about it when we get to the warehouse."

Callum parked the SUV behind an abandoned structure on a fenced-in piece of land, and the second he pulled into a parking spot behind the building, I got out and helped Kelly from the van.

My instincts were all over the place, and so were my emotions, but I'd sort them later.

"We'll have words, but not right now," I told Kelly. Oh, I was fucking pissed. I understood where she was coming from, but I couldn't get over that she didn't stick to the plan. What part of *stick to me no matter what* didn't she understand?

We met Callum at the back of the van. He'd yanked off the atrocious wig and was wiping off the lipstick smearing his mouth. He looked like the clown I hated from that horror movie which made my next action easier.

I punched him across the face.

"Fuck!" he muttered, then spat out blood.

"Levi, what the hell?" my wife yelled.

"Stand back, Kelly," I growled, glaring and pointing a finger at her. "I'll deal with you later."

Her eyes flashed. She fucking knew she was in goddamned trouble.

My attention whipped back to my former teammate. "That's for taking Kelly away from my protection. If you were anyone else, I'd have killed you."

Callum and I locked gazes. That punch confirmed I wasn't dreaming, and he was real.

My SEAL training went to shit. No training could have prepared me for the monumental emotions surging through every vein, muscle, and cell exploding from my lungs. My chest was too small to contain all the words that scaled up my throat, but inevitably failed to come out. Words to convey disbelief, anguish, and anger, yet through it all, there was also relief.

What do you say to someone you thought was dead?

Not just anyone.

A brother.

Finally, I summoned the language a fellow SEAL would understand.

"C'mere, you ugly fuck." I grabbed Callum behind his skull and wrenched him into a tight hug. "What the fuck happened to you?"

When we broke apart, his jaw was hard. "Betrayed."

I gripped his chin, turning it right and left and then looked at Kelly. "What do you think? Fake?"

She puffed a nervous laugh.

"Fuck off," Callum said and glanced warily at Kelly who was still standing beside the back of the van.

"No hug from you, Ki?"

Her mouth trembled, her face turning red, before tears spilled down her cheeks. "Is it really you, Cal?"

He grinned. "Maybe we can binge all The Avengers now?"

Kelly laughed through the flood of tears and started

bawling as she stagger-stepped into the arms of her long-lost brother.

"Five years," I murmured, letting them have their moment. "You've got a lot of explaining to do."

Given the players in the game so far, and having dealt with numerous clandestine ops before, Callum being alive wasn't farfetched. All we needed was for Kelly's brother to complete the puzzle. As my mind defied the logic of his resurrection, seeing him alive was surreal. It was a good thing McGrath in drag queen disguise tempered the shock. A slow recognition. A slow acceptance proving he wasn't a ghost.

After Kelly regained a semblance of composure, we walked into the warehouse. With my head on a swivel, I followed them into the building, still spiked with adrenalin from the shocks of the evening.

There were too many.

"Where's Roth?" I asked.

Callum flipped a lever for the lights. "Five minutes out. He's with your cop buddy. We've been careful not to be seen in public together."

"Is Dmitry coming to Vegas?"

"He's finishing his business with Moretti."

My eyes scanned the area. A sofa, arm chairs, and a wide screen TV sat in the middle. Sectioned off areas were made into other living areas. Two crates loomed in one corner. But despite all these pieces, the warehouse was so enormous, it looked empty.

"Roth stays here?" I asked.

"Yes. It's owned by one of his shell companies." Instead of expounding, Callum asked, "Beer?"

I was still weirded out with the makeup and lipstick. "Point me to the kitchen if you don't mind us ransacking your stash." I grinned wryly. "I'm sure this conversation would go down easier if you scrape that gunk off your face."

He chuckled. "Good idea." He tipped his chin to the

corner of the warehouse. "Fridge over there. Get me a Heineken while you're at it. We've also got whisky."

When Callum disappeared into one of the sectioned off areas, I turned to my wife and collared her with my fingers, easing her to my side. "Still mad at you, Kelly."

"Can we not do this here?" she whispered. "I'm still wrapping my mind around the fact that Cal is alive."

"You and me both. Straight up, I don't know how I feel about it."

She rested her forehead on my chest. My arms came around her. "Let's see what McG has stocked."

It was a decent living space. A microwave sat on a stainless-steel tabletop. Beside it, the fridge contained mostly beer and deli meat. With Vegas nearby, there wasn't a need to go all prepper. I grabbed our beers and Kelly grabbed a coke.

When we returned to the living area, McGrath was back, dressed in gym shorts and a tee cut off at the sleeves.

The man before me was Callum. Yet, he wasn't. The glint in his eyes was flint hard, his face seemed thinner, more angular, yet it had the same crooked smile. Callum had always been a meathead who loved pizza and beer. I used to joke he was more fat than muscle. But that was not the case now.

A choked sob started up Kelly's throat again. "You've lost weight."

I handed him a beer. "I'd say he needed it. They didn't have pizza where you were, bro?"

"Fuck off," he said good-naturedly. "Roth and your detective are here."

As if on cue, the two men walked in.

Kelso walked to our side. "You guys okay? Saw the shootout and saw you get into the van. Roth tells me it was Ford's man."

"Vegas CSI is on the scene," Bristow said in my ear. "I'm monitoring your channel and theirs. I'll go incognito."

"Roger that," I said.

"What did Bristow say?" Kelso asked.

Roth and Callum conferred while I talked to the detective. I kept Kelly by my side.

"CSI is onsite," I answered. "Think you can get details from your buddy in the Vegas PD?"

"Definitely," Kelso said. "What happened?"

I told him how Callum snuck Kelly out, and gave him the gist of the chaos that ensued when the cowboy appeared.

After McG and Roth broke up their meeting and approached us, I stiffened when the fucker and my wife locked eyes.

Hell, no. I tightened my grip around Kelly's shoulder.

Roth smirked, but if he thought I was shy about staking a claim, he must've forgotten our restaurant encounter.

"Levi!"

I ignored Kelly's warning and stepped in front of her.

"The next time you call my wife behind my back, I'm going to bury your body."

The man flicked an amused gaze Kelso's way. "Hear that, detective?"

"I might help him," Kelso told him. "Save the department the trouble seeing that you've cost us enough man-hours looking for you."

Roth's amusement faltered. "Noted."

Having made my point, I looked at McG. "Now would you tell us what the fuck is going on?"

25

LEVI

"I SAW YOU DIE."

We gathered around the makeshift living room. Kelly and Callum were sitting side by side on the long couch. I didn't know who I was jealous of—Callum for having my wife's attention, or my wife who couldn't sit two feet away from McG. As long as Roth wasn't trying to get in there, I would let them have their time. Kelso and I were standing drinking beer. We weren't comfortable enough here to simply relax in an armchair.

Apparently, Roth was more than relaxed and was lounging like he was about to binge-watch TV, unaware of the man in the room who wanted to tear him to pieces.

But my priority was the information McG had for us.

"You saw me in the middle of an explosion. The blast threw me into the sea."

"We looked for you."

"Dmitry fished me out of the water," Callum said.

"Dmitry was aware of the deal between the Russian mafia

and Stepanov," Roth explained. "Russian arms dealers made millions selling Cold War-era nuclear material to terrorists. That was what was on that ship in the Gulf of Aden. Al Qaeda in Yemen was making deals with the Russians, who, in turn, were working with people in the Kremlin."

"Don't tell us things we already know, Roth. Tell us who betrayed the SEALs." I wanted to grill him about his connection to Dmitry, but that could wait.

"Our commander and two SEALs," Callum said grimly.

"Proof?"

"One of them is heading Ford's corporate security. No direct link. None of this leads back to Ford but to a close oligarch associate."

"Fuck. Stepanov has this proof?"

"He has recordings," Roth put in, and I was getting irritated with how he kept butting in. "Dmitry's been keeping tabs on this oligarch for years and he's been feeding me intel."

That time I couldn't hold back and snarled, "Tell me how you seem to be Dmitry Volk's spokesperson."

"It's eating at you isn't it?" Roth taunted. "That I knew Callum was alive before you did."

"You knew Callum was alive this whole time?" Kelly flared.

"No." Roth's gaze softened when he directed his reply to my wife. I clenched my fists. I could take a shot at his jaw later. All of us needed answers. "Dmitry contacted me six months after that op because I was in special activities. I was surprised how he knew I was connected to the agency. He didn't immediately tell me Callum was alive until he made sure I was clean." He switched his gaze to me and I wasn't sure if I preferred the mockery over the sympathy written all over his face. "You were too close to this. You were on the op, your guilt over Callum's death—no way could we burden you with the plan."

"That wasn't your decision. You and Dmitry—"

"It was mine," McG cut in. "I love you, bro. I love my sister. I hated what this shit did to you—"

"Spare me the sentiments," I cut him off. "We can hash out hurt feelings later. Let's get back to Stepanov, and how he seems to be the center of this mess."

"There's a rumor circulating that Stepanov has dirt on everyone, and somehow the information will be released to every news agency if he dies."

"He could be bluffing," I said.

"Maybe."

"So, why did you stay gone, Cal?" Kelly asked softly.

"I was badly injured. Broken bones, burns," he said. "I had amnesia for a few weeks."

"So, what's in it for Dmitry?" Kelso asked.

"Can't speak for him but he has his reasons," Roth said.

"And none of you guys were suspicious that he happened to fish Callum out of the water?" I scoffed.

"He's since proven he's on our side," Callum said. "And you should know. He struck a deal with the agency."

"So after you healed? You stayed gone?" I asked. My mind still couldn't understand why he chose to stay away. And yes, I was pissed he stayed gone, because it broke my marriage and gave an opportunity for this asshole to move in.

"Since I was laid out, Dmitry was this voice in my head telling me returning to the States was a mistake. That I would endanger my family if Ford didn't get what he wanted. It's the mob way—evening the score. So, I agreed to help him."

"Sounds like brainwash to me," I said.

Callum chuckled. "That's what I say all the time."

"We have people, too, you know. Those who could have helped you."

"At that time, Ford was very powerful. The fact that he couldn't stop his mafia associates from having his son assassinated spoke to how loyal he was as a business partner."

"Terrible father," Kelso muttered.

"So, Dmitry proposed we hit him from the shadows and chip away at his power which is tied to his wealth," Callum said.

"What do you mean?" Kelso asked.

"If you check his net worth from five years ago, it's down by sixty percent." Kelly's brother said with relish. "Most of his businesses were with Russian oligarchs and the energy pipelines. With those disrupted, some of them shut down, you can imagine how his influence has plummeted."

"Did they suspect Dmitry was behind the attacks?" the detective asked.

"Not until recently," Callum said. "Dmitry got distracted when his brother was giving him trouble and became careless. But it was time for me to come home. Five years of staying gone … it was getting hard. Don't get me wrong. The first few years we were always on the go …" His eyes gentled when he looked at my wife. "It's time to come home."

Kelly was shaking her head. "I can't believe you didn't let us know. Even signaled at least. I mean you should have known Levi worked for the CIA."

"Yeah, but you had a terrible DNI then," Callum said. "We didn't trust him not to fuck us over. When Admiral Porter returned to head National Intelligence, we saw an opportunity."

We talked briefly about how it had been a relief since the admiral was in the thick of it again. While Porter was DNI, they could respect his competence in handling the strongest intelligence agency in the world, and they had to move quickly.

"So, are you two really back together?" Callum split a wary look between Kelly and me. "You went private when I got killed, right?"

"Yeah, I got disillusioned, bro," I admitted. "I didn't want to stop the search. The window was too small."

"We made an illegal incursion that was off the books,

caused an explosion at sea for everyone between Yemen and Africa to witness. Thank fuck you guys got the nuclear material off the ship by then."

"So what's the plan," I asked. "How do we get proof of Ford's involvement. And why the fuck do you need Kelly?"

McG turned to my wife. "I need you to make us disguises."

KELLY

"WHAT FOR?" I asked. "You're not thinking of staying hidden forever, right?"

My brother's eyes grew troubled. "Ford knows I'm alive, he'll come after the ones I love if I don't get to him first. It's already happened."

I glanced at Levi. "Surely John can do something. I mean, he's got a direct line to the admiral."

My husband crossed his arms and stared at the floor. "I see how this can be dicey." He lifted his gaze to me. "We're not clear where the threats are coming from. Stepanov? Or Ford?"

"Both?" Kelso asked. "My take? If the SEAL op was exposed that would mean treason for Ford and for Stepanov which would be disastrous for Murder Sanctum. He can't operate under the radar anymore because it would be a huge scandal."

"The Sanctum will implode and take everyone down with it," Callum agreed. "We're talking about the Russians—the collective oligarchs and mafia— and Ford. This might have repercussions for the Kremlin, and what do you bet there'll be a race to find people who'll take the fall? The most expendable right now is Stepanov because he's at the center of it all, but he's got too much on everyone to simply roll over. With Ford's reduced power, he's the next candidate."

"Shit." Kelso scratched his jaw. "Let's make sure we have the connections straight. Ford is in business with the Russians."

"Correct," Levi said.

"The evidence from McGrath Investigations sent his son to prison—a scapegoat of sorts, but everyone was afraid that the younger Ford was going to try and cut a deal with the feds."

Everyone started nodding.

"There was no question Ford's associates would have his son whacked. He was fatalistic about this, but he loved making money more, so he did nothing to prevent it," Kelso said. "Enter Stepanov and Murder Sanctum with an enviable roster of the deadliest hitmen. They get rid of Ford's son, the prosecutor's son, Robert McGrath's son—" he looked at Callum. "You."

Again, everyone nodded.

"The Russian mafia agreed to blow up the SEAL operation in exchange for Stepanov to be the distributor of Moscow White in the U.S. because the Russians wanted out of selling Cold-War nuclear material. Higher profits, and it's easier and safer to move illicit drugs. It was a win-win on both sides."

"That's why Stepanov is desperately trying to find answers as to whether Callum was dead," Levi said. "He sent Blaze after my wife. Was that to send a message to you or Roth?" He turned to look at my brother.

"Both," Cal said. "A double-agent on our team sent a picture of Roth and Dmitry to Stepanov. This made him suspicious. So, he sent a man after Roth. That man never came back."

"Then he sent Blaze after Kelly."

"Right. After they sent a video of Kelly's beating we knew we had to act fast." Callum wrapped an arm around his sister.

"Tom was on your tail the whole time. That's why he got to you quickly."

"But what about Alana," I said. "I'm trying to be patient. At this point, I don't care why you faked your death, but we need to get her back."

"Whoever has her, we can lure with the Moscow White we stole," Callum said.

Levi whistled and glanced at the crates. "Are those Stepanov's drugs?"

"Yeah, man," my brother said. "That threw Stepanov off at first, and he suspected Chicago. Moscow is squeezing him for payment. Technically, it's their money—twenty million dollars—with no product to sell. After we got rid of Eisenberg and his crew and stole the drugs, that was when Ford found out I was alive."

"How?" I asked.

"With Stepanov backed into a corner, he probably asked Ford for money and confessed," Callum said. "Ford lost confidence in Stepanov and sent mercenaries after the McGraths himself."

"Let's not forget the cowboy," Levi said. "Bristow just confirmed that the guy was definitely Ford's man, not Stepanov's."

Kelso interjected, "I thought you cut Ford's net worth to forty percent."

"It'll be zero when we get through with him," Callum said.

"So is that why you need a disguise now?" I asked. "To move around? Because that one you wore at the casino was terrible."

"I had to catch you in the restroom because your husband stuck to you like a tick."

"What if I didn't have to go?" I raised a brow.

He grinned. "I made sure the server kept refilling your drink."

I shook my head and laughed lightly. Turning serious, I

said, "Levi has friends who can help. You don't need to do this alone and wear disguises." I glanced at my husband who nodded in confirmation.

"Ford has eyes everywhere. I can't risk facial recognition."

My critical eye took in the angles of his face. "We can use prosthetic transfers, but we'll need to work on your makeup game."

"Hey, I didn't do too badly," Callum grumbled. "Don't forget, I was the one who taught you to use that shit."

"What?" Levi chuckled. "Is there something I need to know about you, McG?"

"Halloween," my brother said. "Kelly's first Halloween she wanted to go as Wednesday."

"Wednesday?" Kelso asked.

Callum rolled his eyes. "*The Addams Family*, dude."

Levi turned to the detective. "One thing you need to know about the McGraths, they're movie buffs. If they throw out some weird statement you don't understand, it's most likely in reference to a movie."

Kelso crossed his arms and squared his stance. "I'm getting that. But what's our plan? How do we get Alana McGrath back and bring Ford and Stepanov down?"

"Our plan," Callum said, pointing to himself and Roth.

"Fuck that," Levi growled. "We're here. Bristow is on board. Use us." He glanced at the detective. "You don't have to."

"Hell if you'll keep me out of it," Kelso said.

"Gabby is going to kill us," my husband groaned.

Callum regarded the other men in the room before turning to Roth, who shrugged. "The more the merrier, but it's not our call."

"What do you mean?" Kelso asked.

"Dmitry," Callum clipped. "He'll arrive in the morning. We used to be a bigger team but after the leak of the picture, he reduced this to me, Roth, and him. All of us have personal stakes in this."

"Well, the CIA has him on a leash," Levi said smugly.

Cal chuckled. "Try not to gloat about that too much. The guy has an ego."

26

LEVI

"I DON'T WANT to leave you," Kelly told her brother tearfully. "I feel like this is a dream and you're not really here."

Callum chuckled. "I'm really here. You've pinched me enough."

As my wife hugged him, Callum and I exchanged looks over her shoulder, an understanding. They had a plan to infiltrate Stepanov's organization, rescue Alana, and take down Ford in the process.

If Dmitry refused our help, he was an idiot. I'd hate to lean on Garrison to call the DNI and force him to include us. The SEAL op gave us justified involvement.

Plus, he had the agency's intel at his arsenal, but I had an inkling he wanted as few people as possible to know what was going down. It was about revenge. It was about protecting the McGraths and about Dmitry's own personal vendetta against Ford. Interagency red tape could curtail their plans and that was why they were going it alone instead of using us for help. Until I had all the intel I could use to make a case for our involvement, I wasn't arguing with McG.

"Kelso is taking us back to the hotel," I said.

"They'll be watching," Callum said. "But it's one of Uncle Cesar's hotels. If he says it's secure, it is."

After Kelly pulled away, I dragged my brother from another mother into a tight hug. "Great to have you back, man," I rasped in his ear then leaned back and squeezed his face between my fingers. "Still want to punch you for what you put the family through."

"Sorry—"

"But," I cut him off. "We're not digging shit up until you're in the clear. Got me?"

"Loud and clear."

After several false starts at goodbye, I managed to pry my wife away from her brother. I didn't even give her a chance to say goodbye to Roth. The two of them knew better, but seeing them exchanging silent communications with their eyes made me gnash my teeth so hard, a dental appointment was in my future.

On our way back to the hotel, we were still reeling from the events of the past few hours.

Kelso, who was driving, glanced over at me. "Surreal, isn't it?" He lifted his eyes to look at Kelly in the rearview mirror. "You okay back there?"

"I didn't want to leave him," she said. "Don't know how I can keep it from my family. It doesn't feel right."

"It's a good thing you don't have your phone then." I twisted around in my seat to look at her. "Don't think I've forgotten you threw all our plans out the window and left willingly with Callum when I repeatedly told you to stay close."

"It was Callum back from the dead," Kelly argued. "It's unprecedented."

"It's been five years, Kelly, he could've changed." I glanced at the detective. "Right?"

"I'm not getting between that." Kelso chuckled. "But if your brother had amnesia in the first few weeks, it's not unheard of that he could've been brainwashed."

"Come on," Kelly retorted. "That's too Hollywood."

"So"—I pointed out—"is this back-from-the-dead plot twist."

"You're such a buzz-kill," she mumbled. "This is huge news."

"No matter how big the news is, babe, your safety is my priority."

Kelly gave an annoyed huff and looked out the window.

Kelso snorted a laugh before focusing on the traffic ahead, but his mouth couldn't stop twitching.

"You'll not find this funny when you find a woman of your own," I muttered.

"Not sure I want such entanglement. Bristow and I are perfectly fine with our bachelorhood."

Bristow had signed off when we left the warehouse. Otherwise, we'd probably hear a wisecrack from him too.

"How are the girls?" Kelly asked. "Gramps and Nana?"

"Bristow said they binged on a new Primeflix series and stayed up late," I said.

Kelso was staying in the same hotel as we were and drove straight to the underground parking. From there, we took the elevator to our rooms. He got out first and seemed eager to leave us alone. I had more words to say to Kelly regarding her escapade with Callum, and there were certainly plenty when we got to our room.

I waved the keycard and opened the door, letting Kelly through. I followed her in and shut the door and leaned against it, casually crossing my ankles and arms over my chest, while my gaze followed her strut into the kitchenette.

"I'm thirsty," she said. "Want anything?"

"I'm good." I had two beers at Callum's. I was plenty hydrated.

When she returned to the living room which was directly across from the door, she frowned at me. "What are you doing standing over there?"

"I don't know," I said. "You tell me."

She rolled her eyes. *Oh, beautiful, you're really asking for it.*

"I need a phone." She made the mistake of walking toward me.

My arms snaked out and hauled her against me. "You sure?" I asked. "Who are you calling? Roth?"

"Stop that. Don't tell me you're still jealous."

"You think I can switch off simply because I'm back in your bed and I've fucked you?"

"How about you sleep on the couch?" she tossed at me.

I chuckled darkly. "You know better than to refuse me access to that sweet body of yours when I want nothing more than to fuck my mark into you."

She slapped a hand on my chest and pushed. "You're not intimidating me."

I didn't budge with my grip on her. "Oh, sweetheart. I don't intimidate. You know that."

Her eyes glittered with heat and annoyance. Her body thrummed with her desire. I could almost smell it. My dick thickened in response, because when we were fired up with each other this way, the sex was explosive.

Foreplay.

I lowered my head and braced her close, so she couldn't escape. "You know what image I have of you right now?"

"What?" She was breathless, and judging from how her pupils dilated, she was wet.

"I'm on my knees and you're on your back with your legs straight up, resting on my shoulders. Your ass is up high, and I'm pounding you so hard, you're begging for me to stop."

Her breath hitched. "That's a terrible position."

"Is it?"

"I'm completely at your mercy," she whispered.

"That's the point." Grinning, my hands skimmed her sides, feathering her short shirt and reaching underneath it.

She shuddered against me, "Levi …"

I trailed my fingers over the back of her fantastic ass and squeezed the flesh there, before I let one hand skim her hip, slip under her skirt and stroke between her legs. "Just as I thought," I groaned. "Wet."

Foreplay over. I set her an arm's length away, bent and shouldered her torso and tossed her over my shoulder.

"Levi!" she screeched.

With my prize struggling, I stalked into the bedroom. "I don't recall the last time I turned that ass of yours red." I was lying. I remembered every blistering second.

"Seriously, Levi. I'm getting dizzy."

"Oh, you were begging for it in the end, weren't you?" I said. Sitting on the bed, I flipped her over, and turned her over my knee.

"Don't you dare!"

"Not the words to say to me right now, beautiful." I grabbed the edge of her skirt and shoved it up, exposing the silky skin of her bountiful ass. The thong left little to the imagination. She squirmed on my lap, hardening my erection. My cock wanted inside her.

"The last time I fucked you, we broke the bed." I stroked a finger across her damp slit. It came away drenched. I lowered my face and inhaled. The smell of her. Christ. It drove me feral. Made me just want to bury my face between her legs and drown in her juices. But the primitive need that I was going to be *the best fuck she'd ever had* proved stronger. I wasn't joking when I told her that. I sucked and licked my finger before returning to its job of priming her for a hard pounding.

"And yeah, you're ready for this," I murmured, continuing the friction against her core.

"Seriously, Levi," Kelly whined. "Let me up."

"I haven't punished you for almost giving me a heart

attack when you left with McG, and that eye fuck Roth was giving you."

"What are you talking about? I didn't eye fuck him," she protested.

"Did I say you did? I said Roth." And saying his name riled me up further.

No kids.

Sound proof room.

Kelly at my mercy.

"How's that even my fault?"

And she was still giving me lip. Perfect. She fed on it. My wife knew exactly what she was doing. She wanted to be fucked hard, and that was the only way I was capable of giving it to her at that moment.

"Hmm, not good enough." I withdrew my finger, and palmed her ass before raising my arm and giving her a slap.

She laughed. "What was that?"

"Just warming up, babe." I was gauging her receptivity. In our marriage, Kelly and I had been creative in our sexual games. We'd used toys and vibrators. We'd done bondage, but it always depended on the mood. I was in the mood to dominate but in order for me to get my thrills, I wanted her willing to submit. With her being sassy like this, she was receptive. My hand came down harder.

She hissed, but didn't say anything.

"You know why I'm doing this?" I brought my hand down again.

Thwack.

"Because I disobeyed, oh lord and master?"

I bit back a smile. She was still being bratty. I gave her a solid thwack.

"Oh my God!" she whimpered. I ran my palm over her reddened flesh.

"Seems, I'm not getting through to you."

Another slap landed.

"What do you want me to say?" she moaned.

I touched between her legs, and my fingers came away slick. I hungered to taste her there. "Damn babe." I gave a smacking sound with my lips as I lapped up the evidence of her arousal around my two fingers.

"Levi," she moaned. "I think I could spontaneously combust with you doing that."

"We can't have that now."

I flipped her on the mattress and hovered above her. "I think I have a better idea."

Her glazed eyes narrowed. "What are you thinking?"

"Had blue balls for a week, babe"

She rolled her eyes. "We were just following what the therapist said and not having sex."

"Are you saying I should stop?"

"Don't you dare leave me hanging, James." When she used my last name, she was definitely fired up.

"So, are you saying the therapist is full of bullshit?"

She awarded me another eye-roll. "You know she had a point."

I chuckled, "A point of giving me blue balls."

"Levi! We discussed this."

"Messing with you, babe," I said, but I turned serious. "I'll make you come if you promise never to leave my protection again."

Her lips compressed.

"What did you do the first chance you were put to a test?"

"You would've done the same!"

"No. I'll always pick you. I learned my lesson the hard way."

"I understand you now more than ever. The stakes when you're on a mission."

With the back of my hand, I caressed her cheek. "Good. But I still need to hammer in a point."

"By punishing me?" Her breath caught on the inhale.

I grinned wickedly. "Gonna be worth it."

"You're not …"

I crawled down her body, and she tried to get up, but I pushed her down. While stripping her undies off, I spread her wide and threw her legs over my shoulders before diving into her wet heat.

She cried out and moaned as I avidly tongued her entrance. She thrashed her legs and cursed my name, but I continued edging along her pussy lips without bringing it home.

"Dammit Levi … let me come," she breathed raggedly. I scooped her ass to bring her closer to my mouth, yet the angle agitated her more. Her fingers clawed at my head, pulling me toward her cunt. I could never stay pissed at her forever. I loved this woman to the bottom of my soul. I would do nothing whatsoever to hurt her, but I could use pleasure to drive home a point.

Or the denial of it.

Her hips continued to squirm.

I should have tied her up.

I raised my head. "Promise me you'll never go off on your own again."

"I promise! Now make me come."

"That was too easy, beautiful. Not sure you meant it." I dipped my head and continued feasting. Her moans of frustration became louder. They were music to my ears. I edged the area around her clit, rimming it to avoid that sensitive bud that would deliver her ultimate release.

"Ahhh…. Levi, you're driving me crazy … ahhhh …"

That's the idea. I raised my head again. "You taste so good. Now, repeat after me. I promise to obey my husband from now on."

There was a slight hesitation, before her "Yes."

"Still fighting it, I see."

"I'm not."

"You just want to come." I dipped my head and got to work again. Kelly continued to moan and whimper, her voice started to get hoarse. Even if it was pleasure ultimately waiting for her in the end, her misery and frustration were getting to me. I didn't have it in me to prolong it.

Lowering her ass, I glanced at her from my favorite vantage point, between her legs, her chest rising and falling, her arms thrown back, and her eyes squeezed shut.

"Are you getting my point, beautiful?" I murmured.

"Yes," she whispered. "I'm never doing it again."

"It would kill me if anything happened to you, Kelly," I said quietly. "More so if it happened on my watch."

"I'm sorry. I really am."

"Love you, beautiful," I murmured, before setting back to my task, no longer teasing, but building. I'd mastered every inch of her sensitized flesh. I licked her in broad strokes, inserted my fingers once more and crooked them touching that sweet spot. I withdrew them and lapped harder before flattening my tongue against her clit, and pushing down on the tip of her mound.

Her body convulsed, her legs squeezed against my head and her cry of release spurred me to latch onto her clit, sucking it hard, feeling the swell of her arousal. I loved on her pussy until she became a melted puddle of limbs and flesh, pliant for my taking.

I pushed up to my knees and began to unbutton my shirt. Kelly watched me through hooded eyes, a satisfied smile on her lips.

"You're so good at that," she whispered. "Even if I hated you in the middle of it."

My mouth quirked at the corners. Tossing the dress shirt on the floor, I started unbuckling my belt.

She licked her lips. "I also love it when you do this strip tease after you've made me come over and over."

"Giving you time to recover." I whipped the belt loose,

and it fell to the pile on the floor. Unbuttoning my pants, I lowered the zipper before I lowered myself over her, propping up on my elbows. "You're so beautiful when you come. All flushed cheeks and eyes craving for more."

I bent my head and kissed her, taking my time to explore her lips while pressing my erection against her pussy to let her know how hard she'd made me. My tongue delved and tangled with hers. We explored each other in slow, lazy kisses, letting her taste how much I'd taken her over the edge.

When I trailed kisses down her throat, she sighed my name in surrender. I kissed her through the flimsy fabric of her dress, nudging the strap to expose a milky globe. She wore no bra underneath, just one of those sticky petals that strippers used. I peeled one away and paid homage to the taut bud, grazing the tip with my teeth before soothing it with my tongue.

"I want you inside," she whispered.

I mouthed my way up her neck, before I lifted my head to stare down at her. I worked my hand between us and released my cock from my boxers. "Oh, I'm getting in there, babe."

She understood my double-entendre and clasped her hands behind my neck. "I'm yours, big man. However you choose to make me yours." She wrapped her legs around me and the tip of my cock touched her entrance. I hissed as I slowly sank in, the urge to shove inside her was overwhelming, but it was no secret I was a masochist in delaying gratification. Inch by fucking inch I slid inside, her inner muscles snug despite preparing her with my fingers.

"Christ, babe, how are you so tight?" I groaned. "It's only been a week."

"Who cares?" she gasped. "Just put it in."

She clenched around me.

"Fuck, don't do that," I warned. Or it would be over before I thrust. I slid all the way to the hilt and hissed out a breath. "You feel so damned good. I want to make this last. But I have to move soon." I looked down at her. "You good?"

Unlike the first time, she was ready sooner. "I'm ready."

I withdrew slowly and squeezed my eyes shut at the exquisite pleasure, not only of the physical, but the pride bursting from my heart. This warm, living, breathing gorgeous woman in my arms was my wife.

My wife.

Those words echoed in my head as I started to thrust.

My wife.

Possessiveness threaded through my entire being.

Pumping, slowly but getting faster, I hooked her legs over my elbows. The pumping became a pounding.

"That's it," she moaned as I rotated my hips and ground against the top of her pubic bone in the spot where she got off during penetration.

"You've always been mine, Kelly," I growled. I continued pounding her into the mattress. "This is everything, you underneath me, in my arms. My cock letting you know who you belong to."

Pounding at a ruthless pace, I forgot everything else. All that surged inside me was the need to make her mine and mark her in every way. Take back what belonged to me. A trace of resentment flitted briefly with the reminder of Roth, but it dissipated quickly. The realness of this moment over-shadowed everything else.

I hardened even more, but again, I held out until I couldn't any longer and I shot forward, jets of cum spurted inside her. I continued pumping. She was going to get every last drop as I wrung out my release. I was primitive, feral in my possession of her.

My staggered thrusts slowed, and I gave her one last nudge before planting deep. I collapsed on top of her, giving her enough of my weight without crushing the breath from her lungs.

I stayed embedded.

Panting, sweat beading, our heartbeats and raspy breaths mingled. I raised my head to gaze down at her face, proud as fuck I put that sated look on her. "I love you, beautiful. Always and forever."

"I've always loved you, big guy. Forever."

Our lips touched and sealed our reaffirmation with a kiss.

27

KELLY

MY LIMBS and back were killing me. I groaned and opened my eyes to a strange ceiling and a weird perspective. I turned to see Levi's broad back, sleeping beside me on the floor, atop the coverlet we must have dragged off the bed. The events after we came back from seeing Callum came back in full color, giving me a clue how we ended up in the living room.

Levi fucked me until the early hours of the morning. He fucked me in every corner of our suite. Sometime in between our carnal activities, we took a shower, only to fall on each other again. We finally fell asleep exhausted.

I had images of me riding Levi on the couch. My cheeks flamed. I wondered if we broke anything that time.

I wrapped the throw blanket around me and sat on the couch, staring at my husband's monstrous physique. He was starting to stir. Since he was on his stomach, his glorious behind was on full display. If it wasn't for the soreness of my pussy, I might be tempted to wake him up for another round.

But anxiety chased away my lust-filled thoughts, leaving me to wonder if Callum's return was a dream.

"Fucckkk," Levi groaned, rolling on his back and turning to face me. "What did you do to me?"

"Me?" I teased. "Don't you remember the creative ways you had me flexed last night?"

He grinned. "Yeah, that." Then his face sobered. "What's wrong, beautiful? Did I fuck you too hard?"

"No, you delivered as I expected," I forced a laugh. "But I think I need a break for the next two days."

He sat up. "What's bothering you?"

"Callum." His name was a croaked whisper as if hearing it aloud would erase him from reality. That he was still lost to us. Alana was still missing. "Tell me I wasn't dreaming, Levi. Tell me he's really alive."

It was silly, I knew. But I still waited with bated breath for the reassurance only my husband could give.

The frown on his face disappeared and was replaced with a tenderness that eased my anxiety. He pushed up from the floor and sat beside me. He took my hand in his.

"He's very much alive," he said. "After our shower earlier this morning I received a text from him."

"What time is it?" The sun was blocked by vertical shades.

Levi picked up his phone on the coffee table and checked. "A little after noon."

As if on cue, both our stomachs grumbled.

"We're meeting him at five today. Will that give you enough time to pick up what you need to create disguises?"

"This is Vegas, big guy. My favorite special effects company has an emporium over here. We'll probably need two trips. Callum wasn't clear about the purpose of their disguise. That will influence material and application."

"Figured it wasn't a one-shot thing." Levi yawned. "But first things first. Why don't I order room service while you check on the kids." He handed me his phone and scrolled to a contact labeled Branna.

"What do we tell them? Gramps and Nana?"

"Tell them Roth didn't show up, but we have a lead. Don't tell her we have proof Alana has been taken. That would only open up questions we don't have answers for. Bristow already knows to tell the same story." He picked up the hotel phone. "Your brother doesn't want anything getting out yet. We don't need the entire McGrath family breathing down our necks. This might alert Ford or Stepanov of our plans."

"Okay." I thumbed the number. Nana answered on the second ring. "Please tell me my granddaughter is okay."

"Nana, it's me."

"Kelly? We were waiting for your call last night. Bristow said everything was fine."

"We're fine."

"Then why didn't you call?"

"We were out late last night following a lead, but we hit a dead end." Shit, I was making it up as I went. Was this what Levi did when he was trying to keep bad news from me? "We didn't want to wake the children."

I heard an extended sigh over the phone. I could imagine her wringing a kitchen towel. "I'm just not used to you being involved in these things. I already have one granddaughter missing."

"Alana hasn't called?" The words scraped out from my mouth.

"If she had I would've told her to call you immediately," Nana said. Grouchiness and impatience laced her tone.

My throat tightened. I really wanted to reassure her Alana was alive. It was only because I trusted my husband and saw first hand what he and his team could do in such situations that I wasn't in a full-blown panic.

"I know, Nana," I said. "And don't worry about me. Levi is taking care of me. Can I talk to Ash and Whit?"

"Cil and Bristow took them for ice cream."

"They left you alone in the house?" My voice rose.

Levi came back to my side and mouthed, "What's wrong?"

I put the phone on speaker.

"Don't worry." Nana's voice held a tinge of excitement. "Declan and Gabby are here to keep me company."

"Ahh, I see where this is going. I didn't think you liked zombie movies."

Once upon a time, Gabby Woodward had been a teen superstar on a cult zombie movie *Dead Futures*.

"I do now," Gram said. "I just watched the first episode of *Dead Futures*. Choppy beginning and Gabby agreed. Listen, I'm preparing them lunch. When will you get back?"

I looked at Levi. "Hey, Branna," he said. "We're not sure yet. We'll keep you updated."

"How are Whit and Ash doing? Are they getting along?" I asked.

"They're fine. Scout has them occupied and they don't have time to get in trouble," Branna said. "The best solution is to have more children so they don't pick on each other." Wistfulness entered her tone. "Goodness, Nana," I laughed lightly. At my grandmother's hopefulness, the direness of the situation momentarily lifted. "Two isn't enough?"

"I want more great grandbabies. Keeps me young," Nana said. "Don't worry about us. Your team has been taking turns checking on us."

"Who all stopped by?" Levi wanted to know.

"Ariana and Nadia and their husbands. Both pregnant." She stressed the word pregnant. And it was funny where she mentioned "and their husbands" instead of saying Migs and John.

"I'm glad they're looking after you," I said.

"They are. Okay, I'm busy," Nana said. "I need to get back to my guests."

We ended the call, looked at each other, and burst out laughing.

"Branna cracks me up," Levi said. "She must be on cloud nine living in Los Angeles near Hollywood."

"She is. And I'm so glad your team is taking turns keeping her mind off Alana's disappearance. It would be harder to keep the news from her if she was idle with crazy scenarios running through her head."

"We'll get her back," Levi said with confidence. "But Nana is right. This time away from the kids gives us the opportunity to focus on us."

My laugh was brittle. "Kind of hard to do with everything else going around."

"I disagree," Levi said. "With Callum showing up, his death is taken out of the equation."

"I don't understand. Are you saying we're suddenly fixed because the source of our guilt is gone?"

"No, babe, Callum's supposed death exposed a weakness in our marriage. It would have come out sooner or later because our issues are buried deep. I didn't get it for a long time, but I'm getting it now. Why you wanted to separate."

"I told you why," I mumbled, getting up and walking to the window to draw the blinds. I stared at the concrete jungle of the Las Vegas strip.

Levi came up behind me. "My anger at myself was not good for the kids, but there was another reason, Kelly. I need you to tell me if you see that."

"We're seeing a therapist next week."

"We don't need a third person to see what our problem is if we could see it ourselves, don't you think?"

He turned me around to face him. "I wrecked the security you had with me."

"My feelings of abandonment."

"Yes. It wasn't until you told me about your epiphany with Sofia, understanding why she'd make that choice—even if you say you don't blame her for no family support because you had the McGraths—it made me see where you're coming from."

"What do you mean?"

Levi exhaled heavily. "You had the McGraths. Mads and Robert are wonderful parents. I've seen you with Callum, Ronan, and Alana. I've definitely seen how you are with your grandparents, but I think …" He sighed again. "I think we have the same issues. I grew up in a group home, abandoned in the hospital. Both our biological mothers gave us up. Your biological dad couldn't be a real dad. But our issues are different. I grew up around kids who had the same problem while you grew up seeing what could've been."

I smiled. "I think we've established that."

"That's just it, babe, you didn't see why it took us a while to get back together. It wasn't only about me abandoning our marriage and making your scar deeper. It was because despite having the McGraths during your life—Whit, Ash, and I were your first real family, one you had all to yourself."

My heart pounded. "I think you're wrong there."

He gave me a tiny smile. "I'm not sayin' the McGraths treated you like an outsider."

"I am lucky to call them family," I said sharply.

"But it's still different," he said gently. "Kelly—the girls and I—we're really yours. I fucked up the faith you had that you had a family to call your own. Just explaining. I understand why it took you a while to give me another chance."

"You're giving me too many passes in this separation."

"We accepted that it was necessary. But we also needed to understand why it took us eighteen months to come to terms with it."

"That's the assignment our therapist gave us," I laughed. "But damn, big guy, you're more intuitive than I am."

"It's always the person on the outside who can see the big picture."

I circled my arms around him and drew him closer. "You're not on the outside anymore."

"I certainly hope so," he murmured. I raised my chin for his kiss, but he gave me a quick peck and stepped away.

I raised a brow.

"Room service is coming soon."

"You didn't have to step back," I teased. I was familiar with the tension radiating from his body.

"I see the bruises on you and I'm not liking it, but on some perverted level, I'm also finding it sexy that I put my mark on you."

He glanced away, and it almost made me laugh given his color-heightened face.

I was still naked underneath the blanket, and he was finding it hard to fight against going another round.

I recalled our sexual acrobatics last night. "We *were* pretty enthusiastic and I'm deliciously sore, but you'll be sorely disappointed. Pardon the pun. I think you've wrecked my vagina."

He chuckled. "Do we need to ice it?"

I teasingly opened the blanket and looked down—whisker burns everywhere, and yep, my pussy feels a bit puffy.

"It needs a break from you."

He went down on his haunches, and drew in a breath as he pressed his mouth against the mound. "I can kiss it better."

"We know where that's leading, and like you said, we've got room service coming."

He got up. "That's true."

"What did you order for me?"

"For us? Steak and Eggs. Waffles. Bacon. A big carafe of coffee."

My mouth watered. I didn't realize how ravenous I was.

"We need nourishment." He waggled his brows; I rolled my eyes.

He nudged me toward the bedroom. "Throw some clothes

on." He bent forward and snagged his boxer briefs from the floor. I threw a look over my shoulder to see him watching me walk away. I shot him a sultry smile and he shook his head and looked at the ceiling before shooting me one of his self-depre-cating ones.

Something changed between us when we had our marathon sex this last time. Something more liberating. A reconnection. I couldn't wait for my family to put all the heartaches of the past five years behind.

Levi

"I'm REALLY DIGGING this super covert stuff," Kelly said behind us.

Callum was driving, and he shot a look in the rearview mirror before glancing briefly at me. "What have we done?"

"You're the one who insisted we needed Kelly," I muttered.

"Hey, I heard that." My wife scooted between our seats and poked my shoulder. "Remember, I saved your asses last year at StreamCon."

"She's right, bro," Callum said. "That was the shit, Ki. So proud of you. Was that Locke Demon really that Garrison guy who Dmitry keeps talking about?"

"Yup," Levi said. "The one who got mobbed by fans."

"And you were the Marsh Man monster," he chuckled.

"Another fan of *Hodgetown* I see," Kelly said. "My girls love that series."

My wife was beside herself with excitement when we switched vehicles at the parking garage where Callum was waiting for us. I didn't have the heart to tell her that it was standard evasion maneuvers just in case someone was watching us. After lunch and another hour simply lazing around the suite—of course Kelly called it cuddling—we hit the strip and drove to the special effects emporium. I pushed the cart while Kelly shopped.

Afterward, we passed the time in the coffeeshop because my wife was still feeling the effects of our active night together.

"Where's Dmitry," I asked.

"He and Roth are meeting us at the warehouse." Callum cast me a brief glance. "There's been a development."

The way he said 'development' gave me pause. "What development?"

"You'll see."

"I hate surprises," I said. "Especially when Kelly is with us."

"I like surprises, but I think I've had my limit," she informed her brother.

Callum drove in silence which made the feeling of wanting him to turn the vehicle around worse.

Finally, he said, "A deal was made in exchange for Alana." He checked the side mirror before changing lanes. "We agree she's priority, right?"

"Not if it puts Kelly in danger," I countered.

"Fuck you. You think I'd put one sister's life in danger over the other?"

I didn't say anything.

The silence spoke volumes and Callum said, "Ki, please tell me you don't think I love you less."

"Of course not!" Kelly snapped. "This is a team effort. Levi's just reacting because I'm his wife. He's not thinking whether you value Alana's life more than mine."

"Sorry if it came out wrong, but Kelly gets it," I said. "After *everything* that's happened, I'm paranoid about her safety."

"It's a controlled situation."

I chuckled darkly. "It would help if you keep us in the loop."

"I don't have all the answers, but I trust Dmitry not to fuck us over. That's why he wasn't with us yesterday. He was ensuring a mutually beneficial alliance."

Somehow, mutually beneficial alliance didn't sit well with me either.

Before I could question him again, which would be a waste of time, he turned onto a familiar road. Even though I was in the back of the van last night, I recognized the fields and the way the road felt. It was a necessary skill to learn as a SEAL just in case we got captured, blindfolded, and taken elsewhere.

Callum pulled up beside a commercial truck. He used an SUV today. The van he drove the previous day was no where in sight.

Getting out of the vehicle, we followed him into the warehouse.

I stopped short. My arms circled Kelly when I saw the men inside.

"What's wrong?" she whispered. "That's Dmitry right? I remember you said he had gray hair and was huge."

That was Dmitry all right. I hadn't seen him since Stream-Con. The Gray Wolf of Odessa watched us approach, his freakishly silver eyes almost made him look as if he was blind, but he wasn't.

But all my attention was focused on the man standing beside him.

Simon Stepanov.

I wasn't expecting *him*. The file Bristow accumulated on the man contained a few pictures. Most were blurry. Clearly, he wasn't a man who liked to be photographed, but I had enough of his features burned in my memory to identify him on sight. He was wearing round frameless spectacles, wore his salt-and-pepper chin-length hair in a ponytail, and with his short goatee and tieless suit, he looked like a cross between a rocker and a scholar instead of the morally corrupt hitman broker for the mob and seedy businessmen.

"What the fuck is he doing here?"

Callum walked over to where Roth sat on the long couch and dropped down beside him. Kelly's brother gestured to the other two in the room who would give an explanation.

"Who is he?" Kelly whispered.

"Simon Stepanov."

My wife gasped and stopped in her tracks.

"Mr. and Mrs. James, glad you could join us," Dmitry said. "I see Stepanov doesn't need introductions."

The man in question smirked before saying, "Pleasure."

"Can't say the same," I snarled. "And if someone doesn't explain what's going on right now—"

"What? You'll walk out of here?" Stepanov said. There was no sarcasm in his voice, merely a-matter-of-fact tone. "Ford has Alana McGrath."

"Did you help him?" I asked.

"No, but I can help you get her back."

"What's in it for you?"

"I want my product back, that's all," he said.

Callum snorted. "We know that's not all you want, Stepanov, so let's cut the crap."

"I'm tired of this game," Stepanov said. "I want to be free."

"Not understanding here," I said. "You want to quit Murder Sanctum? Can't you just turn it over to whoever has the most stakes?"

"Eisenberg was supposed to succeed me, but you all murdered him when you took my drugs."

"He and Blaze conspired to hurt Kelly," Roth growled.

Stepanov shrugged. "I'm not saying it wasn't fair play, an eye-for-an-eye and all, but taking my product put me in a difficult position with Moscow."

"Boo-fucking-hoo, asshole," Callum sneered. "Not our fucking problem."

I unwrapped my arms from around Kelly and stepped protectively in front of her. "Tell me why I shouldn't kill you right now."

"Get in line," Callum clipped.

"He went after my wife," I said.

Callum laughed in derision. "And he instigated the whole shit that cost me five years of my life."

"I sent the man after Tom Roth," Stepanov said. "Blaze and Eisenberg acted on their own without my knowledge."

"But weren't you the person Blaze was talking to on the phone during my captivity?" Kelly asked.

Stepanov nodded. "He made a mess of things and your abduction was all over the news. The Sanctum doesn't care for that publicity."

Taking a step toward him, I snarled, "Blaze nearly executed my wife. You're telling me that order didn't come from you?"

"I merely told him to fix his mess up."

My arms shot out on their own, but Dmitry slid between me and Stepanov. "Let's have cool heads, shall we?"

"You expect us to work with him?" I spat.

Kelly's hand touched my bicep. "We need him to get Alana back."

I stepped back, dragged my fury back into my lungs and exhaled a calming breath before cutting a brief nod.

"Listen to your wife," Stepanov added. "I'm merely the middle man. It was not my intention to drag her into this, but Blaze Ulrich wants to be the new Sanctum boss and offered Ford another way to get proof that Callum McGrath is alive and to prove I failed."

"So Blaze is with Ford right now?" I asked.

"From my latest intel, they're together with several men

from Moscow's mafia," Stepanov said. "Including a couple of oligarchs."

"Ford is trying to escape the country," Dmitry added. "He needs the help of his oligarch friends, but not when there's four hundred million dollars in product missing." A smile touched his lips as he nodded to the crates. "And we're sitting on it."

"Four hundred million," Kelly whispered. "I thought it was twenty."

"That's the street price," I said. "How exactly are you going to help?"

"The Russians want their money with interest," Stepanov said. "I give them back their product plus a fifty percent restocking fee, I'll be free and clear."

The cogs in my mind were turning. "Did Ford nab Alana because of his vendetta against the McGraths?"

"Oh no," Stepanov said. "That's not the point now. Blaze told him Callum McGrath has the product. The Russians want Ford to get it back."

"Why doesn't he just pay them?" Kelly asked.

"He's broke," Dmitry said with relish. "The man who consorted with the oligarchs, who impoverished my town and killed most of my family, is finally broke."

And just like that, Dmitry revealed why he wanted to bring down Walter Ford. Everyone had their stakes on the table.

"I have the information to prosecute him," Stepanov said.

"But you were involved. Or were you going to say you were just a facilitator again?" I said.

"I have enough to put him away and plead immunity. All I want are the Russians off my back," Stepanov said. "Besides, you want Miss McGrath, right?"

Callum shot me a look while Kelly's fingers curled into mine, giving it a squeeze.

"What are you proposing we do to rescue Alana?"

28

L EVI

"T HIS IS A STUPID PLAN ," I muttered. "It's not going to work."

"Oh ye of little faith," Bristow told me. He grinned at me, obviously enjoying the set up of special effects magic Kelly was executing.

Bristow and Kelso arrived just in time to join the fun. Stepanov apparently had done his research as well and was no slouch in computerized special effects software that Kelly used. He offered three of his associates faces we could use to overlay our own and trick any facial recognition into thinking we were them.

Callum, Roth, and Bristow were the main actors picked to go along as Stepanov's bodyguards.

Dmitry and I were too conspicuous because of our bulk and height.

Kelso was staying with Kelly in the command van along with Dmitry. Having run the Argonayts hacking ring before it disbanded, the Gray Wolf was more than qualified to help the detective operate comms and drones.

As for me …

"Why am I always relegated to driver," I grunted my displeasure.

"Because you stick out like a sore thumb," Bristow said.

"Rhetorical."

He shot me another shit-eating-grin which I wanted to wipe off his face. I wanted to have a shot at the man who put his hands on my wife, to tear off Blaze Ulrich's limbs from their sockets and tear off his head too.

Both of us were riveted on the work area Kelly had set up while she was testing proof-of-concept on her brother. After studying everyone's bone structure, feeding photographs to the computer and generating matrix comparisons to the men Stepanov offered up, she said a life casting would be necessary.

Shit, that meant taking a cast of everyone's faces. I sure as hell was glad I wasn't needed for one. If we were to make the meeting in two days with Ford and the Russians—the next thirty-six hours would be critical for Kelly.

I'd seen my wife at work plenty of times, but she never ceased to amaze me. I wasn't surprised with all the awards she'd earned in recent years. I was so fucking proud of her.

"Are you guys paying attention?" Stepanov clucked, tapping the impromptu map in front of us. He, Kelso, Roth, and Dmitry were discussing the plan to rescue Alana.

Ford had her in an associate's compound a few miles outside Vegas.

"The gate is here." Bristow switched to all business. He had brought up a satellite image of the property and used it side-by-side with the makeshift topographical map we had laid out on the table. "There's a barn and several bunkhouses. The main house is a Spanish-style villa located here." He pointed to a cereal box we used as a marker for the main structure.

"You think he has her in there?" I asked Stepanov.

The Russian shook his head. "Ford is a hypocrite, and so

are his friends. They have the women in a different building."
He pointed to the cracker box.

"Wait, what do you mean women?"

The Russian looked at Dmitry before glancing at me. "I
didn't want to say it in front of your wife and McGrath, but
the Russians, who are putting the pressure on Ford, are also
human traffickers."

"Wait a minute … Alana …" Bristow scowled.

"I don't think that will be her fate. She's too old."

"Dammit." It didn't mean some schmuck wouldn't
abuse her.

"I can't keep this from Kelly."

Stepanov shrugged. "That's why I leave it up to you to
break it to them."

I was pissed, but I was glad Stepanov didn't mention it
right away.

I glanced at Bristow, and then Kelso, and finally at Roth.
"All right," I exhaled a sigh. "How many men are we up
against?"

KELLY

"WE'RE MOVING against Ford in two days," Callum said.
"Would that give you enough time?"

"You're talking about doing that life cast?" Tom walked to
our side.

"Yes. Think of what dentists do for your teeth."

Predictably, my husband appeared by our side. I was about
to roll my eyes at him when the expression on his face gave me
pause.

"What's wrong?" I asked.

"Roth, can you give us a minute?"

Tom backed away and returned to the men around the table.

"What's going on?" my brother asked. His jaw clenched hard. "It's Alana, isn't it?" He glanced past me at Stepanov. "He tell you something?"

Levi's chin dipped briefly, and my anxiety skyrocketed. "Is she … she's still alive, right?"

"As far as we gathered from Stepanov—he has a man inside."

"Who?"

"He's not saying."

"Alana?" Callum bit out.

"She's in a group classified as Lillies."

My brother cursed. "That's what I was afraid of."

Levi and my brother exchanged a look.

I crossed my arms and hugged my biceps. "Start talking right now. Don't keep me in the dark about anything. I'm as much a part of this op as anyone."

"Lillies are the prime grab for human traffickers."

"Oh my God." My world shifted on its axis, and I swayed into Levi. He steadied me.

"The Moscow cadre will be picking up a group of Lillies," my husband continued. "That's what Stepanov said. Bristow verified that the code word is used for the Western women for the Russian's Middle Eastern clients."

My stomach turned. "But Alana …"

"She's older than most. That's why we think she'll be okay."

"But that doesn't mean …"

"No motherfucker is touching her," Callum yelled and stood so quickly, it sent his chair toppling. He brushed past me and prowled toward one of the sectioned-off areas. A few seconds later, we heard a crash and roar.

"Levi …" Bile churned in my gut.

He drew me tight into his arms.

"We're going to get her back."

"You can't promise that."

He leaned away and cupped my face, staring at me with fierce eyes. "No, but do you think Callum is going to accept any other outcome except your sister alive? If he's going to lay waste to the compound, you can be sure I'll have his back."

"Thank you," I whispered.

"I guess you told them?"

We both looked over to see Bristow approaching. He stared in the direction my brother disappeared. "McGrath okay?"

"No," Levi said.

I pushed away from the comfort of his arms and tipped my chin to where Cal went. "Go to him."

"You'll be all right?" my husband asked.

"I'll be fine."

He exchanged a look with Bristow, and he said, "I got her."

I was pretty sure that look was about Tom getting close to me, but I couldn't bring myself to get annoyed at Levi. I gave him a light push. "Go."

29

LEVI

I WALKED behind the room divider. McG was usually the cool-headed man on the team. The jokester. But I hadn't seen a trace of that man. The Aden mission changed us. I recovered a part of myself that had been lost, but for Kelly's brother, he'd transformed into someone else.

Callum's back was turned to me as I walked in. He had flipped the cot against the wall and the box that served as a nightstand had been flipped along with it. The LED lamp that must have been on the box lay shattered on the floor.

"McG," I said. "You okay?"

He didn't turn to me immediately, taking ragged breaths. His shirt stretched taut over his back, shoulders, and biceps. My eyes sought our shared tattoo. The Spartan helmet was partially visible under the sleeve and even if I couldn't read the words at that distance, I knew what they were.

Finally, he turned to me. He'd ripped off part of Kelly's prosthetics from his face.

"She's not going to be happy you fucked up her work."

"You think I give a shit right now?"

I narrowed my eyes. "I get you're worried about Alana, but what we're doing here, including the shit you just tore off is what we need to get her back."

He gave a shake of his head, a wry apologetic grin twisting his mouth. "You're right."

"So, I repeat, are you okay?"

He glanced at me. "I'm sorry."

I inhaled sharply. Those words struck deeper. We never got a chance to talk about the Aden mission. My shoulders slumped. "I was supposed to have your back."

"I know, brother," McG said.

Our team changed formations at the last minute.

"Taking the nukes off that ship was too easy. Nothing made sense." I stepped toward him. Emotions burned behind my eyes and rattled inside my chest cavity. "I saw you at the bow." The words barely scraped past my throat. *Right before the world exploded.*

Then, grabbing his nape, I inched his face close and gritted out, "I would've had your back."

"I know," Callum rasped. "And I'm fucking sorry I put you, Kelly, and my entire family through hell."

My mouth flattened, and my jaw clenched hard. I squeezed my eyes shut.

The moments when I thought Callum got incinerated in a ball of fire were forever seared in my memory. I'd buried them deep. The survival of my marriage depended on it. I allowed myself to call upon it now and braced for it.

Comms were chaos.

"Going after tangos!" McG shouted.

"Let them go," I ordered. But something compelled my feet to head in his direction. I turned to the rest of my team with the cache of nukes. "Get it off this ship."

I ran down the port side to Callum's location. We didn't have the arms traffickers. I got why he wanted to nail these motherfuckers down and end this dangerous alliance with Al Qaeda.

I saw him at the bow, looking into the depths of the ocean. Did the guys jump ship?

"I got you, brother," I said behind him.

He turned.

I opened my eyes to ones reflecting the same fierceness I felt. Fierceness that communicated what a thousand words couldn't. If he were drowning, I would've jumped into that ocean and given him my last breath. If he were too wounded to move, I'd have carried him off that ship and dragged him to our waiting speedboat.

He would've done the same for me.

This was our brotherhood.

I tightened my grip around his neck and acknowledged our unspoken words and our current predicament. "We'll get Alana back."

———

KELLY

"How MUCH DO we trust your man inside?" Levi asked Stepanov. When he and Callum emerged from behind the divider, a look of fierce calm had settled on their faces—men on a mission.

"I think 'man inside' might be stretching it," the Russian said. "Mutual acquaintance between Ford and me is more apropos. As far as they're concerned, I found a middleman who negotiated a price in exchange for the product. But as a penalty for losing it, they want it back with interest."

"Like I said," Levi stated. "Bad idea. How do they know that you're not going to double-cross them? Which is exactly what you're going to do. And how do we know you're not leading us into a trap?"

"That's a risk McGrath was willing to take to get close to his sister."

"I smell a setup."

"We don't have time or reason to delay," Callum interjected. The rest of the guys gathered around. "Alana's outta time. We should've been there yesterday."

"And it's not possible to raid it now without the disguises?" I asked.

"No," Stepanov said. "I'm your ticket inside. You'll never infiltrate the compound without me. If you try to force your way in, the driveway is so long, their armed guards would be waiting for you and in position before you even reach the main house. The building that contains Alana is even further back."

"Can't we get around it?" I pressed. It wasn't my expertise, but I knew my husband was well versed in covert extraction. Sending them to the wolves with their weapons not easily within reach set my nerves on edge.

Bristow and Stepanov shook their heads at the same time, but it was the SEAL who answered, "It'll be challenging and risky since the property backs up against Mount Charleston's highest peak. And from what we're gathering, the perimeter is an old-fashioned steel trap. Security can't be hacked."

"How about your friends whose faces we're using for these masks?" I asked. "Are they onboard with the plan? Do they know Ford too? Won't that be a problem?"

"Good question," Stepanov said, smiling at me and then at Levi. "But they won't be an issue."

Levi crossed his arms. "Care to enlighten us?"

Stepanov shrugged. "For one thing, two of them are buried under the desert on Route 15."

"Christ," Kelso said. "Should I be hearing this? You do remember I'm a cop, right?"

The poor detective was getting more corrupt by the second.

Bristow smirked. "Out of curiosity, what happened to the third guy?"

"He's in my basement. He won't be a problem either."

"Interesting. You left him alive." Bristow seemed fascinated by the Russian.

"Of course. He's my friend. I like him."

Bristow barked a laugh. "Sucks to be your friend."

Stepanov merely smiled in a way that reminded me of a hyena.

Levi was glaring at Stepanov. "As the leader of a secret society, you sure have a big mouth."

"Your confidence in this plan is important to me. Granted there are flaws, but if we pull this off, it would solve all our problems, don't you think?" He stared at the lone law enforcement official in the warehouse. "And since he's here, involved in our plans, I'm confident his badge is a little tarnished."

"Helping a friend," Kelso grumbled and muttered about not keeping them in basements.

I reached out to touch the detective's hand. "Thank you for this."

"You guys have become family," Kelso said gruffly. "And it seems I'd do anything for family."

Tom joined the conversation. "I hate to intrude, but don't you think we need to do a supply run now? I'm foreseeing a long forty-eight hours, and we need to get started."

"Yes." It was seven. Even if the mask emporium was open twenty-four hours, I wanted to begin at dawn. I knew how to pace myself and I could function better with a full night's sleep. I started a list on my new phone. "It'd be faster if I do the shopping for the special effects things than hand this over to one of you."

"I'm not letting you out of my sight," Levi said.

"And you're not," I retorted. "You can be my cart man as usual. We get started on casting tomorrow morning at five."

I looked at Tom, Callum, and Bristow. "You guys up for it?"

All three men nodded.

It felt like the biggest job of my SFX career.

30

LEVI

"I'M NOT sure I can sit still for that."

I'd never seen Bristow so pale or ready to pass out after Kelly finished the lifecast on Roth. That was also the one and only single time I was thrilled my wife had her hands on the other guy instead of me. As she poured and slathered that goop on his face, McG assisted his sister by clearing Roth's nostrils so he could breathe. After a few false starts, I wasn't surprised Callum took to it like a pro given how they had bonded over it when they were younger.

"He's doing fine," I informed my friend.

"Easy for you to say," Bristow shot back. "You don't have to sit for that shit. That's like mud boarding."

"It's not like mud boarding," Callum retorted. "We make sure the airways are clear. Are you saying Roth is tougher than you?"

"He's terrified. That's why he's turned into a statue."

Roth, for his part, didn't help much when he gave Bristow the thumbs up.

"See?"

"Stop complaining," I said. It would have been a hilarious conversation if I wasn't on edge about Kelly being part of the mission. Even if I knew she would be safe with Dmitry and Kelso in the command van, I preferred she was nowhere near the compound when everything went down.

My phone buzzed and I was relieved to see Garrison's name. I tried calling him a few hours earlier to see if he had any updates that would compromise the op, but he hadn't responded until now.

"I need to take this."

Bristow gave me a chin lift meaning he would make sure the rest of the guys didn't follow when I took the call. Stepanov and Dmitry sent me interested looks.

Walking briskly toward the exit, I answered in a low voice. "G?"

"You good?"

That was Garrison. Short and to the point. Are we safe? Is everything on track? Is it safe to talk?

"Yeah."

"You asked if there was any chatter of a double-cross since Bristow couldn't find anything. Nadia dug deeper. And yes, my wife insisted, and don't be counting further for her help because I think she's close to popping—"

That was when I detected strain in his voice. "Jesus … is she okay?"

"She's fine or she insists she is—"

"I'm sor—"

"Don't fucking apologize," Garrison grated. "You think I'd let her do this if I thought she couldn't handle it?"

"I see you're learning to compromise." I chuckled despite myself.

"Yeah, I see you with Kelly. You're in a more difficult spot than I am right now."

"Okay, we can table this discussion of being married to

women who wrap us around their fingers later. What did Nadia find?"

"There is concern in one of the assassin's chatrooms about Stepanov's capability of managing Murder Sanctum. There's also chatter of Blaze Ulrich kissing Moscow's ass, so they'll back his claim to dethrone Stepanov."

"Sheesh," I said. "You make it sound like a kingdom."

"It is the underworld kingdom." Garrison gave a low laugh, but his tone turned serious. "I'm trying to get Porter to sign off on making you part of a federal task force looking into this."

"Shit, G. If this blows up without that safety net, Kelso is going to get canned for sure."

"Probably."

"Gabby is going to kill us. Wait, she knows about this too."

Double shit.

"She'll probably get suspended."

I laughed darkly. "You're saying this as if it's a slap on the wrist. Another suspension might very well cause her the badge."

"Look. Quit fretting. It's not the first time they've gone rogue with us. One could say, they're even thrilled doing this. Makes me wonder why they're in law enforcement when they have a tendency not to uphold the law. The Feds are onto the Moscow mob, but they don't want to move in because they haven't identified the kingpin."

This didn't sit well with me. "You know we have a bunch of kidnapped young women and men in that compound."

"I'm aware.

"In short, you have nothing new for me. Just watch our backs since we have chatter."

"Grumblings."

"Okay. Thanks."

"If the missus doesn't pop the kid tomorrow, I'll check back with you guys. Tell Kelly hey, and that Nadia is jealous she couldn't be in on the action. I couldn't keep her from poking her nose around anyway."

"Thanks, G."

I ended the call and returned inside.

Kelly was about done with Tom, who stood up to let Callum take his place. Bristow was going to clear the nasal airway for Kelly's brother.

"Sure you're up to it?" I asked Bristow. "Because I've watched Kelly enough to do this and help."

"Might be a good idea," Callum muttered.

"Hey, I got this," Bristow grinned at me. "This looks like fun. Besides you can thank me for contributing to the harmony of your marital bliss. If I'm the one who messes up, Kelly won't be yelling at you."

My wife's laugh tinkled from the corner where she was making the mixture she used for the cast.

Callum was not amused. "Might I remind you I'm assisting Kelly when she slathers that mud on your face?"

Bristow paled a little, or maybe the contrast was more stark with his red hair.

"Fuck, you're right."

"So do a good job or hand it over to Levi." Callum glared at me. "Though I'm not sure I trust you either."

Kelly bumped me out of the way. "Move over, big guy. Bristow's doing it."

"Hey, I'm hurt, babe. You don't trust me?"

She angled her eyes mischievously at me. "Bristow's got bigger stakes not to mess things up."

"You have a point there, Ki." Callum laughed, although a bit nervously.

I was thankful as fuck I was not getting under all that mud.

KELLY

.   .   .

"You're quiet."

"What did I tell you?" I shushed Callum. "Don't interrupt while I'm applying the prosthetic."

"You're just about to … so I can speak," he mumbled from the corner of his mouth. With the time we'd spent mimicking our favorite characters in the past, I couldn't bullshit Cal with the process. We'd binge watched enough "the-making-of" videos in our teens and when my brother returned home during his downtime as a SEAL, it became our bonding moment.

I sighed and held the appliance away. "I'm just a mass of nerves."

"It'll be fine," he said. "You're just tired and wired. How much coffee did you consume?"

"A lot."

I'd been going at it non-stop for thirty-six hours, sneaking in catnaps in between working and re-working the prosthetic to make sure it attached flawlessly to their faces and passed facial recognition.

The prosthetics I worked with were encapsulated in a type of skin adhesive that allowed for precise placement. Make-up gave the finishing touches. Both cosmetic and prosthetic should hold up to all rough conditions, but I hope to hell they didn't get into a fist fight.

I worked in stages on all three men. Callum's disguise would be finished first.

"I'm worried about Alana," I said.

"She's alive. James assured us, right?"

Levi and Bristow disappeared the day before, leaving Kelso and Callum to guard me. Stepanov had left after the first night and was returning at go time. The Russian didn't make inquiries about Alana in his communications with Ford so as not to tip off the businessman.

"Now I'm shutting my mouth until you're done." Cal glanced over to where Bristow was chatting with Levi while Tom was in a corner staring broodily at us.

Tom and I never had the chance to talk. I had yet to let him know that Levi and I were back together, but it was obvious.

"Good idea."

"We're going to have words about that too," Callum said, knowing where my thoughts had gone.

"How about we're not? Now, quiet."

Callum's mouth flattened, but it was twitching. He was laughing at my bossiness.

It took almost an hour before I was satisfied with the application on my brother's face. I had plenty of time to work on Tom and Bristow who were already half-fitted with their appliances. After surveying the result of my brother's disguise, I was extremely pleased it looked natural. Unlike a full-on-mask, selective prosthetic application allowed natural movement of facial muscles. For the final foundation and skin tone application, I turned Callum away from the mirror. The guys started gathering around us.

"Shit, that looks freaky," Bristow said.

Callum gave him the bird while Levi nudged Bristow none too gently on the shoulder.

"In a good way," Bristow deadpanned.

I laughed lightly. I really loved Levi's buddy. He never failed to bring levity in the midst of tense situations, unlike my husband who'd been a ball of tension since we walked into the warehouse the other day. It was a good thing Dmitry and Stepanov stayed elsewhere, otherwise, Levi wouldn't have been cool with us staying here.

"What do you think?" I spun my brother's chair so he faced the mirror.

"Damn Ki, it's—" Callum stared at his new face and then,

spinning back around, he grinned at the rest of the guys. "My sister is kick ass."

Tom winked at me. "Damn, Kelly, I can't wait for you to get your hands on me.

A frigid blast came from the direction of my husband. I pointed a finger at Tom who clearly wanted to get his digs into Levi. "Behave. Otherwise, I'll make you look like that monster from *Hodgetown*."

Levi walked to my side and slung a possessive arm around me, and planted an even more possessive not-so-light kiss on my lips. "Great job, babe."

I stared up at him. His eyes held pride that calmed my nerves. God, I needed to be permanently attached to him. "Pity, I couldn't work you over."

He grinned devilishly. "You can work me over after this op."

The men gave a collective groan.

"Save that flirting for later," Callum muttered.

"I'll help you with the beard disguise," I told Levi.

"He doesn't need help with that," Bristow said. "That's basic super agent 101."

"I can make you a shade darker," I said, determined to have a hand in my husband's disguise.

"Okay, this is an op, not a fantasy op," my brother interjected.

I ignored Callum's grumblings. "Are you sure the facial hair and fat suit will be enough?"

"It is," Levi assured me. "I'm staying in the truck anyway and will be wearing a cap."

"Here's an idea," Tom said. "I know for certain these guys never want to hire or work with Mexicans. Why not wear a straw hat?"

"Yes." I chewed my bottom lip. "But not the wide brimmed ones for farming. Maybe the ones the day workers wear coming in from Tijuana."

"That's even better," Tom said. "Then you just have to wear a wife beater and a checkered polo."

"That thought did cross my mind," Levi said. And for a second, I thought he didn't like that Tom came up with the brilliant idea, but there was no enmity emanating from either man.

Levi turned to me. "I have the checkered shirt and I'm sure we could find the hat in one of the convenience stores on the way to Mt. Charleston."

"Sounds like a plan. I can deepen your tan with the foundation I have."

He grinned wide. "You're the expert."

I checked my watch. "Okay, who's next?"

Tom raised his hand. "Me."

As Callum got out of the chair, I told him, "Give it another twenty minutes to set."

"Wait a sec," Bristow said, holding up his phone towards Callum's face, using the app that Stepanov used yesterday to do a quick scan.

Two beeps came from his phone. Then he showed us the screen identifying Callum as Aleksey Minkov.

"Better get used to the name," Levi said.

"Not my first rodeo, bro."

"Do you speak Russian now?" I teased my brother.

He rattled off a sentence that sounded Russian. "Five years. Language is my strong suit." And then he rattled off more sentences that might had been Mandarin and Arabic. I knew he spoke Spanish.

My awe was quickly replaced by sibling fondness. "Show-off."

31

LEVI

"COMPOUND IS TWO MILES OUT," Bristow spoke through comms.

The freight truck I was driving followed a black Expedition. Tom drove that vehicle while Bristow rode shotgun with Stepanov and McG in the second passenger row. Behind their vehicle, an RV outfitted as a command center trailed from a distance of a quarter mile. While Kelly was busy making disguises, Dmitry had been getting the RV set up with all its high-tech bells and whistles. From what Callum told me, even Stepanov wasn't privy to the equipment inside.

"Take care of my WASP." A voice came over comms.

"Nadia?" I said with a smile in my voice. The WASP was her favorite drone. A tiny insect device made with reflective surfaces so it was invisible to the naked eye. "How are you doing, lady?"

"I'm so ready for this girl to come out," she groaned. "I've driven Garrison bonkers enough that he allowed me to monitor you guys."

"I don't know how you did it with two girls," Garrison grumbled.

A pang twisted in my chest. Thank fuck I didn't miss their births. That was before that Aden mission. Sometimes one was so blinded by guilt and grief they became selfish about how they affected people around them. Breaking my vow to cherish and protect my wife was unacceptable. My hands gripped the steering wheel.

"I just showed up for the birth," I forced out a laugh when I realized there was dead air. I'd been excited for each pregnancy, and the longest time I'd ever stayed away was six weeks. As a Tier 1 SEAL, I did mostly shorter-duration direct-action missions rather than the typical six-month deployments.

"He was great," Kelly said. "How are the prosthetics holding up?"

All three men she addressed responded positively.

I detected gruffness in her voice. She must have felt the rush of regrets in the same way I had when Garrison made his comment. Thankfully, the subject changed and refocused our attention back on our mission.

"Compound's coming up on the right," Bristow said. "Kelso, Dmitry … you guys doing okay?"

"I'm glad Nadia is monitoring," Kelso quipped.

I was about to bite his head off when Dmitry deadpanned. "This is like child's play."

"Heat signatures are still holding up on the structure near the cliff," Bristow said. "We'll know for certain if Alana is still with the group once we deploy the drone."

The day before, he and I staked out the compound and sent the WASP for reconnaissance. Callum knew what we were doing, but we left Dmitry out of it. The Gray Wolf was pissed, but he didn't tell us about the RV either. We grudgingly accepted that what we did prior to the day's mission was on a need to know, but until this day ended, we were on the same team and we promised to share every fucking piece of intel.

So far, we'd established there was no tail or any signal that showed we were being tracked.

Still, I was paranoid. Bristow and I scanned our vehicles and each piece of equipment we brought with us for every known tracking device known to man.

All clean.

"Go or no-go?" Kelso asked. "You're two minutes to target."

"Go," I responded immediately. We had a weird situation going on here. No one was emerging as the clear leader of the op. I expected Dmitry or Callum to make the call, but Kelso was the one who had his career on the line.

But nothing was more important than getting Alana back.

"Go," Callum answered.

Without hesitation, the rest acknowledged with similar answers.

"We're breaking off. Good luck," Kelso said as their vehicle pulled off the road into a parking lot for campsites in the area. With other RVs in the vicinity, they wouldn't look out of place.

Two minutes later, our vehicles arrived at the entrance of Greystoke Ranch. A tall iron gate with twenty-foot walls surrounded what used to be a resort ranch for the rich and famous. Horse stables, bunkhouses, and a guest house surrounded the grand Spanish-style villa. A quarter-mile driveway led to the main house.

A guard emerged from the pedestrian gate and headed straight for the middle passenger row. Stepanov lowered the window.

The security guy held up a device to Stepanov's face, before doing the same to Tom, Callum and Bristow.

I held my breath.

He turned to me.

Fuck.

He approached the semi. "The registry only specified four people. Who are you?"

"I'm the driver," I told the man in Spanish.

Stepanov leisurely stepped down from the Expedition. "He's with me."

The guard sneered. "I guess it's useless to run a facial scan on him. He's an illegal."

"Look, he's the best I could do on short notice."

"Can't one of you guys drive the truck?"

"We're wasting time here." Stepanov shook out a sleeve from his suit to fix the cuff. "Check with your boss. Otherwise I'm turning around."

The man returned to the guardhouse.

"What's happening?" Dmitry asked.

"Problem with James," Callum said.

Silence reigned for a few seconds and then Tom said, "It'll be fine. I've dealt with assholes like this. Like I said, these men despise anyone south of the border and across the Pacific Ocean, and not all of it has to do with being racist. The cartels have become so powerful and vicious, they're making the Russians look like Disney princesses. And Ford has a hatred for the Chinese, so … "

I snorted, "Just as well. Good thinking with the cover."

The gates opened, and the same guard gestured for the vehicles to pull aside to the corner. "Okay, here we go. Second inspection." Hopefully, they'd be too lazy to check under cushions for weapons."

"Over there." One of the ranch security guards instructed me. Another one joined him.

"Get down from there," First Guard said.

I didn't move.

"Are you deaf or plain stupid?" He turned to his partner. "Damned wetbacks. You'd think if they sneak into this country, they'd learn to speak English."

"Do you want me to shoot you, you stupid fuck?"

I raised my hands and ducked my head. "*No hablo Ingles.*"

"Juanito," Callum called and told me to get out of the vehicle in Spanish.

As I stepped down, First Guard shoved me to the side, and I pretended to stumble and crash to my knees. It wasn't that difficult to pretend with the weight of the fat suit I carried around my torso.

"Jesus, man did you shower at all?" Second Guard put a hand to his nose. The weather in Mt. Charleston was twenty degrees cooler than Vegas. Still, the fat suit was a killer. It didn't take much to burn up in it. I had the AC blasting in the truck, and the suit still carried residual coolness from it.

"Want to search him for weapons?" First Guard asked his companion.

Second Guard grumbled but did as he was told. The suit had a skin-like texture, and I sprayed enough water on myself to make it look like I was sweating through my shirt.

Stupid fuck couldn't even bring himself to touch me. He lifted my shirt with the barrel of his rifle and since the pants were so tight, almost giving me a wedgie, all he did was feel me through my pants.

"He's clear," the man grumbled. "Let's check the truck." It was a case where idiots failed at their jobs because of prejudice. I'd carved out two sections in my suit so I could keep two semi-automatics inside.

"Damn, you're lucky," Dmitry commented.

The guards were more thorough with the vehicle. I had another weapon hidden in a fake compartment built into the console, decorating the surface with loose candy wrappers, a half-eaten sandwich, and finishing my sloth with spilled orange soda.

"Man, this guy is a filthy pig too," First Guard muttered. He turned to Callum. "The truck needs to go to a service entrance. Mr. Ford has important guests. We don't want your driver polluting the air."

Soon, our vehicles were allowed through to the villa. The long driveway was lined with bristlecone pines. Midway to the main house, Bristow said, "Deploying the drone."

"Go ahead," Kelso replied.

After a few minutes, he said, "Relinquishing control. Got it?"

"Affirmative. In control," the detective replied.

Soon, we approached a roundabout where a voluptuous Romanesque statue of a woman carrying an urn stood in its center, pouring water into a fountain. A guard with a long gun strapped to his shoulder directed me to the left while the SUV swerved to the right where a row of luxury cars parked.

My truck ambled around the main residence, straight for the utilitarian facilities in the back, including the guest house where Alana and the other captives were being held.

"WASP is on top of you," Kelso said.

"How are the heat signatures?"

"Same. Clusters in rooms, but the corner room is showing a single occupant."

Bristow reported that they had arrived at the front entrance, and Ford himself had appeared with one of his identified Oligarch partners.

I parked the truck at the back of the house.

A black-clad man exited the rear and approached my vehicle. A gold chain hung around his neck while his handlebar mustache and Stetson were at odds with his mob henchman attire. He walked over to my side and made a sign to roll down the windows.

He spoke in Spanish.

"He's saying 'stay here'," Kelso coached me.

"Sí."

"I'll have someone check the products after everything is clear with the boss."

Kelso translated, but thankfully I understood the gist of it and said, "Sí."

The man waved back at the guard standing in front of our target building and returned to the villa.

"You'd think they wouldn't be so nonchalant about twenty million in product," Kelso commented before continuing, "Moving WASP to the rear room now. Bristow, McG, you guys okay?"

Both men inside the villa cleared their throats once which meant all was still cool.

"Anyone have visibility on them?"

"I just managed to tap into one of the villa cameras," Nadia piped in. "Sorry it took a while. They've got their security locked down. I'm working on another feed including an outdoor one."

"Not tight enough for you apparently. Send it to me, nerd girl," Kelso said. "Holy shit is that …"

"What?" I growled.

"What the hell is he doing here?" the detective growled. "Luca Moretti."

"This is going to be fun," Bristow muttered.

There was a chatter of pleasantries exchanged but tension zapped across our comms channel.

"You didn't think I'd send you guys in there without backup, right?" Garrison said dryly.

Dmitry chuckled. "I wouldn't have agreed otherwise. I've grown quite fond of McGrath."

"Who else knew?" I asked.

"Only Dmitry and I," Garrison said. "The surprise on their faces had to be authentic."

So much for no secrets between us, but Garrison in the know made it go down better.

"And we're sure Moretti is on our side?" Kelso asked. "How did he manage an invite to the table?"

"He has the cash to float the product. The Moscow cadre gets more than double their profit. They get sixty from Stepanov, forty from Chicago."

"And the Russians trust Moretti?"

"Of course not," Dmitry said. "But money talks."

"Kelso do you have eyes on Alana?" I growled because I was getting a bad feeling about this. I wasn't sure I trusted Kelly's stepbrother and I wished I'd done more research into him other than knowing he shot a guy at dinner because he was annoying.

"Almost there," Kelso replied.

"Hurry."

"Cool it, James. Nadia is better at this," the detective said, a trace of annoyance entering his voice.

"Well, have her do it. I have no idea why you guys invited Moretti to the party. That man is a trigger-happy motherfucker."

"Which is exactly what we needed," Dmitry replied.

"That's my brother in there," Kelly's cracked voice reached out to me. "Does Luca know it's Callum?"

"No," Dmitry said. "The fewer people knowing all the pieces, the better this is going to unfold."

"I'm not leaving things to chance," I said. "Kelso!"

"Confirmed. Alana McGrath is in the last room of the structure. She seems out of it. Has something around her ankle. The room is bare except for a bed. Nadia is checking it out now."

"Might be a proximity sensor." I shoved at the door and stepped down from the truck, making a production of hunching over and clutching my stomach.

"Should've eaten more beans, man," Kelso said.

"Shut up." Despite the high-tension situation, a round of laughter burst over comms. Otherwise, it was a string of muffled chatter.

"Where are they?" I staggered toward the guest house, still looking at the ground.

"They've moved to an inner room. Looks like good-natured negotiations," Kelso said.

Before someone raised hell.

"We're running facial recognition on everyone in that house, and, man, we're hitting the motherlode of gangsters."

"Stop!" The man guarding the house where Alana was kept shouted. He didn't move to unsling the rifle from his shoulder which meant he didn't see me as a threat.

"Baño," I muttered.

"Can you piss behind a tree?"

I looked up and did my best impression of needing to shit and clutched my stomach.

"Shit, that's ... shit."

Everyone laughed over comms including Bristow and Callum.

Dmitry shushed them.

"Shit ... sí," I nodded vigorously.

"Dammit. Go over there and poop near the trees, sí?"

"*No hablo Ingles.*"

"Dammit. Come on." He gestured for me to follow him.

When we were along the side of the house and out of sight of the main house, I groaned and doubled-over.

"What the hell, man, did you eat some bad burrito or something?"

I jackknifed up and caught him in the chin with my elbow and said, "Sorry, man." before cracking his head on my knee. He was out cold. I dragged him around the corner of the house.

"Alarms are disabled," Dmitry said.

I removed my belly suit, and my guns fell to the ground. There was also a knife and a couple of zip ties. I used those to secure the guard. I also put a gag around his mouth.

"I'm not liking this," Dmitry added. "This looks too easy. Why only one guard?"

"You're worrying about that now?" I asked. "I'm getting Alana."

"Be careful," Kelly whispered.

"How you holding up beautiful?" I hated that she had to listen to everything but with *everything* she'd done, she was *very much* a part of this team.

"I'm good. Don't worry about me, big guy. Just come back with my sister, and if it's not too much trouble, Callum, too."

A couple of snorts came over comms, but I was proud as fuck my woman was solid under pressure. In a few sentences, she was reminding her brother to be careful and not have a repeat of last time. I'd probably be losing my mind right now if she were the one in danger.

Free of the fat suit, I strapped my guns to a thigh holster, secured the magazines around my belt, and grabbed the guard's long gun. I also took his keys and walkie-talkie.

I snapped an image of the man and sent it to the command RV to process. I needed a name in case the compound's security checked in with him. Slipping beside the backdoor, I tested the handle. The light on the status box was green, and the lever gave in easily.

Raised voices came over comms.

"What's going on?"

"Luca is causing a scene," Kelso told me. "Get Alana out now. We're heading toward you."

"Things are not secure yet," I growled. I did not want my wife in the middle of this shit.

"It's going to happen quickly," Dmitry said. "Luca jumped the gun."

Motherfucking wildcard. I quickly lowered the door handle and peeked in. I was in some sort of utility room. "I'm in."

Sidling around the walls of the room, I poked my head out its door. "Hall is clear."

"I see your thermal," Kelso said. "I'm on you, and Dmitry is on the villa. It's getting chaotic."

I edged toward the room where Alana was located and

opened the door. A woman was hunched against the corner of the bed glaring at me.

"Alana?"

"You fuckers drugged me."

"No visible signs of injury. Confirming manacle around the ankle."

"You come any closer, and I'll castrate you."

"Your sister just threatened my balls, Kelly."

"Who the hell are …" she squinted her eyes. "Levi?"

"Is there an alarm attached to that leg of yours?" I asked, stalking into the room and kneeling to inspect the ankle bracelet.

"Proximity sensor. As long as I stay near the property, it's okay."

Kelso informed me they had not disabled it yet.

"Sitrep at the house?" I asked.

Before anyone could answer, a hail of gunfire erupted outside.

"Holy shit!" Kelso exclaimed. "They just opened fire on each other."

"Get the girls and boys out first," Alana told me. "They don't have any ankle bracelets."

A barrage of artillery erupted over comms like the shooting was right beside me.

"Did you get my sister yet?" Callum yelled. "Damned Moretti drew first blood and shot one of the Russians. It's a madhouse in here."

"Ford?"

"He's down. I'm trapped in a corner with some idiot mobster firing blindly. He'll be out of bullets soon. Alana?"

"She's locked down with an ankle bracelet. Doesn't look incendiary, but the guys are checking." I got up and walked to the hallway, unlocking a room. Two girls who couldn't be more than fifteen cowered behind the bed. Bile rose up in my throat. "We're getting you out of here. You'll be safe soon."

"But there's shooting."

"Don't run outside yet," I told them calmly. "Wait until we give the signal, okay?"

"Why should we trust you?"

"Good question," I muttered. "Wait here."

Ignoring the mayhem in my ear, I opened the next room and it was a young boy of indeterminate age between twelve and sixteen, lanky, with feminine features.

Those sons of bitches. Hell was too good for Ford and his cronies.

"Help is on the way, son." With each room that I opened, my rage escalated. After unlocking the last room, I told Kelso. "We need child protective services on site. We cannot keep this under the radar. I don't care what the fuck you say, Dmitry."

"We're a minute out," Kelso said. "We'll be coming in hot. How's the gate?"

"I don't think you can ram through in one shot."

"I have grenade launcher," Dmitry said.

"Jesus Christ." But even as I said it, I couldn't help but wonder if these were the types of ops I could work in. No rules. Be on the right side of the underworld. There was bad … and there was evil.

The last room was adjacent to the main hallway, and when I turned the corner to head back toward Alana's room, my blood turned to ice.

A man was hauling a struggling Alana out of the room.

Blaze.

My wife's abductor and assailant.

When he saw me, Blaze pointed his gun to Alana's head at the same time I raised my rifle. My mouth curled into a snarl and I stalked toward him. "Let her go. This is between you and me, Blaze."

He smiled derisively. "I'm impressed that you know who I am."

"Blaze Ulrich, real name Hans. Your face is imprinted in my mind."

At Alana's confused expression, I said, "He's the man who kidnapped Kelly and beat her up."

Alana's eyes flashed, and renewed her struggling.

"Is Blaze in there?" Kelso asked. "I didn't see him in the main house."

I cleared my throat.

"Proximity sensor has been disabled," the detective told me.

I cleared my throat again.

"There's going to be a diversion," Dimtry said. "Be ready."

"I'm lowering my weapons," I told Blaze, laying the rifle to the floor. "How about we settle this man to man and you let Alana go."

"How about I get first shot at this asshole?" Alana snarled. Her fingers dug into the arm across her chest.

"Feisty, these McGraths," Blaze said. "I think I'm keeping this one."

"How about it?" I said. "Can you take me in a fight?"

"I'm not stupid," the assassin said. "You have fifty pounds on me."

"Three, two," Dmitry counted down.

My hand went to my Glock.

Blaze's eyes narrowed at my movement and pointed his gun at me. My eyes went to Alana, her eyes communicated she was ready for anything.

"One."

32

Dmitry walked to within twenty feet of the gate and shouldered the RPG. The guards began fumbling with their weapons.

"He's crazy!" I told Kelso, who agreed, but at this point, Levi and Alana needed this. Hell, even Callum. My chest constricted. My family was in there, shooting their way out. I could only hope that Dmitry's wild west action was the diversion they needed.

"Down!" Kelso yelled just as Dmitry fired the RPG.

The blast rocked the RV, and a bright light cast an orange glow around us. Dmitry calmly stepped back into the RV, but he didn't come in, instead he lowered the weapon and picked up an uzi. Kelso straightened in his seat and shot the vehicle forward while I was still trying to find my bearings. Dmitry braced at the RV entrance and prepared to fire as the vehicle bounced on the driveway at top speed.

This was like the movies.

Then my mind backtracked. This was exactly like the movies.

"Keep down," Dmitry ordered.

I obeyed without argument.

As the RV sped through the gates, bullets pelted our vehicle.

It was only after we were a few seconds past the gate that Kelso gave the all clear. "But I want you to stay down," the detective added. "Levi, you there?"

The pit that had taken root in my gut had pushed up against my throat. We hadn't heard from Levi since Dmitry destroyed the gates. I tried to quell the rising panic threatening to take over.

He'd been in a standoff against Blaze who had Alana under duress.

They'll be fine. They'll be fine.

Levi had been in worse situations than this and I knew my sister enough to know she wasn't going to be a helpless damsel. They would get through this.

My breathing hitched.

They had to.

At that moment, I clung to Dmitry's show of force to maintain my sanity. The man was as good at playing politics and giving orders as he was in executing an assault.

Every single man on the team was a deadly weapon.

The RV approached a rotunda, and beyond it, a Tarantino-like gunfight was in full chaotic glory. Fireworks jockeyed from one corner to another.

Kelso swerved to the left.

"Are you there, man?" the detective repeated.

My breaths turned shallow.

Pick up, Levi. Pick up. My jaw was aching from clenching too hard, and my fingers were frozen icicles.

"Should we go check on him?" I was looking at Dmitry.

The Gray Wolf shouted something in Ukrainian and started firing.

Seconds later, the shooting abated, and my brother jogged up to the RV. "Thanks for the assist," he told Dmitry. "Where's Levi?"

"Ulrich has Alana," Kelso said.

"Dammit," Callum sprinted off before I could say anything.

Bile burned a line down my throat, and I must have whimpered because Kelso glanced at me with sympathy in his eyes.

Two of the most important people in my life were in that house. And the one I just got back ran off to join them. The cramping in my stomach intensified and with my chest weighing so heavily, I didn't know whether I was about to throw up, pass out, or have a heart attack.

"If there's anything I know about Levi James, he's the toughest son of a bitch on the planet," Kelso told me. "He's fine. He's got rage on his side."

"That might make him careless."

"Job for you." The detective brushed away my fears. "Clear some room in the RV. Seems like we have a dozen passengers to load."

My eyes strayed back to the guest house, willing my husband to appear, but the door remained shut.

Levi

I surged toward Blaze the second Alana stomped on his foot and managed to break free.

He fired.

Burning singed my shoulder, but momentum carried me forward sending my shoulder straight into his torso. We both fell to the floor. Images of Kelly's bruised face throbbed through my mind, and my fist connected with his jaw again and again. He bucked his hip, but my weight crushed him.

"What about now, eh?" I spat. "How does that fucking feel?"

"Fucking spectacular," he gurgled with blood spilling from his mouth.

"Psycho."

"We're two of a kind."

"No, we're not. Hit me, damn you." I straddled him and leaned away, spreading my arms. We weren't physically matched, but I knew he wasn't helpless. I never underestimated a man's size. Blaze probably had a knife on his person, I was egging him on to use it to give me an excuse to kill him.

I yanked him up and slammed him against a wall.

"Where are you guys?" I spoke into comms.

No answer.

Shit. The receiver must have fallen out of my ear. No time to look for it. Blaze was smiling through his bloody mouth.

"What's so funny, motherfucker?"

"You're not getting out of here alive." He continued his hacking laughter.

I released him and glanced at Alana. "Check the front door and see if there's an RV parked there. Your sensor is disabled. You know Kelso, right?"

"Yes."

I kept Blaze in my periphery.

The backdoor slammed open, and I immediately pointed my Glock at the new arrival.

"Alana," Callum whispered.

"Is this one of yours?" Alana asked warily.

"Yes."

Callum couldn't stop staring at his sister. Now was not the time for an emotional reunion, but Kelly's brother was distracted.

The front door opened again, and Bristow appeared.

I waved him down. "Get them out. Help him, Alana."

She split a look between me and her brother. I clapped Callum's shoulder to wake him up from his trance.

When Bristow approached us, Alana said, "Do I know you?"

Blaze laughed mockingly. "That's because—"

I punched him across the jaw, hoping like hell this time it shattered.

"Fuck!" Blaze mumbled and sank to his ass.

"What's the matter now, motherfucker? Can't take it?"

"You're the ass picking on someone half your size."

"It sure didn't bother you when you hurt my wife. "

Blaze continued laughing like he wasn't in deep shit, or he was laughing like a maniac because he realized he *was* in deep fucking shit.

Alana finally gathered the young captives together, but dawdled back.

"Outside. Now," I told her.

"What are you going to do with him, I want to take a shot," Alana said.

"Jesus," Bristow muttered and shot me a shit-eating grin.

"Alana. Go! Bristow. With her."

"All right, all right," she said and finally followed the kids outside.

"What are we going to do with him?" Callum repeated his sister's question.

"This is less satisfying than I thought," I told Blaze. "Why didn't you put up a fight, you fucker?"

"Because you're going to beat the fuck out of me anyway."

"Let's take this asshole outside," Callum said.

"Wait," Blaze croaked, staggering to his feet. "Let me have a smoke before you lock me up." He reached into his pocket.

Callum and I raised our guns. "Keep your hands where we can—"

He slipped out a pack of cigarettes, but his bloody smile gave me chills.

He's the ordnance expert of Murder Sanctum. He likes to blow up shit.

Fucking hell. Without another thought, I shoved Callum into Alana's room, followed him, and shut the door, leaving Blaze in the hallway. There was no second guessing where the explosives were planted. The blast was simultaneous with the slamming of the door.

It blew the door back open and threw me into the air.

Intense heat wrapped around me, and the building collapsed.

33

KELLY

GUNFIRE ABATED, and the world became quiet.

The team and Luca's men were securing the area when the door to the guest house opened and people walked through.

Children. Boys and girls. My stomach churned. None of them could have been more than fifteen. I got down from the RV so I could help them get situated, my eyes searching for Alana.

She emerged with the sixth child. I started for her. "Alana!"

"Kelly," Kelso growled behind me.

A boom, a flash of light, and an invisible force threw me to the ground.

The roar of an explosion echoed around me, before muffled screams reached my ears. Dazed, I tried to make sense of what happened. Heat singed my skin. The house before me was a wash of orange. Bright and blinding.

"Jesus Christ!"

"Is everyone all right?"

I pushed up on my elbows, spat out dirt, and blurry images came into focus.

Greedy flames licked wood and turned it into falling embers.

"No," I whispered, my mind refusing to accept what I was seeing behind them. "No."

I struggled to my feet, my vision tunneling, and my ears plugged. Still unsteady, I staggered to the burning structure. "Levi!" Oh my god, Callum!

A steel band wrapped around my torso. "Don't." Kelso rasped in my ear. "There could be secondary blasts."

"Let me go!" I screamed.

"Think of Ash and Whit," he growled. "Get it together and help these kids. Let us do our jobs."

The crushing feeling in my chest overwhelmed me, and I sank to my knees and sobbed with the realization I couldn't be a burden to these men right now. I stared up at Kelso. "Go."

An argument called my attention.

"What the hell is this?" Alana shouted at Bristow.

His disguise had ripped.

Shit. I forced myself to get up again, fighting through my shock, and made my way to them, comforting the kids who were crying even while my heart was cracking in two.

"You okay?" A voice said behind me.

I turned to see Luca.

My mouth couldn't form words.

"Levi?" he asked.

I couldn't say anything and just looked at the decimated house.

"Kelly?" Alana shouted.

I ran the few steps toward my sister and hugged her. Over her shoulder, I saw Bristow and Kelso rush around the burning house.

"What are you doing here?" Alana asked. "Oh my God."
She looked behind her. "You shouldn't be here."

I still couldn't speak and, instead, sucked in a ragged
breath.

"They were in the back close to the exit," Alana said.
"Levi and the other guy should be fine."

It's our brother, Alana, but I couldn't say.

"I hope so."

"Your husband is a tank. It's a one-story structure. He'll be
fine." She had no idea how I clung to those optimistic words.

"Alana, can we stay here?" one of the rescued girls asked.
She seemed to be the oldest in the group. Dmitry had already
herded a few of the kids into the RV, but apparently more
than half of them didn't trust him.

Alana hugged her. "Sure, Ceci." When my sister's attention returned to me, a relieved expression transformed her
face. "See, what did I tell you?"

I spun in the direction of her gaze.

Four men appeared.

I ran toward them.

Bristow was helping a limping Callum while Kelso was
Levi's crutch.

"You're both okay," I cried, while my eyes did a full body
scan. Their faces were covered in soot, and their clothes were
ripped in places but they didn't appear to have sustained grave
injuries.

Levi broke away from the group and swept me into his
arms. His mouth covered mine and devoured me in a quick
fierce kiss.

He leaned away and reluctantly released me to my
brother.

"I thought I lost you again," I sobbed.

Callum embraced me tightly. "Not this time, sis."

"So, if that's not Tom ..." Alana said from behind me. I

stepped away from Callum, my lungs filling with apprehension as my siblings came face to face for the first time.

Like Bristow, my brother's prosthetics were toast. The forehead piece was gone, and the ones along his cheeks were out of place.

Bristow and Kelso hurried away from the group to help the rest of the guys secure the area. I wasn't sure if they wanted to give us a moment for our reunion or were just too chicken to be around the unpredictable outcome.

"Hi, Ally Cat," Callum rasped his nickname for Alana. He was the only one who called her that.

"What is this?" Alana's eyes filled with tears, and my own couldn't help flooding with emotions.

"It's Cal," I croaked.

Her face scrunched in disbelief. Three feet away from our brother, she glared at me. "This joke is in poor taste, Kelly."

I threw up my hands in frustration and glared at Cal. "What the hell are you waiting for?"

"Fuck this," Callum muttered and closed the distance between them and dragged Alana in a hug. "You were always a feisty one, Ally Cat."

Alana stood there without returning our brother's hug, arms outstretched as if she wasn't sure what to do with them, but his words and mine seemed to sink in.

Her arms finally wrapped around our brother, and she started bawling.

One thing about that sister of mine. She rarely bawled.

She was the toughest nut among us.

After a while, without looking at me, both of them stretched out their arms and gestured me toward them. I didn't hesitate and walked into their huddle, and my tears flowed. This time because of pure joy. My sister was safe. I had my brother back.

"Oh my God, oh my God." Alana cried.

A helicopter roared above us, and, for a second. Anxiety

swept through me along with not knowing if they were friends or enemies.

Callum set us from him, with each hand gripping our shoulders as he split a look between us. "That's my ride."

"What?" Both Alana and I exclaimed.

"You can't leave!" I said.

"Only for a while," Callum said. "There are things I need to wrap up. Don't tell anyone in the family." He glanced at our sister. "You weren't supposed to know I am alive yet." Then he looked at me. "I need to clean up my cover before I come home."

"Cal ..."

"Gotta go." He hugged both of us and then stepped into Levi to give him a tight hug and walked away without looking back.

Alana and I clung to each other, still in shock and reeling.

Levi

PORTER CAME THROUGH, thank fuck.

The helicopter airlifted Callum, Dmitry, Stepanov, and Roth from the site. Bristow, Kelso, and I stayed behind and were conscripted into the federal task force looking into the Russian Mafia and its numerous illegal businesses, specifically the flow of Moscow White into Chicago and California.

Blaze Ulrich was dead. His remains were found under the roof wreckage. He had the house rigged to blow in some kind of last stand rather than go to prison. Callum and I were lucky we were thrown into the corner where the door and part of the roof fell on the bed to create an air pocket. We belly-crawled out of there just as Bristow and Kelso dragged us clear of the burning structure.

Walter Ford was killed as were two of his oligarch friends. A Russian mafia boss and his oligarch cohort locked themselves in a panic room. Roth stood guard until Kelso took over from him. From what I had learned from Bristow, it was a bloodbath inside.

Moretti and his men came prepared. They left before the Feds arrived.

"You guys off?" Kelso asked from the bottom of the RV steps.

"As soon as Alana and Kelly are ready." I tipped my chin to where they were saying goodbye to the kids. Child Protective Services was called in. The dozen kids were ages twelve to fifteen. Death was too kind for Ford and the people behind the despicable trade. The Feds weren't too happy that they didn't get the kingpin they were after, but before we launched this operation, we'd all agreed that no life was worth collateral damage. And seeing the smiles on those children's faces, knowing they were going to be returned to their parents gave our mission more meaning. It made me think of Ash and Whit, and how their future would be better without men like Ford.

Kelly and Alana appeared beside Kelso.

"You're not coming back with us, detective?" my wife asked.

"Nope. Need to clean up the mess here." Kelso sighed.

"Sure you don't need me?" Bristow asked from behind me. He was packing up the equipment for Dmitry. We were surprised the Ukrainian left the technology for our safekeeping, but we had a feeling it wasn't the last time we'd see him.

"Nah, go on home," Kelso said, then he stilled. "Shit. Can one of you call Garrison and check on Nadia?"

APPARENTLY, before Dmitry fired the rocket launcher, Nadia had groaned in pain, and Garrison immediately cut their feed.

The excitement was probably too much for a woman on the verge of giving birth. Knowing G, it wasn't his idea, and he was probably gnashing his teeth at having his very pregnant wife under so much stress.

We were all married to stubborn women. Must be the requirement to be with men like us.

Bristow took over driving since I almost got blown to pieces. My eyes tracked the sisters sitting despondently in the couch seats of the RV with their hands clasped and staring into space.

I made a quick call to Garrison, not expecting him to pick up, and left a voicemail that we were all good and heading back. I noticed a missed call from Declan. I didn't even bother checking his message and called him.

He picked up on the second ring.

"You guys good?" he said.

"A little battered."

"Yeah, my wife just got off the phone with Kelso. Jesus, man, you and McGrath were lucky to escape in one piece."

"Yeah." It was sheer luck I picked the right room to take cover.

"Garrison?"

"Nadia is in labor."

"You guys heading out there?"

"Soon." He gave me the hospital info and ended the call.

I tossed my phone on the dashboard.

Bristow shot me a brief glance. "Well?"

"G's about to become a dad."

"Straight to LA then?"

"Yeah. He could use moral support."

We both exchanged hearty chuckles, the type we hadn't shared since the attack on the McGraths. It was liberating as well as a promise of a future. Bristow cocked his head toward the women.

I sighed and got up. I didn't know what to tell Kelly and

Alana. Especially Alana. She had her brother for all of two minutes before he disappeared in a chopper.

I sat across from them and addressed Kelly. "Nadia's in labor."

A smile broke through the melancholy of her face. "Trust her to hang on until the last minute."

"Yeah, keeps a badass like Garrison on his toes." I nodded at Alana. "How are you holding up?"

"Physically, I'm fine," Alana said shortly.

"Maybe we should have a doctor—" Kelly started.

"I'm fine," she snapped. "I gave them so much hell the first day they left me alone. It's not the first time I had to deal with lowlifes. It was a walk in the park compared to the scum I have to deal with in New York." She was breathing heavily and I wondered if I should've just kept my mouth shut rather than have Alana go on another tear. "What I want to know is when I'll see Callum again." She directed the question at me.

"I have no say in that."

"What do you mean you have no say? You're CIA."

"Alana," Kelly said. "That doesn't mean he knows. I already told you. Information is compartmentalized to prevent leaks. Callum will come to us when he's ready, and he's counting on us to keep this a secret until he is."

Alana's eyes filled with tears, her cheeks flushed, and her nose flared. "And when is that? Another five years?"

"Isn't it enough to know he's alive?" Kelly said.

"Easy for you to say! You spent days with him."

I shouldn't interfere, but it pissed me off that Alana pushed this guilt on Kelly, but before I could say anything, Kelly whipped an admonishing stare in my direction as if she knew I was going to defend her. My mouth tightened. I understood where Alana was coming from because I was just as pissed when I found out Roth knew McG was alive first and I didn't.

"I'm sorry," Kelly told her sister. I had a feeling she'd been repeating that for a while.

"How can we face Nana and Gramps?" Alana's voice cracked. "And what about Mom and Dad? They're going to call the second they hear I'm back."

"Garrison's our best bet to know what's going on," I said. "But Nadia is his priority right now. We've already asked too much from him."

"Kelly told me how he helped you when they attacked the house," Alana said, then she let out another ragged exhale. "I'm not a good actress, but I'll keep it in as much as I can."

"Thanks, Alana." I got up before she could interrogate me some more.

IT WAS two a.m. when we hit LA. Declan called to tell us Nadia had delivered the baby. A unanimous decision was made in the RV that we wouldn't miss that moment when our intrepid leader's life changed forever. Alana was able to talk to her family, and we were able to hold off going back to the safe house for another few hours.

Giving Garrison a hard time and poking fun at his expense might snap us out of our funk.

I didn't blame Alana for feeling angsty and unsettled. I felt the same myself. It was undoubtedly worse for her. The exhilaration of finding Callum alive was cut short with an anxiety that he would disappear again. In between heaven and hell was always worse—this limbo.

McG better not take his sweet-ass time sorting this shit out.

I wouldn't be responsible for my wife or Alana spilling the beans to their family. The news was huge. Now that I thought about it, I was pissed at Callum that he put such a burden on his sisters.

When we arrived at the hospital, Declan and Gabby were in the waiting room talking to Migs and Ariana.

"So?" Our group strode up to them.

"Fiona, Stephen, and the rest of the MoMoS are with them now," Declan said. The Merry Old Men of SkyeLark apartments, as they were fondly called, consisted of Nadia's dad Stephen, and his friends, Clyde, Arthur, and Dugal.

"I just got off the phone with Kelso," Gabby said. "He's bummed he couldn't be here." She glanced at Alana who had hung back from our huddle. "Glad you're okay."

Alana forced a smile. "Me too."

"When can we see the baby?" Bristow asked.

"Not sure I'm sharing her with you motherfuckers." A voice said from the hallway.

Garrison appeared. It was disconcerting to see him in scrubs. His face was lined with exhaustion, but peace and contentment settled into those indentations too. And his eyes gleamed with unmistakable joy.

Ah, fatherhood.

"Start watching that language." I razzed him before pulling him into a hug. "Congratulations, man."

Back slaps, hugs, and well wishes were exchanged.

When Garrison's eyes landed on Alana, he said, "Sorry these guys dragged you here."

Alana emitted a brief laugh. "I don't know if I want to be left alone with Nana and Gramps. I'm not yet used to the news that my brother is alive."

"How's Nadia?" I asked.

"Exhausted," he said with a wide grin and baffled shake of his head. "But she's deliriously happy. We're fucking thrilled the baby's finally here."

Then he was at a loss for words.

I knew that feeling. My eyes met Kelly's, and she knew exactly what I was thinking at that moment.

I experienced it twice. It was the best fucking feeling in the world.

It was what followed that would test a man's mettle, remembering my struggles with Ash, and then more recently with Whit. Children could bring the toughest man to his knees.

I had a feeling the teenage years were going to eclipse what I'd experienced of fatherhood so far, but I was looking forward to every gray hair they'd give me to be the best dad they deserved.

KELLY

"AND THEN EVERYTHING EXPLODED," Bristow recounted the op.

We all piled into Nadia's room. Ciara Elizabeth Garrison was adorable as any newborn could be. She was sleeping peacefully in the crib set up beside her mother's bed, blissfully unaware of the people in the room.

Despite John's protests that she needed her rest, Nadia demanded to know what happened after Dmitry fired the rocket launcher.

"Damn," she said after Bristow told her that Blaze hid a trigger in a pack of cigarettes that blew up the house. "That man was insane if not a genius."

"Good riddance," Levi muttered. "He got off easy. That motherfucker."

Nadia clasped John's hand. "I'm glad you got them on the Fed task force investigating the Russians."

"That explosion could be seen for miles," Gabby said. "There were bound to be questions. It's better to have our bases covered."

She was in one corner of the room sitting on Declan's lap. It amused me how Levi's friend seemed to do that at every opportunity. It was like a game between husband and wife. Sometimes Gabby got annoyed in a fond, roll-your-eyes way, of course.

"Where the blast came from would be hard to identify without satellite replay," Bristow said. "The locals took a while to get there which was a good thing. It allowed the Feds to set up."

"What about Callum McGrath? Is he coming in?" Nadia glanced at her husband.

Everyone looked at the man expectantly.

John barked a laugh. "Don't look at me. That's out of my control."

His wife gasped. "What? That's unprecedented."

He wrapped his arms around her. "I've got my hands full right here plus my little one. She's got strong lungs. She's gonna be kick-ass."

I looked at Ariana. She and Migs were on the couch in the room. "You're next."

"Oh, yes, please," she groaned. "I need for this boy to come out now."

Everyone laughed.

"Are you sleeping on a recliner?" I asked.

Migs answered with a grumbled, "She is."

"Oh, man, so many babies," Bristow cocked his head toward John. "Maybe your Mom should open a daycare."

"That's a good idea," Declan said.

There was so much meaning to his tone that everyone took notice. Gabby's face was the color of the room's rose-pink walls.

"Should we tell them, babe?" Declan's eyes gleamed.

Bristow's face split into a shit-eating-grin. "Well I'll be damned."

"We already told Kelso before he left for Vegas, but ... baby is due in December."

Nadia squealed and if Garrison didn't remind her that she'd just given birth, she might have jumped down from the hospital bed. I swooped over to give Gabby a hug.

"I'm so happy for you both." Tears formed in the back of my eyes. "You two deserved this, so, so much."

Gabby's own eyes glazed. "Don't make me cry. But thanks."

While the guys were giving Declan a back slap and their own congratulations, mutterings of rapid-fire Spanish erupted behind us. We glanced back to see Ariana struggling to get up, glaring at her husband who had left her on the couch. "Help me up."

Migs growled, "Babe, don't even——"

Gabby laughed and walked over to sit beside her. "No. No. Don't get up."

The two hugged.

Afterwards, Ariana huffed. "I need to get you some vitamin infusions."

"Here we go," Declan sighed.

Levi snuck up behind me and murmured in my ear. "Want another baby?"

EPILOGUE

THREE DAYS LATER ...

KELLY

"LEVI ..."

"Sh ... quiet, beautiful, or I'm stopping."

"You wouldn't dare."

The licking between my legs stopped, and so did the build-up of pleasure that left me hanging on the precipice. I glanced where Levi was busy giving me the goods. Or where he had been. He raised his head and narrowed his eyes, the warning glint in them only making me wetter, more aroused. My juices glistening around his mouth only made him sexier and more primal.

"Are you going to keep it down, 'coz our girls are in the next room?"

It was our last day at the safe house. My parents flew in with my brother, Ronan, the afternoon we arrived from Vegas.

It was time to move out and face the damage at my grandparents' house.

"I wasn't *that* noisy."

"Yes, you were." He flashed a panty-melting smile before giving my thighs a squeeze.

"Fine. I'll keep it down."

He lowered his head and pushed my knees wider, scooped me under my ass and fed my pussy into his mouth again.

My husband was voracious. I tried to muffle my cries while grabbing the sheets. My toes curled at the exquisite pleasure that shot like a live wire through my nerve endings. I was pulsing, thrumming with anticipation and wetter than I'd ever been. The past three days had been a whirlwind of activity and monumental emotions, I was simply too drained. I needed this release. I writhed and clutched the pillow to smother my moan as my climax hit me.

Then, before I fully came down, Levi crawled up my body and slowly pushed inside me.

Inch by exquisite inch.

"I'm going to make love to you," he whispered. "I'm going to go slow, babe. I want to savor you this time."

"I love a hard pounding," I said. "But I'm not opposed to sweet lovin'."

His eyes smoldered, belying the way he gently rocked into me. Even when it was slow, I felt the dominance of his cock. Angling and rotating his hips, he watched my face closely. His fingers gripped my own and slowly placed our clasped hands on either side of my head.

As he continued making love to me, he watched me intently. "There's nothing more satisfying than watching you come apart with me inside you." As if to stress that point, his cock hit my magic spot. I arched and gasped, and his mouth came down to devour my own. His fierce kiss opposed the gentle way he owned my body and … my soul.

Levi

BRANNA AND CILLIAN's house was buzzing with activity. After the LAPD released the property, I hired a crime scene mop-up crew to deep clean the house and remove every trace of blood and any reminders of the night the McGraths were attacked.

Alana was in Kelly's house keeping her and the kids company while we repaired the drywall that Branna's shotgun destroyed.

Ronan, the eldest of Kelly's brothers, took the lead on the job. Not that hanging drywall was rocket science, but he used to build the shoot houses for Ranger's training, so anything construction fell to him. I was the muscle, content to take his orders while Robert and Cillian became the backseat carpenters, although Cillian was more helpful than Kelly's dad. Mostly, they just sat on the stairs and watched us work. Ruger slept at their feet. The German Shepherd was healing by the day.

Keeping occupied with this task prevented Branna and Mads from asking me questions about their daughters. Apparently, both Alana and Kelly's understanding of keeping secrets was to avoid the rest of the family.

"Hold it steady," Ronan said. "I'm going to jack it into position."

"Got it." I was in a crouch, keeping the sheetrock in place.

"Man, it sure is useful having you around."

"Hey, we could have helped," Robert protested.

Ronan glanced back at his father. "We've got this. Really." Then he winked at me before returning his attention to the task at hand. "So you and my sister are back together, huh?"

I stiffened. Ronan was not the type for small talk. He was more introspective than his younger brother. Callum was built like a linebacker, while Ronan was an inch or two taller and leaner.

"Yeah."

"You got your shit straight?"

The burn of his stare was hot down the side of my face, but I didn't look at him. The problems in my marriage were related to Ronan's downward spiral. Neither of us handled Callum's death well. He of all people knew what I'd gone through. I wasn't sure if he'd dealt with his own shit properly. He didn't have the incentive I had of winning my family back.

"We're working on things, but it's looking good."

"Good."

Then he went back to work.

A few minutes later, Branna called us to the kitchen for lunch. She and Mads went to the supermarket that morning to restock the kitchen. We'd been spoiled at the safe house, although the prepared frozen food was nothing compared to what Branna and Cillian could whip out.

"Kelly's not answering her phone, and neither is Alana," Mads said.

I dug out my phone and tried to call her, but she put me straight to voicemail. There were no known threats so I quelled my rising panic. "I'll go get them."

"Wait a minute," Branna and Mads cornered me.

Shit.

I tried to keep a neutral smile. The two women looked at each other before Mads spoke up. "My daughters are avoiding us." A heavy breath passed her lips. "We're fine if they're not ready to talk about it. But if something terrible happened to Alana during captivity, we want to know and help her through it."

When the three men joined them, I glanced longingly at the exit.

"Alana is fine," I clipped.

Branna's eyes narrowed. Madeline raised a brow. "You're hiding something."

"What? No." My words caught in my throat.

Ronan crossed his arms, his eyes narrowing as well. "You're good. But not that good. So why don't you tell us what my sisters are hiding."

"Why do you think they're hiding something?" I asked.

"Because they seem fine around you, but around us they're …" Branna snapped her fingers repeatedly, trying to look for the right word. "Skittish."

"Yes. Like they're hiding something." Mads agreed.

"Exactly like they're hiding something," Ronan added.

They were scrutinizing every change of my expression. Even without looking in a mirror, I knew my face gave away what they suspected. I tried to smile, but I failed colossally. I was sure my smile was a caricature version of a Disney villain telling children he was the hero. Hell, I could face interrogations and grin with sarcasm and make up shit, but the McGrath women made me feel about an inch tall.

"I assure you they're …"

The front door opened, and Alana walked in.

My relief at her appearance was cut short as I took in her ravaged face. She'd been crying.

Fuck. What now?

"Where's Kelly?" I barked.

"She's outside with the kids … and …" she inhaled raggedly. "Mom—" her lips trembled.

"I knew it," Mads glared at me. Actually I could feel everyone's condemnation.

Ronan walked over to my side and slung an arm around my shoulder, drawing me close. "You're in deep shit, man and …Holy mother of God." He looked past me.

I turned. Fuck.

Callum darkened the doorway. Kelly lagged behind him with the two girls.

His eyes met mine. "I didn't think Alana would be able to explain it."

He was right.

Ronan brushed past me and approached his brother, wariness in his step.

Alana was trying to explain but the rest of the McGraths ignored her, seemingly transfixed on the ghost at the entrance.

"Cal?" Ronan choked. "Is it really you?"

"Yeah, man." He gave that crooked grin he was known for. "C'mere" Like he did with Alana, he didn't give Ronan a choice. He ripped off the Band-Aid and hugged him tight.

Mixed emotions expanded my lungs, and there was no room for oxygen. Joy, a bit of sadness, but mostly joy. Kelly appeared at my side holding Ash's hand. Whit flanked me on my right and linked her fingers through mine.

I put my left arm around my wife. Our family was finally complete.

At that moment, the McGraths simply accepted their son was home. As each of them took turns embracing Callum, there was crying, cursing, back thumps, and more crying.

But the questions would come, and it didn't take long.

Finally, it was Robert who asked, "Why'd you stay gone so long, son?"

KELLY

DAD STOOD at the edge of the living room, looking out the bay window. He was having a hard time processing what Callum had told the family. Until that moment, the subject of Walter Ford had been kept from the rest of the McGraths. Only Alana and I knew.

"I saw his obituary," Dad whispered as though talking to

himself. Walter Ford had been born in New York and had
been a U.S. Senator for the state. It didn't surprise me that his
death would be announced in The New York Times. "I actually felt sorry for that bastard."

He turned to look at my brother, anguish in his eyes. "I
cost you five years of your life."

Callum stalked toward his dad, and put a hand on his
shoulder, and brought their faces close. "What did I say?"

Dad had his head hung, and he was sobbing. Callum
spoke to him in a low voice. Dad punctuated his words with
occasional nods.

It was like watching a movie or reading a book where you
knew it had a happy ending, but you had to live through the
heart wrenching scenes, because those parts made the ending
sweeter.

I was sitting beside mom, holding her hand, giving it a
squeeze whenever she dissolved into sobs. The emotions going
around the room ran the whole gamut. First, anger at Callum
for putting us through the grief, and the repercussions stemming from his "death." Then dealing with the breakup of my
marriage and Levi's guilt. Ronan quitting the NYPD and
becoming directionless for a while because of his anger. He
and Levi shared the same trajectory except my husband had
finally stepped off that cycle when he lost us. But, in the end,
every single one of us was happy Callum was alive.

Mom nodded to where Levi stood beside Ronan at the
entrance to the living room. Both had identical postures,
leaning against the arched opening with arms and ankles
crossed, observing. "Is Levi okay?"

I cocked my head. "What do you mean?"

"The guilt. He'd been so angry like Ronan," Mom said.
"You lost five years."

"But what's important is the here and the now, right?"

"Yes." Her gaze meandered back to her husband and son.
The grief-stricken mother I remembered flashed across her

face. "I would go through those five years again," she said softly. "If we'd always end up here."

I couldn't agree more. And as my eyes returned to my husband, I noticed he was staring intently at me.

He smiled. I was more than ready for our future.

CHRISTMAS MORNING

Levi

"CIARA WON'T STOP CRYING."

Blurry-eyed, I tried to shake the remnants of sleep and checked the time. Three a.m. The other night it was two.

"Is that John?" Kelly groaned beside me.

"Yeah. I got this, babe." Somehow my friend thought that having two kids of my own made me the expert when it came to babies. But I'd be damned before we interrupted Kelly's sleep. Our family was descending on us for Christmas lunch, and my wife needed her Zs.

I walked into the hallway, padded down the stairs, and straight into the kitchen of our new house.

"Is she hungry?" I pressed a glass to the water dispenser.

"She just finished a bottle."

"What did the doc say when you took her in the other day."

"She's fine."

"She's not running a temperature right now?" I took a sip of water.

"If she were, I'd've called the doctor, not you." The irritated exhaustion in his voice made me smirk.

"True. Do you pick her up every time she cries?"

We'd gone over this so many times, but it bore repeating. Every. Single. Fucking. Time.

Silence.

I responded with a sigh.

"She screams the whole world down."

"I can hear that. What does Mrs. Mason say?"

"You already know what Ma told me."

"That they are manipulative little demons at that age?"

"We're not talking about me."

I chuckled. "You know what to do, *Daddy*. You just want some company in the misery, and that's why you call me"

He responded with a sigh and I heard him say, "Come on, poppet." And then the jangle of car keys joined the shrieking baby. John was right, Ciara had some lungs on her. "Hang on."

I wasn't sure if he meant me or his baby daughter.

But I hung on. Because apparently this is what badasses do, show support of first time fathers. Damn, how many times had I gotten calls from Migs too? Declan called me once, but their daughter, Madison, born two weeks before, was still in the angelic stage.

I heard car doors open and slam as well as Garrison talking to Ciara. He never did the baby talk with her and spoke to her like an adult.

"You there?" He started the engine.

"I'm here."

"You never told me what the McGraths thought about the arrests."

Hmm. I wondered if he really needed moral support for fatherhood, or it was his way of sneaking out of the house to talk business. A week before Christmas, the Southern District of New York federal prosecutor's office, as well as the JAG made a joint GPS takedown of a current United States senator, the CEO of a defense company, as well as several officers of the Navy, one of them an admiral. Too bad Walter Ford was dead, but his vendetta against the McGraths was only the tip of the iceberg, a speck in the morally corrupt scheme of greedy businessmen and people in power. The reach of the arms dealers ran deep. The officials arrested were charged with conspiracy to derail a SEAL op and looking the other way while letting the Russians do illegal businesses in foreign countries that would fuel war in those nations. The JAG would handle their own court martial of their officers, while the federal courts would deal with the civilians.

"They're thankful it's over. The recordings Stepanov turned over couldn't be entered as evidence, but it certainly identified most of the players."

"Dmitry has been helpful too ... huh," he broke off. "Well, I'll be damned."

"Let me guess ... she's asleep."

"Yep."

"Told you she's got you wrapped around her tiny fingers."

"Yeah, well, I'll try to resist next time."

"Maybe she just likes to hear her dad talk special ops."

"Don't make me laugh and wake her."

"Seriously, *Dad*," I said. "Babies want to hear your voice. It's better for them to get used to that noise and shit."

"So you said."

"Trust me."

"Two kids make you an expert?"

"Well, you called me."

"True."

"You're already back at the house, aren't you? You just wanted to keep on talking so she'll stay asleep."

"Nah, I'm good. Thanks, James."

With that, he ended the call.

I was used to John's abruptness, and I was glad he didn't change much despite becoming a father. I returned to the bedroom and crawled into bed.

Kelly snuggled into me. "You got Garrison squared away?"

"Yup."

"What time is it?"

"You've got three more hours before Branna shows up."

Kelly didn't answer. Her breathing had already evened out. I wasn't sure she was fully awake when she asked the time.

I kissed the top of her head and savored this moment. Last Christmas, I was alone. I didn't have my family around me. I was a miserable motherfucker who thought there was no hope of Kelly and I getting back together. This last New Year's Eve, I was certain we were on the brink of divorce. What a difference a year made.

Not a day went by that I wasn't grateful for a second chance.

I wasn't failing them this time.

KELLY

"DAMN, if I could eat all the Irish Stew," Callum patted his belly. "You make it as good as Nana, sis." He glanced at our grandmother. "No offense."

"Bah ..." Nana waved her hand in a "don't care" gesture.

"I can't quite get Aunt Ava's version," I said. I know it seemed like I was fishing for compliments, but I wasn't.

We had moved into the West Indies style home in early November. It was the house my grandmother had pointed out that could accommodate our family with room to grow. I fell in love with the airy kitchen, and the beautiful dining room lined with a row of French doors that opened into the back yard and pool area. I might have been too eager to offer to host Christmas this year, but with Nana living up the street, it became a no-brainer given what had happened over the year.

Our mahogany dining table accommodated ten. Levi and I sat on opposite ends following tradition as the hosts. On my right was Ash, Nana, Mom, and Dad. On my left was Callum, Gramps, Ronan and Whitney, who—ever the daddy's girl—wanted to be close to her dad. Scout laid beside Ruger in one corner of the dining room, both dogs waiting their turn to have their Christmas treats. Ruger had fully recovered from his gunshot injury.

Uncle Sean and Aunt Ava had their own celebrations with their families and Charles had to take care of Eamonn's which was busy at this time of the year, but on Thanksgiving, the whole clan got together at one of Uncle Cesar's resort hotels.

That turned out well because Levi and I wanted this gathering to be more intimate given how we hadn't spent Christmas together last year.

"Well." My grandmother stood to clear the plates. "Ava altered the recipe for her family, made it more Italian," she sniffed. "I prefer ours." Every now and then, she'd bring up the old Irish versus Italians competition. She moved to pick up Ash's plate.

"Nana, I'm not done." Ash winked at me. My youngest daughter was becoming a smartass. The whole table laughed, partly in relief. If we held lunch at my grandmother's house, everyone would've had to get up and clear the plates. That wasn't happening in my dining room. I wanted to savor the moment and leave the dirty dishes for later.

"Nana, sit down," I ordered. "Let everyone relax."

."It'll be nice to sit down later and not worry about the dishes," she grumbled but did as she was told.

"That's because you'll be too tired from cleaning up," Gramps said. "The guys will clean up."

Levi, Callum, and Ronan protested.

Alana partially rose to lean over and give me a high-five.

At the end of the table, I caught Dad and Mom's eyes, and even from a distance, I could see them glistening with tears. Their faces said it all. Joy.

It was Christmas, and our family was whole again.

Amidst the ensuing chatter, Levi stood and clinked his beer bottle to get everyone's attention. When we all quieted down, he said, "I wanted to do this before dinner, but knowing McG here was grumbling about starving, I decided to wait until after."

Levi was doing a speech? It wasn't his style, and I could see his apprehension. But when his eyes met mine across the table, I gave him an encouraging smile, and his face lit up.

I remembered our conversation about old couples not giving each other butterflies anymore. That wasn't true.

Their fluttering wings were rioting inside me right now.

"At the beginning of this year, I thought for sure I'd lost my chance with Kelly," Levi started. "The McGraths have gone through unusual situations. Some of us forgot how to live on after the loss—"

"Guilty." Mom raised her hand. "And no offense to you, Cal, if I eventually did move on."

"I should feel hurt about that," Callum murmured and snickering went around the table. My brother gave the speech at Thanksgiving dinner leading with how hurt he was that we'd all moved on from him. Not true, of course. But we could find humor in it. It was a relief that even Mom could joke about it. Callum said he experienced a weirdness about coming back from the dead, and the transition into normal life had been tough.

"As I was saying," Levi continued. "Some of us forgot how to keep on living. It took the breakdown of my marriage to hit me in the face and make me realize that the people who could help me move on were my own family. Kelly"— his gaze met mine before wandering to our girls. "Ash and Whitney. I'm insanely honored you all gave me this second chance."

"We love you, Dad." Whit gave his hand a quick tug.

Levi smiled at his daughter before returning his attention to the table. "To the McGraths, I avoided you because I couldn't stand the guilt of coming home without Callum."

It was the first time my husband admitted that to my family.

"F-, fudge, bro." My brother's face turned red.

"But you're here now," Levi's voice cracked with so much emotion, I could feel my own bubbling up.

"We never blamed you and we knew you had this guilt," Dad said. "And I am so sorry that I didn't talk to you about it, son. Maybe it would have made a difference in your problems—"

"Stop," Levi said. "I'm not saying this now for recriminations but to start a clean slate for all of us." His gaze landed briefly on Ronan before roaming the table again. "I'm not good with words, but I'm just so"—he exhaled a heavy sigh that seemed to make him lighter—"so, fu-freakishly happy to see everyone here today in our new home." He spread his arms. "Last Christmas, I had nothing. Today, I have everything I could ever ask for. All I can say is thank you to my beautiful wife and children for giving me a second chance." He looked around the table again. "And to my family." He raised his beer. "To our future."

We raised our glasses and toasted to new beginnings.

Levi

MUCH LATER THAT EVENING, after everyone had gone home and the kids were tucked away in their rooms with Scout and their new toys and gadgets, we retired to our bedroom.

Our room was massive with a little sitting room in front of

a fireplace that would most likely never find any use in Los Angeles even in the winter months. French doors opened to a second-floor balcony overlooking a backyard screened by mature trees.

I'd done many filthy things to my wife on that balcony.

But the most crucial detail in our room—given our broken-bed record that sparked our house-hunting mission—was the sturdiest bed frame we could find, one that could support our sexual acrobatics when my wife was feeling frisky and demanded a hard pounding from her husband.

A duty I had no problem fulfilling.

That didn't solve all our sound problems. The bed didn't creak, but my wife was loud.

"Oh, my God, oh my God."

"Don't you move those hands, babe," I warned as I continued thrusting between her thighs. Under my mercy, Kelly was a beautiful sight to see.

Pliant.

Responsive.

Perfect.

Arms stretched above her with hands gripping the bed rails—we tested the strength of their construction. Kelly's head was thrown back, her eyes at half-mast, her mouth, which earlier was just wrapped around my cock was open. As much as I wanted to shoot my load into her mouth and have her lips dripping with my cum, I wanted to fuck another baby inside her more.

I reached between us and rubbed her clit.

"God, you're good." Her reedy cry could have pierced ordinary walls and might've made our kids worry with what I was doing to their mother, but I'd tested the acoustics of the room.

"It's Levi, babe," I tried to smirk, but my climax was tingling at the base of my spine. Gritting my teeth, I asked, "You good?"

"Yes, yes," she continued to moan, shaking her head from side to side. "If I come one more time, I'll die."

She was dramatic, but I was immensely gratified that I'd made my greedy wife come enough times, she'd call uncle.

I reared back one more time and plunged deep, stilling for a beat, and sent my cum shooting inside her. But moving inside her was too good, so I resumed rocking into her gently until I was spent. I plucked her hands from the railings and rolled off her, gathering Kelly into my arms.

"Wow, I'm glad you convinced me I needed to get laid."

"You were bouncing with exhausted energy." I kissed the top of her head. "Dinner was fantastic."

"The first Christmas dinner since Callum's return."

"The first since we got back together." I tipped up her chin. "There will be more firsts in this house." A grin curved my mouth. "Ash and Whit's first baby brother?"

She raised a brow. "First? How many kids are we planning?"

"Oh, I don't know, I'm feeling left out with so many of my friends becoming dads for the first time."

"You're ahead of them."

I rolled over Kelly again and propped up on my elbows. "And I love you."

"I love you too." A puzzled look crossed her face. "So …?"

"I want to give you the family you deserve."

Her lips quirked up. "You already have."

"I want to give you more. A family to call our own."

She grasped my jaw. "All mine."

"Forever yours, beautiful."

"I'm all for more."

Nine months later, Liam Patrick James was born.

*** The End ***

If you enjoyed this book, please consider leaving a review. It is much appreciated!

If you haven't read the series, the first book is
Gabby and Declan in
The Ex Assignment

Curious about Kelly's McGrath family? Find out more in my billionaire-mafia-lite romance De Lucci's Obsession.

We haven't seen the last of the Morettis as they join the De Luccis in my new billionaire-mafia series. Sign up to newsletter and receive updates.

AFTERWORD

Levi and Kelly's book was supposed to be book number three in the Rogue Protector Series. Because I was far removed from what I originally planned for their story, it took me a while to be satisfied with the manuscript. I started this book in November 2021 and I was almost seventy percent done when I axed 30k words of it because I felt it didn't have the emotional impact and excitement I had envisioned for their story. It was a painful process. But this year also made me understand the type of writer I am. I need time to write a story. I can't rush my process. I can't predict when I'll uncover my story and peeling away layer by layer is the only way to discover the gold underneath it.

To my developmental editor, Geri, I will miss our brainstorming sessions. Our love for the same tropes and our differences fueled my ideation process. You were a great friend and cheerleader, but you also showed me tough love when my ideas went off the rails. I was shocked and heartbroken to hear of your passing, and I am sad that you didn't read Levi and Kelly's story in its final form. In a way I think you've been reading over my shoulder as I finished the manuscript. Publishing this book is bittersweet. I'll miss you so much my friend! I'm forever thankful for your friendship.

My fantastic beta readers helped me smooth out the craziness of my revisions.

Sue, you always go above and beyond. I am lucky to have

an ideal reader like you who not only picks apart aspects of my plot and makes sure the points come across with clarity, but you're also a superb grammar checker. You have such an eagle eye. All your insights and suggestions are much appreciated. I also love our discussions on the shows we binge-watch and the books we read.

To my daily text buddy, Taryn Rivers, thank you for offering to beta read when you heard me lamenting how I performed surgery on my manuscript, leading to my fear that I'd messed up the flow.

Knowing that my purpose was to preserve pacing, both of you didn't hesitate to tell me what to cut or what details to tighten, and on my final read-through, the cuts have been worth it.

To my proofreaders Dana Dunphy of A Book Nerd Edits and Jo West of Turn the Pages Proofreading, I am grateful to both of you for providing the final eyes to my manuscript. This year had been so hectic for me, your help had given me the confidence to send this book into the world.

To my reader friend, Mandy, thank you so much for being you and always being the cheerleader when I'm showing doubts. I enjoy our chats where we swoon over our jealous, possessive alpha males. Thank you for finding images of Levi for me since I was dreading to face stock photo hell. LoL!

To my Very Important Paige readers, booktokkers, bookstagrammers, book bloggers, and all my loyal as well as new readers ... thank you so much! It wouldn't be possible for me to do what I love without your support.

And most of all, thank you to my hubby for continuing to believe in me. You and Loki are my world. I love you both so much.

CONNECT WITH THE AUTHOR

Find me at:

Facebook: Victoria Paige Books
Website: victoriapaigebooks.com
Email: victoriapaigebooks@gmail.com
FB Reader Group: Very Important Paige readers

facebook.com/victoriapaigebooks

tiktok.com/@vpaigebooks

twitter.com/vpaigebooks

instagram.com/victoriapaigebooks

ALSO BY VICTORIA PAIGE

Rogue Protectors

The Ex Assignment

Protector of Convenience

The Boss Assignment

Her Covert Protector

The Wife Assignment

Guardians

Fire and Ice

Beneath the Fire (novella)

Silver Fire

Smoke and Shadows

Susan Stoker Special Forces World

Reclaiming Izabel (novella)

Guarding Cindy (novella)

Protecting Stella (novella)

Always

It's Always Been You

Always Been Mine

A Love For Always

Misty Grove

Fighting Chance

Saving Grace

Unexpected Vows

Standalone

De Lucci's Obsession

Deadly Obsession

Captive Lies

The Princess and the Mercenary

* All series books can be read as standalone

Made in the USA
Las Vegas, NV
14 June 2023

73405569R00208